Praise for
THE RETRIEVAL ARTIST SERIES

One of the top ten greatest science fiction detectives of all time.

—io9

The SF thriller is alive and well, and today's leading practitioner is Kristine Kathryn Rusch.

—Analog

[Miles Flint is] one of 14 great sci-fi and fantasy detectives who out-Sherlock'd Holmes. [Flint] is a candidate for the title of greatest fictional detective of all time.

—Blastr

Part *CSI*, part *Blade Runner*, and part hard-boiled gumshoe, the retrieval artist of the series title, one Miles Flint, would be as at home on a foggy San Francisco street in the 1940s as he is in the domed lunar colony of Armstrong City.

—The Edge Boston

What links [Miles Flint] to his most memorable literary ancestors is his hard-won ability to perceive the complex nature of morality and live with the burden of his own inevitable failure.

—Locus

Readers of police procedurals as well as fans of SF should enjoy this mystery series.

—Kliatt

Instant addiction. You hear about it—maybe you even laugh it off—but you never think it could happen to you. Well, you just haven't run into Miles Flint and the other Retrieval Artists looking for The Disappeared. ...I am hopelessly hooked....

—Lisa DuMond
MEviews.com on *The Disappeared*

An inventive plot and complex, conflicted characters increases the appeal of Kristine Kathryn Rusch's *Extremes*. This futuristic tale breaks new ground as a space police procedural and should appeal to science fiction and mystery fans.

—*RT Book Reveiws* on *Extremes*

Part science fiction, part mystery, and pure enjoyment are the words to describe Kristine Kathryn Rusch's latest Retrieval Artist novel.... This is a strong murder mystery in an outer space storyline.

—*The Best Reviews* on *Consequences*

An exciting, intricately plotted, fast-paced novel. You'll find it difficult to put down.

—*SFRevu* on *Buried Deep*

A science fiction murder mystery by one of the genre's best.... A book with complex characters, an interesting and unpredictable plot, and timeless and universal things to say about the human condition.

—*The Panama News* on *Paloma*

Rusch continues her provocative interplanetary detective series with healthy doses of planet-hopping intrigue, heady legal dilemmas and well-drawn characters.

—*Publishers Weekly* on *Recovery Man*

…the mystery is unpredictable and absorbing and the characters are interesting and sympathetic.

—*Blastr* on *Duplicate Effort*

Anniversary Day is an edge-of-the-seat thriller that will keep you turning pages late into the night and it's also really good science fiction. What's not to like?

—*Analog* on *Anniversary Day*

Set in the not too distant future, the latest entry in Rusch's popular sf thriller series (*The Disappeared; Duplicate Effort*) combines fast-paced action, beautifully conflicted protagonists, and a distinctly "sf noir" feel to tell a complex and far-reaching mystery. VERDICT Compulsively readable with canny plot twists, this should appeal to series fans as well as action-suspense readers.

—*Library Journal* on *Anniversary Day*

Rusch offers up a well-told mystery with interesting characters and a complex, riveting storyline that includes a healthy dose of suspense, all building toward an ending that may not be what it appears.

—*RT Book Reviews* on *Blowback*

The latest Retrieval Artist science fiction thriller is an engaging investigative whodunit starring popular Miles Flint on a comeback mission. The suspenseful storyline is fast-paced and filled with twists as the hero comes out of retirement to confront his worst nightmare.

—*GenreGoRoundReviews* on *Blowback*

We always like our intergalactic politics as truly alien, and Rusch delivers the goods. It's one thing to depict members of a Federation whining about treaties, quite another to depict motivations that are truly, well, alien.

—*Astroguyz* on *Blowback*

The Retrieval Artist Series:

PALOMA

A RETRIEVAL ARTIST NOVEL

KRISTINE KATHRYN RUSCH

*wmg*PUBLISHING

Paloma

Published 2012 by WMG Publishing
www.wmgpublishing.com
First published in 2006 by ROC
Cover and Layout copyright © 2012 by WMG Publishing
Cover design by Allyson Longueira/WMG Publishing
Cover art copyright © Philcold/Dreamstime
ISBN-13: 978-0-615-72699-1
ISBN-10: 0-615-72699-2

In memory of my mother

Acknowledgements

Thanks on this one go to Ginjer Buchanan for her support and understanding, and to my husband, Dean Wesley Smith, who understands my writing process better than I do. I couldn't have done it without you both. Thank you.

PALOMA

A RETRIEVAL ARTIST NOVEL

MILES FLINT'S OFFICE WAS COVERED IN DUST.

He stood inside the once pristine room, hands on his hips, and surveyed the mess. Moon dust—fine and golden—covered everything: his chair, his desk, his computer systems. The white walls—covered with a substance that looked like permaplastic but wasn't—were now dark brown with filth.

The air tasted gritty. The dust had worked its way into his mouth, and he'd only been here a few minutes.

What a disaster.

And he hadn't even seen the back room.

He gave a verbal override command—one of the few verbal fail-safes he'd left from the days when this office had belonged to Paloma—and the lights came up. They were sepia-toned, not because he had commanded them that way, but because the dust had infiltrated their systems as well.

If the dust was in the lights, then it was in the filter systems, the state-of-the-art air purifiers, and all of his sensors.

He wouldn't be able to work in here until this place got cleaned, and he'd have to clean it. He had too many confidential files, too many illegal systems, to allow any cleaning service into the building.

He'd have to find the source of the breakdown, fix it—without help—and then remove all the dust, fine particle by fine particle. How many systems would he have to trash? (And how much work would that be? He'd have to remove all of the data from them—not only the data that anyone could retrieve, but the ghost data, the kind that retained its imprint on the systems long after the files had been removed.)

He sighed and rubbed a hand over his grit-covered face.

This was his own fault. After his last case, he'd just vanished. He had already been in his space yacht, the *Emmeline*, and instead of bringing her back to Armstrong Dome's port, he turned her away from the Moon, going places he'd only heard of.

For a while, he thought he'd never come home.

Then he realized that no matter where he went, he'd always be restless, always be lonely, and always be alone with himself.

He came back—to dozens of messages on his system (none of which could reach him on his travels; he'd been too far away for the standard links to work). Messages from Ki Bowles, a reporter for InterDome Media, who seemed to believe that Flint wanted to talk with her, even though he'd warned her to stay away from him. Messages from possible clients, and messages from Noelle DeRicci, his former partner at the police department, now Security Chief for the United Domes of the Moon.

DeRicci's messages had gotten increasingly shrill over the months he was away—wondering what had happened to him, begging him to contact her so she wouldn't worry, hoping that he was all right.

He did contact her the moment he could—just outside Armstrong Dome's restricted space—and told her he'd been on vacation, and didn't know he had to report in.

He sounded a little annoyed, even though he wasn't. He was surprised at her concern. The annoyance was for whatever authorities had been listening in, so that they wouldn't think anything more important had happened.

All that happened, really, was that he had allowed a man to die. A man who, in all probability, should have died. Only the method forced Flint into reexamining everything he thought about himself and his new career.

Paloma had warned him that he had become a Retrieval Artist for the wrong reasons. *You see it as a way to save people,* she had said early in his training. *In reality, you will kill many more than you save, even if you do everything right.*

He had told her he believed her. Maybe he even had. He certainly thought Retrieving was better than working for the police department, which had him enforcing laws that he couldn't believe in, laws that cost so many lives for such silly reasons, that he couldn't enforce them even if he wanted to.

Anything was better than that.

He thought.

He sighed, swallowed a mouthful of dust, and coughed. Sweat ran down the side of his face. Everything had shut off when it got clogged, so the temperature regulators were gone, too. He might not be able to save his computer systems. They were sensitive; they might have malfunctioned in the warm, dirt-filled conditions.

Something had broken down while he was gone—or someone had tried to sabotage his systems (and succeeded, although probably not in the way they intended)—or the stupid young lawyer next door had somehow compromised Flint's office, accidentally drilling some kind of hole between them or shutting down the power to the entire area (although that wouldn't have caused this; Flint had backups built into his power systems as well) or accidentally cracking the only wall they shared.

That wall was the weakest one in Flint's office. He hadn't been able to reinforce it on both sides because the lawyer's predecessor—an older version of the same sort of incompetent—hadn't allowed Flint access.

They—and a couple other renters—shared one of Armstrong's oldest buildings, put up by the original colonists. The exterior was made of original permaplastic, and a plaque, somewhere on the side of the building, noted all of this as if it were a good thing.

Mostly it had been. The building looked like it was going to collapse at any moment, which hid Flint's wealth and made many of his potential clients turn away.

The last thing any Retrieval Artist—any reputable one, anyway—wanted was a lot of clients.

He slogged over to his desk, the inside of his shoes filling with dust. Everything had to have been off for at least a month, maybe longer, to accumulate this much through the cracks in the walls, the thin line under the door.

The dome filters in this part of Armstrong were poor. Not all of the roads in this section of town were covered, and some were covered in permaplastic, so the dust that made up the Moon itself was an ever-present part of this sector of the city.

And now a part of his office.

He tapped the computer screen built into the top of his desk, pressing his finger down hard so that the machine felt the warmth of his skin, took his DNA sample and his fingerprint, and turned the system on.

For a moment, he thought it wasn't going to work, then a shrill squeal nearly knocked him to his knees. He reached for the system to shut it off, when the squeal vanished, replaced by momentary static.

He frowned. His system had static? He wasn't even sure that was possible.

Then a woman's voice screamed, "Miles! Miles, please! Get here now! Miles—"

Paloma. The voice belonged to Paloma, his mentor.

"—Miles!"

He peered over the desk, trying to see when the call was logged in, how very long ago. He hadn't contacted her since he got back, but it wasn't uncommon for them to go months without speaking to each other.

"Miles! Help me! Help me, please!"

The system hadn't turned on. It was still black. Which meant that the voice was coming through his links directly into his own mind. He hadn't heard that squeal; he had felt it, absorbed it—somehow it had all gotten in—which he hadn't thought possible.

This office was supposed to be protected against any outside access.

"Miles! Heeeeeelp!"

He had no way of knowing if the cries were real or fake. He put a hand to his ear, staggered outside, and pulled the door closed.

The Dome was in Mid-Afternoon, the light sepia because of the dust clinging to the bad sections.

"Miles!"

He sent a ping back through the links—he knew they worked properly here—and got an address reading along his lower left eye—Paloma's residential tower. As far as his links could verify, the cries were coming from her.

"Miles!" She sounded terrified.

I'm coming! he sent back. Then he jogged to his aircar, parked only a few meters from the office. He hadn't locked up. He hoped the office door still locked itself automatically.

He couldn't turn around to fix it, though. He had to get to Paloma. She'd never called him for help before.

Should I send for the authorities? He sent.

"Miiiiiiiiiii—"

And then the transmission shut off. The static reappeared for a brief moment, then disappeared as well.

He tried to reestablish contact, but couldn't. He sent an emergency beacon to her building's security, warning them that something had happened in her apartment, but he didn't send any other transmission along that link.

Let them go up and see what was wrong. Maybe they would scare whoever—whatever—it was away from her.

He unlocked his aircar, slid in, leaving a dust trail all over the seat. He was covered in the stuff. He put the car on automatic, told it to take him to Paloma's and quickly—traffic laws be damned—and as the car jerked into the air, he shook the dust off himself as best he could.

Dust was trace. He was going to leave parts of himself all over the city if he wasn't careful.

He was thinking like the cop he used to be. Something in Paloma's message had triggered that cold, calculating reaction—watch what you touch, what you bring to the scene, what you're doing.

He made himself breathe deeply—the air in the car was clean, at least—and clung to the wheel as the car wove and bobbed its way through traffic, swerving around the tall buildings that composed the section of town nearest to Paloma's.

Alarms beeped in the car's interior as the vehicle flew into restricted airspace or got too close to the dome itself.

He didn't care.

No matter how many more messages he sent, no matter how hard he tried, he couldn't reach Paloma. It was as if her personal system had vanished—as if it hadn't existed at all.

His knuckles were white. His fingers ached. He made himself let go of the steering wheel—shut off because the system was on automatic—and flex them.

It took him a moment to realize why he was so worried.

Paloma had never asked him for help. She was the most competent person he knew. She had been in more terrible and terrifying situations than he could imagine, and she had come out of them unscathed.

And suddenly—surprisingly—she needed him.

She had never needed him before.

She had never sounded frightened before.

He had no idea what had changed.

2

Ki Bowles walked around the *Emmeline*. Miles Flint's space yacht had no external markings, nothing to identify it either as his or as something that belonged in Armstrong.

She had thought such a lack of identification was illegal, but the man in charge of Terminal 25, where the most expensive yachts docked, assured her that most yachts above a certain class had no exterior identification. They had codes and signature signals that got sent from port to port before the yacht arrived.

No one questioned, no one worried, no one noticed.

Because they were paid not to.

She stood as close to the yacht as possible. She was still fifteen meters from it, but the yacht had its own security system, one that sounded all kinds of alarms should any unauthorized personnel step too close.

Ki Bowles was about as unauthorized as she could get.

She tucked a strand of her strawberry blond hair behind her ear, sighed, and stared at the yacht. It was black and sleek, looking more like a bird than a ship. She'd only seen pictures of things like this—had never ridden in one, and had certainly never toured one.

They didn't let impoverished plebs—which was anyone with a reasonable income—into the showrooms where these things were sold. People Might Get Ideas. Although, when she inquired about viewing yachts, she was told that the income check that ran before anyone was allowed in the showroom was to prevent theft.

Not that anyone could just walk off with one of these things. No, the kind of theft the yacht companies meant was twofold: the first for its customers—the companies didn't want someone to see where the standard shipboard security systems were; and the second for the companies themselves—they didn't want some lesser company to rip off the interior designs, produce them with slightly inferior materials, and sell them to someone who wanted the high life but could only afford half of it.

They certainly didn't want a reporter in their showrooms, various members of the sales staff had told her, and even if they did, they would want one with a sterling reputation.

Implying, of course, that hers wasn't even close.

A year ago, she would have bristled at that characterization. Now she accepted it. She was on probation with InterDome Media. Her stories had fact-checkers again, and she had to work with a team, just like she had done as a young "face" who had to prove her journalistic worth.

She had taken on the Moon's new Security Chief, Noelle DeRicci, and had lost spectacularly. The interview Bowles had thought would make her career had nearly destroyed it.

Her boss, Thaddeus Ling, had given her a choice: she could move to InterDome's Gossip Wing (and get twice her pay) or she could rehabilitate her investigative journalism career by, essentially, starting over.

She had chosen to rebuild, even though that meant giving up her two anchor spots and the best live times. She hated working with fact-checkers—she didn't need them. Even though the Moon's governor-general had accused Bowles of shoddy journalism, everything Bowles had reported on Noelle DeRicci had been true, and backed up with the proper sources.

The problem was with the implications: Bowles had suggested a motivation in DeRicci's actions during her first crisis as security chief—a suggestion based on fact after fact after fact. In the height of the crisis, it had seemed like DeRicci was acting out of her prejudices, not out of any facts, but in the end, it became clear that DeRicci, whatever her motivation, had made the right decisions.

Leaving Bowles holding onto a solid story with an incorrect slant, and a ruined career.

Everyone she knew advised her to go the Gossip section. A few idiots had even told her that her skills were better suited to innuendo and career-destroying examinations of celebrity sex than finding out about the truth about government misbehavior, corporate mismanagement, and just plain old greed.

She saw herself as part of a long tradition of truth-telling journalists who'd saved their corner of the universe—and, like some of them, she had to pay the price.

The price, at the moment, were fact-checkers and a research team whom she'd have to fact-check.

She also had to have Ling (or one of his flunkies) approve every story she wanted to air.

She wasn't ready to air this one. She hadn't even told her team (Ling's team, if truth be told—his way of getting baby reporters trained without paying her for it) or her fact-checkers what she was doing.

She was taking her off time, and thinking.

Nothing wrong with thinking, right? She could even prove it: she had all her links (except her emergency links) shut down. None of her chip-sized cameras filming this amazing terminal, none of them examining the ship. No zooms, no audio cards, no memorized scans that she could examine later.

If someone at InterDome asked her what she'd been doing here, she'd tell them, simply, that she had wanted to do a story on luxury yachts (true) and since she wasn't allowed in the showrooms (also true), she had come to Terminal 25 where they were all docked.

She would do an obligatory piece, then, on the extra high ceilings in this part of the port, the tight security for plebs, the lax security for yacht owners, and the fact that yachts above a certain class didn't have to follow the rules of Space Traffic, like every other vehicle that came through Armstrong's port.

Hell, she might even enjoy that story. Maybe it wouldn't be just a cover.

She climbed off the edge of the dock and walked around the yacht, careful to stay behind the yellow line painted there for spaceport personnel—the garbage handlers, the floor cleaners, and their robotic assistants.

No one wanted these specialized security systems to go off just because some dockworker wasn't paying attention to his small team of robots that swept the floors near the most exclusive yacht club on the Moon.

She walked slowly, studying the yacht itself. No signs of damage—the sleek black exterior was as clean as if it had just rolled off its assembly line. No dents, no dings, no laser scrapes. She thought she saw some grappler hook damage near the main exit, but she couldn't tell for sure.

Maybe the stupid yacht was self-repairing, as well.

Or maybe Miles Flint had been telling the truth when he contacted a worried Noelle DeRicci. *I've been on vacation, Noelle,* he said in a slightly chiding tone. *It's my first. I thought I needed one.*

Bowles wanted to say that she'd overheard that message accidentally. But she hadn't. Even though she'd cut off her illegal taps into DeRicci's links, she'd left a tap on Flint's, not expecting much. The taps went through InterDome, and they'd get blamed if she got caught.

So far, she hadn't gotten caught. She doubted Flint would pursue her legally even if he knew.

Bowles had honestly thought he'd left Armstrong for good. He hadn't come back from his mysterious trip for months and months—and he'd disappeared right in the middle of DeRicci's first crisis, which Bowles, looking back, somehow found suspicious.

How suspicious, she didn't know.

But there was a lot more to Miles Flint than she got off personal history and old vids. He wasn't an average Retrieval Artist. He'd kept his friendship with one of the most powerful women on the Moon, and he'd managed to be on the edges of some of the biggest stories that Bowles had covered in her career.

She didn't have a story about Flint yet; she just had a hunch. A hunch that Flint was someone important—that he knew more, not just about DeRicci, but about Armstrong itself, than almost anyone else in the city.

Somehow he would lead Bowles to the story that would rebuild her career.

She would take her time, do the research, and back everything up. And this time, when she had the story, she would defend it. She wouldn't let someone like the governor-general outmaneuver her and make her seem like a fool.

She settled on the dock and stared at the outrageously expensive yacht.

Miles Flint was back, and deep down, that pleased her more than she could say.

3

THE AIRCAR SLOWED AS IT REACHED THE OUTER EDGE OF THE DOME. Flint frowned at the controls; he hadn't programmed in any caution in approaching Paloma's neighborhood.

Then the security lights flared—just once—signaling an external scan. Someone using government technology was probing his vehicle—either the police, the new security squad that DeRicci ran, or some other, less well-known organization.

His stomach churned. He stopped trying to reach Paloma on his links—he'd had no luck, but he kept his system automatically pinging her—and he shut down every system that could be accessed through a general channel.

Odd that this would happen now. He bit his lower lip, took the car off autopilot, and steered it through the high-rise buildings himself.

Paloma had taken the profits she made when she sold him her business and bought an apartment in one of the most exclusive sections of Armstrong. Buildings that originally defied city code rose ten and twenty stories over the then-tallest buildings in the city. These apartment complexes also butted up against the domes themselves— indeed, to the naked eye, they were part of the dome wall—so that each apartment had its own unobstructed view of the moonscape beyond.

Paloma loved the dome wall, the changing light, the view of rocks and dirt and brown emptiness that was the Moon itself. Initially, she would invite him over when the Earth was in full view, and he would marvel at the way the blue-green planet seemed to overtake the moonscape.

But he hadn't visited Paloma in a long time. She had been trying to wean him off her advice—reminding him of her early lessons: Retrieval Artists worked alone. The best ones had no friends and no family, no one that the corporations or the various alien groups could use to blackmail the Retrieval Artist against his clients.

The job she had trained him to do—the job he had chosen to do, over her objections—was one of the strangest in the universe. He searched for Disappeared, people who had changed their identities and fled their old lives rather than face the legal repercussions of whatever crime they had committed.

It seemed an odd job for a former policeman to do, but it wasn't—not for someone who believed in true justice. Many of the laws in the Earth Alliance favored the alien cultures that had signed on. Humans could be—and sometimes were—executed for crimes that, in human culture, weren't crimes at all, such as picking a flower or teaching a child how to read.

In his last cases for the department, Flint faced turning human children over to aliens whose cultures would destroy those children because of a "crime" the parents had committed. He watched families get torn apart for things as simple as choosing the wrong homesite.

When he realized that his entire career would consist of giving people he believed to be innocent over to groups that would destroy their minds, imprison them for life, or kill them, he quit. He went to Paloma—the only Retrieval Artist he knew well—and talked with her about doing a job where he picked his clients, where he chose which cases to take and which to avoid.

So far, the work he enjoyed the most involved finding Disappeareds to give them good news—they'd been acquitted of the crimes they'd committed; or they had a large inheritance coming (and he helped them get it while keeping their identities secret); or notifying them that treaties with whatever alien government held the contract on them had changed and they were now free to live in public again.

Those cases, as Paloma had warned him, were rare. Most of the potential clients who approached him were Trackers—people hired to hunt down Disappeareds and turn them in to the governments that wanted them. The Trackers often came through a front—a lonely elderly person or a lost child—and then used the Retrieval Artist's skills to find the Disappeared—the lazy way of doing the Tracker's job.

So Flint had become adept at saying no. He'd also become adept at investigating possible clients, discovering who they really were instead of who official records claimed they were.

He glided the aircar over Paloma's street, noting the emergency vehicles parked below. Lights flared and warnings sounded. Police lines, marked by laser light and static signs, already marked Paloma's building as a crime scene.

He turned away from the street, now understanding why his aircar had become so sluggish. The police had an emergency band that tapped into autopilots, regulating vehicle speed and investigating any vehicle in the vicinity of a crime scene.

They only used this technology in the most egregious cases or cases that they believed could become a cause célèbre.

He scanned the newslinks, but so far found nothing. That was strange in itself. Something with this much area cordoned off should've been candy to opportunistic reporters like Ki Bowles.

Flint's mouth went dry. He landed the car on a parking roof half a block away, and shut the entire system down. He'd have to reboot when he returned to the car, but it was a small price to pay for keeping his vehicle's information—whatever parts the police hadn't already accessed—private.

He got out, made sure all but his emergency links were shut down, then loped across the roof to the elevators.

Very few cars parked up here. Most locals took public transportation or had private cars with actual human drivers—an expense that screamed wealth. The people who parked in places like this were either visitors to the neighborhood, like Flint, or employees inside the various buildings.

The elevators were on the dome side of the building, and had clear walls. Flint stood inside, alone, leaning against the back wall, watching the elevator's reflection in the building across from him. All of the new buildings had ruined this building's view—which was probably why the owner gave up the rooftop garden with its once-lovely dome view for rooftop parking.

As he finally reached the lower level, he saw the white-and-blue lights of the emergency vehicles, the red of the police-line lasers, and the bloblike movements of various official personnel reflected on the building across from him.

By the time he reached the ground floor, he had something resembling a plan. He hoped that the police on scene were former colleagues of his and they still felt kindly enough to let him into the apartment building.

If they weren't, he would have to talk his way in, since he was well-known in the department as someone who'd given up a real job for a shady career. The police didn't like Retrieval Artists anyway; that Flint—a former detective, considered one of the city's best—had gone to that barely legal world made them angry.

The fact that he had become rich right about the same time made many officers even angrier. Flint could explain that his wealth hadn't come from his Retrieval Artist work, but that would raise even more questions. He actually had become rich saving lives by onetime trafficking in information, something that would please his former department even less than his Retrieval Artist status did.

He decided to play this more panicked than casual (which was how he felt). He jumped down the curb, hurried across the street—narrowly missing a car that had chosen to land-drive its way through this mess—and then ended up near the parked police vehicles.

Three were unmarked, probably detectives' vehicles. One belonged to the city—marked only as a city car by its license—and two vans that held crime scene techs.

He stopped just outside the lights, scanning the milling officers for a familiar face. He finally saw one coming out of the building—Bartholomew Nyquist.

Nyquist had headed the investigation of the death of a potential client of Flint's just before Flint left Armstrong on his so-called vacation. Nyquist was a rumpled man with dark skin and thinning hair. His haphazard clothing hid an athletic body that he seemed to maintain without enhancements.

Everything about him, in fact, pointed away from who he really was—one of the smartest detectives Flint had encountered in this or any other police department.

Even though none of the other police officials at the scene had noticed Flint yet, Nyquist spotted him immediately. Nyquist crossed the real grass that groundskeepers somehow maintained, just so that this part of the Moon would look more like Earth than it needed to, and stopped as close to Flint as he could get without touching the laser crime scene light.

Nyquist had a small shine that ran across his body, which meant he was wearing a protective covering so that he wouldn't contaminate a crime scene.

"Why am I not surprised you're here?" Nyquist asked.

Flint said, "I got an emergency message from my friend Paloma. She's—"

"Your mentor, you mean." Nyquist dark eyes were red and tired. "You've been monitored for the last six blocks. Everyone expected you."

"And they called you from whatever you were doing to deal with me."

"They assume I know you."

Interesting choice of words. "You do know me."

"I've met you, and I'm still not sure what to make of you. But I'm under orders not to let anyone cross that line."

Flint nodded. He'd expected that.

"And I know enough about you to know that if I tell you not to cross that line, you'll find a way to get into the building anyway. Probably through some secret door that I don't know exists. So, it's better to escort you, keep an eye on you, and then send you away."

In other words, to babysit him. Flint's stomach twisted even more.

Nyquist hadn't said anything about Paloma. He hadn't said what happened here. By implication, it seemed to be over, and it seemed to be bad.

Nyquist reached over to one of the laser chips and blocked it with his identification tag. Flint slipped through the emptiness and onto the grass.

"What happened here?" he asked again.

"That's what we're trying to find out." Nyquist led him across the grass, obviously not concerned with evidence down here.

"And Paloma?"

Nyquist didn't answer.

Flint felt light-headed. He made himself breathe. Nyquist wanted a reaction from him—otherwise, he'd tell Flint what to expect—and Flint was determined not to give it to him.

The main doors stood open. The lobby was empty, something Flint had never seen. The black floor, normally polished to a frightening shine, was scuffed and covered with some kind of dirt. The furniture was covered with robotic evidence-gathering equipment, and someone had shut off the automated air, making the entire place seem stuffy and small.

The view through the dome of the moonscape, usually so vivid that it looked like a person could walk from the black floor to the rocks themselves, was gone. It took Flint a moment to realize that someone had shuttered the giant windows, the way the dome walls came down in an emergency.

The elevator doors stood open, but the elevators themselves had been shut down. Techs—human techs—worked inside, collecting, gathering, recording.

Flint involuntarily swallowed against the dryness of his throat.

Nyquist led him to a staircase hidden in the black wall to the right of the elevators. Paloma lived on the eighth floor. It would be quite a hike.

Flint walked up with Nyquist, feeling more and more distressed each level that they climbed. Either Nyquist was taking him to Paloma first because Flint had asked, or whatever happened had happened primarily to her.

As they approached the eighth floor, voices echoed. The door to the stairwell here was open, and, judging from the conversation, techs worked the hallway.

A woman peered through the door as Flint rounded the last landing. She had curly red hair and dusky skin. Her green eyes looked like they'd been added accidentally, but her generous mouth made up for them.

"You think this is wise?" she asked.

For a moment, Flint thought she was talking to him. Then he realized that she was looking past him, at Nyquist.

"He needs to suit up," Nyquist said.

The woman rolled those strange eyes of hers, then vanished into the hallway. She returned a half second later holding a tech suit, one that covered every centimeter of the body and made sure that nothing—not one bit of trace evidence—fell from the wearer to the crime scene.

Flint hadn't worn one of those in years.

She nodded toward Flint. He turned to Nyquist, unwilling to put on the suit without an explanation. The suit made for a great cover story; it could protect the crime scene or double as an evidence-collection bag. Flint had a lot of trace on him. He didn't want to share it, or any part of his DNA, without a reason.

He didn't touch the offered suit. "Before we go any further," he said to Nyquist, "you tell me what happened."

Irritation flashed over Nyquist's features, so fast that Flint almost missed it. He understood it, though. Nyquist had been hoping Flint had forgotten or had been too upset to remember the suit's double uses.

"I'd rather you covered," Nyquist said.

Flint studied Nyquist. Nyquist would rather have Flint's reaction to the crime scene than explain it. All right, then. Flint would have to make a compromise if he wanted to view the scene.

"I'm not wearing your suit unless I get to keep it," he said.

"You know we can't do that," Nyquist said.

Flint shrugged one shoulder. "Then I'm not going to put it on until you tell me what's up there."

"He shouldn't be here anyway," the woman said.

Nyquist glared at her, then at Flint, as if weighing which would be best. Finally, Nyquist said, "Give him the suit."

She tossed the suit down. Flint ran his fingers over the edge, shutting off all the internal sensors and any links the suit had to the department itself. He pulled out chips that couldn't be shut off and handed them to Nyquist, who looked at them quizzically.

"Your file said you had programming experience," Nyquist said. "But I didn't think you worried about every single chip."

"Been checking up on me?" Flint asked as he slipped the suit over his clothes.

"For the last case," Nyquist said. "Then you vanished. I had to close it without you."

Flint shrugged again. "You didn't tell me I had to stay in Armstrong."

"You didn't have to stay. You just had some information that I would have liked."

Flint shook his head. "I gave you all the information I had."

It was a lie, but a small one. The murder victim in that last case had been one of Flint's clients—or, more accurately, had wanted to become one of his clients. He didn't dare give any information, even on a potential client, to the police. He had, however, bent the rules slightly, and pointed Nyquist in the right direction.

Maybe this, going to Paloma's floor, was a return favor. Maybe that was why Nyquist brought up the way they'd met.

Flint pressed a manufacturer's chip on the suit's palm, and the entire thing sealed up around him. Only his face and ears remained uncovered. Everything else made him feel as if he'd been wrapped like a sandwich in one of those automated machines.

He had forgotten how much he hated these suits.

"All right," Flint said. "Now let's see what you won't tell me."

Nyquist shot Flint a compassionate look. "I'm sorry," he said, and started up the stairs.

Flint hesitated before following Nyquist. Was the man apologizing for what Flint was about to see? Or for the way that Flint was—or would be—treated when he reached Paloma's floor?

The nerves that had bothered Flint from the moment he'd gotten Paloma's message grew worse. He had no idea what he was walking into, and it bothered him.

The fact that Nyquist wouldn't tell him anything bothered him as well.

The woman had moved away from the door. The techs' voices grew louder, directing collection equipment toward certain areas, looking for camera chips embedded in the walls.

Flint knew a few of the techs, but didn't acknowledge them. Instead, he stepped across the threshold into a blood bath.

Spatter everywhere. Some of the blood lacked the rich red-black color of drying human blood. Some of it was too thin and gooey, some of it not dark enough, the rest a bit too dark.

The smell, which hadn't reached him in the stairwell, was foul and familiar. Feces, urine, the coppery stench of blood—all odors of the newly deceased.

His stomach clenched so tight he wondered if the knots would ever come out.

The spatter went all the way to the elevator. The carpet, usually a brown that matched the moonscape visible from the elevator, looked like it had been doused with paint. He saw blood squish beneath the feet of some of the techs, rising out of the carpet as if the carpet were made of fluid instead of fiber.

Nyquist glanced over his shoulder, either to see if Flint was following or to see Flint's reaction.

Or both.

Flint decided not to keep his expression neutral. Sometimes a lack of reaction could be seen as suspicious. He took a deep breath through his mouth and felt a sudden queasiness—not because he couldn't handle a murder scene; he could. He'd seen dozens of them—but because Paloma had somehow been involved in this mess.

He didn't see her yet. He hadn't seen anyone except the police. He hadn't even seen a body, although someone had clearly died here.

Nyquist stepped over a marked area in front of Paloma's door. The door, usually impossible to see against the panels of the hallway wall, stood open, revealing the white wall and ancient collectibles—all flat 2-D photographs of the Moon, many of them taken from the earliest missions here.

Only the wall wasn't white any longer. More spatter, some of it swooping in high arcs, crossing the wall, the photographs, the baseboards.

Flint was holding his breath. He made himself exhale.

Nyquist glanced at him again, a questioning glance, asking if Flint was all right. Flint nodded. He could do this. He had once held the battered, bloody, and almost unrecognizable body of his dead baby girl.

He could handle anything.

Nyquist rounded the corner into the main part of the living room, and so did Flint. The windows were open here, the moonscape visible for the first time, looking flatter than it did in other parts of the building, as if the windows rendered it two-dimensional. Nothing marred the view—not blood, not fluids—and Flint let his gaze linger there for just a moment before taking in everything else.

The overturned couch, the toppled armchair, the shattered tables. The hole in the wall leading to the kitchen. The handprint—bloodstained and vivid—on one side of the kitchen's arch. The battered serving trays still struggling to fly, their contents scattered on the carpet. The overturned mugs, the broken tea container, the crushed scones.

Belatedly, Flint brushed the back of his hand, so that the cameras embedded in his skin took pictures. He needed a record of this.

Nyquist looked at him, not the room. Nyquist had seen this all before.

He was waiting, waiting for Flint to see one thing, the one thing Flint wasn't looking at but he had noted, just barely, out of the corner of his eye—

The body, crumpled and broken, huddled up against the moonscape and the brown wall.

Flint took a steadying breath and turned slightly, making himself look.

Crumpled was the wrong word. So was *broken*. *Crushed* was better. Destroyed. Ruined beyond all repair.

Her white hair was matted with blood. Her face, normally so lively, looked like a skull with skin stretched over it. Her jaw had been demolished, and teeth were scattered along the floor like pebbles.

Flint forced himself to remain still, even though he wanted to go to her. To touch her, to make sure it was her.

Paloma had been so strong. She'd been the foundation of his new life, a sturdy woman who could do anything.

Even though she had always looked fragile.

But she was tougher than she looked. She'd once caught him in an armlock that nearly separated his shoulder from its socket. She'd pushed him against wall, bruising his face so badly he'd had to use a repair kit just to go in public.

She'd taken on aliens and won, the government and won, several corporations and won.

She had more enemies than anyone he'd ever known.

And he loved her.

He hadn't realized it until now. Loved her as a friend, but more than that. Almost like a parent, someone who was so central to the universe that she couldn't die, because it wasn't possible.

How had that happened? She'd warned him not to have connections, not to make friends, not to have a family. She'd warned him that such things would make him vulnerable.

They could destroy him and threaten his clients.

He had agreed with her. One of the reasons he'd become a Retrieval Artist was because his parents were dead, his wife had divorced him, and his daughter had been murdered. He had no friends, not really, no one he was close to—although DeRicci had somehow wormed her way into his life.

DeRicci and Paloma. His only two personal contacts in years.

The only two people he really trusted, even though Paloma had told him to trust no one.

And there she was, her bones so shattered that she looked almost like jelly, her clothes holding her together since her frame could no longer do so.

His knees were buckling and he started to catch himself on the bottom part of the overturned couch, but Nyquist offered a hand instead. Flint looked at him, not really seeing him. Flint used Nyquist's arm to steady himself, feeling the blood drain from his face, realizing that he hadn't breathed since he looked at the body.

He'd had families of victims have the same reaction. He hadn't realized it was involuntary.

"What happened here?" His voice croaked out of him. No part of him seemed to function right.

He hadn't done this when his daughter died. Then he'd felt a rage so powerful he nearly destroyed everything around him, everyone around him.

His wife, who thought they should go through the grieving process together, accused him of taking all the rage for himself, as if the crime had happened to him and no one else.

He felt no rage here, only a sense of loss so profound it felt like he wasn't even in the same universe any more.

"We don't know what happened." Nyquist kept a steadying hand on Flint's arm. "The systems are all shut down. Her links are gone."

"Gone?"

He nodded. "They've been removed."

Flint turned toward the body, but Nyquist's hand tightened on his arm.

"You don't want to look," Nyquist said.

To Flint's surprise, he didn't. He didn't want to know, but he had to know. Knowing, he'd learned when Emmeline died, was sometimes the only thing that got you through.

"She has a security system here, but it's keyed to her in some specific ways that we don't understand. We'll have techs on-site shortly."

"I can do it," Flint said.

Nyquist shook his head. "You're a civilian."

"I bought her business," Flint said. "I know how she sets up systems."

Then realized that he probably shouldn't have said that. He probably shouldn't say much. Nyquist hadn't said Flint was a suspect, but he had treated Flint the way suspects sometimes got treated—showing them the crime scene for their reaction, giving them a suit for evidence collection, letting them ramble as they were caught off guard by their emotions.

"We'll contact you," Nyquist said, "if we can't figure it out."

"It looks like a heck of a fight," Flint said.

Nyquist nodded. "She didn't die here."

She died in the hallway, Flint suddenly realized, heading toward the elevator. That mass of blood—was it hers? He wouldn't know without samples, without help from Nyquist, Nyquist who probably—logically—considered Flint a suspect.

Flint felt his old cop instincts fall into place. They shielded him, divorced him from the emotion that only a moment ago threatened to overwhelm him. He had to remain calm, become logical, be as cold as people always believed he was.

He made himself study the scene. If she had died in the hallway, then the fight started in the living room. Paloma hadn't expected it. She had treated this person—human? Alien? Something that could drink and eat human food—as an honored guest. She had brought out those serving trays for Flint, letting them glide toward him, bringing him sweets and her favorite tea, and—

He whipped his attention back. The scene. He had to study the scene.

The person had been an honored guest. And then he—what? Attacked? Paloma would have bested anyone in her apartment. She knew where everything was. She had hidden weapons, stun-blocks, equipment she'd never shown him.

Even those serving trays became weapons. Little whirling dervishes, the kind that could slice a man's head off if he wasn't careful.

Flint folded his hands together so that he wouldn't touch anything, but he stared. The debris near the wall—the damaged trays, the destroyed food, the spilled tea—that had happened…first?

But it made no sense. Paloma would have defended herself here, especially from an attack this obvious.

She had died in the hallway, but her body had been carried here. To stage the scene.

Was the overturned couch part of that stage? The ruined serving trays? The implied meal?

Flint bit his lower lip. Nyquist stared at him, watching Flint's face as if that enabled him to read Flint's mind.

The only thing Flint knew for certain was that Paloma had died in the hallway. Not because Nyquist had told him, but because the evidence did. That mass of blood only happened when a person died.

But everything else was confusing.

"Can I move closer to her?" Flint asked.

"You don't want to." It was a friendly warning, meaning Flint would see things he didn't want to see.

But he didn't want to look at Paloma. He'd let his cameras do that, let his own internal links keep the images, and he'd study them later, in a place that didn't smell of blood and death.

"Can I move closer?" Flint repeated, his voice as cold as he could make it. He wanted Nyquist to know he wouldn't lose control of his emotions, not any longer, and he wanted Nyquist to sense that he could trust Flint.

"Just a few steps," Nyquist said. "This part has been cleared. She hasn't."

The techs weren't completely done yet. That was good and bad. They wouldn't have disturbed anything near the body, but the fact that they'd left her for last also meant they felt they had a lot of ground to cover.

"What'd the neighbors say about this?" Flint asked.

"On this floor, no one was home," Nyquist said.

There was only one other apartment on this floor, a lesser apartment without the dome view. Flint would look it up, see who it belonged to.

He walked toward the edge of the couch, crouched, and studied the rug. Not even footprints, which was odd, given the amount of blood outside. Something should've tracked through that mess, left imprints of its own.

A person would have had to clean up after himself. Some of the aliens that despised Paloma could have flown from that death location to this site.

Flint looked up, saw no smear on the wall, then forced himself to look at Paloma again.

She'd been staged, but not posed. And given the position her body was in, she could very well have been dropped.

The teeth bothered him. He wished he could pick one up, see if it had roots still attached or if it had been broken off.

He gave a silent command to his internal links to zoom one of the cameras in as close as it could get, study the teeth, the rug for any trace, see if there was any blood.

He couldn't see anything with the naked eye. He'd have to wait until they cleared the crime scene, see if they failed to find some of Paloma's internal systems.

The elevator surprised him, too. She shouldn't have died near it. If she was trying to escape—which boggled him; Paloma was a fighter, not a runner—then she would have gone for the stairs.

He backtracked the few steps he'd taken, turned, and walked in the steps he'd initially made when he came into the scene. Nyquist watched him, face a mask. But Flint could sense his fascination and his under-standing.

Nyquist knew Flint was working the scene, and, at the moment, Nyquist wasn't objecting.

The spatter bothered him. Flint had noted as he entered that not all the blood and fluids were human. What if none of it was Paloma's, either. Then this scene had been staged to look the opposite of what it was: that the fight had started here, went to the hallway, and then, when Paloma lost, the murderer had carried her back inside—

"And closed the door?" Flint asked.

"Hmm?" Nyquist took a step toward him.

That was when Flint realized he hadn't asked the full question. "Was the door open or closed?"

Nyquist sighed. "You don't need to investigate, Flint. We'll do a thorough job. I'll make sure of it."

Not as thorough as Flint would do. They didn't have as much reason to care. "Open or closed?"

"Closed," Nyquist said.

"You didn't answer about the neighbors."

"I did. I told you that the apartment across the hall was empty."

"What about below? This should've made a hell of a racket."

Nyquist pursed his lips.

"How'd it get called in? You still haven't told me the sequence, Bartholomew." Flint used Nyquist's first name to put them on equal footing.

Nyquist met Flint's gaze. "We're not sure of the sequence."

He was lying. The sentence was too confident, too practiced.

They were holding back something about the events. Something they didn't want anyone to know.

"So tell me what you think," Flint said. "I won't hold you to it."

Nyquist shook his head slightly. "Right now, we're not discussing anything about the case."

Flint frowned. "With me? Or with anyone?"

"With anyone."

Flint walked toward the door, careful to stay in his original tracks. Once a detective, always a detective apparently. He looked at the splatter pattern, and saw it as an investigator.

Thin on the edge of the wall, almost a spray, most of the drops flowing downward, although some just stuck, which was odd. Blood didn't stick unless it was already congealing.

Although he didn't know about this other stuff, the stuff that clearly wasn't human blood. Something about the smell—rank, almost cheesy—suggested that it was organic, too, which might have been why he thought it was non-human blood or the alien equivalent of blood.

But he wasn't certain now. He wished he could take a sample or be privy to the police reports. But he wouldn't be able to, not through channels, anyway.

He might have to create his own channels.

If he could still do that. He'd been able to hack into the police databases in the past, but he'd become higher profile recently. Those avenues might be closed to him.

"See anything?" Nyquist asked.

Flint started. He hadn't realized he was staring at the wall so intently. Obviously, he wasn't not completely functional yet, no matter how he was feeling.

He glanced over his shoulder at Paloma. He had no choice. He had to work this. She would have wanted him to.

Although that thought stopped him. She might not have wanted him to. She had told him to stay out of relationships and uninvolved with others for a reason.

She wanted him to remain pure.

Would this taint him?

Probably. And he didn't care. No one could do this to her and get away with it. No one.

The techs moved outside the door, sending floating 'bots over the large wet stain in the center of the hallway.

"You never did tell me who called this in," Flint said.

"The entire building got shut down," Nyquist said. "We get notified when security systems activate."

"Shut down?" Flint asked.

"Something triggered the automatic sensors." Nyquist was using that tone again. *Something* wasn't unidentified. He knew; he was just choosing not to tell Flint. "We dispatched immediately."

"A detective team with a full crime scene unit?" Flint asked.

"That's not procedure," Nyquist said.

"I know," Flint said. "But Paloma contacted me down her emergency links. I came here as fast as I could and the investigation was already underway."

"You'd said that before," Nyquist said. "I hadn't realized the contact was so recent."

Flint frowned, and turned slightly without moving his feet. "Why would you assume that? I came here quickly; I used the word *emergency*. I wouldn't wait if she was in trouble."

"She couldn't have contacted you," Nyquist said. "She's been dead for hours."

Flint glanced at the body again. He had shaken his head several times before he realized he had done it, and stopped himself.

"She sent me a message," he said. "I got it just before I came here."

Then his frown grew deeper. He'd gotten the message in the office. Where the links should have been shut off. He had shut them off when he had gone in, hadn't he? Or had he been so surprised by the dust and the level of disaster that he hadn't touched them?

He almost shook his head again, then stopped. He shut off those links automatically. He had no need for emergency lines because, theoretically, no one needed to contact him.

She had contacted him through back channels, that was what he had assumed. She had known how to reach him even with the office's expanded security because she had designed much of it.

But he had taken out most of her design. It hadn't been safe.

Had her message been waiting? Working its way through the system until it reached him—taking hours instead of the speed of thought?

Nyquist was still watching him, evaluating him, trying to figure him out. Trying to figure out how involved he was.

Nyquist believed she was dead when Flint got the message. But no one had examined the body. The first reports were preliminary. There was no way to know, not yet.

"When did you get the message about the building?" Flint asked.

"I didn't get it," Nyquist said. "It came into the department."

"Don't play with me." Flint was suddenly tired. "If you're not going to tell me something, be up-front. But don't play word games with me."

Nyquist's expression flattened. He was a good cop. Whatever emotion Flint had provoked wasn't going to show in his face.

"All right then," Nyquist said. "I'm not giving you any information that isn't going to the press. I did you a courtesy bringing you up here, but that's it. That's all I can do."

"You wanted to see my reaction," Flint said.

"That too," Nyquist said.

"You suspect me?" Flint asked.

"We don't have enough information to suspect anyone right now," Nyquist said.

Flint smiled coldly. "You mean, you suspect everyone right now."

Nyquist nodded. "That's the other way to put it," he said.

4

FLINT TOOK HIS TIME LEAVING THE APARTMENT. HE STUDIED THE spatter pattern, which grew thicker and more elaborate the farther into the hallway he got, and that puddle near the elevator door.

Nyquist wouldn't let him look in the elevator itself, but Flint used as many tricks as he could to get his own internal cameras to zoom into the evidence. He wouldn't get much of it, but he would get some.

Maybe it would be enough.

The techs worked around him. The woman glared at him. Occasionally, she would look at Nyquist as if she couldn't believe what he was doing.

Nyquist also kept an eye on Flint, but he seemed less interested than he was. That could be a cop trick; Flint had used it himself on occasion.

Flint couldn't get any closer to the real evidence. Finally, he decided to let the crime scene techs finish their job, and he took the stairs down.

He didn't remove the suit. He would keep that, just like he had told Nyquist he would. Maybe it had picked up some external trace, things he could investigate.

He had a few others, as well. In addition to the vid footage he just took, he had one rather large lead. Nyquist had told him that the building had an internal security system—one that had worked well enough to contact the police when there was a problem.

Flint could hack into that. He would have to be careful, to make certain he didn't leave any trails or trigger any alarms that the police department techs set.

For all he knew, Nyquist could have told him about this to tempt Flint to access the system. Maybe Nyquist would see that as a sign of guilt.

Flint didn't know. For all his understanding of the other man's techniques, he didn't know Nyquist at all. Nyquist seemed like a good detective and a good man, but Flint based that on a few encounters and a few favors.

Encounters and favors were enough for a casual friendship, but not enough to know how the man conducted his investigations.

Flint pushed open the door to the lobby and stepped into it. A few street cops still milled about, but he didn't see any employees. This building prided itself on human service—no robots, no alien workers (at least in the public areas, which was how they got around the discrimination laws)—and it couldn't run without some kind of help.

Maybe it had an automated backup.

Maybe the residents were all evacuated.

If that was the case, why? Why would people have been thrown out of their homes?

The entire building was a crime scene. The only part of it that Nyquist hadn't protected were the stairs. He'd carefully led Flint inside, probably walking him on an already established path.

One of the street cops looked at him, as if wondering who he was. Street cops didn't know everyone in their department, let alone every police employee in the city.

Flint had to be careful—he didn't want too much more attention on himself, not from Nyquist or the investigation—but he was willing to take a risk. He didn't even look like himself. With the help of that suit, his blond curls were pressed against his skull, and his clothing's cut—certainly not affordable by anyone in the department—wouldn't be as obvious.

"When was the building evacuated?" he asked as he approached the nearest street cop.

She was slender and young—maybe twenty-five. She had regulation-length cropped black hair and skin so white that it was almost translucent. He'd never seen anyone with skin as white as his before.

"Two hours ago," she said.

"Did you help supervise it?" he asked.

"No, sir," she said. "I just made sure they stayed within the marked area as they left. These people were mad. They wanted to know what would happen to their belongings."

"They're not going to be gone long enough to worry about that," Flint said, guessing, hoping that would elicit more information from her.

"We didn't know that then, sir. That report of some kind of bio-chemical goo—that really spooked everyone."

Biochemical goo. He couldn't ask for a more specific term. That would show he truly was out of the loop. But biochemical goo might give him another in into this investigation, one that might provide him with more help than he could get through the department.

He wondered how much Noelle DeRicci knew about the so-called biochemical threat, or how much of it was being handled by her underlings. If DeRicci knew about it, then she would help him.

She owed him.

Although she might not do much, considering that this case involved Paloma.

"When are the residents going to be allowed back?" Flint asked.

The street cop blushed. One of the disadvantages of being so light-skinned. "I didn't pay attention, sir. It was after my shift, so I really didn't…"

She waved a hand instead of finishing the sentence. To imply that she hadn't cared was one thing; to say it was another.

He nodded. "When do you get off shift?"

"An hour, sir."

He thanked her and headed to the main desk. No one stopped him. No one seemed to pay any attention. Whatever part of the crime scene this had been—and it had been some kind, or they wouldn't have had the precaution of people leaving a specific way—it was no longer.

He glanced at the elevators. They were stopped on Paloma's floor.

When he'd come in, he'd seen crime scene techs near the elevator doors. None were there now.

Still, he stayed back. He went behind the long black desk, noted the kind of security system the building had, but didn't touch any surfaces. Better to keep his hands off things.

Better not to give Nyquist any clues as to what he'd been doing.

Flint took one last look at everything in the lobby—memorizing it as well as recording it—and then headed out the way he'd initially come in. The front door, even though it was now marked as a crime scene, wasn't that well protected.

The street cops just shut off the security lights, nodded at him, and then went back to staring at nothing, probably wishing someone had automated the system so that they could get home.

The front yard was empty too, except for police footprints and some equipment waiting to be picked up. The vans were still there, but no one milled around.

A few curious people watched from across the street, but didn't come any closer. The crime scene lights had warnings on them—a mild electric shock to anyone unauthorized to cross.

Flint leaned back in the door. "I'm parked across the street," he said to one of the guards. "Can I get through that?"

The guard shook his head slightly, but followed Flint outside. As Flint reached the red beam of light, the guard stepped into it first, his chips deactivating it.

The cop didn't even question Flint's inability to step through on his own. A lot of detectives refused to wear those deactivation chips, feeling they compromised any undercover work.

Flint passed through the little gap in the light, then hurried to the building where he'd left his car. So much to sift through. So much to do.

He wondered what would have happened if he had gotten Paloma's message the moment she sent it instead of hours later.

Would he be dead now, too?

Or would she still be alive?

He had to know.

But first, he had to know what happened—and that would take some work.

5

NYQUIST STARED AT THE SPATTER PATTERN, WISHING HE COULD SEE what Flint had. Techs swarmed the hallway, their equipment climbing over the walls, finally taking samples from various places in the ruins of what had once been a life.

Nearly three hours before a single sample was taken. That was how deep the scare had been.

He sighed and ran a hand through his thinning hair. His ex-wife used to tell him if he left his hair alone, he'd have hair left. Of course, she'd urged enhancements—some kind of cell replacement so that his hair would grow again.

But he didn't have the time for that. He barely had the time for this—a study of an inexplicable crime scene, one that could have caused a panic through the entire city.

"He left with the suit." Mikaela Khundred said in a disapproving tone.

"I told him he could." Nyquist continued to study the spatter. He suspected Flint had recorded the entire scene, and that didn't bother him as much as it should have. If Flint had been involved, he wouldn't need the recording.

If he hadn't been involved, he might help Nyquist solve this.

It was one of the most savage killings Nyquist had ever seen. He'd seen some Disty Vengeance Killings and a few other alien ritual deaths, but this seemed different. The spatter alone suggested that

Paloma—whose last name he hadn't yet been able to find—put up a terrible struggle.

Flint had been shaken. He'd nearly passed out when he saw the body, but he had recovered quickly. Too quickly? Nyquist didn't know. He'd never brought another professional onto a scene where the professional had known the victim.

"You were wrong to do that," Mikaela said.

Nyquist suppressed a sigh, trying to remind himself that she was new. Promoted from the Space Traffic police because of her great collar rate. She'd saved lives more than once with some creative thinking—something the brass liked to see.

She'd been allowed to pick her promotion path, and like everyone else, she wanted to be a detective. Somehow everyone outside of the detective unit saw this work as glamorous.

In all his twenty years detecting, he'd never use the word *glamorous* to describe the job. Difficult, yeah. A grind, sure. But glamorous? Never.

"He's a former cop," Mikaela said. "He bends the rules. Hell, I saw him manipulate one of the toughest people in Space Traffic to get a yacht out of the port. He takes advantage, you know? And I'd hate to see that on your record. I'd hate it if—"

"It were on your record too?" Nyquist turned slightly.

Her green eyes were cool. She had pulled her red hair back with some kind of barrette and then placed a covering over it. She was wearing a suit as well, even though she hadn't earlier.

"You don't like me much, do you?" she asked.

"I don't know you," he said, and turned back to the spatter. That much was true. She'd been assigned this case because the brass believed he needed a partner. He preferred to work alone.

They'd been working together only three months, and if he based everything he knew about her on those three months, then, yeah, he'd say he didn't like her.

"All I'm saying is that you should've taken the suit, and you should've interviewed him—formally—on the record. I mean—"

"What's to say I haven't?" He couldn't concentrate on the spatter, so he turned all the way around. A couple of techs scurried past. One gave him an odd look, as if he, too, disapproved of letting Flint on the scene.

Flint had arrived just in time. The biohazard had been cleared—it had been a false reading from the building's security system—and people could come and go in the building again.

Of course, Nyquist was using the quarantine to his advantage. He wanted to finish evidence-gathering and start cleanup before the residents returned.

He hadn't told anyone else that, either.

"Does that mean you have interviewed him?" She crossed her arms. She was still young—maybe thirty—with a quick intelligence and an even quicker temper.

He liked the temper.

"I mean," he said, trying not to speak too slowly so that she would know he was talking down to her, "that I recorded Flint's entire reaction. We'll have it analyzed, maybe even by that department profiling thing."

"The program? What about the shrink?"

"Her too." Even though Nyquist didn't put too much stake in human expertise outside of his own.

"You did all of this on purpose?"

He almost snapped, *What'd you think, that I felt kindly toward the man?* Instead, he said, "In an investigation, I do everything on purpose."

Including keeping Khundred out of the loop. Initially, he'd figured she was too green. But now he was thinking she was too literal.

She wanted things by the book, on the record, aboveboard. Which wasn't the impression she'd given the detective squad when she'd been bucking for promotion. Despite what the regs said, the detectives who were the most creative in their interpretation of the rules closed the most cases, and, ironically, had the fewest convictions overturned.

"I wish you would've told me what you were doing," she said.

"In front of Flint?" Nyquist asked. Not that it would have matter. Flint knew what Nyquist was up to. The simple tricks, the one that fooled civilians, hadn't fooled Flint at all.

For a while, Flint had played along. Then he had seen Paloma's body, and his entire attitude changed. There had been that momentary breakdown, and after that, Flint had gathered himself, become cold, if a little distracted.

And he had stared at the spatter.

Which Nyquist was going to do if Khundred would just leave him alone.

"Not in front of Flint," she said. "You could've pulled me aside—"

"And left him alone," Nyquist said.

"Or not let him up here at all."

"Then I would've missed his reaction." Nyquist glanced at the spatter. Part of it wasn't dripping. That bothered him. The rest was slowing drying, but still suggested the extreme violence that had brought Paloma to her end.

"That fake near-faint?" Khundred said. "Please. I could do that."

"So could I," Nyquist said. "But it wouldn't be my choice of a fake reaction."

She tilted her head, encouraging him to go on.

But he didn't. If she didn't know how hard it was to fake buckling knees—that slow-motion movement was something that only happened in deep shock—then she didn't understand what he meant.

Most fakers cried or teared up or gasped theatrically.

Flint had done none of those things.

He had paled—which Nyquist would've thought impossible given his already pale skin—and then he'd lost control of his legs, catching himself in such an awkward way that Nyquist knew that part was real.

What Nyquist didn't know was how much of it was shock over Paloma's death—or shock over the way an expected death actually looked.

He'd seen Flint near a death scene before: he'd had to break the news to Flint about the loss of one of his clients. That day, Flint had reacted with barely a flicker of emotion. Mostly irritation—some of it at Nyquist, although he didn't voice it—and most of it at the client herself.

This was different.

This was interesting.

"He's gone now," Khundred said.

"Good," Nyquist muttered.

"You didn't set up a formal interview."

"Nope."

"You didn't arrest him."

Nyquist bit back another irritated response. "On what grounds?"

"I don't know," she said. "The fact that he was the last one to visit her."

"Says some guy at the front desk. And no one asked him what he meant by *last*. He might've meant last human. He might've meant last person he'd seen. He might've meant last person he recognized. That's not enough for an arrest."

"It's enough for questioning."

"Grilling actually," Nyquist said. "By you."

She frowned. The look added lines to her forehead, lines she was probably vain enough to remove the moment she noticed them.

"Are you saying I should question him?"

"I'm saying you should stop questioning me. I'm senior on this investigation. I've closed more cases than you've read. This thing is a lot more complicated than it looks."

"It looks pretty simple to me," she said.

"It would," Nyquist said, then shook his head. She wasn't going to get it unless he was blunt. "Look, we don't just follow rumors and gossip. If we decide to take action against Miles Flint, I'll do it."

"Because you're his friend?" Khundred asked.

"Because he's too smart for you, little girl," Nyquist snapped, and then wished he could take the words back. Those were the kind of words that got him warnings. Those were the kind of words that had prevented his own promotions.

Those were the kind of words that would someday get him fired.

Khundred's dusky skin turned even darker, and her green eyes narrowed. Her entire expression told him that she'd take him down for that if they were somewhere else. If they were other people entirely.

She was still too green to take him on.

"He is your friend, though, isn't he?" she asked, a little too loudly, apparently trying to set up some kind of case against Nyquist—separating herself from him because she believed he was doing this wrong.

The techs would overhear, and she probably believed they'd back her. The techs didn't back anyone. They overheard but they didn't get involved.

"I've met him before," Nyquist said. "I've read his files here. I've followed up on a few of the rumors. Otherwise, I have had nothing to do with him. He's an interesting man. I have a hunch he'll be important to the investigation, but how, I don't know yet—and neither do you."

She glared at him. He had to remind himself: she had an ego. She needed it for this job. He had to accept that he would run into it as well.

He just hated how the ego dominated her, making her forget her inexperience.

"You seem awfully sure of yourself," she said.

He smiled at her. "I'm always sure of the things I don't know." he said.

6

NOELLE DERICCI STOOD IN FRONT OF THE WINDOWS OF HER OFFICE, staring out at the City of Armstrong. The damage done to the dome more than a year ago by a bomb was nearly repaired. She could still see the scar—the condemned buildings, the hole in the once-familiar network of streets.

But the dome itself looked perfect. The dome workers had just replaced the last panel two days before. She had gone to the ceremony, had spoken about loss and sadness and rebirth just like she was supposed to, and she kept her left hand beneath the podium, her fist clenched.

No one seemed to notice that they—the police, her office, the other teams assigned to the investigation—had never figured out the identity of the bomber. They didn't even know what had happened in that neighborhood, not really.

The theories got bandied about all the time, and the government had settled on one—terrorists from outside Armstrong, angry at the policies of the Earth Alliance, had set off the bomb to coincide with some meetings on controversial issues inside the Alliance.

But that was as big a guess as the one she'd heard only two days ago—that the government itself had blown a hole in the dome to scare the populace so that they'd be more complacent as the United Domes of the Moon gained more power over the citizens of the Moon.

That last rumor—that the government had done it—was the only one that DeRicci knew to be false. The rest could be true, for all she knew. The investigations had stalled nearly a month after the bombing, and nothing she did could revive them.

So she stared at the remaining destruction, using it to remind herself that she had gotten this job under false pretences. She was being rewarded for a heroism she never felt, for work that she felt was incomplete.

That she had saved Armstrong once before that hadn't mattered—that nearly disastrous Moon Marathon was a long-forgotten event. It hadn't even been mentioned on the two-year anniversary.

Of course, why would the sponsors mention a near disaster at Armstrong's most popular athletic event?

DeRicci shook her head, hands clasped behind her. She wore an expensive suit, complete with skirt, because she could afford such things now. But she kept some grungy work clothes, the kind she would have worn when she was a lowly police detective, in one of the nearby closets.

She'd learned last year that she needed ratty clothing in case she had to oversee a crime scene.

She should have gone to the scene this afternoon, but the phrase *biochemical goo*, stopped her. Maybe it provided her with her first real chance to act like a governmental official.

She didn't have to go to a crime scene, particularly one contaminated with some kind of biochemical goo. That was for flunkies, her nominal boss, the Moon's governor-general, Celia Alfreda, would say.

Biochemical goo scared DeRicci. She had been too close to a biohazard in the past, and it was not an experience she wanted to repeat.

At least that part of the crisis was over. The building had been evacuated, HazMat teams had gone in—first the robotic units and then the human ones—and they had found nothing.

She sighed and ran a hand over her face, then turned away from the destroyed part of the city. Her office was more to her tastes than it had been a year ago. She'd gotten rid of the clear furniture—so very trendy—and replaced it with expensive antique wood furniture, much of it purchased from shops in Armstrong's reviving historic area.

A few of the pieces she'd purchased herself. Then the governor-general had noticed on some visit or another here and authorized payment for a complete overhaul of the office.

DeRicci left the green plants that spilled off most of the surfaces. They added a warmth and freshness—and she didn't have to take care of them. Someone else took care of that.

But everything else she had picked out. Right down to the rugs, woven in Tycho Crater, which added a touch of color to the entire place.

She finally felt safe here. She finally felt at home. She finally felt like she belonged.

Although she had to keep looking at that mess out her window to remind herself that she hadn't deserved that promotion, despite what she had done during her first few months on the job.

She had to remind herself so that she wouldn't make any more mistakes.

Contacting Flint, telling him about Paloma's death, would be a mistake.

Much as she wanted to. The news hadn't leaked to the press yet—all they knew was that someone had died in Paloma's building—and they were only identifying the building by neighborhood, to stem any kind of panic.

Paloma had no next of kin that DeRicci knew of. But the police would research it anyway, and until someone was satisfied that Paloma either had no loved ones or the loved ones were notified, her name wouldn't hit the media.

As long as a pariah like Ki Bowles didn't find out about any of this.

DeRicci crossed to her desk. No matter what, she no longer needed to worry. She had to turn to other measures—whether or not Armstrong Dome needed a full-time security force; how many of the paltry funds that the United Domes of the Moon authorized her should go to large domes like Armstrong and how much should go to smaller ones like Glenn Station; and the big one, whether or not the presence of various alien groups inside the cities led to civil unrest.

She sighed. She wasn't designed for these kinds of decisions. But she was learning about the other kinds—the political ones.

Keeping Flint in the dark was political. Who knew what he would do when he found out? This case was probably going to be public anyway—the city would have a mild panic when it became clear the building had been evacuated—and any investigation that would tie Flint to DeRicci wouldn't be good.

Still, she felt odd not telling him. Paloma meant a lot to him. In many ways, he was her next of kin.

DeRicci sighed and forced herself to focus on the decisions she was being paid to make. As it stood, her office hadn't had much involvement. The governor-general would be pleased that a crisis was averted.

DeRicci should be, too. A biohazard of any kind inside a dome was more dangerous than fire.

But she was uneasy, and not just about Flint. Something about this case, the way it started, the direction it was going, bothered her.

Something she couldn't investigate because it was no longer her job.

But she knew whose job it was.

She sent a message down her links to her assistant. *Tell Nyquist to report to me as soon as he can.*

Maybe he could let her help with the investigation—just enough to get rid of this nagging sense of unease.

7

FLINT HAD NEARLY MADE IT TO THE OFFICE BEFORE HE REMEMBERED that the place was a ruin. He would have to clean up everything and rebuild entire systems before he could trust it again.

Right now, the only safe place he had to view all the material he'd recorded at the crime scene was the *Emmeline*.

So he parked in his assigned spot at the port—not caring if someone (like Nyquist) thought he was leaving Armstrong again—and headed to Terminal 25.

No one seemed to notice him. Back when he'd been a cop in Space Traffic, people used to watch him out of the corner of their eyes. They would try to judge if he was coming after them or if something bad was about to happen.

He would pretend to ignore them, but he would judge them in return. He would see if they needed examination, if they were truly pursuing some kind of illegal activity, if they were afraid of him because of his uniform or because they knew he could arrest them if they were doing something wrong.

Now they just treated him like another passenger, hurrying to a ship, heading out of Armstrong on business. He couldn't change who he was, though. He still watched everyone—from the group of young men exchanging information outside one of the restaurants to a Disty couple shrinking away from all the passing humans to half a dozen Rev who plowed through this part of the port as if they owned it.

Flint was happy to go through the secondary identification door at Terminal 25, the one that used to ask him, a Space Traffic cop, if he had any reason to be in this restricted area of the port. Now the door simply opened for him, recognizing him as one of the elite who belonged.

He hurried past, feeling time pressure. He wanted to study his recordings. He wanted to make sure he hadn't missed anything.

But as he scurried down the ramp that led to the yacht bays, he realized he could do one other thing while he was here. He could examine Paloma's yacht, the *Dove*.

He doubted the police had even thought of it. In fact, he bet that they didn't even know about it. Only DeRicci had known—and that was because Flint had used the *Dove* to help her with a case back when she was still on the force.

But DeRicci wasn't on the force any more, either.

He had some time.

The question was whether or not he wanted to take it.

He was already a suspect—Nyquist had made that clear. And, to be fair, Flint would have considered anyone close to Paloma a suspect at this moment.

But did he want to compound it by entering her space yacht right after he had found out about her death?

He stopped, glanced at the fork that led to the various docks. His was to the right; hers to the left.

He'd go to his first—if nothing else, he'd make copies of the recordings so that he wouldn't lose them—and then he'd figure out what he wanted to do.

He had to hurry.

He wasn't sure if the police were ahead of him or not.

8

Ki Bowles stood. Her knees cracked and her back ached. She'd been on this dock longer than she had planned.

The silence felt good. It was impossible to maintain all her links in this shielded section of the port. She didn't even try. Instead, she'd been staring at the *Emmeline* reassessing her life.

She stretched. She'd been here for hours, wishing her life were different. Thinking about Flint, wondering what he was really like—not the harsh man she'd met on a few occasions, nor the broken man she'd seen on that vid she'd played over and over again, the man who had barely held himself together when his baby daughter died.

But the man who named his space yacht (of all things!) for that daughter. The man who vanished for long stretches at a time, who sometimes made choices that seemed inconsistent with the job of Retrieval Artist. The man who also made choices inconsistent with those of a cop.

He had fascinated her, and he was inspiring her—although she wasn't sure of the route he was unconsciously encouraging her to take.

She'd been thinking of him so much that she wasn't surprised when she saw him on the edge of the dock. She thought he was a figment of her imagination.

He had to be, because Flint never looked like this—his curly blond hair messed as if he'd been in a Terran wind storm, his face blotchy and streaked with dirt, his eyes red. Usually he looked like a cherub or one of those drawings of Cupid she'd studied back when she had been an art history major, deep, deep in her secret and idealistic past.

Not even when his daughter died had he looked so wild.

He froze in place, and something in that movement made Bowles realize he was really here—she hadn't conjured him up from her imagination by thinking about him so very hard. He had actually come to his yacht.

And he had caught her staring at it.

"What do you want?" he snapped.

She deserved that. She deserved worse, really. She'd hounded him for weeks, trying to get dirt on DeRicci, and he'd repeatedly told her to leave him alone.

Then, when the story had backfired, it was his voice she'd heard, telling her she couldn't be trusted. Maybe that was why she had focused her attention on him, why she had studied him, why she was here now, staring at his yacht and thinking of him.

"Well?" he asked.

She licked her bottom lip, feeling like a schoolgirl caught staring at her first crush. She didn't have an answer for him.

"I don't have any comments about any story," he said. "So if you're here to dig up dirt, I'm not going to help you."

"I know," she said quietly.

He stared at her, as if he couldn't believe she had said that. "I mean it. And if you took footage of my ship, then I ask you to delete it or give it to me."

"I didn't," she said.

"What the hell are you doing here, then?"

She shrugged. "It's quiet here."

"It's private here. People like you aren't supposed to get in."

In the past that would have angered her. In the past, she actually had been somebody who thought highly of herself, who thought she had a right to be in places like this.

God, she'd been arrogant. She was as tired of herself as everyone else was.

"I know," she said. "I can still talk my way into any place."

His gaze met hers on the word *still*. He had always unnerved her a little, the way he seemed to see right through her.

"You don't belong here," he said. "I'm going to make sure you won't get in here again."

She held up her hands. "Don't get anyone in trouble. It's my fault, really."

Now he was staring at her as if she weren't quite human. Maybe he'd heard the panic in her voice. She didn't want to get Laxalt in trouble. She didn't want anyone to get in trouble, not any more.

But if she said that, Flint wouldn't believe her—and who could blame him? She hadn't always thought about the consequences of what she did. She used to think everything took a back seat to the story—that once the story—the truth, whatever it was—came out, then people would be okay with the way she had acquired it.

She had learned how wrong she was the hard way. The truth hadn't impressed anyone, and nearly got Bowles fired.

That had certainly gotten her attention.

"I don't have time to deal with you," he said and pushed past her. "Get out of here."

He smelled faintly of sweat and something else, something a little foul. And his pants legs were covered in a fine dust that looked like Moon dust.

Her stomach clenched. Something was happening here, something important. Maybe that story she'd been waiting for.

But his face was wild and sad. And scared.

And reckless.

Something had happened. Something awful. But if she pushed, she would be back where she had been only a short time before—following gut instinct and ignoring the people around her.

He had asked her to leave.

She would, as soon as she figured out where she was going to go.

9

FLINT STOPPED JUST OUTSIDE THE *EMMELINE*. HE COULDN'T BRING himself to open the yacht's doors until Ki Bowles left.

He hadn't seen her so subdued before. Even her clothing was subdued—dark pants, a dark sweater, and no scarves at all. Her hair was a strawberry blond that suited her and made the decorative tattoos across her face seem like etchings.

She clutched a bag to her chest and watched him as if she couldn't quite believe he was there.

"Leave," he said again.

She nodded, bent her head, and walked off the dock, heading down the long port tunnel and back to the main area.

She was behaving oddly. If she had come here because of Paloma, she would have asked him a series of questions. But she hadn't. She acted as if she didn't know at all.

Had Nyquist kept this information from the media? Or was Ki Bowles still off InterDome's main reporter list? They'd pulled her after those disgusting stories about DeRicci. The stories—at least the ones that Flint saw—made DeRicci seem mean and vindictive, two words he would never use to describe her.

He waited until he couldn't see Bowles any longer, then he went to the side of his ship, climbed the ladder that led to the main hatch, and pressed his palm against it.

On his trip, he had upgraded the security even more. The door now used a palm scan (from living tissue), a DNA scan, and a retinal scan, followed by a vocal ID once he was inside the airlock. There he had to go through two more layers of security before entering the ship itself.

For a while, he had thought the *Emmeline* would be his only home, and he wanted it to be as safe as possible. When he arrived back on Armstrong, the precautions seemed a little silly. But now that he had found Ki Bowles, of all people, right beside his ship, he no longer doubted his methods.

The door finished its scans and whooshed open. He entered the airlock, and the door closed behind him. Then he said his own name, so that the system could double-check his vocal imprint, plugged in two different codes into the systems on the far side of the interior door, and watched as that opened for him.

He stepped into the *Emmeline*. Usually he relaxed the moment the airlock door closed behind him, but today he did not. He couldn't.

He couldn't get the image of Paloma's ruined body from his mind.

He took the bag with the tech suit and placed it in one of the coded lockers near the door. The lockers were hidden to the naked eye. They seemed like part of a larger wall. Only the manufacturer and the owners of these yachts even knew the lockers were here.

Space yachts of this level had all sorts of secret compartments and hidden storage areas. Flint had never used all the storage spaces on the *Emmeline*, not even when he spent months on her like he had recently.

It made him wonder if Paloma had used her storage spaces on the *Dove*, and that made the urgency rise in him again. He had to get there before Nyquist did, or at least try to get there first.

But first, Flint had to stop leaving bits of himself everywhere.

He went into the main cabin, removed his clothes and set them in a special evidence bag. He was glad he had purchased those a few years ago, when he started as a Retrieval Artist, glad he had continued a number of the habits he'd learned as a detective.

Then he took a quick shower, using the water option because he was in the port and he could hook the *Emmeline* up to the port's water system if his own supply grew low. So far, he hadn't used the water at all since he replenished it after his trip.

The water was hot, and it scrubbed his skin. He needed the scrubbing. He felt dirty after being in Paloma's apartment. Odd that he didn't feel so dirty after being in his own office, filled as it was with Moon dust and debris.

But the fetid odor of Paloma's apartment clung to him—or seemed to—and the air itself had felt contaminated. No wonder someone had become frightened of "biochemical goo." The air felt soiled, and maybe, on some lower, unimportant (at least to the city) level, it was.

As he got out, he had the drain catch remove every bit of dirt and debris and place it in a small storage container—another of the yacht's many perks. The system was designed for stays in foreign ports so that the yacht could hook into foreign systems without releasing anything unusual or alien into their own supplies.

It also prevented DNA from getting into alien hands without going through the usual protocols.

He programmed the drain catch to keep the little storage box in a secure area, to be released only if he needed it.

Then he stepped out, used the hot air vents to dry himself, and got dressed, putting on a black shirt, black pants, black shoes. He didn't notice, until he was nearly dressed, that he'd reverted to an outfit that looked like one he might have worn as a detective.

He would consider the psychological impact of that later. Right now, he had work to do.

First, he went to the cockpit and downloaded all the material he'd recorded at the crime scene. Usually downloads happened in a microsecond, but this took longer, partly because he was making secondary and tertiary backups. One he removed and placed in one of the escape pods on the side of the yacht. Just in case someone managed to breach all of the security systems here, take the information he'd removed, and then delete it.

He knew he was being paranoid, but he had learned, in the past few years, that sometimes his paranoia had helped him survive.

Then he used the ship's security cameras to see if Ki Bowles had snuck back into this section of the terminal.

She hadn't. She was gone. There wasn't even a heat signature remaining.

He shook his head. He wasn't sure what she wanted, and when he didn't know, he got nervous.

But he couldn't focus on her.

He had to get to the *Dove*.

He took a laser pistol from his stash under the console and stuck it in the waistband of his pants, pulling his shirt so that it fell over the pistol's shape.

If someone was looking, they'd see that he was carrying a weapon, but the casual observer wouldn't notice. Nor would the security system in Terminal 25. It purposely ignored any weapon carried by a licensed Armstrong resident who docked a ship here, a security flaw that Flint had been planning to mention to DeRicci, but somehow hadn't gotten around to yet.

Then he headed out the airlock, down the steps, and across Terminal 25 toward the *Dove*.

10

Nyquist sat in his office, working the very slow terminal built into his desk. He was trying to access information outside of the department, something he wouldn't get reimbursed for if he used some of the faster systems throughout the city.

On his personal links, he subscribed to the most basic services. He didn't like a lot of information flooding him, and he had always figured he could go elsewhere for more.

That theory was beginning to annoy him.

His office was small, barely larger than a closet in his apartment across town. His desk and chair fit into it, plus another chair in case someone wanted to sit and visit (for the record, no one ever had), and a perpetually dying plant that some long-forgotten girlfriend had given him when he'd gotten his own space.

Unlike the other detectives on the fifth floor of the First Detective Division, he hadn't covered the remaining wall space or shelf space with personal items. They distracted him. If anything, he would put an occasional memento of the current case within eye view, something that would remind him of the things he had yet to do.

Right now, the Paloma case was too new for him to gather mementos, and he doubted he would need them. Even though no one had said so yet, this case would be one of those that had to be closed even if there were no suspects.

He tried to stay away from cases like this, but because he'd been on rotation this time (and because the chief, bless her, hadn't wanted the rookie team that was, ostensibly, ahead of him in rotation to handle such a touchy case), he'd gotten this one.

If he had to put something up in his office to make himself think of this case, he'd put up a 3-D image of Paloma's body. No one should die like that, not for any reason.

Although he was beginning to get irritated at her. She—or someone with a lot of computer experience—had gone into all of the public records he'd accessed so far, and erased most of the information pertaining to her.

All that remained were the handful of items a person needed to survive in this society—current address, at least one bank account, and a work history. Apparently, a person didn't need a last name, because he still hadn't been able to locate hers. Her work history was also quite vague. It simply listed her as self-employed for more than seventy years, and then after that, retired.

He was beginning to wish he had never stopped at the office. Noelle DeRicci had wanted to see him for an update. She had told him to come as soon as possible—she might even have said immediately upon leaving the crime scene. He couldn't remember and he didn't care about that sort of nicety.

He had come here first, partly because he wanted more information, but in truth because he wanted to impress her. She had been a good investigator in her day, and her unorthodox ways appealed to him. He was as unorthodox as a man could be inside this department, so unorthodox that he'd had to learn important secrets about his co-workers just to keep from having too many reports written up about him, so he appreciated that trait in others.

The interesting thing about DeRicci was that she had managed to survive this cutthroat department while being unusual and without using the strong-arm tactics he'd sometimes employed.

He wished he could ask her how she had done that, but he couldn't, not yet. He didn't know her well enough. He might never know her well enough.

He sighed and punched into two other databases, finding the same information on Paloma. He had never seen a record so thoroughly scrubbed.

She had to have had a personal life. She had to have had parents and probably some relationships, even if she never formalized them.

He only knew about Flint because Flint had bought her business—and that was in Flint's record, not Paloma's. Flint's record was a lot more complete: the early death of his parents, his marriage at a young age, the birth and death of his daughter, and the ultimate dissolution of the marriage. His various job changes were well documented in police department files, and so was his tendency, ever since he'd gone to the academy, to work alone.

Even his meeting with Paloma was documented, since it happened while he was on a case.

But Nyquist couldn't find corresponding information on her, and it frustrated him. Older information left ghosts, trails of what had been.

He wasn't good enough to find those ghosts, especially when he was in a hurry, especially working on this slow equipment they'd requisitioned for detectives who were never going to get promoted, so he'd have to assign the search to someone else.

Which also frustrated him. Someone else—no matter who that someone was—wouldn't do as thorough a job as he would. Someone else wouldn't pursue that last lead, that fragment of a fragment that might actually bring him to the only remaining piece of information.

Nyquist put his face in his hands. He was running out of time. Soon DeRicci would summon him again, and that would put him at a disadvantage with her.

So he needed to find someone in tech who had the time to pursue this, someone he trusted, and then he needed to head to DeRicci's offices and tell her everything he didn't know.

11

THE *DOVE* WAS DOCKED SEVERAL BERTHS AWAY FROM THE *EMMELINE*, in a part of Terminal 25 reserved for yachts that weren't flown very often.

Flint made himself walk calmly toward the *Dove*. There were so many monitors, so many sensors, that any unusual movement would be recorded. He wanted to hurry, but he didn't dare.

Ki Bowles had left, just like she said she would. That surprised him. He had expected her to accost him as he got farther away from the *Emmeline*. But as he crossed areas that led to other yacht berths, he saw no one else, not even police officers.

Either Nyquist's people had already come and gone or they hadn't arrived in the first place. Flint would wager they hadn't arrived—he doubted Nyquist knew of the *Dove* yet. Digging into yacht registrations was hard, and unless Paloma had left some indication of ownership in her apartment, Nyquist wouldn't even know to look.

Flint knew, because he'd bought this version of the *Dove* for Paloma after borrowing, and then destroying, her first yacht. Paloma had flown him around the Moon that first month she owned the new *Dove*, and declared she couldn't tell the difference between the new and old (she was politely lying), but to his knowledge, she never took it to Mars or Earth, let alone anywhere farther away.

She was content, she said, to stay in Armstrong and live a quiet life.

At the time, he didn't believe her.

Now he wondered. What had she known? What had she been afraid of (if anything)? What had she expected?

He finally reached her berth, as far down the docks of Terminal 25 as she could be. The *Dove* had been moved even farther away from the main areas of activity. He half expected to see dust on her exterior.

She looked a lot like the *Emmeline*, sleek, black, and birdlike, her nose turned downward to give the ship added speed. But she was smaller and even more luxurious, built for comfort on long trips rather than Flint's need to make sometimes dangerous journeys with more than one passenger.

Flint wasn't sure he'd be able to even get close to the *Dove*. His rights as an owner of a yacht in Terminal 25 did give him free reign to go where he wanted, but that didn't mean he could get close enough to touch other yachts.

He hoped Paloma had kept him on the list of cleared pilots who could fly the *Dove*. He had never thought to ask.

When he reached the painted yellow lines that warned away terminal workers and Space Traffic police, he crossed without hesitation.

Silence surrounded him, and he let out a small sigh of relief. If he hadn't been on her cleared list, warning sirens and bells would have gone off. Lights would have flashed and a clear barrier would have fallen to protect the *Dove* from him.

But none of that happened.

He was free to board.

If only he could remember Paloma's codes.

He crossed the black floor to the black ship, wondering how much she'd changed things. He had known the codes for the old ship, and the original codes for this one. But he hadn't been here in more than a year. He had no idea what was different.

Still, he walked to the main door with confidence. He pulled down the exterior ladder, then climbed to the opening under the wing and placed his hand on the concave handle.

The door clicked three times, then the lock sprang open. An automated voice said, "Welcome, Miles Flint" as the door eased inward.

He hadn't expected that at all.

He climbed inside. This entry was less involved than his, designed for easy travel, not for protection. The *Dove* had an airlock with an interior door, but the door was unlocked, at least for him. The required thirty seconds inside the airlock was being counted down on the door's small diamond window. When the countdown ended, that door, too, sprang open.

Almost as if Paloma had expected him.

The hair rose on the back of his neck.

The main door closed and locked. As he stepped through the airlock into the heart of the *Dove*, the interior door closed and locked. He jumped, turned, and nearly grabbed that door's handle, worried that he wouldn't be able to get out.

Then he made himself breathe. Even if the ship trapped him, he was still inside the port. He could get someone from terminal management or Space Traffic to free him.

In a worst-case scenario, he could probably contact Nyquist and beg the man's indulgence.

Flint would find a way to free himself before that happened.

The lights slowly rose around him, bathing the interior hallway in yellow softness. She had remodeled since he last saw the ship: it hadn't been this bright before. Nor had it had a yellow carpet throughout the interior. It had been plain black, like his, the floors made of the same material as the ship and just as easy to maintain.

Now there were even seats near the airlock door, as if someone would wait there while other passengers went through the exit procedure. Art—most of it that two-dimensional imagery that Paloma had loved—was bolted to the wall.

The shape was the same as the corridor into Flint's ship, but the décor made it seem like an entirely different structure. He felt disoriented, like he had the first time he visited Paloma's apartment.

He peered into what was, on his ship, the common area. She had decorated it in soft blues, and then framed the portals so that they looked like a continuation of the art in the corridor. The seats were plush and deep. Only an extra glance at the sides made it clear that the regulation safety equipment had been attached as well.

He would save her private cabin for later. Since she hadn't used the ship much, he could only assume that she kept any important information in the cockpit because that was what she had done before.

Although with all these changes, he could be making a false assumption. He glanced over his shoulder, even though he knew no one else could get in—not easily, anyway. He felt like he was being watched—monitored somehow—but he had a hunch that was the ship itself.

He would check when he got to the cockpit. He would check on everything.

He hurried down the corridor. It felt narrower than the main corridor in the *Emmeline*, partly because of the art. He made himself stop, turn, and record an image of the corridor. In fact, he left one of his recording chips on as he moved through the ship.

He probably should have done that from the beginning. That way he could show Nyquist exactly what he'd done, that he hadn't taken anything (at least, at this point, he didn't plan on it) and that he wasn't trying to impede the police's work.

If anything, he could say he was worried for himself, since he had bought Paloma's business. He had to find out what was going on, just to make sure he wasn't next.

He doubted he was. If any of her former customers wanted her dead, they would have done so long ago. But he supposed the police considered him both potential victim and potential killer.

He knew Nyquist thought of him as a suspect; he wasn't sure if Nyquist had realized yet that he might be a possible victim, too.

Paloma left the cockpit door open, something Flint never did. He walked inside, pressed the door release, and listened to it whoosh closed. Then he locked it, just in case the police had been waiting for a warrant and arrived while he was working.

The cockpit of the *Dove* was smaller than the *Emmeline's*. The *Dove's* didn't have to be as big; the ship didn't command as many disparate elements as the *Emmeline* did. No weapons, only a few extra escape pods, no brig, no warning devices. The *Dove* was, at heart, a pleasure vehicle.

The *Emmeline* was, at center, a warship disguised as a yacht.

He sat down in the *Dove's* captain's chair. He placed his hand on the smooth black console before him and felt a sudden jolt.

Instantly, his recording chips shut off. His emergency links sent a small tone—the one that let him know they were shutting down—and then the white-noise hum that seemed a part of him vanished.

The ship had shut off all of his circuitry.

Paloma had set up the office to do that, using very old technology, and he had had to redesign it. He hadn't expected anything like that here.

He removed his hand, looked at it to see if that jolt had done any damage, and was about to stand when light filled the center of the cockpit.

Maybe he had underestimated her. Maybe Paloma had set up some weaponlike safeguards after all.

If she had, he was in trouble.

The light coalesced into a holographic image. Paloma stood in front of him, looking like she had before.

Before someone had taken her and destroyed her, leaving her like discarded clothing at the base of her living room wall.

"Miles Flint," she said with a familiar smile.

His heart twisted. Her hair was like a nimbus—brighter than it had been in life. Her face was wrinkled—she only went for enhancements that strengthened her; she didn't care about looks—and her black eyes seemed all-wise.

It seemed like he could reach forward, touch her, and pull her to him.

But he knew that he would never have done that. He hadn't hugged her in all the time that he had known her, and even if he discovered that she were alive now, he wouldn't be able to do that.

"You have to answer me, Miles, or this entire recording will vanish without serving its purpose."

Her voice sounded the same, too, strong and commanding and a little too powerful. The hologram was staring at him as if it were alive—as if Paloma were alive—and waiting for the answer to her question.

"I don't—um—yeah," he said, not sure what to say.

An androgynous voice filled the cockpit, the voice of the ship itself. "Voiceprint verified. Proceed."

The hologram folded its hands in front of itself—*Paloma* folded *her* hands in front of herself, or she had, whenever she made this recording for him.

There was no doubt this was all for him. From the moment his hand touched the console, maybe from the moment he entered the ship, this hologram waited for him, waiting for him to get here so it could start up.

"Miles," Paloma said with a sigh. "The fact that you're watching this means I'm probably dead. The *Dove* is linked to me through a special chip, one that senses my body's functions. It's also linked through the standard emergency lines. If the emergency links go down, the ship does nothing. If my body stops working—or somehow gets out of range—the ship is supposed to contact you. You've probably heard the recording—I set it up to call for help in my voice, so you wouldn't think someone was trying to fool you."

The message that had come to his office.

"I used some illegal techniques. If the police are investigating anything, they'll figure out that I didn't follow Armstrong regulations. That could get you in trouble. I'm sorry."

She didn't sound sorry. She didn't even seem concerned.

But why would she? She had been alive when she made this recording—as some kind of precaution—she had no idea what had actually happened.

"If both my emergency links and my personal functions shut down, then the ship was instructed to play this hologram for you. There is a slight chance that somehow I could be off-world when this happens, but you would know if I'm traveling. I will make certain of that."

He leaned forward, feeling very unsettled, questions already filling his mind. What had prompted her to do this kind of preparation? Had something happened? If so, why hadn't she told him about it?

"Of course, if I were traveling off-world, I should be in the *Dove*, so you can see how unlikely that scenario is."

She smiled, and it startled him.

"Nope. I'm probably dead, and you're watching this, surprised that it's even here. I only hope I went peacefully in my sleep, but I've always doubted I would go like that. I suspect it was something sudden and unexpected, and now you're here either looking for information or trying to figure out how to reregister the ship so that you can sell her."

Paloma's smile grew, as if she were satisfied with herself. "Yes, you've inherited her, in case you didn't know. You get most everything, which will also create problems for you. For that, I'm sorry."

Then she waved a hand.

"But I get ahead of myself."

Flint was holding his breath. He made himself exhale. Inherit everything? Why would she do that? He didn't need things—he had enough money to take care of himself.

But she probably had no one else.

"Obviously, I can't know what happened," Paloma said. "With all the advances in technology, they still haven't figured out how to let us see the future with any degree of certainty. What I can tell you is this: If you're watching this and I died in my sleep, then don't worry about anything."

Flint sighed. He wished she had died in her sleep, for her sake instead of his own.

"But if I died any other way, or if I've mysteriously disappeared and the ship is still showing you this message, then you're going to have to go through my files. And if I was murdered, that's probably why you're here."

For the first time, Flint smiled. She did know him well.

Or at least, she had.

"There are extra files. I've kept them here in the port. They're in a ship called *Lost Seas,* as in sailing ships, not letters of the alphabet. That ship is registered under the name Lucianna Stuart, which was once, I'm sorry to tell you, my legal name."

He'd always known that Paloma wasn't her full name, but he had thought it was part of her name. He hadn't expected Lucianna at all, and he wondered why she changed it.

"It's no longer my legal name," Paloma was saying, "but I never changed the ship's registration, for fairly obvious reasons."

He wasn't sure what the obvious reasons were. He'd learned, with Paloma, that what seemed obvious to her often wasn't to anyone else.

"However," she said, "you have to get to the ship as soon as possible. Because I didn't change the registration, there will be competing interests for it, interests that have some considerable legal muscle—"

She waved her hand again, that dismissive gesture he suddenly realized he would miss.

"I get ahead of myself again."

She cleared her throat and rubbed her hand over her chin. Such familiar movements. He threaded his fingers and clenched them together, hard. He had to concentrate on what she was telling him. The holorecording would go away, she said, and if he was wrong—if she had somehow designed this one right—he wouldn't be able to get it back.

"I was born Lucianna Stuart in a place called Los Angeles, which is on Earth. It's a sizeable city; you should be able to find it if you need to. I doubt you will need to. I changed my name forty years ago. I made the change legal because I felt that my own name would never come back to me. I needed a fresh start. I'm sure you understand that."

Flint did—at least for himself—but he wasn't sure about Paloma. She had told him so little about herself over the years, no matter what he asked, that learning anything about her from her (even after death) surprised him.

She shifted slightly and her gaze became more penetrating. "I can almost see you, Miles. I know what it's like to teach you. If you were sitting here—"

I am, he thought. *You're the one who's not here.*

"—you would say, 'Why are you telling me all this now? Why not before?'"

He nodded almost involuntarily. She had captured his thoughts before he even had them.

Again.

She took a deep breath.

"I'm telling you this for a variety of reasons. Let's start with the important ones first. I have always admired you. From the moment I met that young police officer with the cold determination and such a firm sense of justice, I've admired you. I loved the questions you asked me, and I'm sorry I didn't have most of the answers."

Flint started. He always thought she had the answers. He never noticed that she hadn't.

"When you bought the business, I thought you wouldn't last. I was tired. I wanted out. But you asked me to train you, and I realized then that there was more to you than some gritty determination and too much money."

A laugh forced out of him. When he bought her business he had just come into his money, and she knew it. Apparently, she was ready to rid him of it as quickly as she could.

"You have integrity, Miles," she said. "I can't tell you how rare that is in my world. You have integrity and heart and a terrifying moral ethic that you haven't entirely realized yet. In some ways, I've held you back from that. I've given you rules, said they were hard and fast, and tried to steer you in the right direction, and still you forged your own path. It's a path I would never have chosen, a path that has all sorts of dangers, and yet it works. It works better than anything I've ever seen."

She paused. Her skin had grown slightly darker. She was blushing. He'd never seen her blush before.

"I couldn't say that to you if you were here," she said, her voice softer. "I can barely say it now. I'm going to disappoint you, Miles. Worse, I'm going to disillusion you. Everything that you're going to find—because I can't be specific, because I don't know why you're watching this holo—is going to shatter your life. I'm so sorry. But it will all come to you—either through me or people who believe they're my agents. So I thought I'd tell you first."

The image wavered, and for a moment, he thought it was going to fade. Then it came back even stronger.

"I'm leaving you everything as part of my apology. But I'm also leaving it to you because I know that you, unlike everyone else in my life, will respect me, my choices—even if you disagree—and my decisions. You will put yourself back together, and you will be a stronger man."

He stared at the image. It was partially translucent. He could see the back of the cockpit through her. Had she done that on purpose or was there something wrong with the transmission?

"Here's your first problem, and the only one I can truly foresee in its entirety," she said. "I told you that Retrieval Artists should work alone. They should have no ties—not of love, not of friendship, not even casual ones. You had some trouble maintaining that, but mostly circumstances—"

And her voice shook on that word

"—ensured that you would have no close ties. What I told you is not how I've lived. It's what I've learned."

She looked away from whatever had been recording her. She steeled her shoulders. Flint had never seen her make that movement before.

Then she raised her head.

"I have two children, both sons. And I think if you consider for a moment, you'll realize who they are."

Flint clenched his fingers even harder. He had no idea who her children were. He couldn't even deduce who they were.

He couldn't imagine Paloma with children at all.

"I made a classic mistake," she said. "I fell in love with a man I worked with. Even when I tried to extricate myself from the relationship, I couldn't. You can't, you know, when there are children."

The only man that he knew Paloma had worked for had been a regular contract job she had done as a Retrieval Artist with a law firm—Wagner, Stuart, and Xendor, Ltd.

Wagner, *Stuart,* and Xendor.

Flint's cheeks heated. That couldn't be. She couldn't have been deeply involved with WSX, could she? But she had kept detailed files on one of the sons of Old Man Wagner, files Flint found on another case.

"You've met one of my sons," Paloma said. "I told you Ignatius wasn't the brightest Wagner. He was merely brilliant, not a genius like his father or his brother, Justinian. Justinian's mine, too. The older three Wagner children—all of whom have left Armstrong—are not mine. They left with their mother when she found out about me. About Lucianna Stuart, the second partner. I had been a lawyer once, Miles. I'm sure you find that funny. I would if I hadn't been so good at it. See? We all have our pasts."

Ignatius Wagner was her son? Justinian Wagner, the one who had protected a mass murderer? How had Paloma dealt with that? Why had she allowed it?

Why hadn't she gotten involved in that case when Flint was working on it? Was that why she had given him the first *Dove,* because just from the cursory information that Flint had given her, she knew her sons were involved?

Her sons.

Whom she would not allow to inherit anything of hers.

Sons.

Flint felt lightheaded. He had had more shocks this day than he knew what to do with.

The hologram continued. "My sons have always wanted more of me than they could have. I wasn't maternal. I had them on the condition that Claudius—their father—would raise them. He wanted an empire, and I was in love enough to give him one."

Flint frowned, not entirely understanding. An empire—built with children? Perhaps sons to continue the Wagner name?

He wanted ask her what she meant, but he couldn't. The hologram was not interactive, for all its resemblance to the real Paloma.

She was gone, and he could never ask her a question again.

"Of course, nothing lasts forever," she said. "Especially love."

She sounded rueful. Then she gathered herself and looked back at the camera that made the recording.

"My sons will fight you, Miles. They'll want everything, particularly the files that pertain to WSX. I've remained a partner in the firm—that's my last name on the door—but I put the money in a trust so that none of us could get to it. Those funds will go to various charities. A lot of them will help people that WSX has hurt."

She took another deep breath—or she had, way back when she made this. Flint flashed on her body again, how crumpled it had been, how it couldn't breathe even if it tried.

He wanted to stand, wanted to pause this thing, but he was afraid if he did, it wouldn't come back. He would miss the rest.

He wasn't sure he could process much more, though. He was already stunned at Paloma's family, the fact she'd been a lawyer, the fact she'd been good enough to become a partner—a senior partner (a founding partner?) in WSX.

"I wish I could say I got ethics. I wish I could say—like you did when you finally realized what the laws were like, and how you didn't want to uphold them. I wish I could say I had a change of heart, but I didn't, Miles, not at first. I left the law, even though I was good at it. I left Claudius. I was the one who did everything she could to force him to dissolve the relationship, and when he refused, I dissolved it anyway."

Flint shook his head. He didn't want to believe that of her. He didn't want to believe any of this.

"I needed a change of pace. I trained with some Trackers." She crossed her arms, looking defiant. "I signed on with one of the major corporations as their chief Tracker, and I was good."

He had heard rumors that she tracked, and hadn't believed it. When she trained him, she had had only contempt for Trackers, saying that they piggybacked on the real work that the Retrieval Artists did, and when they found a Disappeared, they simply turned that person in with no regard for the consequences.

Had she been speaking of herself?

"But the big money was in Retrieving." She shifted a little. "And yes, Miles, it does come down to that."

He ran a hand through his hair.

"You were so shocked that I bought my condo, so shocked that I ran through money the way I did, buying and spending and acting rich. You thought that wasn't me. But you never really investigated it. You thought I was what you found, an old woman ready to retire, ready to achieve her dreams. I am so much more than that, Miles, and so much less."

He frowned. He wanted to stop her—he could stop her, he supposed, but then he would always wonder what else she had planned to tell him.

"I became a Retrieval Artist, and I soon learned that I would have to work very hard to earn the money I thought I deserved. So I Tracked on the side for WSX. We always called it Retrieving, mostly because I never brought former clients back into the fold, but it was Tracking, and they paid me well. Claudius thought it was funny—I had left the fold only to return in what he saw as a lesser capacity. It wasn't. It gave me deniability, and it let me walk away."

Her lips thinned. She tucked some of her floating hair behind her ear, then shrugged.

"There's a lot in these files," she said. "A lot of regrets, a lot of possible enemies, a lot of information that could damage not just WSX but some powerful people in various domes, as well. It's not pretty, Miles. I was starting to realize that before I met you. Then you came in with all that bluster and strength, and I understood I could have done so much more. Just like you wanted to do. I taught you to be the kind of Retrieval Artist I always admired, Miles, not the kind I was."

His shoulders ached. He was sitting in an awkward position, half-leaning forward, half-twisted away from her.

"That's what I needed to tell you, Miles," she said. "I needed to disillusion you myself. I couldn't let some investigation do it. I couldn't let you go down blind alleys, not with Justinian on your back. He'll be vicious. He was raised that way—not just by Claudius, but by my example. He'll want everything I leave to you. Don't let him have it. He'll use a lot of it in the wrong way. I'm sorry to put you in this position, Miles. I had hoped I would have a lot more years. I planned to update this every year, but if you're watching it now, then you need to know this is only the first of these I've made. Something has gone wrong for me, and I'm leaving it to you to fix things if you can."

He was shaking. He wasn't sure why. But he was. His legs barely moving, his hands shaking, his teeth chattering. He wasn't cold. He was just shocked. Deep-down shocked.

"If you find, after all this, you can't do it for me," she said, "do it for the people in the files. Don't let my sons destroy everything. Don't give them more power than they already have."

She reached a hand forward, as if she could touch him.

"I trust you, Miles," she said, and vanished.

12

Ki Bowles stepped out of Terminal 25 into the main section of the port. Tourists from various places passed her, all in a hurry to get to their destinations. The humans carried their own bags, nearly running to make whatever shuttle they were going to. Several Rev—large creatures with a ginger odor and a bowling ball shape—cleared the entire corridor as they hurried through.

They were followed by a group of Tegarkian Lap Dogs, who, despite their names (which was not what they called themselves), were fierce negotiators and even fiercer competitors on the intergalactic economic stage. They were tiny, though—not quite as large as Bowles' foot—and they did look like small dogs.

It was amazing that the Rev hadn't stepped on them.

This part of the port was heavily decorated—the black walls covered with rotating art from various cultures—and filled with comfortable chairs for any traveler who wanted to rest. Most of the port was utilitarian; this was the only area that had any comforts at all.

It also smelled of real coffee and freshly baked breads, scents that made her mouth water. She ducked into a café near the entrance of Terminal 25, then ducked out again when she saw the Terminal 25-level prices.

She went farther down the corridor until she hit a bakery that was part of a Moon-based chain. She went in, sat at the human-designed tables with real chairs (unlike the larger tables set to the side for the

Disty, who preferred to sit cross-legged on tabletops), and stretched out her legs.

She punched her order into the tabletop, used her thumbprint to register payment, and then leaned back. She was tired, and she hadn't done anything.

Except walk away from a visibly agitated Flint.

She switched her links back on, and winced as a variety of messages clamored for her attention. News also blared through her inner ear, and a major program—all updates—ran across the bottom of her left eye. She shut that off: she would deal with updates later.

First, she had messages to sort through. She had one of the high-level programs InterDome Media had paid for when she became a top reporter sort through each message by priority, sender, and time stamp.

The first that came through was from her boss at InterDome, Thaddeus Ling.

Contact me quick, Ki. I have an assignment for you. It's important.

Then, about ten minutes later: *Ki, I hope to hell you're at this murder thing.*

And fifteen minutes after that: *Ki, I have no idea why you're not answering me, but it better be good. We're losing ground to the competition on this story, and you're the only reporter I have who can give it good coverage.*

She put a hand to her ear, then ordered the system to play the messages with video in vision of the lower corner of her right eye. Ling hadn't used the words *reporter* and *good* referring to Bowles in months.

On the next message, he showed up, face red with pressure. His eyes seemed wild. *Bowles, I'm sending in your team. I'll send you the address. Meet them there.*

That had come in three hours ago.

The serving tray floated toward her with her tea and a scone, covered in real clotted cream. The real cream at the same price as the fake stuff probably came because of her proximity to Terminal 25.

She took the food, set it on the table, and waited for the next message to scroll up. Several others came in, mostly from her so-called team, informing her that she was missing the story of the century (as if she hadn't heard that before), and then Ling showed up again, his face bright red.

Bowles, if this is some kind of game, stop right now. I need you at that site, but you no longer get on-air coverage. You're background now. I've assigned a new reporter. When you get to on-site, give her everything you know about those Retrieval Artists you are so fascinated with, and do not *mention Security Chief DeRicci.*

Bowles nearly put her hand in the cream. What was he talking about? She had done stories on only one Retrieval Artist that Ling would know about—and that was Miles Flint.

Who had just gone into his yacht, looking agitated.

But the address Ling kept spouting was nowhere near Flint's office or his apartment.

Bowles turned on the public terminal next to the order menu on her tabletop. She plugged in the address, and got this:

QUARANTINED AREA. INFORMATION
RESTRICTED UNTIL FURTHER NOTICE.

That startled her. Another message from Ling started in front of her right eye, and she froze it. Instead she called up an Armstrong map on the small screen on her tabletop, and searched it manually, looking for the address.

It was at the edge of a newer section of the dome—one of the ritzier neighborhoods in Armstrong. The condos there were actually built (illegally, some thought) onto the side of the dome so that the inhabitants could have their own private views of the moonscape.

She knew of many people who lived there—the rich and the famous and the well-connected—but she only *knew* one of them personally—and that one she hadn't met more than once.

A former Retrieval Artist named Paloma. A woman who served as Miles Flint's mentor.

The tabletop screen asked for some credits. She used her thumb-print again, and then called up recent news, using the name Paloma.

She got nothing. But she let that screen blink, waiting for her to ask for more information.

Then she unfroze the message from Ling.

He looked furious. *This could've been your comeback story, Bowles. If you hadn't shut off your links—*

It wasn't by choice, she wanted to tell him. No links except emergency links were allowed in ritzy places like Terminal 25.

—then maybe you could've worked your way back into my good graces. As it is, we got scooped by Armstrong Multimedia and United Domes Galactic Network. We've been playing catch-up while I waited for you. Now the police have left the scene, and what little you know is probably what everyone else will find out.

She gripped the warm mug of tea, feeling the plastic burn into her skin.

Forget coming back here. I've had your desk cleared and your personal items sent home. We don't need grandstanders who disappear when they're actually needed. And don't come crying back here, asking to go to Gossip. That time's past, too.

He actually time stamped the message and put his signature on it, so that it was an official firing letter. One that would be in the link system for anyone to pick up if they were really searching.

Tears filled her eyes. She hadn't expected this. What was the story that had him so upset? And why had he fired her?

She took a deep breath. She knew the answer to the second question. He had been waiting for this moment since the DeRicci story. When it broke and then shattered, and left its ruins all over Ki, she had been a popular and well-respected local reporter. People thought they knew her. They recognized her, said hello to her on the street, sent her messages whether she wanted them or not.

Since then, he had marginalized her. He had taken her off her regular time slot, airing her pieces at all hours of the day so that only the most dedicated fans could find her, and often truncating long, involved stories so that they made little sense.

She had been willing to put up with all of it. She figured the only way to get her reputation back was to earn it.

But apparently, she had miscalculated. Ling had never planned to let her back into the fold. He had always planned on firing her. He just hadn't had an opportunity before now.

She leaned back in her chair, blinked, and willed the tears to recede. She wasn't going to feel sorry for herself. She had covered high-level firings in the past, and the response of the fired had always irritated her.

It wasn't their fault. They hadn't known. They had no idea what was coming. They hadn't realized how much their boss hated them.

Ling hadn't hated her. But she had thought he respected her. She had actually thought he'd been giving her a second chance. She was as big a fool as the clueless people she had interviewed.

And, of all people, she should have seen this coming. The offer to go to Gossip had been a real one: a person could report lies there and no one cared. The label *Gossip* and the subheading: RUMORS OVERHEARD AROUND THE CITY protected InterDome against all kinds of lawsuits.

Ling had just never trusted her to do real reporting again. That was why he had assigned the team; not because he was demoting her, but because he didn't trust her.

She slid her tea mug away, so that she couldn't reach it easily. The old Ki Bowles, the arrogant one who had reported that story on De-Ricci, would have thrown that mug. But this Ki Bowles knew better.

Something big had happened, and the old Ki Bowles would have run to that address Ling gave her, fired or not. Maybe Ling was actually doing this as some kind of reverse psychology. Maybe he felt if he fired her, she'd work even harder and give him what he considered to be the story of the year.

But she wasn't going to run. She wasn't even going to backtrack and talk to Miles Flint, who clearly knew something. He deserved his privacy. He had begged for it, and she had never really respected that.

She sighed. She was different. The DeRicci story had shaken her up, too. Ki had once had such faith in her own ability to interpret facts, to understand how one action led to another.

She hadn't expected DeRicci to be good at her job. She hadn't expected the Disty crisis to be something that required quick action. She hadn't expected to find shades of gray in the universe.

Perhaps that was the problem—the shades of gray. They made being a hardheaded, judgmental, holier-than-thou journalist—the kind she had always admired—impossible.

She had to figure out who she wanted to be. What she wanted to be. Obviously, hardheaded and judgmental didn't work for her. Neither did Gossip. She actually cared about accuracy, even though Ling probably didn't believe that.

She had some savings and a bit of time.

She needed to figure out what came next for her. Who she was, and who she wanted to be.

Who she was capable of being.

She couldn't run from one story to the next. She needed some time to reflect, some time to chose.

The very things journalists never had.

The firing gave her the luxury to become someone new.

She needed to take advantage of that.

13

FLINT SAT IN THE *Dove*'s EMPTY COCKPIT, HIS HEART POUNDING. He couldn't move. Paloma still felt very real here; the shock of her disappearance—her *hologram's* disappearance—hit him almost as hard as the sight of her body.

It felt like he had lost her twice in one day.

He forced himself to stand up. He shoved his hands in his pockets and paced.

He had to assume his movements would be tracked, not just by the police but also by the Wagners, maybe even by Paloma's killer, whoever or whatever that might be. If he went directly from here to the *Lost Seas*, he would lead everyone there. But the Wagners already knew about it; they might even have secured that site, if they knew of Paloma's death. Had she rigged something to notify them as well?

Or maybe she even left something old, something she hadn't thought to undo. Flint had found all sorts of old systems still running in the office long after Paloma had left. She was good at setting things up, but not so good at remembering they existed.

Which reminded him: he had better make sure the *Dove*'s internal system hadn't recorded anything that transpired in the cockpit. It would be just like Paloma to set up her hologram to work only on Flint's voice print after the ship had confirmed his presence and to destroy itself when it was done, but not to set the other systems to work properly.

He sat back in the pilot's chair and immediately called up the last hour's security recordings. Sure enough, there was the hologram, with all of its explanation.

When he was a new Retrieval Artist, he had thought Paloma would do these things with some kind of devious purpose in mind. Certainly then, he might have thought she left this so that her sons could find it and know exactly what Flint was working on.

But after years of dismantling Paloma's systems, Flint knew she had simply forgotten that the ship itself was designed to keep track of all that happened inside it. She was careless—*had been* careless (damn his mind, unable to accept that she was gone)—and because of that, he gave a lot more credence to her words than he might have if she hadn't been.

Lucianna Stuart. Part of Wagner, Stuart, and Xendor. Lucianna, reborn as Paloma. No wonder Ignatius had spent so much time with Flint when WSX had tried to hire him. Ignatius had known his mother had never treated anyone like she had treated Flint, not even her sons.

Flint rubbed his eyes, feeling an exhaustion he knew hadn't come from any physical activity. Paloma had been right: it was wrong for a Retrieval Artist to get involved with anyone. Then he wouldn't feel so betrayed.

But how could anyone stop involvement that he hadn't even realized was happening? If asked, he would have said he liked Paloma, and that he respected her greatly (although, over time, he had lost respect for her computer skills and her attention to detail), but he never would have said that he cared for her deeply enough to mourn.

He shook his head. He didn't have time to mourn. He had information to deal with, a murder to solve, and an entire intergalactic law firm to fend off.

He had to move quickly.

Still, it took him nearly an hour of searching before he found the security recording that showed Paloma making the hologram. Flint fast-forwarded through it—the perspective was very different from the one he had seen (in two dimensions instead of three)—and he couldn't bear watching her vanish yet again.

Only when he got to the end of the sequence did he realize she wouldn't vanish. She simply reached out, shut off the equipment, and then leaned over the controls, setting up the entire system that had snagged him when he came into the ship.

He looked at the time and date stamp. She had made the holo-cording only a month before. Had something prompted it? Or had she simply intended to do so and finally gotten around to it?

He had no way of knowing, no way to ask her. He felt like a child who had just lost a parent—all guidance in his small world had vanished.

He truly was on his own now.

He downloaded the security files onto one of his personal chips, then, on a whim, added everything from that past month. Then he wiped the security system clean. The police department's computer techs would know he had done this, but he didn't care. All they would be able to figure out was that he had been here and decided something in the security recordings couldn't be seen by anyone else.

That made him even more of a suspect, he knew, but his very presence on the *Dove* had done that. And it would keep some of the information from the Wagners.

He hoped.

He stood and paced again. He wasn't sure how to proceed from here. He had two ships now—the *Dove* and the *Lost Seas*. He could claim ownership on both, but that wouldn't help him. The Wagners and their staff could just as easily get into the ships and tamper with them just like Flint had.

He could take the ships out of Moon territory, but there were drawbacks to working alone. No one could ferry him back to Armstrong. Besides, he would have to go a long, long way to get out of Alliance territory. And the Wagners clearly knew more about interstellar law than Flint did. There was probably something in the various Alliance agreements that gave the Wagners the right to confiscate a ship even though it was light years from its home base.

What he had to do was twofold: he needed a lawyer to help him secure both properties, and he had to take as much information from those properties as he could get. The problem was that the lawyers he knew, with the exception of Ignatius Wagner, were lawyers who worked for the City of Armstrong. They wouldn't help him. And he wasn't sure how many of the lawyers who practiced privately in Armstrong had the ability or the money to go up against Wagner, Stuart, and Xendor.

Finally, his last problem was one of logistics. He had no idea where the *Lost Seas* was docked. Paloma said it was somewhere in the port, but Armstrong's port was the largest on the Moon. It went on for kilometers, and finding a ship that someone had been intent on hiding wouldn't be easy.

Unless Paloma hadn't been intent on hiding the *Lost Seas*. Flint returned to the pilot's chair one final time. He had the onboard computer search for the *Lost Seas*.

To his surprise, the ship was in Terminal 35, in a dock marked secure. Flint sighed. Secure docks meant that the ship had been seized, but because the ship's owner had standing (usually meaning clout in the community, a significant bribe paid to port officials, or both), the ship hadn't yet been turned over to the proper authorities, whoever they were in this case.

What it did mean was that Flint would have to figure out which port official was in charge of that ship. Then he would have to find out how to get a release to enter it.

Sometimes his past history as a Space Traffic cop helped him. In this case, he suspected, it would hurt him. He had had a reputation for extreme honesty in the port; someone who took bribes wouldn't admit anything to him.

Unless he reminded that person that Retrieval Artists worked on the edge of the law.

Or unless he found a way to bribe that person himself.

Flint shuddered. He was crossing lines he didn't want to cross.

He had a hunch he would cross a lot more before this thing was over.

14

Nyquist had just stepped out of his office, feeling frustrated, unable to find any information on Paloma but knowing he couldn't put off his meeting with Noelle DeRicci any longer.

He would seem like a fool in front of her. Normally, that didn't bother him—not knowing things was often as much a part of investigating as knowing things—but in this case it did. He really wanted to impress this woman and he had a hunch he never would.

As he rounded the desks that made up the First Unit of the Detective Division, he saw a man step through the door. The man was short, with black hair and a long tailored coat that only the well-to-do in Armstrong wore. He looked around for a moment, as if he were unfamiliar with everything on this floor, and then he saw Nyquist.

Nyquist cursed under his breath. The last thing he needed was some civilian with a lost dog. Judging by the way the man moved—head up, arms swinging easily as if the unfamiliar surroundings were merely an inconvenience to him—Nyquist wouldn't be able to easily shake him off.

Nyquist looked around to see if someone—anyone—was nearby. But no one was. Everyone else was on a case or had hidden when they saw the man come through the door.

"Detective Nyquist?" the man said as he approached.

Nyquist stared at him. He'd never met the man before. The department didn't keep its detectives secret, but it also didn't broadcast their images, trying to give them as much privacy as possible so that they could do their work. The man would have had to do some work to identify Nyquist by sight.

"Do I know you?" Nyquist asked.

The man extended his hand. It was long and slim, the fingers manicured, the nails covered with some kind of gloss to make them shiny (or worse, had been enhanced to look that way). Nyquist didn't want to take that hand, not even to be polite, but he did.

"I'm Justinian Wagner," the man said as he shook Nyquist's hand. "I'm a lawyer in town."

Not just a lawyer, but one of the best lawyers in this section of the galaxy. Word was if you had a problem that wouldn't go away, you went to Justinian Wagner.

"I've heard of you," Nyquist said.

Wagner smiled. His teeth were a shade too white. His eyes also sparkled like a glass of water in Dome Daylight. If Nyquist had to guess, he would wager that the sparkle and the teeth were part of the same enhancement.

"Well, good, then," Wagner said. "I don't have to do many preliminaries."

Preliminaries. This could take forever. Nyquist took his hand back, resisting the urge to wipe it off.

"I'm afraid I don't have time for any preliminaries," he said. "I am late for a meeting."

"A meeting when you have a murder to investigate?"

Nyquist made certain his expression remained the same. Still, he felt a little jolt run through him. The department had been careful not to leak too many details to the media. One of the details it held back was the name of the investigating detective.

"There's always a murder to investigate," Nyquist said. "Now, if you'll excuse me—"

"Yes, there's always a murder." Wagner blocked his way. "But this is the first time the deceased is related to me. I insist you give me some time."

Nyquist didn't say anything. Sometimes lawyers used tricks like this to find out information from police officers. Still, Nyquist would have expected more from The Wagner of Wagner, Stuart, and Xendor, Ltd.

Wagner's smile was gone and so was his sparkle. Now he seemed powerful and somehow dangerous. Nyquist wondered if the enhancements actually changed his features slightly with his moods. Nyquist had heard of such things, mostly on lower-level actors who couldn't make the changes themselves.

He supposed it made sense for attorneys to do the same thing.

"You're not saying anything." Wagner crossed his arms. "Have I surprised you?"

"I'm waiting for you to move, so that I can leave," Nyquist said.

"You're investigating the death of Paloma. Her real name is Lucianna Stuart." Wagner's mouth was a thin line. "She's my mother."

"Very effective," Nyquist said. "Very dramatic. Now, if you'll excuse me—"

"You still don't want to talk to me?" Wagner asked.

Nyquist did, but he also felt like he was being manipulated. He loathed being manipulated. The last thing he wanted to do was talk to Wagner, then find out the man had lied to get some version of the truth.

"If you'd like to discuss something with me," Nyquist said, "make an appointment. Otherwise, I have nothing to say to you at this moment. Excuse me."

He pushed past, but Wagner caught his arm. "I have all the documentation. I also have sources that told me the moment my mother died. I have information that you might want, things that she did, things that she knew, cases she worked on, and enemies she made."

Nyquist shook his arm free. He was getting angry. "I'm sorry," he said, not feeling sorry at all. "We can discuss this at your appointment. I must get to my meeting."

"It's more important than a grieving citizen?"

In no way did Justinian Wagner look like a man who was grieving. He looked like a man with an agenda, a man who was used to getting his own way.

"Mr. Wagner," Nyquist said. "I'm sorry to hear about your loss—" he hoped that was good enough to cover himself, so that he wouldn't get blamed for telling Wagner Paloma was dead if, indeed, Wagner was lying to him "—but this meeting is critical for a variety of reasons that I can't go into. So if you would like to have a discussion with me, make an appointment. Otherwise, I will find you when I have a chance."

"I need to talk with you now. There are important legal matters—"

"I've explained my position," Nyquist said.

"And if you do not make me a priority, I'll go to the mayor," Wagner said. "And if he won't listen, then I'll go to the governor-general."

Nyquist would have called that bluff if Wagner had stopped with the mayor. Nyquist was convinced DeRicci would have protected him against the mayor. But she wouldn't go against the governor-general who was, ostensibly, DeRicci's boss.

Nyquist sighed. "I'm not going to use your information. Give me a minute. If what you say checks out, then we'll talk briefly."

Wagner's lips turned upwards slightly, just enough to make him seem self-satisfied. If he truly had emotion enhancers, he needed to have them calibrated to have the smarminess removed.

Or maybe Nyquist just didn't like self-important rich men, no matter who they were.

"Thank you," Wagner said, trying and failing to sound grateful. "I'll wait here."

"Yeah, you will," Nyquist said. In no way was he letting that man into his office, at least not until the information checked out.

Nyquist threaded his way around the desks, then went to the office next to his. He wasn't going to use his: he'd heard too many stories of information getting tampered with even within the department. If Justinian Wagner could manipulate his eyes so that they had just the right amount of sparkle, he could manipulate information on such a fine level that it only appeared on Nyquist's system.

Nyquist smiled to himself. He was being paranoid. But he still didn't go into his office. He sat behind the desk of the other office, activated the desktop screen, and searched for Justinian Wagner's birth records.

They were easy to find. Wagner had been born only a few blocks from here. His arrival into this universe had been recorded—date stamped, time stamped, image stamped, and DNA stamped—and the exhausted mother in the background, a woman who had clearly gone through normal childbirth although other options existed, looked nothing like the body Nyquist had found in Paloma's apartment.

That meant nothing, of course. Decades had gone by. Enhancements made people look different from moment to moment. There was no way to identify people based on a simple glance any more.

The birth record listed the mother as Lucianna Stuart, and the father as Claudius Wagner, both of Wagner, Stuart, and Xendor. Nyquist felt a shiver run through him. Affairs between lawyers left him unsettled. The fact that these two who, according to the preliminary bios that came with the birth records, were the founding partners of WSX, had created the galaxy's best (or perhaps best-known) attorney, unsettled Nyquist even farther.

He couldn't find a DNA comparison that showed him Lucianna Stuart and Paloma were the same woman. He supposed he could run a comparison between the DNA of Wagner's birth record and DNA taken from Paloma's death scene, but that would simply put too much information in a not-well-protected system.

For all Nyquist knew, that kind of information was precisely what Wagner wanted.

Instead, Nyquist looked for evidence that Lucianna Stuart had changed her name. And he found it more quickly than he would have expected—a court record from forty years ago, making the name change legal, and transferring all of Lucianna Stuart's assets to her new identity.

Wagner wasn't lying, at least about his parentage.

Nyquist sighed. He sent a message to DeRicci on his links: *Surprise interview subject just walked into the office. Can we reschedule in two hours?*

Instantly, a reply flashed under his left eye. *Trouble?*

Don't know yet. I'll tell you when I see you.

Okay. I'll be here.

He signed off, set an internal timer for ninety minutes in the off chance that he got involved in the discussion with Wagner, and went back into the mass of desks.

Wagner was where Nyquist had left him, standing in the same position, as if he expected to get sued if he moved. Of course, Wagner knew that the department had a high level of surveillance and probably knew that any move he made would be suspect.

Which made Nyquist think of a question he hadn't asked. "How did you get in here?"

"Didn't my information check out?" Wagner asked.

"You need a code to enter—" That was a lie. The door was actually primed to the various detectives' DNA. "—And I know you don't have one."

"I'm an officer of the court," Wagner said with a smile. "I can get in anywhere."

"With the help of the right judge," Nyquist said, letting the bitterness he felt fill his voice. He hated the way that people like Wagner manipulated the system. He felt it endemic of the way that the entire Earth Alliance catered to money and power instead of valuing human life.

The rise of corporations, Nyquist's old history professor had said, was the death of compassion in the law.

If there ever had been compassion in the law. Nyquist had studied enough Earth history to know that the law used to vary from human culture to human culture, and often didn't have compassion for anyone.

But he liked to imagine a time when it had been incorruptible, when judges didn't open doors for famous lawyers, when Disappearance Services didn't exist, when people took priority over aliens.

He surprised himself. He had thought the job had beat the idealism out of him. He could hardly believe that it hadn't.

"A person has to take advantage of every opportunity," Wagner said with a shrug, responding to Nyquist's bitterness as if he hadn't even heard it.

"You mean create those opportunities."

Wagner smiled, but this time his eyes didn't sparkle. That made the look seem slightly terrifying. "A man does what he has to do to get results."

Nyquist didn't like to be called a "result," but he didn't argue any longer. Instead, he led Wagner to the office he'd used before. For some reason, he didn't want the man anywhere near his personal space.

Nyquist shoved a chair toward Wagner and waited for him to sit in it before taking the chair behind the desk. Even then, with a desk between them, Nyquist felt as if he were at a disadvantage. Wagner wanted something, and he wanted it from Nyquist.

Nyquist wasn't sure if the blunt approach was best or if he should dance his way around the subject.

He finally decided that Wagner was better at the dance than he was. Nyquist would be better off being blunt.

"You seem to believe there's some kind of time crunch," Nyquist said. "I have a hunch that crunch has to do with your interests, not your mother's. So tell me what you want."

Wagner raised his eyebrows. The look was theatrical and had an edge of contempt, but like his other looks, it was effective. "Is this how you treat all grieving children of murdered parents?"

Maybe that comment would have shamed Nyquist when he was a young cop. But he had seen enough misery to know that a lot of children didn't grieve when their parents died. And so far, Wagner had shown no sign of grief.

Nyquist was also smart enough not to comment on it. He valued his job too much to hand Wagner something that potentially dangerous.

"Forgive me," he said, mimicking Wagner's smooth tones. "I was being insensitive. It's just that time is of the essence here, and I need to get to the point."

"You don't think that I know something about my mother's death?"

Nyquist suppressed a sigh. By not dancing, he'd ceded control of the interview to Wagner. Wagner was going to play this for all he could, no matter what.

"I think you've already given us valuable information. All of the information pertaining to the name change had been filed under Lucianna Stuart, not Paloma. By giving us next of kin, you've enabled us to announce what happened, which might help us gather more information. You've already helped us by saving me countless hours. I appreciate that. Now I want to know what brought you here when you could easily have sent that information through the links."

The bite was in his last sentence. Wagner caught it, and acknowledged it with a nod.

"My parents were estranged," he said.

Not divorced, which Nyquist found interesting in and of itself. Since they had kept their names, there was no easy way to tell if they had been officially married or just had a legal partnership.

Either way, the investigation had just gotten tangled because of Paloma's involvement with one of the best legal minds of his generation.

"My mother took many of the files pertaining to her clients in the law firm," Wagner said.

"When?" Nyquist asked.

Wagner sighed. He clearly didn't want to discuss this part in detail. "After my brother was born, my parents separated. My mother took her legal files and left. She changed her name. She began a new profession which, oddly, led her back to our firm in a new capacity. But we never did get those legal files back. And when my parents became completely estranged, my mother went into business for herself and took the remaining files from her work with us."

"You want the files back," Nyquist said, astonished by Wagner's coldness.

"Of course I do," Wagner said. "But that's not what interests me the most. My mother knew a lot of secrets. She hinted at many things."

Blackmail? Nyquist wondered, but didn't ask. Not yet.

"If you believe knowledge is power, then you must know that my mother was one of the most powerful people on the Moon."

Another shiver ran through Nyquist. If she had that kind of information—the kind that gave her a great deal of personal power—then it stood to reason that she had a lot of enemies, too.

"You want her power," Nyquist said.

Irritation flashed through Wagner's eyes, but didn't reflect on his face. Nyquist had a hunch that was the first real emotion he'd seen from Wagner since this conversation began.

"I'm sure we'd all like that kind of power," Wagner said. "But I was thinking that my mother's murderer might be profiled in those files."

"You think someone had cause to hate her that much? Someone she worked with?" Nyquist asked.

Wagner's face became completely smooth, no emotion reflected on it at all. "We all hated her that much, detective. Everyone who knew her."

"Even Miles Flint?" Nyquist asked.

Wagner shrugged. "I have no idea. But I suspect he is as big an opportunist as my mother was. He was the only person I know who could manipulate her. Or maybe she was ready for a young, exotic lover. I'm not sure and I don't want to speculate. Would you want to speculate about your mother and her lovers?"

Nyquist tried not to let the image penetrate, although it did for just a moment. His mother still lived in the house he grew up in, not far from the center of Glenn Station, and to his knowledge, she hadn't had a lover since his father died.

But then, Nyquist hadn't asked. As Wagner said, he didn't want to know.

"I thought Flint's relationship with your mother was purely professional," Nyquist said.

"Then why does he inherit everything?" Wagner asked.

"You've looked at the will?" Nyquist asked.

"Of course I did. Legal matters are usually the last thing taken care of, and they should always be one of the first."

Especially when you stood to inherit a large estate. Nyquist didn't say that, however. Instead, he asked, "So you're sure Flint inherits everything?"

"I haven't seen the most recent draft. Mother's lawyer has yet to contact us. But the copy she placed into safety storage a year ago names Flint as her primary beneficiary."

"Not the sole beneficiary?" Nyquist asked.

"A few charities." Wagner shrugged, as if charities didn't matter. "A couple of smaller heirlooms to me and Ignatius. Nothing more."

His face was still smooth, as if he didn't know what emotion to plug into it so he didn't plug in any.

"Does Flint know this?" Nyquist asked, doubly glad now that he had brought the man to the crime scene. Flint had just become the main suspect, and Nyquist knew his reaction to finding the scene.

"How should I know what he knows?" Wagner asked. "I've never spoken to the man."

That reaction sounded genuine, as well. Wagner's irritation was growing, even though he kept his face controlled. Nyquist resisted the urge to smile.

Somewhere along the way, he had retaken control of this interview.

"I'm sorry," he said, pretending more deference than he felt. "I still don't understand the time crunch."

"My mother had a ship. It's called the *Lost Seas*. It's still registered to Lucianna Stuart."

"It doesn't matter what name it's under," Nyquist said. "It'll still be part of your mother's estate. It'll go to Miles Flint."

"No, it won't," Wagner said. "At least, not for a while, anyway. You see, the Space Port confiscated that ship."

"You want us to find it," Nyquist said.

"I know where it is," Wagner said. "The port confiscated it, but never turned it over to any authorities. It still sits in its dock in Terminal 35. It has space-port locks and warning lights all around it, but anyone with authority can go in and out."

"You want me to go in," Nyquist said.

"You need to get the port to turn the ship over to the police."

"I'm sure you're doing this to aid in the investigation," Nyquist said, not bothering to hide his sarcasm.

"My mother kept everything in that ship," Wagner said. "I'll help you go through the files. I'll help you understand them. I won't take a document from it—"

"So long as you can look at them," Nyquist said.

Wagner smiled. "You're quite bright, you know that?"

He left off "for a police officer," but it was implied. Nyquist tried not to bristle. He wasn't being that successful at it.

"All right," Nyquist said. "The moment the ship's in police custody, I'll contact you. We'll go in it together."

Wagner nodded. "It's a pleasure doing business with you, detective."

"Really?" Nyquist said, and couldn't resist added, "I wonder what I'm doing wrong."

15

Flint decided to leave the information on the *Dove*. Before he did, he made sure her systems were set to admit no one but him. They were. Paloma had seen to that as well. That would hold the ship for a few hours, maybe days, depending on how long it took Nyquist to discover Paloma's ownership of the vessel.

It might also keep the Wagners out, even if they had some kind of court order.

Flint had to gamble on that because he knew the *Lost Seas* wouldn't wait for him.

He left the *Dove* and returned to the *Emmeline*, storing a lot of the information he'd downloaded in his own ship's systems. He knew the encryptions there were excellent. If he got arrested for the things he was about to try, he could delete the downloads from the *Dove* from his personal system, and know he had backups.

He knew how it was starting to look. If he were the investigating officer, he would think his own actions seemed guiltier by the moment. But it was a risk he had to take. He didn't know what Paloma had left him—at least in terms of information—and he had to protect it.

Flint hurried out of Terminal 25. He couldn't act like a rich yacht owner now. He had to call in markers left over from his days in Space Traffic Control, if he still had any. So many police of all ranks hated

Retrieval Artists that even if he had saved their lives in the past, they might not be willing to help him now.

He went down the back corridors that no civilian was supposed to use. No one stopped him. The security systems, set up to keep the civilians out, either weren't updated or had never bothered to remove his profile from the system.

Flint suspected it was even simpler than that. He doubted that level of security existed in most of the port. He had long believed that the signs posted at every entrance, which stated such security existed, were the only piece of that security system put into place.

It took him nearly fifteen minutes of walking, putting his head down when he passed traffic officers or Port Authority personnel, before he got to the Port's Administration Center. All of the bureaucrats for all of the agencies had offices here. The center was just off the port's main entrance, and had official-looking signage—all of it rotating by topic—that tried to point him in the right direction.

They had even installed a few robotic helpers, one of whom greeted Flint. He told it to do something anatomically impossible and walked past it, leaving it to devise an appropriate response.

He should have gone directly to Port Authority and asked for the unit in charge of confiscated vessels. Instead, he headed for Space Traffic's Port Headquarters.

The headquarters sounded more official than it was. Space Traffic had a large room as a staging area, even though it did most of its business out of the port.

The room had dozens of windows, all of which opened onto the hallway. Behind the main desk, a mural of the various ships that used to land here when this part of the port had been built covered the entire wall. The mural looked yellowed and battered, less attractive than Flint remembered it. The room seemed smaller, too.

Once this had been the center of his universe. Now it seemed tiny and grungy, at the end of a long corridor, in the back of an out-of-date port building.

The man behind the desk was small and elderly. He had a wizened face and a shiny bald scalp. Flint smiled. He hadn't expected Murray to still be on the job. Murray was retirement age when Flint started in Space Traffic.

"You," Murray said, pointing at Flint, "aren't supposed to be here."

"I know," Flint said.

"I heard you went over to the other side."

"I'm a Retrieval Artist, if that's what you mean," Flint said.

Murray waved a bony hand in dismissal. "I don't talk to criminals."

"I'm not a criminal," Flint said.

"But you help them."

"I find them," Flint said.

"And don't turn them in. That's collusion or assistance after the fact or just plain criminal involvement, that's what that is. I don't need that in my part of the port."

Flint swallowed. He had expected this, but not from Murray, who had always been kind to him.

"We could get into a philosophical discussion about how unfair the laws are," Flint said.

"And you won't convince me," Murray said. "Laws reflect the society that made them. Yeah, sure, we got to accommodate some alien stuff we don't like, but they got to accommodate us. It all works out in the end."

"And a lot of people die needlessly," Flint said.

"Says you. Says the aliens those people crossed, the law works. Get out of my office."

Flint took a deep breath. "I didn't come here to argue philosophy. I came here to talk to you."

"Bull," Murray said. "You didn't even know I was still here, you and that fancy yacht of yours over in 25."

Flint grew warm as a flush built in his cheeks.

"You think I didn't see you flaunting your wealth all over the privileged section? Now you need something and you come running to me, when you could've come a dozen times before, just to chat. Nope. I don't got nothing to say to the likes of you."

So Murray wasn't as angry about Flint's new profession as he was about Flint's insensitivity.

"I didn't think you'd want to see me," Flint said. It was only a partial lie. He also hadn't come because of Paloma's injunction about continuing relationships, however casual they might have been.

"Yeah," Murray said with great sarcasm. "You didn't think to ask me, now, did you?"

Flint shook his head. "I'm sorry."

"I'm not covering your butt about breaking into the *Dove*," Murray said. "I been watching. What'd you steal, hmmm? You know that ship is privately owned."

"I do," Flint said. "The woman who owned it was murdered this morning. She was a friend of mine. She asked me to secure her things should something ever happen to her."

"Sure she did," Murray said. "If that ship's part of a criminal investigation, you know we got to report your entrance."

"You have to give any and all pertinent information to the detective in charge," Flint said. "I used to work that beat, too."

"So you know your actions are pretty strange," Murray said. He now sounded less like an aggrieved man and more like a friend.

"I know," Flint said. "and they're about to get stranger. I need to find out who is in charge of confiscated vessels."

"The *Dove* ain't been confiscated ever, although once we thought you stole it."

"It wasn't this *Dove*," Flint said. "It was a different version. Same owner, similar registration, older space yacht."

"Covered your butt then," Murray said. "You never came in to thank me."

It hadn't even crossed Flint's mind. "I solved a problem two of your officers lost their lives combating. We're even."

Murray frowned. The wrinkles he'd allowed to remain in his skin gave the frown extra power.

"You're cheeky," he said.

"I am," Flint said.

"You're breaking the law," Murray said.

"Not at the moment," Flint said. "Unless talking with you is illegal."

"You know what I mean. That job of yours."

"We'll agree to disagree," Flint said. "I like to think I do some good."

"Sneaking around in other people's ships," Murray said.

"If I were sneaking, I'd disable your security systems first."

Murray glared at him. Flint's computer skills were legendary in Traffic, since most officers could pilot their ships and do little else.

"You know any conversation you and I have gets reported to the detective in charge, whoever that may be," Murray said.

"His name is Bartholomew Nyquist," Flint said. "He's a good man."

"Friend of yours?" Murray asked.

"No," Flint said. "Although we've run into each other before. He'll do a good job."

"So you don't object to me talking to him."

"Why should I?" Flint said. "You're both members of the same department."

Murray grunted and shoved his chair backwards. Then he stood, put a hand on one of the ships on the mural, and a tray eased out of the ship's image. He pulled some information flats off of it, as if he were going to get back to work.

"You were right," Flint said, not wanting Murray to get too involved with whatever he was doing. "I came here because I need help."

"Ain't it always the way?" Murray took the flats—at least three of them, all of them crammed with the records of the port that dated back to the time that ship was built. At least that was how information had been backed up here when Flint worked in Traffic.

"I need to get inside a ship named the *Lost Seas*."

Murray dropped the information flats. He crouched, picking them up slowly. Flint watched, knowing better than to offer any help. He didn't dare touch anything in this room except the desk and the nearby chairs.

"You need to stay away from that ship," Murray said. He hadn't looked up from the spilled flats. His hands shook as he picked them up.

"Because it's confiscated, I know," Flint said.

"Because it's quarantined," Murray said. "We don't have the authority to send HazMat on board. There's no way a civilian can get near it."

Flint started. Paloma had said nothing about that. "Quarantined for what?"

"You got me. But the quarantine isn't just Earth Alliance. There are at least five other united governments that want that ship destroyed because it's some kind of toxic. That's why it's in Terminal 35 under security protection, instead of Terminal 81."

Flint shook his head, not understanding. "I thought all quarantined ships went to 81."

"They do," Murray said. "But they gotta be moved there, flown there, or delivered there. The *Lost Seas* had a berth in Terminal 35 and suddenly appeared there one day. There's no record of its arrival or who flew it there. The quarantine order followed its arrival by a matter of hours. By then, the pilot was gone and we couldn't move the damn thing. We can't get near it. So the best we can do is seal off the area and hope at some point regulations loosen enough or the quarantine lifts so that we can deal with the ship."

"You don't know who flew it in? What about security?"

"Cleared," Murray said. "The visuals stopped working that day. The backups failed. No voice prints registered."

"How long ago was this?"

Murray shrugged. "I'd have to dig into the records. Before your time, anyway."

"Before my time as what? A Retrieval Artist?"

"Before your time in Traffic," Murray said.

Shock slid through Flint. "A quarantined vessel has been out in a public docking area for more than a decade?"

"We send for updates every month, just like we're supposed to, and every month, the status is unchanged."

"You knew who the ship's owner was, though, right? Couldn't she do anything?"

"The ship's registered to some big lawyer. Your murdered lady, right? A lawyer?"

"She used to be," Flint said, feeling numb.

"Well, she always sent back some legal document, saying that we had no right to tamper with her ship. Which wasn't exactly true, considering it's got some kind of biocontaminate. But it was enough to scare the people in charge here. Not that they'd touch anything quarantined without following every single regulation to the letter."

Flint nodded. They wouldn't. They didn't dare. The port was the first line of defense against disease or contamination spreading in the Dome. Armstrong had always been very strict with incoming vessels and personnel to prevent contaminations, but had gotten worse two years ago after a deadly virus had nearly gotten loose in the dome.

"Any way I can see the documents the lawyer sent?" he asked.

"Any way I can get half the money you've made at your illegal job?" Murray sat at the desk again, the information flats spread out before him.

"I'm sure it won't matter," Flint said. "She is dead."

"Lawyers never die," Murray said. "Their manipulations live on long after them."

"True enough," Flint said. "But they don't create any new manipulations after going to the Courtroom in the Great Beyond."

Murray snorted. "You're still as naïve as ever. I can't let you near the thing. If you try to shut off my security, you'll get flagged."

"Has anyone been on it since it docked?" Flint asked.

"Nope, and no one's going on it, not while it's labeled this dangerous. So find some other thing to waste your time on. You're not getting in there," Murray said.

Flint nodded. "Did you manage to access any of its systems from outside the ship?"

Sometimes ship's manifolds and transport logs could be downloaded by the port without accessing the ship at all.

"I'd have to check." Murray looked at the information flats meaningfully. For the first time, Flint wondered if Murray had taken them out for a reason.

"Would you?" Flint asked.

"Maybe," Murray said. "If I get the time."

Flint smiled. "You're a good man, Murray."

"And you're an ingrate. You gotta promise not to be a stranger."

Flint promised, but he didn't mean it. He still believed in this one of Paloma's injunctions. He had to stay away from contacts, however distant. Because they'd betray him.

Just like Paloma had.

16

NOELLE DERICCI'S OFFICE WASN'T FAR FROM NYQUIST'S, AT LEAST AS
Dome distances went. He only had to take a short walk from the Detective Division to her building, even though she worked outside the
City Center Complex. She was part of the United Governments of the
Moon, and yet somehow independent. He didn't entirely understand
the structure, even now, of the security department. He only knew that
it could override any orders given by him, his boss, or his boss's boss.
Not even the mayor had more power than DeRicci did. He wasn't even
sure if, in a serious emergency, the governor-general had the power to
override DeRicci.

And he certainly wasn't going to ask.

He waited outside her office, in a reception area that had improved
since the last time he was here. The last time, he'd been working on a
case that he later learned was tied into an emergency that started on
Mars and eventually threatened the Moon itself.

He hoped the case he was working on now wouldn't be that big.

He sat in a blue overstuffed chair that leaned against a small ex-
panse of wall. Most of the reception area was made up of windows
that gave him a spectacular view of the city. DeRicci's office, he knew,
overlooked the damage done by the bomb blast of a year ago. He wondered why she had chosen that view when she had this one—rows and
rows of pristine buildings, glinting in the fake sunlight of the dome. He

suspected that, on those rare occasions when the city government let the dome become clear, she had an excellent view of the moonscape and the Earth beyond.

Finally, the assistant told him that he could go into the main office now. He thanked her, stood, and gave himself a mental shake.

DeRicci had made it clear that she wanted to talk with him as soon as possible. She had even set up a time when he hadn't been able to come as expected.

Then she kept him waiting for nearly an hour.

Immediately seemed to have other meanings the higher up in authority a person went.

The door to her office slid open, and he stepped inside. DeRicci stood near the floor-to-ceiling windows on the other side, looking at the very view he'd been thinking of. Disaster front and center. How he would have hated it.

The room smelled of coffee and green plants, scents he rarely found outside the richer parts of the dome. DeRicci wore a suit that seemed tailored to her muscular body. She wasn't a beautiful woman, but she was a striking one, with her dark curly hair and bright, intelligent eyes.

He'd been attracted to her from the beginning, an emotion that always made him nervous. He'd seen too many colleagues misjudge a situation because of attraction.

He never wanted to be one of them.

"Detective," DeRicci said as she turned. Her expression was soft, warm, and somehow distant.

He didn't remember that. But their last face-to-face meeting had been awkward. He'd fled because he hadn't felt like he belonged.

Her office had changed since then. The old décor had been see-through, the furniture almost invisible against the white carpet. Only the plants on the surfaces had defined them.

Now there were fewer plants, and they looked sturdier, and the furniture looked like Earth-based antiques. Lots of wood, lots of upholstery.

Solid. Strong. Like DeRicci herself.

"Chief," Nyquist said as he walked toward her, hand extended.

She took his hand, shook it gently—something she hadn't done before (before she had always crushed his fingers with her grip)—and let it go. "I prefer Noelle."

"Noelle, then." He couldn't have her call him by his first name. Only a handful of people had done that his entire life, and then they'd been close to him. He needed to keep this relationship professional.

"I'd've come to the scene," she said, leading him toward a couch with rather fragile curved wooden feet. "But I was told there was a 'biochemical goo' that later turned out to be harmless."

"We're still not sure what we have," he said. "But there were some early false alarms."

He sat down, feeling awkward. The easy flow between them that he remembered from a few months ago seemed to be gone. Maybe he had imagined it.

"Update me," she said.

So he did. He told her about the scene, about the blood and the complete destruction. He didn't tell her about Miles Flint, though, although he did tell her some of the conclusions he'd come to after looking at the same evidence that Flint had—that Paloma may have been killed near the elevator and the rest of the scene staged.

He didn't tell DeRicci that he suspected there was more than one victim—there was a lot of blood in that small space and not all of it human. He hadn't had time to double-check all of the evidence. He didn't want to seem stupid before her if his assumptions didn't pan out.

DeRicci listened intently, hands clasped over her knees, her gaze remaining on his as if she were going to be quizzed on the information. For all he knew, she might be later on. She would nod occasionally, or make encouraging sounds so that he knew she was listening.

He hadn't had someone give him this kind of undivided attention in a long time. Maybe years.

Finally, he told her about his meeting with Justinian Wagner. She seemed surprised. When he finished, she let out a soft whistle.

"I knew this case would be a problem—a murdered Retrieval Artist always is—but I had no idea WSX was involved."

"I didn't say he was involved," Nyquist said.

"But he has to be one of your main suspects now," DeRicci said. "A son who clearly claims his mother abandoned him, a woman who left her business with all kinds of secrets, secrets that gave her 'power,' at least according to him."

"I plan to investigate him," Nyquist said. "It'll be hard."

"Because he has so much power himself," DeRicci said, as if she were going to participate in the investigation.

"Power that goes back generations. His grandmother was mayor, you know."

DeRicci nodded. "There were Wagners at the founding of the United Domes of the Moon, and I think they belong to the First Families of Armstrong, as well. They've been around. Have you looked into the Stuarts?"

Nyquist shook his head. "I came here as soon as Wagner left my office."

"I'll be interested to hear," DeRicci said. "What about the ship he mentioned?"

Nyquist felt his shoulders tighten. He had promised to give Wagner information the moment he secured the ship. Wagner had left happy, but Nyquist wasn't. He didn't want to fulfill that promise. He'd never planned to, but he also didn't plan to lie. The only way he could do both was to get DeRicci involved.

"I was hoping that your office would claim the *Lost Seas* for the United Domes of the Moon."

DeRicci frowned at him. "It's part of a police investigation."

"One that already has had your interest." Nyquist had thought his argument through on the way over. "That 'biochemical goo' would have caused your office to take over the investigation—"

"I never would have taken it over," DeRicci said. "I would simply have monitored it."

"Well, we still have goo, although the experts don't think it's toxic, and we still need supervision. Right from the start, this has not been a simple murder."

"As if there's any such thing." DeRicci stood. She went back to her window and didn't say anything else.

Nyquist forced himself to sit still. He had a thousand things he needed to do. He had to check on Mikaela Khundred. He had to oversee the evidence results. He had to research the Wagners and the Stuarts, as well as WSX. And he had to find out what Miles Flint was doing.

Miles Flint, who, according to Wagner, inherited everything.

Nyquist hadn't told DeRicci that, either.

"Technically," Nyquist said into DeRicci's silence, "you're still overseeing this investigation. I'm here now, instead of finishing my work."

That came out sharper than he intended. DeRicci turned, a smile on her face.

"Speaking to your superiors that way can get you into trouble," she said. "I should know."

There it was, that connection. It had formed over their rebel spirits. Only DeRicci seemed to be taming hers. Or maybe she had finally found the job that suited her.

"You're not my superior," he said.

Her smile widened. "But I do outrank most everyone in Armstrong Dome. I assume that includes you."

He shrugged. He wasn't going to play this kind of game. He didn't know if she was flirting or exercising her power, and he didn't care.

"Look," he said. "All I'm doing is asking for a favor. If I take control of that vessel, Wagner can take it from me. He can go to the chief and get her to let him inside or, if she decides that he doesn't belong there, not that I would expect it, then he can probably get some kind of court order. He can't do that against you."

"At least," DeRicci said, "it's never been tried."

"I think, if you do this right, he won't even know who has taken charge of the ship. Only that it's not the police."

"I'd have to give you some kind of dispensation to go inside," DeRicci said, "so that we don't have a lot of legal wrangling later on. The last thing I want to do is muddy up evidence that could convict someone."

"First things first," Nyquist said. "We need the evidence. I'm not even sure how the ship fits. I think Wagner wants it to improve his standing within the community, not because it has any bearing on this case."

"You can't know that," DeRicci said.

"No, I can't," Nyquist said.

"And I'm not sure he can improve his standing," DeRicci said. "He's already at the top of the heap. I think he believes there's damaging information there, and he wants it, either for his own blackmail purposes or because it damages him."

"Or both," Nyquist said.

DeRicci studied him for a moment. Then she sank back onto the couch and resumed that demure, ladylike position she'd been sitting in. It didn't suit her.

"I've never met Justinian Wagner," she said. "Tell me honestly, did you like him?"

Nyquist stared at her. Like, dislike, usually didn't factor into his cases. Although sometimes it did. Despite himself, he liked Miles Flint. He'd still convict the man if Flint killed Paloma. But he'd bent a few rules for him.

He wouldn't bend any rules for Wagner.

"No," Nyquist said. "I didn't like him."

DeRicci nodded. "Because of his job or because of his personality?"

"I'm not sure I ever got to his personality," Nyquist said. "He seems purposely hidden, and deliberately snide."

"The lawyer persona," DeRicci said. "There've been rumors about him forever—how he's helped some of the solar systems most notorious criminals escape justice—"

"Like a Disappearance Service?" Nyquist asked.

"Like the best defense attorney in the system," DeRicci said. "I don't think he's ever counseled anyone to use a Disappearance Service, although I do think he's kept some of his people hidden long after the authorities stopped looking for them."

Nyquist had heard the same rumors, but he'd never had the need to track them down before. "Does that make him a bad person or just someone who's good at his job?"

DeRicci shrugged. "Do you think he could have killed his mother?"

Nyquist remembered the carefully manicured hands, the expensive suit, the attention to the slightest detail of his personal grooming. A man like that couldn't do messy work. It wasn't in his nature.

"I don't think he committed that murder," Nyquist said. "At least, not hands-on. But I think he could have hired someone to do it."

"Then there'd be a trail," DeRicci said. "You said he has a brother."

"Who sounds a little less competent," Nyquist said.

"His brother said that?"

"The Moon's gossip mill says that," Nyquist said.

"So the brother could have done it," DeRicci said.

"I don't know," Nyquist said. "I'm not hurting for suspects. I am hurting for a reason to do this now."

DeRicci nodded. "You think that reason is on the *Lost Seas*?"

"I don't know what's on that ship." Nyquist shifted slightly in his seat. He wanted to continue investigating, not speculating. "I won't know until I get aboard."

DeRicci's smile returned. "You're a cautious man."

Nyquist thought of Flint, of the tech suit that he let Flint take with him. "A lot of people wouldn't use the word *cautious* to describe me."

"But you want protection for this one thing," DeRicci said.

"I do," Nyquist said.

"You know that means I could take over the investigation of the ship," she said. "I could fail to release it to you. I could assign someone else to examine the contents. I would never have to say another word to you about this. I could, if I wanted to, screw up your case by not allowing you what's on that ship."

"I know," Nyquist said. "I'll take that risk."

"Have you investigated me?" DeRicci asked. "Is that why?"

He hadn't. "I know enough."

"You know that Miles Flint, the man who bought Paloma's business, is my old partner. We're still friends."

"I know that," Nyquist said.

"Flint could have had reasons to kill Paloma," DeRicci said.

"I know that too," Nyquist said.

"Yet you didn't mention him." DeRicci studied him.

Nyquist wasn't going to answer that. He knew better.

Slowly, DeRicci leaned back on the couch. She toyed with the leaf of a nearby plant. "You don't trust me."

"I trust you as much as I trust anyone," Nyquist said.

She tore off the leaf, then ripped the leaf in half.

"If I didn't trust you," he said, hoping he didn't sound desperate, "I wouldn't ask you to take over the *Lost Seas*."

DeRicci crumpled the leaf in her right hand. "I'd like to come with you when you go onto that ship."

"I prefer to conduct my own investigation," Nyquist said.

"You're involving me," she said. "I will step in as far as I can."

She raised her chin, meeting his gaze. He sighed. She had a point. If she had a hand in the investigation, she would be less likely to pull the plug on him.

Even though she could at any time.

"Does that mean you'll take over the *Lost Seas*?" he asked.

"Yeah," she said. "But before I do, I want a report listing the concerns that still exist over that biochemical goo."

He smiled. She was becoming more political. She wanted him to write something that would cover her ass.

"It'll be on your desk in less than an hour," he said.

"Then we'll be able to go to the ship in two," she said. "Unless we stop for dinner."

He looked at her, startled, not sure if he had heard her correctly.

She shrugged again. The movement didn't seem as casual as the previous shrugs. "We have to eat, you know."

"I know," he said. "I just tend to eat on the fly during an investigation."

"Then it'll be on the fly," she said. "I'll meet you at your office."

His mouth opened slightly, but it took him a moment to realize that he hadn't said anything.

"Sure," he said. "I mean, that would work."

She smiled. "It'll work for me too," she said. "Maybe then you'll have some updates and I'll have a ship."

"Yeah," he said, thinking he sounded awkward. A ship and some updates. Dinner and an investigation. And a woman smart enough to figure out what he was holding back.

Maybe he was making a mistake. But it was too late to change his plan. He had to move forward, even if he was making the wrong choice.

17

FLINT STOPPED AT HIS OFFICE ONLY AS A MATTER OF FORM. HE figured he was being watched—if not by the police, then by WSX. Or perhaps someone wasn't actively watching him yet, but later would track his movements. He wanted those movements to be as far from suspect as possible.

Although that was hard. If someone was tracking his movements, he would seem suspicious, first with his activity near the *Dove* and then with his return to the *Emmeline*. He had a hunch his visit to Traffic's office in the port's Administration Center would only raise a level of confusion, particularly if Murray didn't tell anyone why Flint had visited.

The interior of Flint's office still defeated him. The dust looked thicker than it had before. At least it showed if someone else had been here. So far, he only saw his own footprints.

The air smelled slightly stale. He still had the environmental systems off.

Maybe he would take the equipment from this place and put it up for sale, letting the new owners deal with the mess.

But even as he had the thought, his heart twisted. No matter how he was feeling about Paloma—betrayed, confused, heartbroken—he still cared about her. And this place was as much a part of her as it had become a part of him.

He couldn't sell it. He would have to fix it.

But not now. Now he needed only to use its back door.

He made sure the front was locked, slogged through the dust in the main room. Dust rose, fine and irritating, making him cough. He wished he had put on some kind of environmental gear. He didn't want this stuff getting inside him.

Although it was too late. He made his way to the back room, which was, if anything, more of a disaster than the front. Then he covered his mouth and nose with his hand, and turned on the environmental controls for thirty seconds.

The dust swirled, getting in his eyes, his ears, and through the cracks between his fingers into his mouth. His teeth felt gritty. He resisted the urge to cough again.

He made sure he made the full thirty count, then shut off the environmental systems. Now if anyone managed to break in, they wouldn't know that he had walked through and left through the back. The dust was too thick and too smooth to tell them anything.

Of course, he was coated. He slipped into the small bathroom off the back, wiped off his face and arms as best he could, and changed into fresh clothing. He always kept at least one change here—after he had gotten caught once without enough clothing. The clothes were in a drawer, so they weren't coated at all. Only his feet and shoes would show where he had been, and Armstrong locals would simply assume that he had been walking in a poorly filtered part of the dome.

He slipped out the back door, made sure it too was locked, then went to his favorite sandwich shop. The proprietor greeted him, gave him a sandwich for half price (the man was too poor to offer it for free) as a sort of welcome home gesture, and Flint ate part of it right there.

The sandwich, made of bread with Moon flour and some kind of processed fake turkey breast, tasted rubbery and old. Flint smiled as he chewed. No matter where else he ate, no matter how many expensive foods he could afford, he loved these old Moon meals.

They tasted of home.

He thanked the proprietor and left, drinking a bottle of very expensive purified water and eating the rest of the sandwich. The neighborhood hadn't changed much. A few businesses had gone out, a few new ones had come in.

But the one he was looking for remained, half-hidden in a dilapidated warehouse. Like his business, this one showed no sign of the money it raked in almost daily.

In all practical ways, this place was the source of his sudden wealth.

And he hadn't returned since the day he traded information for money—the day he had saved countless lives by breaking the laws he had sworn to uphold.

He pressed a button against the front door. A beam touched his face, turning everything reddish for a brief moment. Technology was sophisticated enough so that an examination beam could be invisible. But Data Systems wanted its potential clients and visitors to know that they were being investigated from the moment they stepped on the warehouse's threshold.

As the beam touched him again, he said, "Miles Flint for Colette Bannerman."

The beam shut off without finishing its task. The door swung open. The interior was as filthy as he remembered, only the dirt here was deliberate.

Data Systems was a Disappearance Service. It wanted to make certain that its potential clients couldn't be scared away by the appearance of a difficult existence. There were other kinds of traps set up through the entry into the main part of the building.

Flint had gone through them all years ago, when he had tried to see Bannerman the first time.

This time, he didn't have to go through the series of questions, the hordes of middle managers, all wanting to know if he was legitimate. Data Systems probably kept track of him, like they did so many others.

And, in his own way, he had kept track of them.

A lower-level employee—a woman—led him to the very room where he had brokered his deal with Bannerman. He hated the room:

it had no windows, although it was cleaner than the front of the warehouse. The environmental controls worked here as well. He did have to go through a decontamination area before entering, as well as a rather intrusive examination to see if he was carrying weapons or some kind of listening and/or recording devices that couldn't be shut off by conventional means.

Data Systems, like his office, shut down people's links the moment they entered. He had shut his off when he stood outside, not wanting any information accidentally left from his download of Paloma's systems to get into Data Systems' records.

The woman left him without a word. He sat in a large chair—updated and more comfortable than the one he'd sat in all those years ago—and stared at the walls. On them were scenes of various cities. When he first came, he only recognized New York and London from Earth. Now he saw New Orleans, which he had visited a few years back, and Miami, as well as Ottawa and La Paz.

A wall to his left showed some cities from other planets and other moons. He could guess at them—he knew the reddish dome with the Disty buildings had to be Sahara Dome, and the cold, bluish looking dome was on Io. But he didn't know the rest, even though he'd just spent months traveling all over the solar system.

Mostly, he hadn't stopped anywhere interesting, just some fueling and recreational bases in the long distances between settled colonies. He hadn't been as interested in sightseeing as he was in moving, getting as far away from himself and his past as he could.

And now he sat square in the middle of it. His decision to come home had seemed right at the time, but he wasn't certain any longer. Paloma was dead, his office was ruined, his ideals were crumbling.

A door swished open. Colette Bannerman entered. She had always been gaunt, but these days she looked positively skeletal. Her hair had thinned on top, revealing part of her skull. Her enhancements stood out, like grafts of real wood on a permaplastic building.

She looked exhausted, overworked, and a little frightened.

"We don't deal with Retrieval Artists here," she said as coldly as she could.

"I'm not here as a Retrieval Artist," Flint said. He had expected the greeting. In theory, Retrieval Artists and Disappearance Services were enemies. Retrieval Artists were supposed to find Disappeareds, often destroying the careful work of Disappearance Services and causing the death of the Disappeareds.

In practice, Retrieval Artists and Disappearance Services sometimes worked together. More than once, Flint had helped a service find one of its own Disappeareds who had dropped the new identity and gone on to some other kind of life. Usually those cases were about Disappeareds who no longer had a reason to run, only they didn't know it then.

Once in a while, they were about a severing of the agreement between the company and the Disappeared. And once, he'd turned down a case in which a Disappeared used his knowledge of a Disappearance Service to attempt to destroy it. In that case, Flint had recommended a Tracker, feeling that the Disappeared needed to face the legal system he'd fled.

Flint believed Disappearance Services had their place in this culture. He also believed that his job was just as necessary.

"I don't understand," Bannerman said as she sat behind the heavy desk near the scenes of Earth. "If you're not here as a Retrieval Artist, then what do you need?"

They had played a bit of this dance a few years ago, when he had first come here. Then he had been a newly resigned police officer with a list and an agenda.

He didn't feel as altruistic now.

"I don't have lives to save this time," he said, although he wasn't completely sure. He wasn't sure what was at stake. He knew only that Paloma was dead and she had believed that something on the *Lost Seas* would help him. "I've heard over the years that you've gone to court against Wagner, Stuart, and Xendor, and won."

She let out a soft laugh. "A few times."

"So it's true, then?"

She ran a hand through that thinning hair. Had she given up on enhancements? Or had she simply been too busy to take care of herself? He couldn't tell and didn't know how to ask.

"We've gone up against them too many times to count," she said after a moment.

"And won?" he asked.

She paused as if weighing her words. "The later cases."

"Because of the cases or because of your lawyer?"

"We need a good lawyer," she said. "Some would view what we do as illegal."

He knew that Disappearance Services skirted the law by never keeping records of their clients. If a client approached them because they had violated a Disty law, for example, Data Systems would make certain the client had a new identity that kept them as far from the Disty as possible. But Data Systems—and reputable services like them—never asked for the particulars of the crime. Sometimes the company didn't even ask for more than a financial history.

Just because a person helped someone who broke the law didn't put that person at odds with the law. Knowledge counted. Otherwise, a waitress at a restaurant who fed a criminal on the run could be indicted for aiding and abetting.

At least that was how the Alliance laws read now, and some of that was because of the corporations. Corporations invented Disappearance Services. It was the only way to go into uncharted areas and keep the natives satisfied. If a corporate employee broke some native law, the corporation vowed to cooperate with the native law.

But while the corporations did that, in part to help their bottom line, they also protected their employees by giving them new identities and new lives. Eventually, a number of those services branched off, became independent.

Some, like Data Systems, started without corporate sponsorship.

It cost a lot of money to disappear. Sometimes it cost the Disappeared's entire life savings.

When Flint had sold Bannerman his information all those years ago, she had paid him ten million credits immediately, with a minimum of complaint.

"You've always had good lawyers," he said. "What makes this one different?"

"This one isn't afraid of people who have reputations," she said. "She likes to shred them. She believes in what we do, and she'll fight for it as hard as I will."

"Does she fight for all her clients?"

"What's this about, Mr. Flint?" Bannerman asked.

He decided to be as truthful as he could. "I have just received an inheritance that will put me at odds with the Wagners of WSX. I'm not trying to protect money. I'm trying to protect confidential information. The kind that should never be in the hands of unscrupulous people."

Bannerman studied him. She knew that he had initially come to her because he felt being a police officer violated his own personal ethics. Yet she also knew that he had a touch of shadiness to his own dealings, because he had wanted money for that information he brought her, money that would enable him to live for the rest of his life without working.

That wasn't his only reason for asking for ten million credits. He also knew that people like Bannerman never trusted anything they got for free. They expected to pay exactly what something was worth.

"You want the name of my lawyer," she said flatly. "You want a Disappearance Services lawyer to represent a Retrieval Artist."

"Yes," he said.

Bannerman laughed. She seemed almost pretty for that brief moment. "That'll shock her."

Flint waited.

Bannerman stopped laughing, wiped at her eyes, and leaned back in her chair. "You trust me, Mr. Flint?"

"Yes," he said.

"Enough to rely on my lawyer for something this important to you?"

He nodded. "I know a lot of lawyers in this city, and the ones I trust could never go head-to-head with the Wagners of WSX."

All the laughter had left her face. She studied him for a long moment. "You want to win."

"I *need* to win."

"You know that winning is nearly impossible with them," she said. "What they can't get legally, they get illegally."

He had suspected it. He knew that they knew how to manipulate systems to a degree that he had probably never seen before.

"They're ruthless and they're vicious," she said. "If they can't beat you in a courtroom, they'll destroy you personally."

"They haven't destroyed you yet," Flint said, although he wasn't entirely sure. She looked a lot worse than she had when he met her years ago.

"I hide behind a corporate veil," she said. "They've tried to destroy Data Systems. They haven't yet. But they've come close. I shudder to think of what they'd do to an individual."

Flint straightened. He wanted to tell her that he wasn't just an individual here in an impersonal case. He was going up against the partners of the firm in a case that involved their mother.

Their estranged mother.

"I know you're strong," Bannerman said, "but if you have any choices at all, avoid WSX."

"I wish I could," Flint said.

Bannerman sighed. "You could always disappear," she said, and they both knew it was only half a joke.

"No," he said. "Not in this case."

Colette Bannerman looked at him with something like pity. "My lawyer's name is Maxine Van Alen," she said. "Don't take advantage of her."

Flint thought that was a strange thing to say about a lawyer, particularly one who'd won cases against WSX.

"I'll treat her well," he said, and meant it.

18

DeRicci stared at the door long after Nyquist left. She had never had anyone ask directly for her help before, not in her new job as Chief of Moon Security.

His request was odd and he hadn't told her all of the reasons for it, even though his logic was impeccable. He was keeping something back—something more than his suspicions of Miles Flint.

She stood and headed toward that window, using the view to remind herself of her duties. She'd nearly screwed up in the past telling Flint things he should not have known.

But on the flip side, he had always come through for her, always helped her.

But she still didn't make a move. If the past few months had taught her anything, they had taught her how important her job was—and how fragile. Flint had told her back when she was considering taking it that the job was a dangerous one. In the wrong hands, it could lead to an abuse of power that would harm the Moon, not help it.

Of course, people like Ki Bowles had already accused DeRicci of abusing power in that way. The fact that DeRicci's efforts had stopped a major crisis had helped, but the accusations would come again.

DeRicci ran a hand through her hair, then stood. She went to her most secure node, attached to a desk near the windows. This node had more security precautions on it than her own private links. The computer techs had explained everything to her, and she hadn't understood a word of it.

Except that she would have to trust them to protect her most private information, and when they installed that link, she hadn't been in the mood to trust anyone. She wished she knew more about computer tech herself, all that junk that Flint had learned in his first job, way back when.

She envied him a lot of things, particularly his freedom to choose what he was working on. Maybe that was why she had agreed to help Nyquist. It was more than simple curiosity or the possibility that the investigation might return to her. It was also a way of choosing her own work, rather than having it thrown at her.

A way of preventing a crisis instead of reacting to one.

She activated the node and shut off the voice controls. She had several ways to access information on this machine. She could use voice commands, or call up a hands-on screen, or she could use the keypad, which she had insisted the techs install. Flint had taught her that with keypads the strokes she made weren't traceable from within her office.

Only if someone had already tapped into the system and was monitoring what she was doing. And if that happened, every form of communication she used with this node would be compromised.

She hauled out the keypad, turned on the flat screen but left it on the desktop, and activated the securest part of the node. She didn't even want her assistants to know what she was doing.

Then she called up the name of the ship through the standard registry, just like she used to do when she was a detective. The *Lost Seas*, current/former owner Paloma/Lucianna Stuart.

Immediately, the screen lit up with a warning. The vessel had been quarantined. All inquiries had to be made to Space Traffic Control.

The word *quarantined* stopped her. She had seen the records for confiscated vessels before. No one had ever used the word *quarantined* to describe them.

She accessed other registries, got the same listing, and then went to the private site for Space Traffic registries, the site that only officials were privy to.

The *Lost Seas* wasn't just quarantined by one source. Several different agencies had slapped quarantines on it, as well as the Bixian Government.

DeRicci had never heard of the Bixian Government. She looked at the *Lost Seas* travel log and saw no reference to the Port of Bix or the planet Bix or the City of Bix. She also tried Bixian, but found no reference to that, either.

She shook her head and went to her regular search area. She typed in *Bixian Government* and got this:

The ruling class of a small country within the Hazar Empire. The Bixian Government has independent authority on all local and regional matters, but on matters of a grander scale must answer to the Hazars.

There were links to more informative sites, historical documents, and a history of the Bixian Government before the formation of the Hazar Empire.

DeRicci had heard vaguely of the Hazar Empire. It composed part of a large sector several light years from here, and was still negotiating its place in the Earth Alliance. Some said the Empire would never join the Alliance because the trade rules were too strict: The Hazars wanted to export their legal system to all other governments, rather than bow to the Alliance system, which allowed legal precedent of a region or government to stand no matter who committed the crime.

DeRicci had some sympathy with the Hazar position and yet she knew how unworkable that would be within the Alliance itself. If she had more time, she would see what slowed down the negotiations with the Hazars.

But right now, she didn't have time to look. She had no idea why one of the quarantines would come from a small group within a large empire, so she went back to the original quarantine citing to see if it said any more.

It did not. So she looked at Space Traffic regulations to see what a quarantine from the Bixian Government meant. The legal language seemed unclear, but from what she could gather, any ship that had a flight plan to Bixian territory could be confiscated if it were under quarantine from the Bixian government.

DeRicci's head hurt and her eyes ached from the unfamiliar way of searching for information. She had never been good at legalese. She opened a link and sent a message to one of her assistants, asking for legal clarification from one of the government lawyers of the meaning of a Bixian Government quarantine for a ship docked in Armstrong's port.

The reference was obscure enough, she felt, that no one would understand it was tied to Paloma's ship. Not even Nyquist seemed to know about the quarantines, and he had been investigating the entire case.

She leaned back in her chair. She would have to tell him. The quarantines did give her the right to confiscate the ship in the name of Moon security, but she wasn't sure she wanted to. She still had some documents to dig through; she had to see what triggered the quarantine and why it still stuck to a ship in legal limbo.

Then her stomach twisted. Maybe this wasn't uncommon. Maybe a number of ships, docked in unsafe areas like Terminal 35, were in the same kind of limbo.

She went back to Space Traffic's main information screen, typed in *quarantined ships not located in Terminal 81,* and sat back, appalled, as a long list scrolled across her screen.

She saved the list, then downloaded it to an information chip on her right thumb. She got up, downloaded the same information onto another node, and cleaned off all references to the security alerts from her most secure node. Then she sent the list to Rudra Popova.

Popova had been DeRicci's de facto assistant when she became head of Moon Security. They had clashed almost from the beginning,

Popova believing that DeRicci wasn't qualified for the job and DeRicci, for the most part, agreeing with her.

The Disty Crisis had changed Popova's opinion of DeRicci, as it had for so many others, and now Popova was the number two operative in the department, with a real job title: Deputy Chief for Moon-Based Security. She still had to approve everything through DeRicci, but she didn't seem to mind. And she had proven herself valuable on more than one occasion. She specialized in research, rules, regulations, and the fine art of Moon-based diplomacy.

DeRicci's door opened. Popova stuck her head in. Her long black hair touched the floor, making it seem like she was attached to the ground by a pool of blackness.

"What's this?" she asked.

"I hadn't finished the instructions yet," DeRicci said. She couldn't count how many times this had happened between them—she'd send Popova the first part of a task, and the woman would enter her office rather than wait for the second part of the message.

"So finish," Popova said, her black eyes snapping. She was intelligent and impatient, one of the best researchers DeRicci had ever seen, partly—Popova once admitted over drinks—because she had such a short attention span that she flitted from one fact to the next, collecting them the way some people collected old Earth coins.

"Looking for something else, I stumbled on a list of quarantined ships not housed in Terminal 81," DeRicci said.

Popova frowned. "If they're not in 81, where are they?"

"All over the port, from what I can tell. That's what I sent you. I need them researched. I also need the law researched that allows this, or I need to know if this is some kind of accepted way of handling quarantined ships."

Popova let go of the door and slipped into the room. She folded her hands behind her back as if she were standing to attention. "I sure hope that isn't the case."

"Me, too," DeRicci said. But in her work these past several months, she'd learned that the legal way of doing things in many of the domes did not match the actual way of doing things. One of her jobs as security chief was to get rid of potential hazards from common practices like this one.

"How bad do you think this is?" Popova asked.

DeRicci shrugged. No sense panicking her most competent aide. "A lot of these ships have been in quarantine for years. I often can't even figure out who ordered the quarantine or why it exists. I looked up one ship, found it had been quarantined not just by the Port of Armstrong, but also by a government I'd never heard of, and I just didn't have time to research it all."

"So you want me to do that," Popova said with a slight smile.

DeRicci nodded.

"How did this come up now? I thought you were talking to a police detective a few minutes ago."

"He left," DeRicci said. "I checked on a few things he said and stumbled on this."

"It's related to the Paloma case, then?" Popova asked.

"It started from that," DeRicci said truthfully. "I found a notation in one of the files that Nyquist had given me that made no sense. Then I continued my research and found all of this. I don't think any of these ships relate to Paloma's case—"

At least, DeRicci hoped not; she hadn't searched for any connections other than the *Lost Seas.*

"—but if you find that they are, let me know."

"Of course," Popova said.

"And I don't have to remind you that this is all confidential," DeRicci said, doing just that.

"Of course not." Popova seemed to stand at even greater attention. "How soon do you need this?"

"As soon as possible," DeRicci said.

"You think we have a budding crisis on our hands?" Popova asked.

"No," DeRicci said. "I'm afraid we have an old neglected one."

19

KI BOWLES ARRIVED AT HER APARTMENT TO FIND PILES OF THINGS outside her door. All had been neatly boxed, labeled, and laid out in a pattern that effectively blocked her entrance.

All of the boxes had come from InterDome, and they contained a career's worth of things—her possessions, her research materials, her demos and production recordings, and her best-stories archive. Everything she had ever brought or ever created at InterDome was in these boxes.

Everything she'd thought she'd been.

Someone had dumped them here without a care as to what was inside. Someone had set them where they could be stolen or destroyed or just plain lost.

She had gone from being InterDome's most important young employee to its whipping girl. She was afraid to watch anything on her link, afraid that she'd be mentioned in terrible tones.

Or worse, that she wouldn't be mentioned at all.

She tried to shove a pile aside with her foot and found that she couldn't budge it. Robots had packed these things and probably brought them here. Which explained why they were in such neat rows. InterDome hadn't even had the courtesy to send a human with her belongings. They had sent a group of anal-retentive robots.

Which, of course, was an oxymoron. Robots were what robots were. But she hated the gesture nonetheless.

She sighed and leaned over the boxes so that she could put her palm on the door, activating the security system's retinal scan. As it went through its varied procedure, the system sent out pulses of light—something she'd designed so that she wouldn't be standing here, waiting for the system to unlock, only to discover (after maybe a half an hour of nothing) that it had somehow malfunctioned.

She'd had too many problems like that over the years, and too many "interested fans" whom the law sometimes called stalkers, to allow that much time to pass while she waited.

The door clicked and slid open. Interior lights turned on. She cleared her throat and called for her own house robots, small machines that were little more than cleaners and serving equipment, demanding that they pick up the boxes and move them inside.

As the first robot appeared—a small dervish that she usually used for drinks—she commanded it to start with the boxes in the center. That way, she could get inside quickly.

Levers came out of the robot's thin sides and hoisted the box on top of the dervish as if the box weighed nothing. Half a dozen other robots appeared, all working off the same instruction, making the slight, low-pitched humming noise that robots were required to make by law so that no one would be surprised when they approached.

Each 'bot picked up a box or two or four and carried them inside, heading down the hall toward Bowles' home office—or the room she called her home office. She'd never been home enough to work out of it. She used this place mostly for sleeping.

Meals were eaten on the fly; research done in the office; any relaxation—holotales, 2-D flat movies, books—were enjoyed in a special room at InterDome, in one of Armstrong's many libraries, or in a corner of her favorite restaurant.

Mostly, she had worked—interviewing potential subjects, filming anything she saw that seemed unusual, stopping at crime scenes just to make sure everything was aboveboard. Even her interests had been work-related: she'd taken courses in the Disty language after the most recent Mars crisis, and spent some time studying the rudimentary elements of Earth Alliance law, learning that what she thought she knew hadn't been anything at all.

She stepped through the opening the 'bots left and went inside the apartment. Except for the hall light, which came on automatically, the place was dark. Usually, she commanded lights up the moment she entered a room, but this time, she paused.

The living area looked unfamiliar to her. She had bought the couch and the three extra-wide chairs, thinking them perfect for the kind of review that happened during research, but she'd never used them. She had a wall of screens, all framed as if they were art, but they looked strangely empty without anything playing on them, almost eerie, as if they were waiting for some family pictures to appear and give them life.

The place smelled dusty and abandoned—no lingering food odors, no programmed odors like ocean or evergreen, not even a hint of the body perfumes she wore. The 'bots cleaned the air as a matter of course; apparently, with nothing to clean, they had eliminated most odors entirely.

The last 'bot came in with the final box, disappearing down the hall into that hidden office. The main door closed behind it.

"Lights up," Bowles whispered.

The room looked no better with its lights. It was dingy and unwelcome, like a showroom that had been abandoned. No pillows on the couch, not even a body dent. Had she sat on it for more than a few moments? She couldn't remember, which meant she probably hadn't.

"Depressing," she muttered as she headed to the kitchen. She kept it well stocked, just in case she wanted to eat in. Keeping up the food gave the 'bots something to do. She paid a lot for this place and the 'bots that kept it functioning. She always felt that they needed to be busy, even though they probably wouldn't notice if they weren't.

She took out a bottle of Real Earth Water and opened it, tossing the cap into the recycler, and then headed down the hall.

By Armstrong standards, this apartment was large and impressive. The neighborhood wasn't the most upscale in the city. It wasn't even as tony as Paloma's had been. But it was a good, prestigious address, in an improving area. By the time Bowles retired, she'd thought when she bought the place, it would be worth millions of credits more than it was now.

A gamble she had taken. One of many. Now the upscale address didn't mean as much, and the apartment seemed more a symbol of the life she'd lived this morning than the one she was living this afternoon.

The boxes filled her small office. She didn't even look at them. Instead, she walked into the guest room, a space no guest had ever stayed in. She wasn't even sure why she had had a second bed made up, furnished a comfortable discussion area in the corner, and added a small cooking corner to the side.

Maybe it was the presence of the en suite bathroom, or maybe it was because she'd been taught that all homes had a guest area. Or maybe she had hoped, way back when she'd bought the place, to have guests.

She'd once believed reporters were popular people. She'd never really understood until a year or two into the job that they were hated. The hatred became fascination as the reporter gained fame. Then she had to deal with hatred or worse, people who became her friend because she could get them something—whether it was a job at Inter-Dome, some measure of their own fame, or a bit of prestige just from knowing her.

None of those people had ever been invited to her home.

The only people who had come to her home, besides the service people who were the human faces of management here, had been her colleagues for her annual private party, which she'd always held on her birthday.

She'd never told anyone it was her birthday, so she never got gifts. Her parents were far away, and their presents were always sent a long time in advance. She'd open those when the gifts arrived, not on the actual day, but she'd always felt the need for a celebration.

This year, she'd even had a large cake. No one asked about it, but everyone had enjoyed it.

Everyone except her.

The guest room smelled even mustier than the main room. She ran a hand along the comforter, noting that it was a bit clammy, and wondered if she'd ever instructed the 'bots to clean here.

Probably not. She probably hadn't seen the point.

Her bedroom was the only room in the place with any personality. It smelled faintly of her soaps and perfumes. The bed looked a bit rumpled, its bright red comforter familiar and welcoming.

She resisted the urge to sprawl on it—if she lay down, she'd never get back up again. Depression, in the form of an understandable pity party, waited to take her in its blackness and hold her there as long as she wanted to stay.

She wasn't going to do that.

She sank into the fourth oversized chair in the apartment, the only one that had an impression of her body, the only chair that ever got used. She ran a hand over her face and leaned back.

What she needed was a plan. She had options. She could apply at the other media outlets. They'd know InterDome had let her go. They'd assume they knew why. She would explain her side.

But they'd probably want to put her on Gossip, too. She hadn't repaired her reputation, and now the dismissal from InterDome would simply make that reputation worse.

She could volunteer to work for minimal salary, be treated as the lowliest intern, just like she had done when she started at InterDome, but the very thought of humbling herself that much made her stomach hurt.

She could produce her own 'casts, send up stories without the benefit of InterDome's connections, using the public access areas of the newslinks. She could make her 'casts personal and chatty or cover riskier topics than InterDome allowed her to do.

But she would know—and some of her fans would know—that she had settled. That she was doing this because she could no longer function on a Moon-wide level. Her stories would only reach Armstrong, and then only parts of it. She would have to rely on word of mouth to get any buzz at all.

She sipped the water. It was cold and fresh. Moon water had a flatness, an almost metallic taste that probably came from all of the recycling. It was probably healthier than the stuff imported from Earth—who knew what germs that stuff had—and it was certainly less expensive, but it didn't have the taste.

She would have to let her parents know she'd been fired. They liked watching InterDome's Alliance-wide reports, hoping to see something she had put together. The last thing she'd want was her parents to find out her career was over long before she told them.

Only a few things to do—talk to her parents, figure out a plan— and already she was overwhelmed.

She supposed she could contact her lawyer and see if InterDome had the right to terminate her contract in such a preemptory manner, particularly when she had been cooperating with them.

But she'd always hated whiners, people who sued rather than solved. Besides, the case would eat her alive, keep her focused on past injustices, rather than make her future.

And she was afraid, ironically enough, of the publicity. If she took on InterDome, the gossips would cover the story as if it were the destruction of Armstrong media. She would have to face former colleagues and tell them to leave her alone, or pretend to confide in them so that she could manipulate them.

Her name would be all over the news, but as a newsmaker, not as a reporter.

She couldn't stomach that, either.

She leaned the bottle on the arm of her chair and closed her eyes. Maybe she would follow Flint's example. Maybe she would get a completely new profession. She never trained as a journalist. She'd been an art historian.

There were museums all over the solar system that needed an expert in multicultural art. She could revive the career she'd abandoned.

But she'd abandoned that for a reason. It seemed like a waste to spend her life managing someone else's art, even if it were the most respected art of various cultures. She wanted to create on her own. She had no artistic skills—she couldn't draw or paint or sculpt—but she could tell stories, and she adored doing that.

Reviving the art history career wasn't for her.

But she could revive her own career somewhere else. Take her credentials and show up at the outer reaches of the solar system, maybe even go farther into human-settled territory, and report from there. Not as a link to InterDome or any of the other Moon-based media, but for the local media in whatever place she'd ended up in.

She would tell them she needed a change of pace, or she wanted to become a real reporter, one who explored the dangerous parts of the Earth Alliance, rather than sitting in its tame hub.

But the thought of danger worried her. She wasn't that courageous. She'd often thought of those Disappeared, average people who, because of circumstances, had had to give up everything and start all over again.

They didn't even have their names to work with. They couldn't mention their personal histories.

They only had their pluck and their willingness to live a new life.

And people like Paloma and Miles Flint destroyed those lives.

Bowles sat up, her eyes opening. No one had ever done a long, in-depth study of the Disappeared. No one had done more than a series of reports on the phenomenon. Everyone was afraid of it.

But she had some contacts and she had a hook—Paloma's murder. She could do the series freelance, or maybe even do it as a nonfiction study, one of those week-long things that people downloaded, then watched in pieces, sometimes over the space of months.

She had the credentials to pull this off. And the ability, although she'd never done anything so in-depth.

What she needed was help from her manager getting a deal with one of the outlets—not a news outlet, but an educational one—and maybe some assistance, like an educational grant while she put the entire thing together.

Her heart started pounding the way it always did when she felt like she had a good story. She could even use some of her back pieces, pieces that went nowhere, like the Child Martyr story. She could look at Noelle DeRicci in context and see if the rumors that DeRicci had helped some Disappeareds vanish were true.

Bowles sent a message to her manager, asking for a meeting, and then she got up and went into that home office. She summoned a single 'bot and got it to move some of the boxes so that she could sit at her desk.

There she started a file of notes, ideas for the longer piece, things she had to investigate.

On her own. Without a team of rookies mucking her up. Without a boss overseeing her effort. Without a group of lawyers worrying about her every word.

If she did a good enough job, this story would open doors for her and give her a new career that used the skills of both of her old careers—investigating the past, and digging into the present.

She smiled. One thing she had learned at InterDome. She would survive this. Even if they publicized why she was no longer there, people would forget by the time this long piece hit the links. Her reputation would have a black mark, but the mark would mean little compared to all the accolades she'd received over her career, the award-winning stories she'd told, the scoops she'd broken.

She would survive this, and she would do better than she ever had.

She was amazed she hadn't made a change like this a long, long time ago.

20

MAXINE VAN ALEN HAD OFFICES IN A FIVE-STORY OFFICE BUILDING that had once been Armstrong's first courthouse. Called the Old Legal Building, the place was on the historic registry for the Earth Alliance, and was even considered a tourist attraction.

Flint thought that a good omen.

The neighborhood wasn't as old as his and it was better kept up. But it was in Old Armstrong, and the dome filters here were as poor as the ones near his building. A fine layer of Moon dust covered everything. A few locals wore breathing masks over their mouths and noses. The masks were designed to look like skin, but because they had to have a small space for oxygen, they looked like enhancements gone wrong.

The buildings themselves looked fine in the dust. Most were made of Moon brick here, so the dust seemed like part of them. In fact, Flint couldn't guarantee that the dust didn't come from them. In the last few decades, early Moon brick had started to crumble because it was made with the wrong combination of ingredients. The early colonists hadn't had the resources or the know-how to make proper brick, but had done the best they could.

Inside the Old Legal Building, the walls had been fortified, first with permaplastic (probably by the old colonists, when it became clear that their brick might not hold up) and then with various modern substances. The Old Legal Building's brick covered the outside like a disaster waiting to happen, but the inside, for all its historical significance, was as much a modern building as the one he'd worked in when he'd been with the police.

Maxine Van Alen had the entire fifth floor. At the moment, elevators made Flint think of Paloma, so he took the stairs.

The stairs ended not in a hallway, but in a fully functional office space that had no entrance door. Desks were scattered about the wide room and employees scurried about as if each person's mission was important.

'Bots picked up leftover equipment, probably to protect confidentiality, and made certain no coffee cups or half-eaten sandwiches marred any surface. The air smelled faintly of lavender, which was one of the soothing designer scents often sold to large office buildings. The smell always made Flint sneeze.

His sneeze caught the attention of a red-haired young man with muttonchop whiskers. He wore a long paisley coat and carried actual files, probably for effect.

"May I help you?" he asked.

"I'm here to see Maxine Van Alen," Flint said. "Colette Bannerman set up the appointment. I'm Miles Flint."

"Yes, Mr. Flint," the young man said. "Ms. Van Alen is expecting you. You do realize you're six minutes late."

Flint hadn't realized an exact time had been established. He thought he was to get to the office as quickly as he could. But he didn't say any of that to the young man. Instead, he allowed himself to be led through a nearly invisible door at the back of the room, and into a large, well-lit corridor, filled with moving pictures of attorneys in courtrooms.

Flint assumed those attorneys were actual employees of the firm, and he suspected if he touched any of the images, he could hear the most masterful moments of the trials, trials that they had most likely won.

The corridor ended in another wide space. Only this area had the hushed reverence of a library. The young man bowed to Flint, then stepped aside, letting Flint go in ahead of him.

A tall woman with hair as blonde as Flint's leaned against a desk. She wore a red silk dress that ended at midthigh. On her, it looked like business attire. Her legs were crossed at the ankle and her hands rested easily on the desk's surface. Her skin was a dusky rose color, as false as the color of her hair. Only her eyes seemed unenhanced. They were black, almost fathomless, and looking into them made Flint feel momentarily lost.

"Colette Bannerman says you have a proposition that will amuse me." The woman's voice was husky, as if she spent most of her time in minimal oxygen.

"Does she?" Flint asked.

The woman stood. She was taller than Flint, and broader, although she had no fat. She looked like she could take him and toss him through the nearby windows with minimal effort.

She held out her hand. "Maxine Van Alen."

He took it. Her skin was hot and dry. "Miles Flint."

"You're a Retrieval Artist."

"Last I checked."

"I represent disappearance companies."

"You also win cases against WSX, from what I hear."

Her smile was slow and easy, but it didn't reach her eyes. "I figure I have another year, maybe two, of winning cases against them."

"And after that?" Flint asked.

"My answer to that question depends on how I feel at the moment."

"How do you feel at this moment?'

"Divided." She took her hand back and rested it on the desktop again. "Either WSX will buy every judge in Armstrong by then, or they will have figured out a way to destroy me. Or both."

"Do you think they're that powerful?'

Her eyes narrowed. "Are you naïve, Mr. Flint, or are you testing me?"

He shrugged. "Pretend I'm naïve."

"Every long-established city has a law firm like WSX. It's just a testament to the corruptibility of public officials as to whether or not the power law firm invades the judiciary or city government. WSX has done both."

"I know we have some corrupt judges here," Flint said. "I never thought all of them could be corrupted."

"See?" she said. "This is what gets people in trouble with lawyers like me. I said in a few years WSX *will* buy every judge in Armstrong. I didn't say they *had.*"

Flint nodded to her. "Good point."

She swept a hand around the room, as if she were inviting him to dance. "Find a chair."

He had a lot of choices. Most seemed functional—fake wood chairs that dated from one hundred years ago, when Earth items were valued but impossible to obtain. A few near the wall were actual wood and obviously never used. The rest were modern, heavily upholstered, and looked too comfortable for a business meeting.

Flint sat on the arm of one of the upholstered chairs. He didn't want to commit to a long conversation, and figured this was the best way to hint at his intentions.

"Shy man," Van Alen said.

She had noticed, then, and wasn't afraid to comment.

"Cautious," he said.

Even though he sat, she leaned back against the desktop, extending those long legs. They were her best feature, and the most imposing.

"So," she said, "tell me what makes you believe you have a case against WSX."

Flint crossed his arms. "First I need to know if client confidentiality applies to this meeting."

"One hundred percent," Van Alen said. "Every meeting I have in here is confidential. We don't even have an active security system that records what's happening here. You could toss a chair at me if you want, and no one will come running."

He was half-tempted to try it, just to test her.

"You didn't shut my links off," he said.

"That's so crude," she said, standing up and walking around her desk. Finally, she sat behind it, using the smooth surface as a prop for her elbows. "You're the client. If you want to reveal what's said in here, then that's your prerogative. It's just not mine."

"I'm not a client yet," Flint said.

"My philosophy is this," she said. "Anyone who comes in here testing the waters is a client for the duration of the first meeting. Even if we decide not to bond."

Then she smiled. Slowly. As if she were making him some kind of proposition instead of talking about lawyer-client privilege.

"Whatever you say to me, Miles Flint, will remain confidential. Even if you tell me you've committed mass murder, I will remain silent. I will agonize over it, wish I hadn't heard it, and decide that I don't like you, but I will not tell anyone, not even my pet cat."

She didn't look like a woman who had a pet cat. She looked like someone who had no ties at all.

Flint sighed. He'd come here to see if she'd assist him. Now he would find out. "Do you know of the Retrieval Artist named Paloma?"

"Of course," Van Alen said. "She found a few of my clients, people who didn't want to be found. She was good at what she did. She retired a few years back, right?"

"Right," Flint said, and paused just slightly, like he would have done if he were the investigator on Paloma's case. "She was murdered today."

All the expression left Van Alen's face. For a moment, she seemed vulnerable, and those eyes seemed empty and lost. Then she swallowed hard and nodded, as if acknowledging what he said.

"Murdered," she said. "You're certain?"

Flint nodded. "I saw the crime scene."

"Because you're…?"

"A friend," he said.

"Police don't let friends on scene," Van Alen said.

"They do when the friend is a former detective," Flint said, stretching the truth a little. "It turns out that I stand to inherit most everything Paloma had."

"Congratulations," Van Alen said dryly.

"You won't congratulate me when you hear my dilemma," he said. "Her name before she took on the Paloma identity was Lucianna Stuart. Does that ring any bells?"

The rose color had completely left Van Alen's skin. "Of Wagner, Stuart, and Xendor, Limited? That Stuart?"

Flint nodded.

"But she's the mother of—"

"The Wagner brothers, I know," Flint said.

Van Alen cursed. "You want me to protect your inheritance against them? Are you kidding?"

"No," Flint said, "I'm not. There's a reason Paloma picked me to keep everything, and I don't think it has to do with money."

He explained that he had his own personal wealth. He also talked about the files he'd found when he'd taken over her office years ago, and the files that Paloma had been worried about before her death.

"I thought you didn't know you'd inherited until today," Van Alen said when he finished.

"I didn't," he said. "Paloma left me a holographic explanation."

"One of those disappearing kinds?" Van Alen asked with a bit of sarcasm.

Flint nodded.

"I hope you had the presence of mind to make a copy," she said.

"I have one," he said. "I'd like to show it to you if you want to handle this case."

She let out a gusty sigh. "Let me think. Do I want to handle a civil case for the heir of the murdered and estranged mother of the Wagner boys, the most powerful attorneys in all of Armstrong? Do I want to delve into the private records of one of the most notorious Retrieval Artists of our time, with the caveat that I can use nothing in my good-deeds work for the Disappeared because this includes client confidentiality? Do I want to look at tangled records that might have their own confidentiality issues, not just from Paloma's Retrieval Artist days, but also from the days when she was a member of that elite and powerful law firm?"

"I guess that's what I'm asking you," Flint said. "And probably a lot more."

Van Alen leaned back in her chair, tapping her fingers against her chin. "I've taken on the Wagners before, which makes me unstable. Taking your case would make me suicidal."

Flint's breath caught. She was going to turn him down. He wasn't sure where else to turn.

"I've always wanted to go down in a blaze of glory." Van Alen stood and extended her hand over the desk. "I'd be happy to serve as your lawyer on this case, Mr. Flint, if you'll have me."

He stood too and shook her hand. "Consider yourself hired," he said.

21

NYQUIST CLEANED THE OLD COFFEE CUPS OFF HIS DESK. HE FOUND a half-eaten donut behind a large mug, and removed both of those, as well. He was alternately too hot and too cold, which had nothing to do with his health or with the environmental systems in the Detective Division.

He had felt like this as a boy on his first date. He'd felt like this when he first took out his ex-wife, and he'd felt like this when he tried the inevitable reunion.

He was smitten, he knew it, and he hated it. He hated relationships. They never worked and they made him nervous.

But he couldn't change how he felt. Nor could he change how he reacted to DeRicci, no matter how much he wanted to. He'd decided not to pursue her, but her suggestion of dinner had changed that.

Which made him even more nervous.

He'd managed not to think about her arrival until five minutes ago. He had had a lot to do. First, he had gone to the forensics lab to find Khundred. She had stayed with most of the evidence and with the body, making certain nothing got missed as it went through the log-in procedures.

He learned little from her and even less from Ethan Broduer, the coroner. Nyquist had always suspected that Broduer was a political appointment, but couldn't prove it. The man seemed singularly uninterested in anything that caused people to die in the City of Armstrong.

Even though Broduer had started his examination of Paloma's body, he refused to speculate about the exact cause of death. He also had no theories, as of yet, as to what administered the horrible destruction that Paloma had suffered or whether she had been alive when the worst of the damage occurred.

"Here's the thing, Nyquist," Broduer had snapped when Nyquist pressed him. "There are a lot of aliens out there, and this woman worked against most of them. I'm not familiar with all the weird forms of death that come into this city from faraway places. This woman was a Retrieval Artist, and I'm assuming she had friends and family. So her death could've been caused by anything—some alien ally I'd never heard of performing a legal ritual, or some angry spouse who decided to rip her from limb to limb. I just don't know."

Which meant that Nyquist didn't know, either. It also meant that he had nothing to go on, nothing that he hadn't already seen for himself.

Farther into the forensic unit, the techs had started analyzing that bloodstain—or whatever it was—that had been on the wall. No one would talk to him, afraid, apparently, that they'd be accused of causing a public outcry if they used the words *biochemical* and *goo* in the same sentence.

Nyquist was stuck on the technical side of the investigation, stuck and unable to move it forward. He gave an order to Khundred to get some results immediately, but he figured he had as much clout with her as he did with the forensic team.

So he came back to his office and started through the cleaned-up security vids from Paloma's apartment building. The entire system shut down shortly before she died—the building itself claiming an organic malfunction (was this the source of the biochemical-goo rumor?)—but he was able to get a bit of information off the screen.

Paloma had arrived at the front door of the building midmorning, greeting some friends as she went through the full lobby, and headed toward the elevator. Two serving 'bots trailed her, their saucerlike tops covered with packages.

She had been shopping and she had come back with a lot of merchandise. He needed to check two things about those 'bots: whether she had left with them in the morning (he would have to look at more security video for that) and whether they were the 'bots that were crumpled near the kitchen door of her apartment.

He also had no record of packages inside that apartment. If she had time to put them away, then she had been inside the place longer than he thought.

Either that, or the 'bots went blithely on, putting away her newly purchased items while she was being brutally murdered just a few meters away.

The security vid ran for a few seconds after she got onto the elevator alone. No one had joined her at the last moment, no one was waiting for her when she got on.

He would need security recordings from the other floors to see if, in those few seconds, the elevator had stopped at those floors and let someone else on.

He still had quite a bit of searching to do, but he had stopped with the tedious moment-by-moment work to do a bit of research on Lucianna Stuart and her family, before eating with DeRicci.

Which actually meant that he had been lying to himself. All along, he had been marking time until their dinner. He had planned his last two hours around it.

He would be horribly disappointed (and, at the same time, relieved) if she didn't show.

He moved a chair closer to his desk, brought in one more chair so that it looked like his office was more welcoming than it usually was, and then he settled in his own chair, peering at the scratched screen on the desktop as if he could actually concentrate.

He couldn't. His nervousness had reached a high pitch. He silently cursed himself and his overactive imagination. He needed to focus on this crime (and the dozen or so other investigations he was running, all of which had been reduced in importance when he got assigned this one), and not on the schoolboy infatuation he had with the Moon's Security Chief.

Someone knocked on his half-open door, and he jumped, then silently cursed himself again. He'd been expecting a visitor. He was so on edge that he'd let his nervousness show.

He looked up. DeRicci peered into the room. She looked smaller here, her curly hair pulled back as if she had tried to control it, her clothes a casual pair of pants with a dark shirt—something most plain clothes officers wore when they knew they were going to a crime scene.

She was supposed to come with him to the *Lost Seas*.

In her left hand, she held a large, grease-stained bag. It smelled of garlic and some hard-to-define spices.

His stomach rumbled.

"I thought we were going to eat on the fly," he said, then realized how ungrateful that sounded. He hurried to make it sound better. "If I'd known you wanted to eat here, I'd've made sure we had something good."

As if what she brought wasn't good. He was glad he no longer blushed. If he did, he would have blushed now.

He hadn't felt this awkward since he'd been a teenager.

DeRicci grinned. "I'll take that as a 'come-in.'"

She did. She set the bag on the corner of his desk like an old pro. Most nondetectives set anything they brought in the middle of the desk—not used to the flat screens.

"I brought some curried beef, garlic chicken, and an Ilidio dish that they swear doesn't use vast quantities of *beltle*."

He raised his eyebrows. *Beltle* was an herb found only on Ilidio. Humans imported it under the Alliance's Dangerous Substance Ordinance, but only in miniscule quantities and then with the understanding that it wouldn't be eaten. It had some technical function for some of the equipment used in Moon-based farming—making plants grow quicker or something along those lines. He'd never learned the details, only that it made real food grown in the Growing Pits come to maturity quicker, as long as it was in the soil only.

If it were ingested in any quantity, it caused a grotesque and rapid death in humans. Earth-grown plants did not absorb the harmful elements of *Beltle*, which was how it could be used in agriculture, but when it first got introduced into Moon culture, it became a favorite murder method for disgruntled agricultural workers.

Ilidio restaurants had to have special permission to use *beltle* in any off-Ilidio location, although they often protested. *Beltle* was considered a delicacy on Ilidio; to ban it from Ilidio cuisine was like banning garlic from most Earth-made delicacies.

"I would hope that there's no *beltle* in that dish," he said.

Her smile widened. "Don't worry. I've had this before. The Ilidio restaurant is next to the Chinese restaurant, so I brought both. You can be noncourageous and eat the Chinese food only. It's probably sensible; in case the Ilidio dish does have some *beltle*, one of us will live to tell the tale."

"Why would you even try something that adventurous in the first place?" he asked.

She shrugged one shoulder. "Now that the word *security* is in my title, I have to take a few risks now and then."

She opened the bag and pulled out chopsticks, containers of rice, and some wriggling noodles that had to be part of the Ilidio dish. Then she grabbed three other grease-stained containers, some plastic-wrapped cookies, and a large brown root.

Nyquist tried not to grimace, but he doubted he was succeeding. He pulled some disposable plates from his top desk drawer—testimony to how many times he ate dinner here alone—and set them near the food.

DeRicci put most of the containers near him, sticking the restaurant supplied spoons in them. But she opened the Ilidio dish, squeezed the root so some of that brown substance dripped into the food, and then poured it on the wriggling noodles.

Some of the stuff splashed on Nyquist's screen. DeRicci wiped it off with one finger, then licked the finger clean.

"If you knew how long it's been since that screen was cleaned, you wouldn't have done that," he said.

She sank into one of the chairs. "I do know. It's been two years. I used to have the office next door."

Hair rose on the back of his neck. "You were here when the bomb went off."

Although numerous bombs had gone off in Armstrong over its long life, there was only one that locals called "the bomb." It was the bomb that destroyed part of the dome.

"I was in my office," she said. "We lost power to the entire building. No air movement, no environmental controls, nothing. And we shook from the dome walls coming down. A lot of people got injured."

Her smile was gone. She had grabbed a plate and just held it, not dishing up any food.

"I hated that day," she said.

Nyquist nodded. "I was investigating a murder."

He'd always thought that ironic. When a lot of people had died in a deliberately set bomb attack, he had been across the city, investigating a simple domestic—wife stabbing her husband with a kitchen knife.

"Nowhere near the bomb, I hope," DeRicci said.

"No, but I was holed up with a crazy woman and the man she'd stabbed to death, for nearly four hours." He grabbed his own plate. "Keeping her calm took some fancy talking on my part."

"I'm amazed you did it," DeRicci said.

"Me, too," he said. "Looking back, no one would've even noticed if I killed her instead of arrested her. But how was I to know that?"

DeRicci shook her head. "You would've known."

"Yeah," he said quietly. "I would've."

That was a day he didn't want to relive. But there were a lot of days like that in his career. A new partner—he didn't know how many partners ago—had asked him why he stayed on the job. He'd said it was because he didn't know how to do anything else, but the honest answer was that on the good days he loved it, and on the bad days, he felt needed.

No one else had ever really needed him. Not his ex-wife, not his family, not even the handful of people who passed for his friends.

He didn't even like having a partner. Even though he complained about them, the problem never really was with them. It was with him. He preferred to be alone and answering to no one.

Maybe that was why he got so nervous when a woman attracted him. He had no real idea how to operate in any kind of partnership. He wasn't sure he was capable of doing so.

"The bombing's always a conversation-stopper, isn't it?" DeRicci said. "We all go back to that day."

He nodded, then started to dish up some rice. He threw garlic chicken on top, a bit of the curried beef to the side. Then he grabbed one of the chopsticks and dipped it into the wriggling, crackling mess that was the Ilidio meal.

"What is this?" he asked.

"It's called *yringen*," she said. "I'm told it's better with arsenic, but I'm not going to try it that way."

He shook his head, certain she was joking now. Arsenic, a metal, was used as a poison a lot in the old murder mysteries. It was considered an arcane form of murder, until one of the poison squad's symptoms tests, given to detective cadets, cited it in a major quiz. No case like that had ever appeared on the Moon, so the poison squad had to back up its question with all sorts of old entertainments, from 2-D movies, to murder novels that had survived from previous centuries, to actual cases, all of which had occurred in pre-twenty-second-century Earth.

"They couldn't serve it that way, anyhow, could they?" he asked.

"Sure they can," DeRicci said. "Arsenic is allowed, even here, in very small doses for a lot of the alien cultures. No restaurants serving humans use it, though, because in its mildest doses, it causes severe stomach upset."

He paused as he held that chopstick, still not sure he wanted to taste the Ilidio dish. "How come you know all of this?"

"I could lie to you and tell you it's because I aced the poisons part of detective school or because I'm the Security Chief and we have to know everything."

"But?" he asked.

"But," she said, "for a while, I was considered the poisons woman on the detective squad, mostly because those cases were considered at the bottom of the rung. A person might've died from deliberate poisoning or, hmm, they ate something they shouldn't've accidentally. More often than not, they ate something they shouldn't've."

His stomach continued to growl, but that was the only sign he felt of continued appetite. He still hadn't moved the chopstick out of the Ilidio dish.

"You're not giving me much confidence in this food," he said.

She took a spoonful of the wriggling noodles, added something fat and squishy that vaguely resembled a prune, and ate.

"I know more about strange foods than anyone," she said as she chewed. "And you should feel reassured, not frightened. If I'm gonna eat it, then it's trustworthy. I've seen too many poison deaths to risk going out that way on my own."

He gave her an uncomfortable look, then used the chopsticks to grab a squirming noodle. He knew the noodle wasn't alive—a number of multiethnic cuisines used these noodles because they seemed exotic—but it made him queasy to look at it.

He put it in his mouth, bit down, and got the expected crunch from the noodle. He hadn't expected the sweet-bitter taste of the sauce, however, or the peppery aftertaste.

He sighed, then dished some onto his plate.

"You liked it," DeRicci said.

"Against my better judgment," he muttered.

She laughed and finished dishing up her own meal. Then she ate the Ilidio portion quickly, washing it down with some liquid he hadn't even noticed.

"It's goes with the meal," she said after a moment. "Trust me, you'll want it when the pepper and the curry collide."

He probably would want it, but he worried about trying so many new things, particularly when he was already on edge. Still, he took the other container, which he had initially thought held more food, and took a tentative sip.

It tasted like a cross between real orange juice, fake strawberries, and some kind of cream. It was extremely sweet and tart, but it did cut the peppery aftertaste from the *yringen*.

He ate some more, not sure how to proceed. The food was better than he expected. If he had been the one to choose, he would have picked up some Moon-built hot dogs with his favorite fresh-from-the-carton rolls and some coleslaw made with reconstituted lettuce and Moon-grown carrots.

"Were the last couple of hours productive?" DeRicci asked, moving to the garlic chicken on her plate. She ate a lot faster than he did, maybe because she was used to the food.

"Not as much as I'd hoped." He briefed her on the slowness in forensics, the uncooperative nature of Ethan Brodeur ("at least he doesn't hate you," DeRicci muttered. "He's always hated me."), and heavy detail work he was going to have to do on the security vids. "I did find out a few things about the Stuarts, however."

"The Stuarts," she said, looking up from her plate. "There's more than Lucianna?"

"A dozen more. They've settled all over the Moon. One of the Moon's first families, as well, only without the Wagner's illustrative modern pedigree. The Stuarts have mostly become big fish in the smaller domes. Lucianna was the star of her branch of the family, and here's the thing that amazes me. She never let them know she changed her name."

DeRicci frowned. She clearly didn't understand what he meant. "So?"

"So," he said. "By doing so, she effectively cut off all communication with that part of her family. In many ways, she tried to cut off her entire past, although it didn't work. She went back to WSX, but in a different capacity."

"I don't understand," DeRicci said.

"I don't either. But here's what I get from the official family history—and they have one of those special family sites, with vids and oral histories and all kinds of testimonies about how important they are to the Moon—"

"Ick," DeRicci said.

He nodded, but continued. "What I get is that Lucianna started WSX with her own money. She's the one who made the firm what is, not Claudius Wagner. She merged with his smaller, less prestigious law firm after hers became the do-not-mess-with firm in Armstrong. And she became that kind of firm doing work for her family."

"What kind of work?" DeRicci asked.

"Something corporate," he said. "Something to do with the Earth Alliance. Something that maybe might have led someone to disappear. I don't know. It's too buried in the family myth to tell."

"Was she the only Stuart here in Armstrong?"

"Not then," he said. "But when she went through the name change, she was. By then, some of the older, more impressive Stuarts were dead, and a few just vanished from the family chronology."

"Vanished?" DeRicci asked. "As in disappeared?'

"As in there's no history of them past a certain date, but no death date, either. For a family that's so proud of its heritage and history, I find that unusual."

"It sounds like a mess," she said.

Nyquist nodded. "This whole case is a mess of details. And I can't even get Brodeur to tell me what Paloma died of."

"Except that she was murdered," DeRicci said.

"You'd know that, too, if you saw the body," he said.

"It's not a death ritual of some kind?" she asked.

"Brodeur isn't willing to say, and to be honest, I'm not either. None of us know enough about the aliens around us to know if this is some new wrinkle on a Disty Vengeance Killing or something like that."

"It doesn't sound like it from what you describe," DeRicci said.

"It doesn't look like it, either." Nyquist sighed and set down his half-touched plate. "I do understand why Brodeur doesn't want to commit. I'd be the same in his shoes. But I'm worried. I'm worried that I'm running out of time."

"For what?" DeRicci asked.

He shrugged. "I wish I knew."

She took some more curried beef, even though she hadn't touched most of hers. Then she sipped more of that noxiously sweet Ilidio drink.

"Well," she said when she finished. "I have some bad news."

He braced himself.

"The *Lost Seas* is under quarantine."

"Quarantine?"

She nodded. "And not just from our government. Three other Alliance governments have placed a quarantine on the ship, not to mention something called the Bixian Government."

"What's that?"

It took her about ten minutes to explain the Bixian Government to him, and he still wasn't sure he understood. He picked the chicken off his plate while she talked, ate some of the rice, and then grabbed one of the wrapped cookies.

DeRicci took the other, as if she were afraid he was going to steal it.

"It took one of my assistants most of the last two hours to find out what a Bixian Government quarantine means," DeRicci said. "With the other governments, it's fairly simple. The ship has been contaminated somehow, and has to be inspected by their government regulators before it's allowed in any of their ports."

"It means something different for the Bixians?" Nyquist asked.

"Oh, yeah," DeRicci said. "It means the ship is cursed."

22

It took Flint longer than he expected to show Van Alen the security recording of Paloma's holographic message and then to explain what he had learned about the *Lost Seas*. He half expected Van Alen to call an end to their meeting, claiming his time was up and he had to make a return appointment.

Instead, she gave him her full attention, pausing only to ask the occasional question.

When he finished, she templed her fingers and frowned. "Do you really think it that important to get into the *Lost Seas* before the Wagners? They'll be bound by the same quarantine orders that you will."

"I think it very important," Flint said.

She let out a small sigh. "You could be risking all kinds of horrible diseases or something else that we can't even fathom right now."

"Or it could simply be a bluff," he said, "something to keep people off the ship."

She frowned at him. "Paloma would have had to do that."

"Possibly," he said. "Or the Wagners themselves."

"I thought you said the quarantine orders had been on the ship for some time."

"I did."

Van Alen tapped her fingertips against the desktop. She was an active thinker. It was probably a learned trait so that her clients would give her a moment to figure out what she was going to say.

"It makes no sense to me," she said finally. "After several years, anyone can contest the quarantine."

"Even if they didn't initially own the ship?"

Van Alen nodded. "They'd still have to get the original owner's permission to enter, but the law firm could have done that, I'm sure."

Flint stood up. This meeting had already gone on too long for him. "So I could contest the quarantines."

"It would take forever," Van Alen said, "and cause a lot of interest in that ship. It wouldn't be in your best interest."

"See? The quarantine works, then. It would have worked against Paloma, as well."

"Or against the Wagners," Van Alen said. "Or anyone else who wants to go into the ship."

Flint walked to the far side of the room. Behind a large, real (which surprised him) plant, an overstuffed chair leaned against the wall. A footstool was pushed slightly away from it, and a table near it held several empty glasses.

The part of the room where Van Alen did most of her real work.

She said nothing as he stood there, probably not to call attention to its importance.

"Why wouldn't she have told me?" he asked without facing Van Alen. "On that hologram, why wouldn't she have said anything to me about the quarantine?"

"You knew her," Van Alen said quietly. "I didn't."

He shook his head. "That's what bothers me the most. She told me to get information off of it, knowing there was this big hurdle, and she never said a word."

"Maybe she thought because of your police experience, you could go around the regulations. You thought that."

He sighed, then turned. She was watching him, catlike, from her desk. Except for the drumming fingertips—which had actually stopped—she hadn't moved.

"I did," he said. "And you're right. She would have. She's seen me go around a lot of regulations."

"Not really something you should tell your lawyer," Van Alen said primly.

Flint raised his eyebrows. "I thought everything is confidential here."

"I just don't want to get implicated in too much. Believe it or not, lawyers have ethics, too."

"Some lawyers," he said.

"Like some Retrieval Artists," she snapped.

He felt his cheeks warm. That was a partial dig at Paloma, and it was probably deserved. He still admired her too much.

Van Alen saw his reaction and it must have bothered her. She stood and gave him that warm smile again. "Look," she said, "there is something we can try. It's risky, and it brings the ship and all its contents to everyone's attention."

He bit his lower lip. He hadn't expected one final solution. "What's that?"

"We have to assume that Paloma was the owner when the quarantine happened. We will never know who requested the quarantine, at least from Armstrong's side, only who administered it. That would be Space Traffic, but there was a reason why they hadn't put the ship into Terminal 81."

"I know," Flint said. "I couldn't get that information."

"It may be irrelevant." Van Alen's voice got a bit breathy. Obviously she had remembered a point of law that had gotten her excited about this case. "If Paloma was the owner when the quarantine occurred, and she failed to request that all the data be downloaded from that ship before it went into permanent stasis, then we might have a chance to download it ourselves."

"How?" Flint asked.

Van Alen smiled. "A little-known regulation from the early days of the port. At that time, so many ships were coming in, bringing God knows what with them, that they all went into quarantine."

"Like anyone coming from off the Moon now," Flint said. "Automatic decontamination."

"Yes, but now we use a quick procedure for the humans and an even quicker examination for the ships, something automated."

Flint nodded. Rookies in Space Traffic always got a few days working with quarantined vessels. The rookies were always worried about what faced them, while the veterans added to the worries by recounting stories of their own illnesses.

It was only when the rookies actually reported for quarantine duty that they realized all the work was done with long-distance scans as the ships came into port. Only experts worked on flagged ships, and only then because the dangers were great.

"But in the old days," Van Alen was saying, "a lot of the stuff had to be done by hand. Humans in HazMat suits had to go inside and inspect for themselves. Computers only analyzed where ships had been and the possible hazards. They didn't find the hazards."

Flint knew that bit of history. It had been covered in some damn lecture back when he was starting out, and it had stuck, mostly because he had a vivid imagination and he could always picture himself as one of the unlucky few, searching a ship for some microscopic problem.

"So?" Flint asked. "What does this have to do with the law?"

She grinned. It was an impish look. "Legal history is a specialty of mine. If you know how laws evolve and why, you can sometimes find their hidden loopholes."

"You're not getting to the point," he said, only slightly annoyed. She was trying to impress him with how brilliant she was, and she was succeeding.

"A lot of ship owners began to lie about where they'd been. It kept their ship and its contents out of the mandatory weeklong quarantine. It kept them from losing precious time."

Flint's breath caught. "So the government made a law demanding the ship's log."

"And since the ship was under quarantine, the government then found ways to examine everything on the ship's computers, learning about all kinds of illegal activities."

"You're telling me," Flint said, "that the owners somehow got permission to download all the other incriminating stuff *before* they let the government into their ships?"

"Not permission." Van Alen's eyes sparkled. "They got it written into the law. The ship owners had a lot of clout in those days. Remember that Armstrong got most of its goods from somewhere else at the time."

Flint nodded. Every kid who went through Armstrong's school system learned how dependent Armstrong used to be on shipments from Earth.

"But," Van Allen said, "Armstrong found a way to modify the law. Ship owners had to request the download. A lot of them didn't know that. They asked informally and got denied. But somewhere along the way, a clause got added that if the ship owners made their request through an attorney who put a request in to a judge, who had to act *that same day*. If they did that, then the request had to be honored."

"No matter what was in the ship."

"They wouldn't know," Van Alen said. "They couldn't. They had to release the information *before* they examined the computers and the logs."

"Wouldn't that enable the owner to alter the log, anyway?"

Van Alen shook her head. "The owner didn't do the download. A specialist on the HazMat team would."

Flint walked back to his chair and rested his hands on the back of the seat. The fabric felt cold to the touch, even though he'd been sitting there only moments before. "You're telling me this law still applies?"

"It's never been wiped off the books," she said.

"Has it been used in the last hundred years?" he asked.

She smiled. "Once or twice."

"By you," he said.

She shrugged. "The more tools you have, the better case you build for your client."

He smiled too. "This is why you win against the Wagners."

"No," she said. "I have won against the Wagners because I'm too stubborn to give in. At some point, they'll beat me, and then some other attorney, just as naïve and stubborn, will take my place. And more power to that imaginary young thing. I'm getting tired."

Flint hoped her exhaustion didn't hit in full force until she had finished with his case. "You're telling me that I can use this law as the ship owner?"

"If Paloma hasn't," Van Alen said. "And given what little we know about the *Lost Seas*' strange quarantine history, I'll wager she hasn't."

Flint wasn't ready to wager on anything. He'd had too many surprises that day already. "So after you file with a judge, what then?"

"He rules for us, and then a HazMat team shows up."

"How long will this take?" Flint asked.

"If you stop quizzing me," she said, "I should have the first information from that ship in an hour."

"An hour," he breathed.

"Provided Paloma hasn't tried this before," she said.

"Right," he said.

Van Alen returned to her desk, looking like a woman who was ready to work. Then she gave him a sideways glance. It would have been almost flirtatious, if it weren't so proud of itself.

"You know the best thing about this?" she asked. "I mentioned it in passing."

"You mentioned half the history of Armstrong in passing," he said.

She laughed. "Yes, but this is the important part. The information is downloaded and removed from the internal systems of the ship. Once you have every bit of information Paloma stored on the *Lost Seas*, no one else can get it without getting to you."

23

THE BIXIAN GOVERNMENT—WHOEVER THEY WERE—CONSIDERED the *Lost Seas* cursed? Nyquist couldn't quite process that information. He'd heard some strange things in his time, but he had no idea why a ship would get quarantined because of a curse.

He set down his plate, leaving most of the wriggling noodles with their peppery sauce, and got up, mostly because he felt too confused to sit still.

"You want some coffee?" he asked DeRicci.

"Good old detective-area coffee?" DeRicci asked.

"Yes," he said.

"Believe it or not," she said with a smile, "I miss that slop."

He didn't believe it. No one could miss coffee that was made from hybrid beans grown in the cheapest part of the Growing Pits, then ground and cut with something else, something that—if he had to guess by taste—was probably Moon dust.

Still, he drank the stuff as if it were as important as water. And maybe it had become that important. He had no real idea. Maybe he would crave it when—if—he left the force.

He found two clean mugs (he hoped they were clean; they looked clean) and poured the last of the only remaining pot into it. Then he set all three pots on their machines and pressed the start button, a simple procedure that everyone else in the department had apparently never learned how to do.

He left before the liquid finished brewing. Anyone who thought the coffee smelled foul when it was lukewarm had never smelled it as it squirted fresh into the pot.

DeRicci took the offered mug with a smile. She wrapped her hands around it and inhaled. Then she coughed.

"God, as awful as ever," she said.

"You asked for it."

She smiled. "I need to remind myself that my current job has better perks than my old one."

"Your current job doesn't seem that bad," he said.

Her smile faded. "Do you know none of the domes have evacuation procedures in case of a slow-dome breach? No real plans for an epidemic or for a biological attack? Everyone thinks the dome walls will protect them, but half the domes on the Moon haven't isolated their environmental systems, so anything that contaminates the eastern section of the dome will automatically contaminate the western section."

He picked up the plates, not sure he wanted to know any of this. "I didn't think you dealt with dome safety."

"I deal with everything," she said. "At first, the position seemed advisory, even though no one knew what it was supposed to do, not really. But it became clear in the Disty crisis that *someone* had to make emergency decisions for the entire Moon, and that no politician was going to do that, not and keep her job."

"You mean the governor-general?" he asked.

"I mean anyone," she said. "I studied what happened on Mars after the whole crisis ended. A lot of government officials there just didn't respond. And a lot of people died."

He looked at her, wishing he could end this conversation, but also knowing that she had to get it out. She was trusting him with this, talking to him because she probably didn't get a lot of chances to talk to anyone else.

"They have a different governmental system than we do," he said after a moment. "The Disty are in charge."

"Actually, it's similar," she said. "Our domes are loosely confederated here. The United Domes of the Moon is relatively new, considering how long the Moon has been settled, and it has almost no power at all. Not overall power. Any decision it makes can be overruled by a dome mayor, did you know that?"

"Not for the whole Moon," he said.

"Only for that dome, but still." She shook her head. "I have to come up with advisory plans and mandatory plans and then I have to do the political song and dance to make everyone believe me."

She wiped a hand over her face. There were shadows under her eyes that were so deep, he wasn't sure why he hadn't noticed them before.

"I'd much rather solve a murder," she said. "It's easier."

He smiled and set the plates down. "Even with the Wagner family's involvement."

"Even with," she said.

"You know," he said, "if you were here, solving a murder, you'd have to drink that coffee all the time."

She sipped and grimaced. "I know. That's why I'm drinking it now. Trying to remind myself that I have perks."

"Perks," he said.

"They even gave me a clothing allowance," she said, and then she grinned. "And when I still didn't dress better, they hired someone to shop for me. Apparently, appearance is everything in government."

"Apparently," he said.

She sighed and set her coffee down. "There's one more thing I have to tell you, although you may already know it."

He frowned.

"In addition to the *Lost Seas*, Paloma owned a space yacht. It's registered in the name Paloma and the secondary registration, in case something happens to Paloma, is in the name of Miles Flint."

Now DeRicci was bringing up Flint. Nyquist took the plates out of his office and tossed them in the already overflowing recycle bin near the coffee table. Apparently, the bin had broken down again.

"You hear me?" she asked.

She was leaning against the doorjamb into his office, her arms crossed. In the half-light of the hallway, she almost looked beautiful.

He nodded. He had heard what she said and what she meant. She had told him facts, but had also trusted him with some personal information. Now it was time for him to trust her with personal information, and she even guided that part of the discussion.

She wanted the information he had on Flint.

Her old partner.

"I didn't know she had a space yacht," he said, pretending he didn't understand the subtext of their conversation at all. "I had been looking up historical information. Stupid me, huh? I should have looked at all the current things first."

DeRicci studied him. For all her unorthodox manners, she missed nothing. She knew he wasn't going to trust her with Flint. Nyquist needed to keep some things for himself.

At least that was what he told himself. Deep down, he worried that DeRicci wouldn't be interested in him any more if Miles Flint became the main suspect.

"You need to get to that ship before Flint does," she said.

Nyquist closed his eyes for a brief moment. He had let Flint go free, after investigating the scene, after taking his suit with him.

DeRicci might not have been playing games at all. She might have been warning him.

But if she was, how come she waited until the end of the conversation to tell him about Paloma's ship?

"Bartholomew?" she asked.

He opened his eyes.

"You think Flint knows about the registration?" DeRicci asked.

"I think Flint wouldn't care," Nyquist said. "I hadn't even thought about some kind of space yacht. I'm sure he's been there already. I hope to God he left something on board that we can use."

24

THE *LOST SEAS* WAS PROBABLY THE MOST DILAPIDATED SHIP FLINT had seen since he quit Space Traffic. It almost hid in the corner of Terminal 35, a section so poorly lit that the HazMat team had had to ask the port to put up extra lighting before they approached the ship.

HazMat's own warning lights did work properly here, though. The lights, built into the ceiling, glowed bright orange, letting Space Traffic know not to have any other ship dock here until the team was through.

Flint stood at the edge of the docking area, as close as the team would let him get. Van Alen stood beside him, towering over him in a pair of high-heel boots that made her outfit seem both sexy and macho at the same time.

He had told her that he didn't need her here, but she insisted. And he was beginning to realize that Maxine Van Alen was a person to argue with sparingly.

The ship was at least fifty years old, maybe older, and of some kind of alien design cobbled with some ancient human technology. Its center core looked like a bubble. It even had the iridescent coating on the outside edge—or it appeared to; he wasn't sure if that was caused by time or was part of the original design.

All sorts of components had been added to the side of the bubble— hatches and bays and smaller bubbles, not nearly as well designed. Someone had even added a crude docking block, so that a nearby ship could grapple on.

"Ugly damn thing," Flint said to Van Alen as the HazMat team examined the outside. They were going slower than he liked, using instruments and all sorts of equipment he didn't recognize to see if the hull itself was a hazard.

As far as Flint was concerned, HazMat should have done that a long time ago, given how many quarantines this ship was under. But there were no records of any kind of inspection, thorough or otherwise, so HazMat had to follow modern procedure.

"It's yours now," Van Alen said with a smile. "The proud owner of that ugly damn thing."

"Lucky me," Flint said.

The team, six members in all, moved around the ship as if they were a multiunit creature with a single brain. He didn't get a formal introduction to them. He did meet their captain, a slender woman with unenhanced skin that was an odd greenish color. It came, someone told him after she had left the staging area, from a decontamination gone bad. She kept the skin color to remind everyone what carelessness could do.

The rest of the team simply nodded to him, their faces masked by their environmental suits. These suits were especially designed for HazMat. They covered the team like a second skin, obscuring their faces and making them seem not quite human.

If, indeed, they all were human. Flint had no way to tell.

He watched the team record the ship as if it had just come in, examine the results of some of their on-site tests, as if the ship hadn't been sitting in the open for decades, and treat everything nearby as if it were already contaminated—which, Flint supposed, it probably was.

Then the team leader gave a hand signal. A siren went off, warning everyone out of the area in case the contamination spread. Flint grabbed Van Alen's arm, moving her as far back from the staging area as he could.

A squeal sounded above him. Dust rained down, followed by the protective barriers that surrounded every dock in every terminal.

These were so old that they were scratched and cloudy. Flint wondered if they were effective any more. It seemed to him something could get through one of those scratches and contaminate the entire port.

He glanced at Van Alen. She was watching the HazMat team through the scratched protective barrier. Mostly, they looked like colored blurs against another colored blur, but he could guess at what they were doing.

After they ordered the protective barrier down, they would open the hatch. Then they would test the air—or whatever it was—that came out of the hatch. They would examine the area around the hatch for dangerous materials, and then the least experienced member of the team would enter first, in case there were booby traps of some kind.

Even if Flint couldn't see what was happening, he would be able to tell at this distance if there were booby traps. He'd been unlucky enough to be primary Space Traffic cop on a case in which the cargo ship had been trapped. He'd stood outside a barrier like this one and listened to an entire HazMat team scream in panic and disgust.

They stood in silence for several minutes and then someone shouted. Flint jumped and squinted at the protective barrier, as if he could see what was going on inside it.

Only when there was a second shout did he realize the noises had come from behind him.

He turned. Two Port Authority security guards trailed two other men. One of the security guards slapped the side of the tunnel door, and more warning sirens went off.

Flint recognized these. Years ago, when he worked here, a sound like that would have brought him running.

"Shut the damn thing down," one of the men said, waving a hand. "We're officers of the court."

"I don't care who you are," a guard answered. "You don't have a right to be here."

"It's all right," Van Alen said smoothly, that lawyer persona back. "They're with us."

Flint looked at her with surprise. Her lids were half hooded over her eyes, and her face revealed nothing. She stood, her body at alert, as she watched the two men come down the ramp.

"You sure?" the other guard asked.

"I am," Van Alen said.

The first guard kept following. "You were supposed to name your entire party before coming in here."

"Sorry," Van Alen said. "I forgot."

She said it with such guilelessness that Flint almost believed her, even though he knew Van Alen was not the kind of woman who forgot anything.

"They're your problems, then," the guard said, waving a hand in disgust. He looked at his partner, and they headed up the ramp, slapping the sirens off as they disappeared through the door.

Flint started to ask Van Alen what was going on, but she made an almost imperceptible gesture with her right hand, silencing him. So he studied the two men instead.

They looked familiar. The taller one had flowing white hair and a long patriarchal beard. He wore a dark suit that needed a cleaning, but his shoes shined and his hands were manicured.

But the other man drew Flint's eye. The man was shorter—short by most standards, actually—with a bullish build mostly hidden by his long, stylish suitcoat. His hands were manicured, as well—their fingernails actually shone in the orange light—and his eyes had a sparkle that only came from enhancements.

"Miles Flint," Van Alen said with just a hint of disgust, "meet Judge Garton Antrium and Justinian Wagner."

Flint recognized them now. He'd only seen them on news vids, never in person, and Judge Antrium only because he was a noted philanthropist throughout Armstrong. He didn't look like a philanthropist now. He looked like a man at the end of a very long day, who needed to go home, change his clothes, and relax.

He remained half a step back from Wagner, as if communicating his reluctance to be here—whether that was because the ship might be contaminated or because he didn't like Wagner, Flint couldn't tell.

Wagner was watching Flint closely, almost as if he could see inside him. Flint turned to him slowly, as if he were the least important person in the area. That movement didn't escape Wagner; something flashed in his eyes before they narrowed.

"You realize you're breaking the law, Flint," he said.

Flint started to answer, but Van Alen put her hand on his arm. "Mr. Flint is the legal owner of this vessel. He's following the law, which, it seems, his predecessor and the port did not do."

"You have no claim on this vessel," Wagner said, still talking to Flint.

"I am his lawyer," Van Alen said. "You will address me."

Wagner didn't move. Only the judge watched her.

"Flint," Wagner started.

"Justinian," the judge said in a tone that brooked no disagreement. "Give the woman her due."

Van Alen nodded slightly at the judge, a small smile playing at the corner of her lips. Flint kept his gaze on all of them, not entirely understanding the game.

Wagner shot the judge a furious glance. The judge lowered his own gaze, and Flint felt a surge of disappointment.

Was Judge Antrium in Wagner's pocket? If so, had the judge become a philanthropist to keep some kind of balance between the bad deeds he did for Wagner, and the good deeds he did on his own time?

"I prefer to talk with Mr. Flint, who seems to believe he has rights to my mother's estate."

Van Alen's grip had tightened on Flint's arm, warning him to remain quiet. It was harder than he thought it would be.

"He does have rights," she said. "We have a statement of her intent, completed less than three weeks ago, as well as a copy of her will. Miles Flint is Paloma's heir."

"Paloma." Wagner spit out the word. "But the *Lost Seas* is registered to Lucianna Stuart, my mother."

"Who had her name legally changed to Paloma," Van Alen said calmly. "She was thorough enough to have the court add a cautionary statement to the document. The statement says, in part, that anything still in the name of Lucianna Stuart should be considered Paloma's under the law. It's in the court records. I can give you the reference number if you like."

Wagner flushed, but his enhancements scrubbed the color from his skin quickly. Interesting that he didn't get an enhancement that would have automatically blocked the color. Maybe he saw a use for blushing, one that would help him in his trial work.

Wagner still hadn't looked at Van Alen. He said to Flint, "You have no legal standing. She's my mother. My brother and I are her nearest relatives. We will sue you, citing coercion, so that you could get her estate. You have to understand—"

"Coercion? Mr. Flint has been off-Moon for most of the past few months," Van Alen said. He'd told her that in her office, as they struggled for ways to find short-term answers to any question Wagner might bring up. "How could he coerce from light-years away?"

"Before," Wagner said. "He wants her estate, and he made sure he'd get it."

"Why would I want her estate?" Flint asked. Van Alen's nails bit into his arm, trying to stop him from speaking. "I already have more money than I know what to do with. She sold me her business and its records. What else is there?'

The judge frowned, as if he hadn't realized that Flint had money of his own.

"Whatever's on this ship," Wagner said.

"I didn't even know this ship existed until this afternoon," Flint said. "I—"

"He learned of it," Van Alen said, talking over him, "went to see if the registration indeed belonged to the Lucianna Stuart who became

Paloma, and in the course of doing his job as heir, learned that the ship is quarantined and not in the proper part of the port. He called me. I've been worried about liability, so I advised him to have HazMat take care of this immediately."

Not exactly a lie. She was good.

"Do you honestly plan to stop something that might prevent a hazard to the entire city?" she asked Wagner. "Do you know something about this quarantine that you're not telling us?"

The judge looked at Wagner, and Flint thought he saw a glimmer of independent thought in the judge's face.

Wagner hesitated for just a moment, but it was long enough to see that the question had thrown him. No wonder Van Alen won cases against him. She thought differently than he did.

"I'm sure the cause of the quarantine is in the records," Wagner said smoothly, as if he hadn't hesitated at all.

"No," Van Alen said. "And it's not just one quarantine. There are several, some from outside this region."

"It seems to me this investigation should continue." The judge's voice was stentorian. It echoed in the shut-off terminal. "If this man is trying to steal from you, Justinian, he's certainly going about it in an unusual way."

"Judge, he has no rights to my mother's estate," Wagner started.

"That remains to be seen," the judge said. "Ms. Van Alen, do you have the documentation that shows Mr. Flint as the sole heir?'

"I have it," she said, although there was no way at this point she could know with any certainty that Flint was the sole heir.

"Can you access it for us now?"

"No, your honor. It's in a secured file. I can, however, show you a segment of the holographic message in which Paloma states her intentions to Mr. Flint."

Flint's mouth went dry. Paloma hadn't wanted anyone else to see that message. He'd already stepped over the line she'd set by having Van Alen see it.

"It's not necessary," the judge said. "At the moment, Mr. Flint is operating under the assumption that he is the legal heir. He's not pilfering the estate. He's taking care of a hazard. I suggest, Justinian, that the next time you take me from my well-deserved dinner, you have greater cause than this."

So Judge Antrium wasn't in Wagner's pocket. Antrium was just the only available judge at the moment, and Wagner had enough clout to get him to come to the port to make a ruling.

"But Flint will have everything from inside the *Lost Seas*," Wagner said, dropping any attempt at finesse.

The judge looked at the protective walls, then lifted his head toward the blinking orange security lights. Then he sighed.

"In the unlikely event that Mr. Flint will remove something from that ship," the judge said, "then bring your complaint—along with your dispute of the will—to the court. But I see nothing here that leads me to believe Mr. Flint or his attorney are stealing from your mother's estate. Indeed, they're taking better care of it—and by extension, the entire city of Armstrong—than your mother ever did."

The judge nodded at Flint, then as he looked at Van Alen, he touched a hand to his white hair as if he planned to doff a cap in her direction. Then he pivoted, and headed back up the dock.

Wagner looked after him, waiting until the judge went through the door into the tunnel. "All right, Flint. What do you want?"

Flint blinked at him, feigning surprise. He had a hunch Wagner would try to negotiate, just not this soon. "What do you mean?"

Van Alen let this conversation happen. Apparently, she'd been waiting for it, as well.

"Money, a new job working with WSX, maybe? Some political capital? A say in the way things work around here?" Wagner's face had lost all of its enhanced charm. Flint was probably seeing the real man for the first time. "What'll it take to get my mother's estate from you?"

"Are you acknowledging that it's his?" Van Alen asked, before Flint could say anything.

Flint suppressed a grin. He hadn't even thought of that. If he had to lay money, he would wager she had also recorded the conversation. He'd been relying on Port backups, an old police habit. But considering the firepower that Wagner had walked in here with, there was a chance that the Port had shut off all of its cameras around this area.

Wagner turned toward her for the first time. "I'm not acknowledging anything."

"Then why would you offer to give my client something for something you claim he does not possess?"

"I want him to leave us alone."

"By bribing him?"

Flint felt like he had vanished. Neither person seemed to remember he was there.

"By paying him to go away," Wagner said. "He can stay out of my family's business."

Van Alen was about to say something, but Flint put his hand on her arm for a change.

"Did she abandon you?" Flint asked, trusting that Van Alen was recording this.

"What?" Wagner whispered the word, but it echoed with shock.

"Paloma. You were older than your brother. You remember her and your dad together. Did you always feel abandoned? Is that why the fact that she didn't remember you in her will is so very hard to take?"

The flush returned, followed by its sudden erasure. Wagner's face looked pale and artificial, his eyes bereft.

"You're a son of a bitch, you know that?" he asked.

"Yes," Flint said.

"You have no right to make comments like that. None." Wagner was shaking.

"You accused him of stealing your inheritance," Van Alen said blandly. "I think that gives him the right to ask you a personal question or two."

Wagner took a deep breath, then steadied himself. He seemed, for a moment, like a man torn between how he felt and how he should behave. Finally, his legal training took over.

"You're right," he said in a calm voice. "I'm reacting like her son, not like a lawyer. Maybe I should hire someone."

He clearly meant that as a joke, but it fell flat.

"It's just—she was my mother. You said it, Flint. You don't need the money. You don't need that apartment or her yacht. Why are you hanging on to this so hard? It means nothing to you."

Flint felt a surge of compassion for the man. It might have been an act, but Wagner seemed truly sincere, truly confused as to why Flint would want any part of Paloma's life.

"I respected her." Flint wasn't going to admit he loved her. Wagner would take that as an admission to a romantic relationship, and Flint hadn't had that with her. "She asked me to take care of her things. She said she didn't want them to go to anyone connected with WSX. I'm sorry."

Wagner stiffened. "You're making that up."

"On the contrary," Van Alen said, "we have your mother making that statement in more than place. Her words are recorded and written down. I'm afraid any challenge to this will won't work. Mr. Flint is her legal heir."

"How come I haven't seen these recordings?" Wagner asked.

"Because we just came across them," Van Alen said, before Flint could answer. "I'll make certain you get copies of the pertinent information by tomorrow morning."

Flint didn't want him to have the security recording of the holographic message, but he wasn't going to say that in front of Wagner. He'd discuss that with Van Alen after they finished here.

He also wondered, yet again, where she got the written part of this. Had she seen some documentation she hadn't yet told him about?

"Recordings can be faked," Wagner said.

"They can," Van Alen said. "We didn't alter these."

"I'd need the original for proof," Wagner said.

"You know it doesn't work that way, Justinian." Van Alen used her personal voice, not her lawyer voice, for that. "If you want an expert to examine the original, we'll do so in police laboratories with observers, so nothing else gets altered."

"So that it goes his way?" Wagner gestured at Flint. "Don't forget I know about his ties with the police department. They let him onto a closed crime scene today. He didn't even have to turn in his tech suit when he left. This man gets special treatment from them. Going through the Armstrong Police will simply guarantee that they'll confirm everything he wants them to confirm."

"Then we won't go to the Armstrong Police," Van Alen said. "A neutral police department of some random judge's choosing. *Not* someone like Judge Antrium."

Implying that he was in Wagner's pocket after all.

"The judges here respect me," Wagner said.

"Not all of them," Van Alen said.

"I won't participate in a setup," Wagner said. "She was my mother."

"Which, oddly," Flint said, deciding he no longer felt any compassion for Wagner at all, "she never mentioned to me in all the years that I knew her. How often did you see her?"

"Often enough," Wagner said.

"How come she let your father raise you?" Flint asked.

"That's none of your business," Wagner said.

"It seems everything becomes everyone's business, if you chose to fight this." Van Alen smiled. "Won't it be fascinating to have the Wagner dirty linen aired in front of all of Armstrong? Imagine how many people will tune in to all the gossip shows. Imagine what it'll be like, having the press chase you constantly, asking why your mother changed her name as well as her profession. Won't that be fun?"

"It's worse for him," Wagner said, nodding at Flint. "His profession is based on secrecy."

"Yes," Van Alen said before Flint could answer. "But he already told you that he doesn't need money. He can quit any time. Can you?"

Wagner looked back and forth at both of them, as if he was assessing them. When he was done, his face had flushed and kept the color. Flint's guess had been right; Wagner manipulated his visible emotional responses to let people think he felt one way when he really felt another.

"You don't want to fight me," he said to Flint.

"Good," Flint said as calmly as he could. "We're agreed. The estate won't be challenged."

Wagner's flush deepened. "That's not what I meant, and you know it."

"You don't need the money, either," Flint said. "So what is it that's driving you here? And don't pretend that it's some kind of ancient childhood vendetta because your mother abandoned you. You both could have settled that at any point. Neither of you was interested in the other."

"You don't know that," Wagner said.

"I know that you're afraid of something," Flint said. "Is it something she owns? Or something she did, something you're afraid I'll tell the wrong person? Or is it more complicated than that?"

"Her estate should remain in the family," Wagner snapped.

"You know," Flint said, not caring how much he angered this man. "If you had been just a bit nicer, we might have worked this out. I could have given you whatever it was that you wanted, and you could have left me alone."

Wagner glanced at Van Alen, then back at Flint. "You wouldn't have hired an attorney if you were going to be that cooperative."

"That's where your logic fails," Flint said. "I grew up here. I know the name Wagner. The moment I heard it, I hired an attorney, knowing that legally, I was outclassed. I didn't realize I was sending you any kind of signal."

He must have been doing all right, because Van Alen didn't interrupt.

"You'll work with me?" Wagner asked.

"Why should I now?" Flint asked. "You've threatened me, all but accused me of murdering your mother, after you accused me of having an affair with her and manipulating her, which, if you knew Paloma at all, you would have known was just about impossible, and you've tried to bribe me. Why should I do anything for you?"

Wagner sorted through the various answers, obviously discarding some. Finally, he said, "Because you have no need for her things, just like you said."

"She asked me to protect them," Flint said. "From you."

Wagner's color faded. He shook his head. "You don't want to get into a fight with me."

"You said that before," Flint said. "I agreed. Yet you're the one who won't walk away."

"She's my mother," Wagner said.

"She obviously put less stock in that relationship than you do."

"You're doing this to harass me," Wagner said. "Just get to what you really want."

"I really want to do what your mother asked me to do," Flint said. "I want to honor her memory. Maybe, after you see the documentation, you'll do the same."

Wagner shook his head. "If what you say is true, my mother stuck you in the middle of something that's too big for you. You don't belong here."

"I didn't," Flint said quietly. "But I'm here now. And this is exactly where I'm going to stay."

25

SPACE TRAFFIC CONTROL HAD A SECURITY VID OF MILES FLINT entering the *Dove* shortly after he left the crime scene. Nyquist cursed himself as he stood outside the space yacht. He had brought a crime team with him, not that it mattered; this scene had been compromised after Paloma's death by someone he'd more or less trusted.

The question was: did he arrest Miles Flint for tampering with an auxiliary crime scene, or did he wait to see where else Flint would lead him?

He hadn't decided yet. He wasn't even sure where Flint was. He sent a street unit to Flint's office and to his apartment, just to find out that information. He wasn't going to contact Flint on his links—not yet.

Nyquist was glad DeRicci hadn't come along. She felt she couldn't justify it, considering the fact that the *Lost Seas* was under quarantine and couldn't be viewed. She decided to let him handle the *Dove* alone.

The *Dove* wasn't impressive. Or maybe Nyquist just didn't like giant black ships that were built to resemble one kind of Earth bird and were named after another.

When he'd first arrived, brandishing a warrant so that he could get into Paloma's ship, no one would talk to him. It was almost as if he wasn't even part of the police force. When he finally did get someone to pay attention, that person, an older man, had seemed angry he was asking about the *Dove*.

"If you wanted the ship protected, you should've called us," the man had said, and he had a point. After Nyquist had learned about the *Dove*, he should have called in an order to seal the ship. Of course, even that would have been too late. DeRicci had told him about the *Dove* only an hour before; it was everything he could do to assemble a team and get over here quickly. He hadn't even thought of sealing the ship.

Flint had been half a day ahead of him. And, according to the security footage, he had been inside the *Dove* for a long time. To make matters worse, he had spoken to a reporter just before he went inside his own ship, the *Emmeline*.

Nyquist had a request in to a judge to seal off the *Emmeline,* as well. But he wanted to do that without Flint's knowledge, something he wasn't sure was possible under the rather loose laws governing ships in port.

"You want us to go in first?" asked the woman beside him. She was tall and thin. Her name was Deepa Zengotita. She was one of the best in the department, and she specialized in information gathering from movable technology—ships, aircars, bullet trains. He had been lucky to get her on such short notice.

"No," Nyquist said. "Once you've cleared it, I want to join the effort."

Clearing it meant that a team member or a couple of team members went in first to make sure there were no surprises on board. Each investigative team did this differently. Nyquist had never worked with Zengotita, so he wasn't sure what her procedure was.

She had put together the rest of the team. Three men and another woman. None of them had worked on the crime scene at Paloma's apartment. Nyquist had specifically requested a fresh team. He didn't want this team going in with any preconceptions.

He did, however, tell Zengotita that a possible suspect had gone into the ship this afternoon. She made the instant leap, knowing that any information accessed since the morning would be the first thing to focus on.

The other woman approached the ship. Zengotita remained beside Nyquist. Security protocol insisted that any area where a suspect had gone after a crime had to be considered a potential booby trap. Too many detectives and crime scene techs had died going into a scene without protection.

The other woman wore a uniform similar to HazMat gear, designed to protect her against whatever she found. Everyone else wore the standard-issue tech suits, protecting the scene from anything they dropped and protecting them from contaminated trace.

She moved easily; even though she was the most junior member of the squad, she had a confidence that came from long practice. Before she reached up to touch the outer door, she examined it, using not just her eyes, but also her information chips and handheld scanners.

Then she looked over her shoulder, and nodded at Zengotita.

"Good luck," Zengotita called, and from the shake in her voice, that wish was a superstition among the team. Had someone forgotten to say it once? Had someone died on that mission?

Nyquist didn't want to know. Even though he tried to have no superstitions either, he developed a few—double-checking the lock on his apartment door when he left each day; making certain he greeted the people he cared about whenever he saw them, even if they'd only been separated for a few hours; and touching the grip of his laser pistol before he went into any building, just to make sure he knew it was where it was supposed to be.

The woman touched the hull door, opening it.

"I hate this part," Zengotita said to him softly.

The rest of the team couldn't hear her. They were setting up the exam 'bots, making certain the interiors were empty and the exteriors were clean. All exam 'bots got cleaned when they were returned to the lab, but it was good to check them in the field as well. No one wanted cross-contaminates.

"Ships are the worst," she continued, staring straight ahead, "because most of them have shielding, so we don't know what's inside. Even if we do know, things don't always go according to plan. You know that guy who killed cops on a city train a few years back? That was us. They thought the site had been clear for two days, and then the next thing we know, he's up from some kind of compartment, laser-rifle firing. I lost four good men that day."

"Dead?" Nyquist asked.

She shook her head. "Two critical, but they made it. The others just couldn't handle the stress. We can fix the physical part, but the folks who were on that team, with the exception of me and Naree Lind-strom, never got back into the field. Too much fear."

Nyquist understood. He had had close calls himself, and he thought of them too much. But he'd never admit that to one of the department shrinks. As long as he functioned on the job, he didn't need special help, or so he told them.

In reality, he figured he only had so much time to do his work before his system broke down, just like everyone else's did. He'd do what he could while he could, and wouldn't worry about the rest.

"It's taking a while," he said.

"She's got to wait out the airlock. Who knows how long it's timed for? The personal ships don't follow any regular protocol. They—"

An explosion resounded through the bay. Nyquist saw it before he heard it—light blowing outward, light filled with something, piec-es—part of the ship? He couldn't tell—and then the sound, deep and resonant.

He grabbed Zengotita and threw her down, landing on top of her as the pieces – oh, God, they were bits and pieces of a person, the other team member, the woman who went in alone—rained around him.

Another explosion sounded, and then one more.

"We gotta move," he said, pulling at Zengotita. "That ship might go."

Which was the least of his worries. If the ship went, then the blast walls inside the building would fall, and who knew where they'd land. He had to get out of the open and into the doorways, the only safe part of the bay.

"My team..." Zengotita tried to turn in his arms. He wouldn't let her. He used his full strength to drag her away.

If the team lived, they'd get themselves out. If they hadn't, they'd be found soon enough. It wasn't like the six of them were in the middle of nowhere. They were in Terminal 25, the wealthiest section of the entire Port.

Blood and other fluids continued to rain from above. How much liquid composed a single woman? Or was this rain something else, something deadly?

He couldn't tell. It smelled of blood and flesh and ozone, like something had burned, but he wasn't sure if some of that scent came from the destroyed ship itself.

Warm liquid ran down his face, coating him. His clothing was drenched. Zengotita continued to struggle in his arms. He clutched her so tightly, he wondered if she could breathe.

It took forever to get up the dock. The floor was slick. Sirens had started to go off. Lights swirled, making it hard to see. An androgynous voice made some kind of announcement, but he couldn't understand it. His ears had worked fine when Zengotita spoke (or had they? Had he merely guessed what she said? Because it was what he would have said in that circumstance? Or because he just expected her to be that kind of woman?), but they rang now, the other noises trumping the human voices.

He nearly lost his balance, put out his hand, and caught the edge of the wall. It was slick, too, or maybe that was just his skin, covered with goo.

Biochemical goo—wasn't that the phrase used at Paloma's building? Was this what they meant?

But there had been no explosion there, right?

Somehow, he reached the door frame and leaned against it, Zengotita still in his arms. He glanced at her. Her eyes were open, unblinking, but he could feel her breathe. She was staring at the space yacht.

He looked, too.

The *Dove* was still intact, except for the main hatch, which had blown open. Inside, he could see lights—or it seemed that way. The air was filled with a fine red mist that covered everything and didn't seem to want to dissipate.

Of course it didn't. The environmental systems had been turned off just in case something toxic had been released into the environment. With the systems shut down, the theory went, that something toxic wouldn't get released into the rest of the port.

But the *Dove* had been standing here, idle, for weeks, maybe months. Who knew what it had released?

He blinked. Goo ran down his cheeks, but he didn't wipe it away. Instead, he released his grip on Zengotita. She stayed beside him. Her team was sprawled against the floor, the 'bots scattered.

Had the explosion been that forceful? He wasn't sure. But he knew that the woman—the lone team member to venture inside—hadn't survived it.

Which was odd, because Flint had. Flint had been in there hours earlier. Flint, who had just found out that Paloma was dead.

Flint, who had gone to his own ship first.

To get supplies?

Had Miles Flint, former Space Traffic patrol officer, former City of Armstrong detective, set a trap guaranteed to kill anyone who entered the *Dove*?

Was he that ruthless?

Was he that desperate?

Nyquist didn't know. But he had to find out—and soon.

26

THE DATA RETRIEVAL WAS TAKING A LONG TIME.

For some reason, Flint had thought it would only take a few seconds. But the HazMat team had been inside for fifteen minutes now, and he was still waiting.

At least Wagner was gone. He stomped off, literally, shaking the floor as he marched away. Van Alen had chuckled beside Flint.

"That's his mad act," she said. "It's not his best routine, but it's my favorite."

"Sounds like you two have had a lot of run-ins," Flint said.

"Enough," she said. "And each one is memorable."

"You handled him well," Flint said.

"*We* did," Van Alen said. "You surprised him. Not a lot of people do that."

"I suppose not." Flint stared at the door. Wagner had surprised him too, arriving with a judge, ready to take care of the problem immediately, outside of the courtroom.

"I will have you notice, however," Van Alen said very softly, "that neither Justinian nor Judge Antrium knew about that little quirk of the law. The judge left happy, thinking we're being good citizens. If Justinian knew what was going on, he'd've bought another judge, and everything would've stopped."

Flint glanced at her. "Another judge? For a purchased judge, Antrium didn't perform very well."

"I'm not so sure he was purchased," Van Alen said. "Maybe just borrowed."

Then she grinned. Flint smiled too, although he didn't feel any real levity. The stresses of the day had started to get to him.

He rocked on his heels, wishing the day was nearly done. Then the hatch opened and one of the HazMat team members leaned out. Another member hurried to the side of the ship. Flint hadn't even seen the others who had been left behind. He had been too involved with Justinian Wagner, apparently, although the HazMat team's protective clothing did blend in with the ship.

The member took a bagged handheld and pointed it at the person on the ship. Flint sighed. He was going to get a copy of a copy of a copy of the information, but it would have to do.

It was better than not getting the information at all.

The hatch door closed, and the team member who hadn't been on board brought the bagged handheld to Flint. Van Alen stopped him. The man, face flattened by the protective suit, waited patiently, handheld extended.

"Is this everything?" she asked.

"Everything in the main systems and stored in all the logical places. We haven't been to the hold yet or looked to see if there are auxiliary systems. If there are, we're required by the same law to give what we find to you. We'll notify you, Mr. Flint."

"No," Van Alen said. "You'll notify me."

She took the handheld. Flint frowned. The information was his. He wanted to snatch the handheld from her and run off with it. But she had gotten him this far.

"Very well," the team member said. He half bowed at them, a courtly movement that suggested he wasn't human after all, and then headed back to the *Lost Seas*.

"Let's download," Flint said.

"Not here," Van Alen said. "Anything transmitted through the air here can be ruled public domain. If Wagner was waiting outside and he captured it, the law says that he has a right to that information. It's as if he overheard a conversation."

"We're not in Armstrong," Flint said, knowing he probably shouldn't argue law with her. "We're in the port. Neutral territory."

"Really?" she asked. "Courts fall all ways on that one. There's no accepted law. Just so-called common knowledge, which is wrong. We're taking this to my office, and downloading the information there—"

A huge bang interrupted her, followed by warning sirens and flashing lights. An overhead voice announced a ship breach, possible contamination, and warned that environmental systems had shut down.

Flint could feel it already—the growing heat as the temperature regulators stopped. The air would last quite a while in here, but it would become uncomfortable.

And since this had been triggered by a ship breach, the call for evacuation would start at any moment.

He grabbed Van Alen's hand. "Come on."

"What the hell is this?" she asked.

"One of those weird emergencies," he said. "We have to get out of here before they decide to lock us in permanently or initiate a stampede."

"A stampede?" she asked.

"A total port evacuation," he said. "I've seen them before. They're not pretty."

He was shouting over the repeated automatic announcement. The lights were flashing orange, white, and blue—code for possible biohazard, a call for the HazMat teams and Space Traffic officers to check with their leaders for instructions, and a count-down before the interior walls fell, protecting the affected area of the port.

"This is bad, isn't it?" Van Alen yelled.

"Oh, yeah," he said, but so softly she probably couldn't hear him. "This is as bad as it gets."

27

THE DOORS HAD SHUT, SIRENS WERE BLARING—NYQUIST COULD barely hear them through his shocked ears—and lights were flashing. A red haze coated everything. Nyquist swayed as he surveyed the scene, knowing he had to act, but not sure how.

His ears weren't the only thing that suffered from shock. He did, too. And he couldn't. Not now.

Zengotita leaned against him. She was warm and felt fragile. Like him, she stared at her team.

She was almost unrecognizable. She was coated in fluids, mostly red turning black (that had to be blood), although there were several other colors, as well. Human fluids? He couldn't tell. It wasn't his job.

He was just investigating.

Investigating.

God, his brain was on autopilot. "I need your handheld," he said to her.

Zengotita frowned at him. At least, he thought that's what she was doing. She might have been staring at him blankly. Her face was nearly unrecognizable, her hair plastered against it, the streaks of goo running down like too-thick water.

He held out his hand, miming holding an exam computer. "Your handheld," he said again, very slowly.

He could hear himself—the words sounded hollow, echoey, from the aftereffects of a blast. She wouldn't be able to hear that. She might not even hear the warning sirens, which sounded far away, but which had to be on so loud that they were palpable.

Finally, she fumbled against her side, found the handheld, and scrubbed the screen. She knew what he wanted. They had to know what this stuff was made of.

She pressed the sides, turned the thing toward her, and winced. Was she injured? He couldn't tell. He couldn't even tell if he was.

He leaned so that he could see the small screen. It was working. Chemical codes flared across it, information written in a language he—a lowly Humanities major with a masters in criminal proce-dures—didn't understand.

Her lips moved. He shook his head, felt slightly dizzy, and decided not to do that again. So he shrugged.

He was right. His hearing was damaged.

"I can't hear you," he said, as if she could hear him.

She thrust the handheld at him. He stared at it, expected more of those chemical codes. He got something like that—a composition chart, all in CO_2 and similar notations.

He almost shook his head again, remembered, and handed her the handheld. Then he shrugged.

She tapped the screen and handed it back.

Composition:
Unknown human female. DNA not in registry.
Assume disease-ridden AMoP (examination continuing).
Blood, brain matter, fecal matter...

He couldn't read any more. He thrust it back at her.

AMoP meant "as a matter of practice." All bodily fluids from an unknown source were considered disease-ridden until proven otherwise.

Zengotita tapped it, then handed it to him again.

Secondary composition:
Metal (examination continuing), oil, chips
(examination still continuing)…

The bomb. Or the ship itself. Something else, but nothing dangerous. Except the body parts. He shuddered, and looked back out at the mess.

The red haze still hung in the air. The lighting was strange: the flashing oranges and yellows made the large dock visible, but the regular overheads were off now, as if someone had cut the power.

And they probably had. The environmental system had shut down as a matter of procedure, leaving everyone in here to survive on the remaining air. It wouldn't get cold—not for a while, not with the other parts of the port surrounding this section—but the air would get dicey soon, unless the port had a separate environmental system for this area.

The team was moving. He hadn't seen that before. Hands pushing underneath, legs bending. He would have to go back down there, see how badly they were injured—

And then, one by one, they stood. Procedure again. This team was good. They checked themselves from the downed position, probably with their own handhelds, and then they pushed upward, after deeming the area safe enough.

The 'bots were intact. The shiny things along the ground were metal pieces from the ship itself.

No one was injured. Except the woman who died.

Because of Flint.

Nyquist shut his eyes. They felt gummy and not his own. He had to get to decontamination. He had to make sure everything was all right.

Warm air hit him. He turned. The doors behind him had opened, and teams of people streamed in, all wearing HazMat gear. Someone in a suit—someone he couldn't recognize—grabbed him, moved him away from the door and toward a side of the terminal.

He dug his feet against the slick floor, trying to stop them.

"Wait," he said. "We know who did this. He could still be in the port."

The person—very strong—kept dragging him. He stuck out a hand, touched a metal wall, now covered in slime.

"Stop!" Nyquist said. "I'll go with you. Just let me get notice out on the man who did this."

The person dragging him stopped. Maybe that person was talking to him. He couldn't tell. Then the person's hand went up, and they waited like that for just a moment.

Finally, someone else came over, slight like Zengotita. He looked for her. She was walking toward whatever it was they had tried to drag him toward, her head down. The rest of the team was following, some with the needed help of the people in HazMat suits.

The person who came toward Nyquist also had a HazMat suit. He thought he could see skin inside, but he wasn't sure. He hated those things.

"Look," he said. "I can't hear you. I have ear damage. But I need to tell you something. My name is Bartholomew Nyquist. I'm a police detective."

The person—a woman? He didn't know, but he was going to guess, just to make things easier—nodded. Then a scroll ran through Nyquist's links, words appearing in the lower part of his left eye's vision:

Make it quick. The longer you wait for decontamination, the greater chance you have of serious illness.

He noted that the person didn't tell him who she was.

"Okay," he said. "I got that. I'm going to send you the files—

No sending. I can contact you, through a series of links, but you can't contact me. You might have acquired some kind of virus.

It took him a moment to realize that she meant an information virus. He shuddered. The person holding him looked at him as if the shudder were worrisome.

Nyquist ignored that. He sighed, then wished he hadn't, as something got into his mouth. "Look, we know who set the explosion. His name is Miles Flint. He's a Retrieval Artist and a former police detective."

We'll send someone to pick him up. The person in front of him reached for him. *Now you have to go to the decontamination chamber. You'll go through at least three of them. It'll take a while...*

"I think," Nyquist said, interrupting the flow of words, "that he's still here. Somewhere. In the port. The quicker you move, the quicker you'll find him."

I've already sent the message. The person took his other arm. Together, the two first-responders in their HazMat gear led him toward the far side of the Terminal. *They'll catch him if they can.*

"In the port," Nyquist said.

In the port. Stop worrying. We'll get him, and we'll get him soon.

Nyquist hoped that was true, but he had his doubts.

He was beginning to worry that Flint was smarter than them all.

28

Kɪ Bowles had cleaned up her new office herself. She had banished the 'bots. They creeped her out, something she had never admitted to herself before. She kept two of them running because she was lazy—she didn't want to get out of bed at three in the morning if she needed a drink of water—but she had relegated them to the corner of her laundry room, so that she didn't have to see them.

It felt good to arrange her stuff in her apartment. She put the disks of her important stories on the top shelf of her newly created library, and before she did anything else, she downloaded all her other work from the InterDome site, just in case they decided to delete her connection to them forever.

She bought some storage space on an off-world server and she kept the reports there, using as much encryption as she understood, so that no one could access them and no one could delete them.

Anything to prevent herself from becoming that whiny ex-employee of her imagination.

She had sent a message to her manager, promising big money, and had gotten no response, which made her stomach tighten. Her manager had probably heard about the firing. Bowles had gone against her manager's wishes in the first place by not going to Gossip. Maybe this would be the end of their relationship too, and she would have to find new representation.

Maybe that wouldn't be so bad.

Her hands shook at that last thought. She'd been putting her awards as data dividers on that top shelf, and she nearly dropped one.

For a woman who hated change, she was going through quite a bit of it at the moment. She had lived the same kind of life for nearly a decade now, and she had liked it.

But she hadn't realized how isolated she'd become. She only saw the people at work every day. She arrived there so early and left so late that she didn't even see the other people who lived in her building. She'd gotten dispensation when she moved in to avoid the owners' meetings, so she didn't know the politics of the apartment building she'd bought into.

She didn't know if they'd make it hard for her to stay because she wasn't famous any longer.

Then she sat in her chair and made herself take some deep breaths. She was still famous. Famous didn't go away just because the job did.

She just wasn't employed, and that wasn't as serious a problem as she had initially thought. One of the benefits of never doing anything except work meant that she had a lot of money stored up. She traveled, but it had been work related; she bought clothes, but only on the company's credit; she ate out every day, but at company-approved (and company-billed) restaurants.

Since she had become an employee of InterDome, she had hardly spent any money on herself at all. Just for this apartment, and while that had seemed like a stretch, given her monthly income, the fact that she spent so very little on anything else made it a wise purchase.

Over time, she had even built in some equity, which surprised her. She was better off financially than she expected.

While she unpacked her boxes, she'd had her apartment system download all the information it could find on the history of the Disappeared system from various public databases. She'd start work tonight because, she knew, not working would drive her crazy.

She needed a focus, and the focus couldn't be getting fired from InterDome or even reassembling her slightly shattered life.

Eventually she would know everything there was to know about Disappeareds, Retrieval Artists, and the most hidden secrets of the society she lived in.

29

FLINT LED VAN ALEN THROUGH THE BACK AREAS OF THE PORT, areas that only authorized personnel saw. Those areas were the only places that Flint could guarantee the interior protective walls wouldn't lower.

Van Alen clung to the bag containing the battered handheld. Flint wanted it, just in case they got separated, but he knew she wouldn't hand it over.

She was moving slower than he liked—her boots had enough of a heel that she was unbalanced running, or maybe she just wasn't used to moving this quickly. He had a firm grip on her left wrist, dragging her forward as if she were a recalcitrant child.

Along the way, they'd seen half a dozen HazMat teams going toward Terminal 25 and another half-dozen heading toward other areas of the port. The announcements were so thick and so loud in back here that Flint had started to ignore them.

Instead, he tied his links to the port systems, watching for any new announcements to crawl along his left eye.

So far, they only told him what the first broadcast announcement had—that a ship had breached and the port was in a state of emergency.

"Where're we going?" Van Alen managed to gasp.

Flint ignored her. The less she knew at the moment, the less trouble she'd be.

No one seemed to care that they were in these corridors, going against the tide of HazMat workers, security personnel, and Space Traffic police. The tide got thicker the closer he came to the Port Authority Center. People, mostly uniformed, hurried past him, all trying to get to the crisis.

He needed to get away, but before he did, he had to know what was going on.

Finally, he was able to turn down a familiar hallway. It took some tugging to get Van Alen through that crowd and into the mostly empty space.

"What the hell are you doing?" she snapped. "The announcements said to stay put."

"Do you want to be in the port for the next eight hours?" he asked.

"No," she said, "but—"

He didn't want to hear her argument. It would probably be well thought out and carefully reasoned and even amazingly logical. But it wouldn't factor in the fact that Wagner had just left, after losing a verbal battle with Flint.

Wagner could have orchestrated this. Flint wouldn't put it past him.

This corridor was one of the oldest in the port. It smelled musty, even though it was heavily used. It had flaking walls, made of some substance between permaplastic and that half-plastic so many modern buildings used. This substance was hazardous, but impossible to remove; he always tried to avoid touching these walls. He even felt that the corridor was an affront—putting everyone who used it in danger.

Now he was relieved to be here.

Van Alen was looking over her shoulder, watching to see if they were being followed. He tugged her, gently this time, and she stumbled with him. He glanced at that bag, still clutched in her hand.

"You think some alien vessel breached?" she asked. "Not using our atmosphere?"

"It could be anything," he said. "It could be that. It could be improper decompression in one of our ships. It could be an on-board explosion. There's no way to tell this early on."

"Unless you're one of the privileged few," Van Alen said.

"Unless," he agreed.

He was walking now, but walking fast. Going the other way in the main corridor was enough to get them noticed, but probably not yet. The port was too busy dealing with the emergency.

Finally, he got to the dark, unmarked door that led into Space Traffic headquarters. It was the door the cops used most of the time. He just hoped it wasn't locked.

He grabbed the well-used knob and turned it. The door pulled open just like it used to.

Van Alen had come up beside him. "Where are we?" she asked softly, which showed that she was at least being cautious.

"Let me do the talking," he said, without really answering her. "I used to work here."

She frowned at him. She knew his résumé—at least, he thought she did—but he wasn't going to illuminate her on any part of this. He wanted to find out what was happening and then leave the port, as invisibly as possible.

The door opened into a filthy hallway that branched in several directions. Most of them led to various locker rooms and a few meeting rooms. Only the hallway to the right took them to the main part of Space Traffic Control.

Van Alen clutched Flint's arm, as if she were afraid to be in this part of the port. Most people never saw this area. It wasn't pretty—it still had the same flaking material on the wall, and the signs were old-fashioned scrollers rather than blinking repeaters. Most of them used only Spanish and Disty, the main languages of the Earth Alliance, although a few of them also used English and a few other Earth-founded languages.

Van Alen didn't ask where they were. The signs helped her. They told rookies where to stash their uniforms, reminded veterans to check their laser pistols before leaving the area, and warned that any suspicious vehicle should not be allowed into port. An emergency sign had been turned on, and it repeated all the information that had been blared overhead in the public areas, as well as the words that were still running across Flint's left eye.

Flint led her down the hallway to the right. The muscles in his shoulder had tightened. He could be making a mistake here, getting them into even more trouble than they had been in near the *Lost Seas*.

But he was going to risk it.

The hallway opened onto a side door that led to the area behind the main desk. Murray sat there, monitoring screens that showed him all of the Terminals. He was focused on Terminal 25. That screen was yellow and orange with hazard lights and some kind of debris that Flint couldn't see.

"Murray," Flint said.

Murray jumped. Flint had never startled him before. He had always thought Murray was all-knowing and all-seeing. Then he realized that Murray wasn't really watching the other screens. He'd only been focused on the disaster.

"Oh, crap, kid," Murray said. "You have to get out of here."

Flint nodded. "I know. The port's closing down."

"You don't know," Murray said. "You're wanted for blowing up a ship."

Van Alen gasped. Murray peered around Flint. Apparently, Murray hadn't seen her before.

"Who's that?" he growled.

"My lawyer," Flint said.

Murray's mouth thinned and his expression went flat. He clearly didn't want anything to do with her.

"She got me into the *Lost Seas*. That's where we were when the alert came down."

Murray grunted, then nodded, as if he had forgotten that. "Still, you gotta leave. If you do it soon, I'll pretend I only saw the lawyer."

Flint pulled Van Alen in so that the door did close.

"What did I allegedly blow up?" Flint asked, praying it wasn't the *Emmeline*.

"The *Dove*," Murray said.

"Paloma's ship?" Van Alen asked.

"It's been blown up?" Flint asked.

Murray pressed the wall unit with the back of his hand. Then he peeled out a chip and handed it to Flint. "Take a look, but not here."

"You're not holding me?"

"Why should I?" Murray asked. "You didn't do it."

"You base this on my kind personality?" Flint asked.

"I base it on something you said." Murray grinned, revealing yellowing teeth. "You said if you wanted to do something illegal, you woulda disabled our security systems first. Besides, an officer is down. You wouldn't set nothing up that would hurt a person, especially not a fellow officer. You've saved too many to do that."

Flint smiled at the words *fellow officer*. He had been right earlier. For all his gruffness, Murray had believed in Flint.

"But they think you done it. A crime scene tech was inside when it went. She's dead, others might be injured."

"The ship?" Van Alen asked.

"The ship's lost its hatch. I think it was some kind of booby trap designed to catch whoever went in. You coulda set that off." Murray was still talking to Flint. The last was speculation.

Flint shook his head. "I didn't set anything off. Although the ship recognized me when I went in the first time."

"If it hadn'ta, you think it woulda blown on you?"

Flint frowned. If that was the case, then Paloma had set up the explosives. Why would she do that? It didn't seem like her.

Then he closed his eyes only for a second. Nothing seemed like her.

"I don't know," Flint said. "When did they start looking for me?"

"Call came down a few minutes ago. I'd get if I were you, and I wouldn't go to none of your usual haunts."

Flint nodded. He turned toward Van Alen and the door, then he stopped. "Is the *Emmeline* all right?"

"Dunno," Murray said. "The ships in that area mighta gotten hit, might not. But if it is, it's just space debris."

Meaning the damage would be minor.

"Thanks," Flint said.

"Don't mention it," Murray said. "I mean it. Don't."

Flint grinned, then pulled the door open. "Don't worry," he said. "I won't."

30

DERICCI SAT ON HER OFFICE CHAIR, CHIN RESTING ON HER PALM, staring at the list of ships Popova had sent her. Sixty-five ships, all of them under various quarantines, none of them in Terminal 81. Some of them had been allowed to rust and decay at their berths for more than a hundred years.

DeRicci shuddered, not wanting to think about all the problems this could have caused. Illnesses, deaths, some kind of radiation poisoning from the proximity to the vessels. Who knew what kind of contamination had spread through that port?

The decon units helped a little, she knew, but certain species were allowed to forgo strenuous decon. For all she knew, certain people—certain groups—had spread all kinds of nasty stuff through Armstrong for years.

But she couldn't be alarmist. Instead, she had to be organized. She had to have her staff research each and every ship, and then the staff had to propose what to do about the problem.

Which would take more time, and would create all sorts of political problems. Because once the news broke—and it would—the stupid reporters would wonder how come DeRicci hadn't acted the moment this came to her attention.

Or the moment she became Security Chief.

It could blossom into a scandal—why were these ships left to rot in public areas of Armstrong's port?—and, honestly, it was a scandal.

A serious one, one that would have long-term repercussions. Not just political ones, but health and safety ones.

In truth, she only cared about the health and safety repercussions. But she was being paid to care about the political ones. As soon as she had preliminary information on all the ships—what kind of quarantine they were under, how long they'd been there, who owned the ships— then she would have to notify the mayor and the governor-general.

DeRicci leaned back in her chair and surveyed the room. The dome lights had dimmed to night, putting everything in her office in relief. Now that the place was filled with plants and antique furniture, she liked it here. Before it had seemed cold and imposing. Now it was more familiar to her than her own apartment.

Sixty-five ships. She shook her head. Then her screen pinged. Popova sent her the notes on the Bixian government's quarantines. DeRicci had asked a specialist at Armstrong University to research this for her, and do it quickly.

Even if the specialist had leaked the information, no one would understand it. There wasn't a hook yet. No one except DeRicci and her staff had context.

She wasn't even sure her staff quite understood what DeRicci was searching for.

DeRicci sighed and glanced at the notes. They'd been put in a vid file, probably because the specialist wanted credit for his work and this was the best way to get it.

DeRicci shook her head. It was also the slowest way to pass information. "Computer," she said with another sigh, "transcribe and organize."

She was taking a few risks having the computer organize the material. Sometimes, a computer's organization was based on key words, not on concepts.

But she figured it would be just as easy to scan out-of-order information, written by computer, as it was to listen to every word of some professor's lecture. If this professor was anything like the ones she'd had at the academy, he would give the lecture out of order as well.

The image had frozen on the screen as the computer did her bidding. It wasn't the transcription that took a long time; it was the organization part.

DeRicci stood and walked to the windows. Lights were on all over the city. They reflected in the dome's interior surface, making it look like another city—rounder, a little chubbier—floated above them, the buildings upside down.

She loved Armstrong at night. It had a warmth that it lacked during the day. It didn't matter to her that it wasn't as safe as it was in Dome Daylight. She just liked the light show.

Her computer pinged, and an image flashed across her right eye, asking her if she wanted the information downloaded into her personal system. She declined, and went back to the desk.

Then she scanned the professor's two-hour-and-twenty-minute lecture. The computer had organized the material into information on the Hazar Empire, the history of the Bixian Government, and the quirks of both. In its zeal to get every piece of information correct, the computer also listed the areas that the professor plagiarized from published material.

The plagiarism caught DeRicci's attention, until she realized that the professor had been repeating information he'd provided to some vid on the Hazar Empire, and regurgitating—line by line—stuff he'd written in his poorly published (available only through the Armstrong University System, and only on this region of the Moon) treatises on the Bixian government.

The upshot was a little simpler than DeRicci expected. The Bixian government was allowed to keep its traditions because a number of people in the Hazar Empire exploited them. It seemed that the Bixians weren't really a tribe at all. Instead, they were a loosely connected group of assassins, isolated within the Hazar Empire so that they could be controlled.

That control had continued for hundreds of years, and as a result, the Bixians married into the empire and created a whole bunch of little assassins. Their traditions weren't so much religious as trade craft.

Occasionally groups from the outside used the Bixian's services, often with permission of the Hazar Empire. And there were code words for the bizarre series of political maneuvers that allowed the group to enter Bixian territory.

One of the code words was *quarantine*. The Bixian government could—and often did—quarantine ships that had never entered Bixian territory. Often the ship hadn't even been to the Hazar Empire. The Bixian word for quarantine, often misinterpreted as curse, was simply code for "target."

Anyone who had a ship under Bixian quarantine was a target for a Bixian assassin.

DeRicci felt cold. Paloma had been murdered. Had the assassin been Bixian? And if so, how could she tell?

Then she leaned back. It wasn't her job to tell. It was Nyquist's.

She needed to do more research. She needed to know Armstrong's relationship with the Bixians, and whether or not Bixian traditions were allowed on Armstrong's soil. From her own preliminary work, it seemed like they weren't.

But her initial research had also told her that Bixian quarantines were curses. So she couldn't trust everything she found on her own.

She was about to summon Popova when the door opened. Popova slipped inside.

DeRicci would have made a snide comment about Popova's psychic abilities if it weren't for the expression on her assistant's face.

"We had an explosion at the port," Popova said. "People are dead."

DeRicci's first thought—that the explosion couldn't have been very big because she hadn't felt it like she had felt that bomb two years ago—shamed her. She didn't say it.

"How many?" she asked.

Popova shrugged. "But that's not our biggest problem."

"What is?" DeRicci asked.

"The ship that blew belongs to Paloma. It's called the *Dove*. They think your friend Flint set the charge."

DeRicci stood and went back to her spot by the window, careful not to let Popova see her reflection. She wasn't sure how to react. Nyquist had gone to the port. He'd gone to see the *Dove*.

Flint wouldn't murder Nyquist. Flint was capable of killing people, DeRicci knew that. DeRicci knew of one occasion.

He'd thought the circumstances justified, and so did she.

Had he thought so now?

"Is Detective Nyquist okay?"

"I don't know," Popova said softly. "You want to go there?"

DeRicci shook her head. She could almost hear the governor-general exhorting her to delegate. She wasn't an investigator any more, and in this case, she wasn't sure she could be.

She couldn't be objective.

"No," DeRicci said. "I'll get in the way."

Besides, the port had procedures that wouldn't allow her to go in unless she pulled rank. If she did that, she would be in the way.

She took a deep breath and steadied herself. She had to handle this from here, and not think about Nyquist. "Seal the area around the port. Get someone to handle the media so we don't have a panic. And find out what's really going on."

"What are you going to do?" Popova asked.

DeRicci normally would have found the question cheeky. At the moment, though, it seemed logical.

"I'm going to contact Nyquist," she said.

She wanted to reassure her that things weren't as bad as they seemed.

31

BARTHOLOMEW NYQUIST WAS UNAVAILABLE TO EVERYONE, INCLUDING Noelle DeRicci. His links were shut down.

He was in a decontamination chamber unlike any he'd ever seen. It was large and high-ceilinged. The door locked behind him. He couldn't get back out if he tried. He had to go through the entire process.

He was told, in a variety of languages and in a variety of ways, to remain clothed for the first part of the decontamination. The signs flickering all over the walls made him dizzy. The voices, speaking in more languages than he could recognize, made him feel crowded.

He followed the directions and went up two steps into another chamber. As the door closed behind him, he watched the first chamber fill with small 'bots. They were supposed to pick up any trace he left behind before the water and then the lights cleaned up after him.

The port had several of these. He hadn't realized one was so close to Terminal 25, but it made sense. It also made sense that this decon chamber was the ritziest he'd seen, given where he was.

Rich people needed to feel like they were being treated with style.

But as the process began in the second chamber—which seemed like nothing more than a giant tube to him—he realized that he wasn't being treated with style. He was getting the most thorough cleansing of his life.

The lights that ran across his clothing actually had heat. Something moist coated his hair. At first, he thought it a kind of shampoo, and then he realized it was some kind of nanocleanser—tiny 'bots that took more debris from him and stored it who-knew-where.

More instructions in all those languages (no signage this time) came with the lights—turn this way, lift that arm, move that leg—and he felt crowded again, even though he knew he was alone.

He wondered if Zengotita had already been through this decon chamber or if she had gone into a different part of the unit. He had no way to find out.

Nor could he discover how the search for Flint was going or if the techs, all of whom had stood, had really survived after all. His ears itched, and as he clapped his hands onto them, he realized that the voices he heard weren't coming from overhead, but from something inserted in his ear, something that dealt with the severe trauma that had happened to his hearing.

Either that something healed the trauma or avoided it; he didn't have enough medical knowledge to tell the difference.

When the stuff floated out of his hair and the light show ended, more voices instructed him to go to the dressing room between chambers. Again, that room was through the only open door.

There he had to remove his clothing. A claw-handed thing, another 'bot apparently, pulled the articles away, and after a moment, the voices told him he wouldn't see his clothing again. It was evidence in a criminal case.

He wondered how it could be evidence when they had removed all the trace from it. But this case, being at the port, wasn't exactly his concern. Since he was a victim of the explosion, he wouldn't be able to investigate it. Whoever got the call from his office would have to share duties with port security and whatever jurisdiction held title to the yacht or its berth.

Just because Paloma had owned it and just because she lived on Armstrong didn't mean the *Dove* had been registered here. A lot of yacht owners registered with other governments who provided tax breaks or even stipends for running such an elaborate vehicle.

The voices came back and directed him into another decon chamber. This one was even smaller than the second one. He pressed against the wall and let the light work on his skin. That substance coated him again, and he watched with a sick fascination as it floated away, giant globules carrying bits of whatever had clung to him.

The substance left him feeling sticky and wanting a water shower, which he wasn't sure he was going to get. He wasn't even sure he would get clothing from the port, since his own wouldn't come back to him.

It would be hard to maintain his dignity while he was waiting for someone from headquarters to bring him clothes. He hoped he wouldn't have to do that.

His face itched. He wanted to rub his nose, but he couldn't. The voices had instructed him not to touch anything except the walls.

Light came on again, this time making sure he had no breaks in the skin. The voices explained it all as the work occurred. The examination showed several breaks in the skin (*Cuts*, he muttered), and as a result, the voices directed him to yet another chamber.

That one was dark and tiny. The walls pressed against him, and there was barely any place for his feet. It felt filthy in there, even though it couldn't be. A decontamination chamber wouldn't work if there was filth.

Still, the sensation left his skin crawling. He cringed as the lights invaded all of his orifices. More small 'bots took readings, some from his skin, some from his blood, and some from his other bodily fluids. His eyes were forced open, his mouth probed.

He was beginning to feel more like an assault victim than a bombing survivor.

He knew better than to struggle, though. The decontamination process was supposed to help him, to protect him from whatever dangers had been found in that explosion. Still, he hadn't been through anything quite like this before, and he was sure he didn't want to go through anything like it again.

Finally, the lights shut down, the voices told him in all their languages that he could wait in the next room. His skin burned. He felt worse than he had when he entered the decontamination chamber.

He found himself in a small room, furnished with heavily upholstered furniture and a thick carpet that soothed his bare feet. A robe, sealed in plastic, waited on one of the couch cushions. He knew it was his, even without his name on it.

He pulled the plastic off, put on the robe, and felt the material caress his skin. The robe probably had some soothing fibers, something that was supposed to calm him, and he didn't care. He needed some calming.

He needed to get out of here.

After a few minutes, the doors clicked open. His links powered on, identifiable by a small hum that he hadn't even realized was missing. His hearing was back—whatever they had done to let him hear the voices had repaired the damage to his eardrum.

A list of what had been removed from him scrolled along the bottom of his vision; he instructed the links to save the information and send it in a compacted file to his desk at headquarters. He would look at the information later.

Right now, all that mattered was that he was cleared enough to leave.

As he walked through the doors, a woman wearing a port security uniform met him. She handed him a suit of clothes remarkably like the ones they had taken from him.

"You're lucky," she said. "Nothing permanently damaged."

Just cuts and bruises and repaired ears. He nodded at her, and hoped she would leave without him telling her to.

This room wasn't as comfortable as the last. It was some kind of exit chamber. Dressing rooms were built into the walls.

"Is everyone else all right?"

She nodded. "Only Theda died in the initial blast."

Theda. The woman had a name, and he didn't learn it until she was dead. "Did you find Flint?"

"Flint?" she repeated as if she hadn't heard the name. "Was he in your group?"

Nyquist sighed. "I'm going to change. When I get out, I want to meet with whomever is in charge of the bombing investigation, and anyone left from my original team."

"I don't think—"

"I don't care what you think," Nyquist said. "I'm investigating a murder that just got compounded by another murder, and the killer might still be in the port. We need to act quickly. Make sure your people are looking for a Retrieval Artist named Miles Flint, and do it fast."

She frowned at him. "The former police officer?"

"Yes," Nyquist suppressed a curse. He hated repeating himself. "Quickly. We're running out of time."

She nodded, then tilted her head the way people did when they sent confidential information along their links.

He stepped into the dressing room, noting for the first time that they had forgotten to supply him with shoes. Everything was screwed up, including him, and he wasn't sure how to make it right.

32

THEY GOT OUT OF THE PORT, WHICH SURPRISED VAN ALEN BUT
not Flint. When he'd worked in Space Traffic, there'd been several similar incidents—five bombings, two bomb threats, and one serious ex-
plosive decompression—and each time, the port had responded with
remarkable chaos.

He took advantage of that.

He had also caught a glimpse of Murray's screens, and knew which
parts of the port had already sealed down. Flint couldn't have gotten
to the *Emmeline* if he wanted to, since the explosion happened in Terminal 25. Everything from Terminal 8 to Terminal 33 was blocked off.

But the exits from the port weren't. He kept hold of Van Alen's
hand and tugged her through various corridors toward the main exit.
Travelers, both human and non-human, ran out as if they were personally being pursued by the bombers.

Flint made sure he and Van Alen kept up with the crowd, finding
it ironic that everyone was panicked except him, the one man who
might have something to worry about when it came to being pursued
by bombers.

Had that bomb been placed in the *Dove* after he left? If so, had it
been placed there for him?

Chaos was worse outside the port—people trying to get in, emergency services personnel carrying equipment, and panicked travelers

scattering in all directions. Flint continued to tug Van Alen, who seemed distracted by everything.

Finally, he reached down, grabbed the plastic bag with the hand-held, and clutched it to his own chest.

Van Alen didn't even notice.

Nor did she seem to notice when they reached the lot that held her aircar. He was glad they hadn't taken his here, glad they had decided it would call too much attention to their plan. He hadn't figured it would keep the authorities from finding him.

"I'm driving," Flint said. "Give me the codes."

She blinked as if she hadn't heard him. He sent a message across her links, and she blinked again, this time looking directly at him.

"No," she said.

"We have to get out of here," he said.

"I'll be fine." She shook free of his hand and hurried through the rows of cars. Right now, no one else was in the lot—maybe everyone who had parked here was trapped inside. This was short-term VIP parking, after all, and a lot of the VIPs would be in Terminal 25.

Flint didn't want to think about that. He didn't want to think about the damage that the bomb would cause.

Van Alen jogged toward her car. Flint had to hurry to keep up with her. Maybe he should have spoken to her earlier instead of trying to pull her wherever they needed to go. A simple sentence had done a lot to revive her.

Although so had the relative quiet of the VIP lot. The cars were, for the most part, expensive and new. A few of them beeped to life as Flint and Van Alen hurried by—a little electronic query, wondering if the emergency required them to start up as their owners got near.

But once the cars figured out that their owners weren't the people rushing by, they retreated to quiet again. This electronic beeping was a fail-safe, something the truly expensive cars had in case the nets had shut down and no one's links worked.

Flint wasn't sure he wanted a car that would run off with anyone who could convince it that the end was near. He was glad his model was ancient and crusty, and he wished it was in the lot, instead of parked outside Van Alen's office.

She found her car easily. It didn't beep at her, which relieved Flint. As she headed to the driver's side, he tried one last time.

"Let me drive. I'm certified for emergency vehicles."

"I'm sure we won't need anything like that," Van Alen said.

Flint extended a hand toward the sky. In the distance, black dots covered the area between the buildings and the port. Dots that could only be aircars and emergency vehicles.

"Are you sure?" he asked.

She smiled. "I have my own tricks."

His door unlocked and opened. The car welcomed him with a little greeting message, something he had shut off in his own vehicle. As he slipped in, the car closed the door, put the protective belts on him, and asked if he wanted his belongings stored.

"No," he said, preferring not to send it messages along his links. Then he blocked the car's access to his personal network. He'd have to purge when he got back to his office, make sure that he hadn't acquired any bugs that Van Alen's law firm thought necessary for clients.

She got into the driver's side and was going through a similar protocol. As she let herself get strapped in, she said, "We are in a port emergency. I'll be needed at court. Let's stop first at the office."

The car immediately flung into gear. The automated system took over the steering, and along the sides, warning lights showed, just as if the car were an emergency vehicle.

As they soared out of the lot, Flint asked, "How did you get permission for this?"

"I don't need permission," Van Alen said. "I'm an officer of the court."

"Like every other lawyer," Flint said.

"And they're all entitled to this."

"How come they haven't done it?"

Van Alen shot him an evil grin. "Maybe for the same reason they don't know about the quarantine rules. They don't research the arcane aspects of the law."

He leaned back, still wishing he was doing hands-on driving. The car was using emergency-services lanes, dodging vehicles coming at them, trying to deal with the port emergency.

But he knew protocol well enough to know this took the car off most surveillance equipment. No one watched the emergency vehicles. Just the regular vehicles, the ones with normal registration.

Now he understood why Van Alen wanted to be in the driver's seat. Most designated vehicles—vehicles which weren't designed as emergency vehicles but had altered equipment—only responded to one particular driver in an emergency.

That driver wouldn't have been him.

"Where are we going?" Flint asked.

"My office." Van Alen had recovered most of her poise. "Even if they think to look for you there, you're protected. My staff can't even let them know you're there, since you're one of our clients."

"I can't stay there forever," Flint said.

"They can't consider you a suspect forever," Van Alen said.

They could. Right now, everything at the port was fluid. No one knew anything, and no one would for many hours, maybe days.

Then, if there was no obvious suspect, they'd pick a convenient one, something to keep the press busy while the detectives went to work.

They'd have a theory of the crime, and if they solved it, good; and if they didn't, the general public would be satisfied because the theory let them believe the crime was solved.

It had happened with the dome bombing. Most people thought that crime solved, even though it never was.

"You don't believe me," Van Alen said.

"I know that part of the system better than you," Flint said.

She glanced at him. She had a smudge of dirt along one side of her face. "How come you can still go in and out at Space Traffic?"

So she had noticed. He wasn't sure how much she'd been registering.

"Once a cop, always a cop," Flint said.

"Is that why you're a suspect?" she asked.

He shook his head. "I'm a suspect because it's logical. Even if I had done it—and I haven't—there will always be cops who believe I couldn't've done it, just because we used to share a uniform."

"So you took advantage of that."

"If I have to be on the run, even for the short term," Flint said, "I'm taking advantage of everything."

She grinned. "I'm beginning to like you."

Flint grinned back at her, hoping that the trust he was starting to feel for her wasn't misplaced.

"I'm beginning to like you too," he said.

33

SOMEONE GAVE NYQUIST SHOES OUT OF A LOCKER. THE SHOES WERE one size too small. They pinched and poked, but they'd do.

He had been told to wait for the investigating officer, but he was waiting for no one. He had a hunch that no one else was searching for Flint—not yet, anyway. When the port got past the explosion itself, then it would turn to finding the bomber.

The new suit had a scratchy warmth that he had finally worked out of the old suit. He tugged on the sleeves, wishing he had time to shower. But he didn't. He would have to leave this place, feeling itchy and covered with that slimy stuff that the decon units had used on him.

He wanted to find Zengotita, but he knew he didn't have time. As soon as her links were operational, she'd find a message from him, wishing her well and asking her what she needed for her team.

He managed to get out of the decontamination area and down the hall before his port escort noticed he was missing.

He continued along the corridor, keeping to one side so that he didn't run into the flood of emergency personnel going the other way. It astonished him how many people were being used in this investigation. Granted, one person was dead, and several were injured.

But it seemed to him that these scores of emergency personnel would be better suited doing something else, anything, other than cluttering up the hallways. If they wanted to find out whether other ships had similar explosives, they would use handhelds and 'bots. If they wanted to talk to every person in the area, they were better off holding them and waiting for the police to arrive.

He'd been in circumstances with mass witnesses before, and he knew the emergency teams would only screw up the preliminary interviews. Better for the police to screw them up. Then they could only blame themselves.

He swayed a little as he walked. It wasn't just from the inner-ear thing—he assumed the medical patching he'd gotten in decon had taken care of that—but also from the crisis itself. It had happened long enough ago that the adrenaline had worn off. He was left with that heavy exhaustion that only came from a combination of shock, fear, and joy at survival.

It took him fifteen minutes longer than he wanted it too, but he finally got to the main part of the port. He'd had to use his police identification, embedded in the working chip on his hand, to get through a number of the blocked areas, but he had managed.

Just as he had managed to send half a dozen messages through his links to various agencies within the port, reminding them to search for Flint. He'd gotten nothing back from most of them, a curt "we know" from another, and an odd acknowledgement from SpaceTtraffic.

He hasn't left the Moon, one of the people in charge had sent. *We've been monitoring ships to make certain.*

Nyquist was surprised that anyone had left the Moon, and said so. The Space Traffic officer reminded Nyquist that there were other, smaller ports in the smaller cities, and Flint could have taken off from them.

But it seemed like an odd statement nonetheless. Even if Flint had left the port immediately after he had visited the *Dove*, and the vids indicated that he hadn't, he would have had to take a bullet train to the nearest dome, hire a ship, and get permits to leave. That would have taken hours at best, and the permits would have shown up on everyone's links.

So Nyquist made his decision in a corridor not far from the main doors. He went to Space Traffic Control first.

It looked less chaotic than he expected. No one scurried through its reception area. The cops in the back seemed calm, and everyone in the nearby corridor moved at a leisurely pace.

The man behind the desk had been there when Nyquist arrived. He was older, with a bald head and beady eyes.

"Heard you were right near the explosion," the man—Murray, his name was; it took Nyquist a moment to remember—said quietly. "You should probably be seeing some medical personnel."

"I need new clothes," Nyquist said, tugging on his sleeves again. "But I'll take care of that when everything settles down."

"Ain't got much to tell you," Murray said, looking down. The over-head lights reflected off his pate.

"No sightings of Flint?" Nyquist asked.

"Heard they got a new investigator on this." Murray tapped a few buttons in front of him. Nyquist leaned over the desk so that he could see what Murray was working on.

"They have a dedicated investigator working on the bomb," Nyquist said. "But I'm still in charge of the Paloma murder."

"Since the two are obviously related," Murray said, still not looking up. "It would seem to me that the new guy would be more objective."

Something in his tone made Nyquist realize that Murray was the man who had sent the messages from Space Traffic.

"You think I won't be objective." Nyquist figured low-key was the best way to handle Murray.

Murray finally looked up. He had bags under his eyes. His entire face was drawn with exhaustion. Nyquist wondered how long Murray had worked that day.

"I wouldn't be objective if I'd just gotten bombed," Murray said.

"You think I'm pursuing Flint as some kind of vendetta?" Nyquist asked.

"I think you have him in your head, and you figure you'll go after him, no matter what the evidence."

"There's evidence that he didn't do it?"

Murray folded his hands over his stomach and leaned back in his chair. "He's a good man. He's saved I don't know how many lives. He's ethical. He wouldn't kill innocent people, especially not cops."

"You know this how?" Nyquist asked. "Because you've met him?"

"I know him," Murray said.

"Then you know he's a Retrieval Artist." Nyquist couldn't quite see the screens, carefully placed under the desk's lip. He had a hunch he couldn't patch into them, either. There'd be too many safety features and fail-safes, all to prevent others from getting inside, as well. "Retrieval Artists aren't ethical."

"He wouldn't do something like that." Murray leaned back. He was watching Nyquist, as if he knew what Nyquist was thinking.

"Look," Nyquist said. "You're the one who showed me the vid. He was the last person in the *Dove* before it blew."

"That's not evidence," Murray said.

"It's more than you have," Nyquist said.

"It's the same, actually," Murray said. "I trust his character. I've known him for years. You've known him—what?—an hour, and you think because he went into a ship and it later blew up that he set the charges. Why would he do that? Why would anyone ethical do that?"

"I don't see any evidence that he's ethical," Nyquist said, although he did have evidence. Flint had worked with him on a case not too long ago in such a way that Flint hadn't violated any confidentiality rules of his profession, and Nyquist didn't violate any of his, and yet they both got results they wouldn't have gotten if Flint hadn't been involved.

"What you got is just circumstance," Murray said. "He came in, he went out, it didn't blow. He wasn't close enough when the thing went off to remote detonate, no matter how sophisticated his equipment. Maybe somebody set that door to explode on the second opening. Maybe someone else set it to explode at that exact time on that exact day. Maybe someone made a mistake and pressed the wrong wires together, causing the explosion. We don't know until the techs get done with their examination."

Nyquist opened his mouth to argue more, when he realized what Murray had said, buried in that entire argument. Flint had been in the port when the explosion happened. Nyquist hadn't been sure of that.

"Where's Flint now?" Nyquist asked, leaning forward.

Murray tilted back even farther, looking like he might tumble into the mural that graced the wall behind him. "How should I know?"

"Because you knew where he was when the bomb went off."

Murray's cheeks grew pink. He brought his chair forward with a thump. "I didn't say that."

"You said he wasn't close enough for remote detonation, which means you know where he was." Nyquist came around the desk and yanked on that door. It was locked. "Is he back there?"

"He's not there," Murray sounded sullen, but he didn't force Nyquist to leave the private area.

"Where is he?"

"I don't know," Murray said.

"Then where was he when the bomb went off?"

Murray sighed.

Nyquist turned, hand still on the doorknob. "I can get the information from damn near anyone who works here. Hell, I can pull it off the computers myself if you give me enough time. So just tell me."

Murray pursed his lips.

Nyquist leaned toward the row of screens, not sure where the computer access was. But he'd press surfaces until he got the information he needed.

Murray grabbed his hand. "He was with his lawyer."

"Where?" Nyquist asked.

"Terminal 35."

"And what was he doing there?" Nyquist asked, even though he had a hunch he knew.

"Supervising data removal from a ship called the *Lost Seas*."

"I thought it was under quarantine," Nyquist said. "I thought no one can go in."

"HazMat crews were working it until the explosion," Murray said.

"Still, Flint couldn't go in, could he? He couldn't have access until the HazMat team was done."

"Maybe you should look at port regulations, Detective," Murray said.

"Maybe you should tell me," Nyquist said.

Murray shrugged. "It's hearsay."

Nyquist sighed. He could be arguing with Murray all night. He'd look at the regulations when he got a chance. Or maybe he'd ask De-Ricci. She probably had someone who could research that stuff in a heartbeat.

"If Flint was near the *Lost Seas* when the explosion occurred, where did he go next?" Nyquist asked.

Murray raised his eyebrows. "I didn't keep track."

"No, but your system did. You want to program it to follow his movements, or should I?" Nyquist poised a hand over those screens again.

Murray batted his fingers away. "Flint was a Space Traffic cop."

"So?" Nyquist asked.

"He knows where the dark spots are."

"He stayed out of camera range?" Nyquist asked.

"Mostly," Murray said.

"So you did track him," Nyquist said.

"I couldn't," Murray said.

Nyquist let out a large breath, making his exasperation known. "Is he in the port?"

Murray grinned. "Now you should've asked that in the first place."

"I've been trying to." Then Nyquist realized that Murray had distracted him again. "Is he?"

"In the port?"

"Yes," Nyquist said.

"Not anymore," Murray said.

"When did he leave?" Nyquist asked.

Murray touched a screen to the far left. An image of Flint hurrying out the main doors, clutching the hand of a woman who looked vaguely familiar. Murray peered at the timestamp.

"Looks like you just missed him," Murray said.

"How much is 'just'?" Nyquist asked.

"Maybe five minutes," Murray said.

"Give me surveillance from outside the port, and order any vehicles leaving this area to be stopped." Nyquist pushed away from the back and headed toward the door. "*Now.*"

Murray nodded. He pressed a few screens, then sent everything to Nyquist's links. Nyquist saw the message scroll by as Murray sent his instructions to every cop in the vicinity, along with that image of Flint and the woman.

Nyquist headed toward the main door. From behind him, Murray said, "Aren't you going to thank me?"

"For stalling long enough to make sure your friend got off port property? No," Nyquist said.

"Give him a break and start looking for the real bomber," Murray said. "I'd start with Wagner's minions. He was here tonight too, you know."

Nyquist hadn't known. Seemed like Wagner had been everywhere since Paloma died.

Nyquist slammed his hands against the door and headed out of Space Traffic without saying more to Murray. He'd send someone—someone with ties to the new investigation—here to get all the surveillance vids from the last eight hours. Maybe even from the last two days.

He'd find something.

He had to.

34

Van Alen's office was mostly empty. Only a handful of employees were at their desks as Flint and Van Alen hurried through. As Van Alen passed each one of them, she pointed at them and said, "I'm alone. You got that? Everything else you may or may not see is confidential."

And to a person, the employees nodded or gave a verbal acknowledgement. Flint didn't feel comforted. He recorded the entire interaction as he passed through, in case someone from the firm leaked any information concerning him. As much as he liked Van Alen, he wasn't above suing her for breach of attorney-client privilege if he had to.

He clutched the plastic bag holding the battered handheld as tightly as he could. If things had gone the way he wanted them to, he would have been in the *Emmeline* now, looking at all of this.

But he wasn't sure when he'd get back to his ship, nor was he sure his office was secure. He had no real equipment in his apartment, which was a utilitarian place where he slept. He didn't even eat there.

Van Alen entered the wide area that marked off her office. Flint had forgotten that he had seen no doors on his first visit. He felt even more uncomfortable. Then she waved her hand at some motion sensor, and glass doors slipped down from the ceiling, like dome dividers.

Only the glass was frosted. The parts nearest the door handles (apparently, they could be pulled open or closed as well—he looked for hinges and saw none; they had to be carefully balanced) were etched with floral versions of MVA intertwined.

Maxine Van Alen had a vanity that intrigued him.

"Let's play those things," she said, "and see what we have."

He wasn't even sure "those things," which he saw as only one thing—the handheld—had any video component at all. He suspected he was looking for something buried deep inside files, files upon files upon files.

"I need a system that's dedicated," he said. "Is everything in your office networked?"

"Would I be a good attorney if it was?" she asked. She pushed a panel on a nearby wall, and four desks rose out of the floor, all of them with surface screens. "Take your pick."

He went to each, touched it on, and ran through his own diagnostic. Two of the screens had too many users in the past. Another still had case files from something Van Alen had been doing, although he didn't tell her. The fourth—the one closest to the wall and, as a result, very uncomfortable to work on, had no recent user log-ins and no case files. In fact, it looked neglected.

He stood in front of it and went deeper into the system, looking for hidden tracers, something an unscrupulous lawyer or another client might have put into the system.

"I have it debugged every other day," she said. "It's safe."

She was standing behind him. Her perfume was faint but rich, as much a part of her as her enhancements and her flamboyant clothing. He didn't like how close she was.

"Still," he said, "I'm going to check a few things."

"Suit yourself." She went to the stuffed couch on the far side of the room and flopped down. Then she pulled off her boots and rubbed her feet. "I do not want another day like this one."

He didn't either, but he didn't voice the sentiment. Instead, he dug deep into the computer's memory, looking for ghosts, looking for traces of hidden users.

He found none.

"You're being awfully cautious," she said.

"I've only known you a short time." He shut down all the computer's networking systems and its ability to link with anyone else except someone he determined. He added six different passcodes, all of them too long to be quickly cracked.

"Yes, but you hired me for my skills and the confidentiality they provide."

"I did, didn't I?" Flint said, knowing that wasn't an answer. He took the handheld out of the plastic. The handheld had a greasy feeling to it, as if it had been encased in slime.

"You sure that's safe?" she asked.

"They decontaminated it before they handed it over." At least, he hoped that was what the slimy feeling was. He didn't really have the time to check.

He had to hook the handheld directly into the computer; it was the only way to keep the information from being snatched up by any systems in the room. Even then, he wasn't sure how confidential all of this would remain.

"You think this is what got her killed?" Van Alen had lain back on the couch. The position wasn't provocative. The events in the port had clearly exhausted her.

"At this point," he said, "I have to think everything she touched is tied to her death."

"But are you going to know it when you see it?" Van Alen asked.

She had voiced his main fear. "Probably not," he said.

She shook her head and then sighed. "I feel like I should be doing something."

"Maybe getting us dinner," he said. "This is going to take a while."

He didn't want to tell her that she could leave. It was her office, after all. Part of him wanted her to remain. He wanted her to run interference for him. But part of him wanted complete privacy.

"Any thing in particular you want?" she asked. She hadn't moved off the couch.

"Nope." He pulled over a chair, attached the handheld to the computer, and downloaded the data. The HazMat team had compressed the data. As he watched the screen, the information streamed so fast that it looked like bits of light instead of data, and he realized that his initial plan wouldn't work.

He had hoped to isolate the most important information—the stuff from the bridge, most likely, and transfer it from the computer to the data chips on his hand. Then he'd take the handheld and he'd use his own chips as a backup. He'd work on pieces of the information at various places around town.

But he wasn't sure, first of all, that he could isolate the important information, and even if he did, he wasn't sure the chips he wore had enough room for this much data. He didn't want to leave any of it in Van Alen's office, either. He needed to get it out of here, but to where he did not know.

No wonder HazMat had told him they had done the best they could. Old ships like that usually carried one-eighth the data of a space yacht like *Emmeline*. Somewhere along the way, Paloma had boosted the capacity.

Or the HazMat team had taken information off systems other than the ship's. He hadn't thought to ask what that might be.

"Problem?" Van Alen still hadn't ordered any food. From what he could tell, she hadn't even moved off the couch.

"No," he lied, wondering if he'd made a face. "Except that I'm hungry."

"Nag." She swung her legs off the couch. "I suppose you don't want me to use my links at this sensitive time."

"It doesn't matter." He wasn't using anything networked, and he was relieved to realize she didn't know that.

"Good," she said. "Then I'll get someone to bring us a small feast."

His stomach growled. He was amazed he could be hungry after the day he'd had.

He sat down. Van Alen had that vacant look people sometimes got when they were sending messages along their links.

When she blinked and looked at him again, he said, "This is probably going to take me a long time."

"Weeks, months, years?" she asked.

He wanted to answer *yes*, but instead, he said, "At least until tomorrow."

She sighed, glanced around her office as if it had suddenly changed color, and then stood. "Well, lucky for us there's a full bath right through that door."

She pointed behind one of the tall trees pressed up against the wall.

"You can have a shower and everything," she said.

"Everything except a change of clothing," he said.

"Give me sizes and I'll send one of the associates out."

"You don't think that'll look suspicious?" Flint asked.

She tilted her head and then smiled. "One of the male associates. Who's going to question him?"

Nyquist, Flint thought, but didn't say. The handheld had almost finished dumping the information. He glanced at the sofa, hoping it was long enough for him to catch a comfortable nap.

"You need help on any of this?" Van Alen asked in that tone people used when they really didn't want to help.

"No," he said.

"Good, then I'll get down to business."

He frowned at her.

"I do have other clients, you know," she said.

His frown deepened.

She smiled. The smile was cool. "Much as I like you, you're not staying in my office alone."

"Because of your other clients," he said.

"And that prodigious skill I just saw with computers. That was a bit scary. I had no idea people still knew how to dig into machines like that."

"People don't," he said.

"Oh, that's right," she said, waving a hand. "You were some kind of computer whiz once."

222

Some kind, he thought. He wished she'd shut up. He wanted to work. He wanted to work alone.

He didn't want anyone to see his reaction when he learned what other surprises Paloma had in store for him.

35

DeRicci sat at her desk, studying ship specs and worrying about her friends. She hadn't heard from Nyquist, although she'd been pinging him for the last hour.

Finally, she got a response, and she sighed with unexpected relief. She was glad she was alone in her office with the lights dimmed, because she felt unexpected vulnerable.

DeRicci put him on visual, something she usually never did because she hated having two images play in front of her eyes. But there he was, superimposed over the antique desk as if he were nothing more than a disconnected head.

She shuddered at the image, thinking of the explosion. She'd seen disconnected heads before, and much as she tried to harden her heart to that kind of thing, she hadn't been able to.

Nyquist looked a little matted. His hair was combed wrong, and his skin shone. His eyes were bloodshot. His collar was turned up, and his suit looked unfamiliar.

"You haven't answered my pings," DeRicci said.

"I was in decon," Nyquist said. "I was near the blast."

DeRicci's breath caught. All her annoyance vanished, and she felt a greater than normal concern for Nyquist.

She liked him too much.

The thought annoyed her, and she pushed it aside.

"Are you all right?" she asked.

"Cut, bruised, and cleared by the computers," he said. "Just peachy, considering how much brains, blood and fecal matter landed on me."

He didn't even grimace as he said that. She wondered if he was in shock. She didn't know him well enough to tell.

"We only have confirmation of one dead," DeRicci said.

"That's enough," he said.

She nodded. She'd never been near someone who'd exploded, but she'd been close to a couple of blasts, and even closer to people who'd been shot. Being covered with the remains of someone else was one of the worst sensations she'd experienced.

"Maybe you should take the evening off."

"Would you?" he asked, with a little too much edge.

Of course she wouldn't. But it was easy to see from the outside how ridiculous that was.

"We have reports of biochemical goo," she said, "Just like Paloma's murder."

"Yeah," he said. "I think it's just as false. Everyone on the tech team and me have been cleared. We'd've been covered with it if the reports were true."

She let out a small breath that she hadn't even realized she'd been holding. She was more worried than she wanted to think about. "You know what caused that report?"

"Probably the sheer destruction of the poor woman who went into the ship," he said. "I'm not in charge of that part of the investigation, though. Theoretically, I'm only taking care of Paloma's death."

DeRicci liked the *theoretically*. It meant Nyquist was going to do what he could.

"Do you know where your friend Flint is?" Nyquist sounded exhausted, almost defeated, as if Flint had betrayed him, too.

DeRicci found herself wondering if she had failed to contact Flint not because of any misguided loyalty to her office, but because she actually believed he could have done this thing.

"No," DeRicci said. "I've deliberately avoided contacting him until this thing gets resolved."

"You think he did it?" Nyquist asked.

"You're the one with all the information," DeRicci said. "I've only gotten what's come through the secure links."

And a bit from the media, although it didn't seem like the usual feeding frenzy. The reporters were confused; they couldn't get into the port, and very few people had gotten out.

"Do you know how to find him?" Nyquist wasn't quite tracking. Maybe he wasn't looking at the camera, or maybe he was more injured than he thought.

DeRicci knew better than to say anything. She would have resented it if someone had pointed out that she wasn't functioning at full capacity when she was on a case like this.

"Flint's a creature of habit when he's not on a case," DeRicci said, surprised to hear the words come out of her mouth. She hadn't expected to betray him so easily. "You can find him at his office or on his yacht. He catches about six hours' sleep at his apartment, but otherwise he's not there. He likes to eat at the sandwich shop behind his office or at the Brownie Bar. Sometimes he does his research at the public links or in Armstrong University's main library."

"And when he's on a case?" Nyquist asked.

DeRicci shook her head. "It depends on the case. If it takes him off-Moon, he'll go. He's been known to go pretty far to find out information."

"Far physically or far in the bending of laws?"

DeRicci almost said, *Both*, then didn't. Not because of Flint but because of some weird sense of self-protection. She had a hunch this was going to get a lot worse before it got better.

"I meant far physically," DeRicci said.

"Although that was a long pause." Nyquist's gaze finally met hers— or what passed for hers through the links.

"I guess it was," DeRicci said.

"You think he did this thing." That wasn't a question. Nyquist had an uncanny sense of her, something that should have bothered her more than it did.

"I don't know enough about it," DeRicci said.

"But you wouldn't put it past him," Nyquist said.

"Flint and Paloma were close," DeRicci said. "He doesn't react well to the death of people he loves."

There it was. The thing that had disturbed her. She had seen him years after the death of his daughter, and he never seemed quite sane on the subject.

"You think he loved Paloma?" Nyquist asked.

"He did," DeRicci said. "But more than that, he admired her. She was his ideal. He felt like he could never measure up to her."

"She was a Retrieval Artist," Nyquist said as if he didn't understand.

DeRicci nodded. "Flint sees it as a noble profession."

Nyquist frowned. "Do you?"

She had when Flint dropped out of the police force. For a year or so afterward, she had thought of becoming a Retrieval Artist herself. To be on her own, to make her own rules, to decide which rules she'd follow and which she wouldn't felt noble, but in the end, she had decided that she needed the structure.

She wasn't wise enough to determine which laws were just and which weren't. She just wasn't that smart.

"Noelle?" Nyquist asked, prompting her.

The use of her first name startled her. It sounded almost intimate.

"What?" she asked.

"Do you think being a Retrieval Artist is a noble profession?"

"I think there's no such thing," she said.

"As a noble Retrieval Artist?"

"As a noble profession," she said, and severed the link.

36

Van Alen had unimaginatively ordered pizza. The difference between the pizza she ordered and the pizza Flint used to have on late nights when he was a detective was that this pizza had real ingredients. Sauce made from real tomatoes, fresh herbs, real cheese, real pepperoni, and sausage made from real meat.

The first bite he took tasted so unexpectedly rich that he almost spit it out.

He whirled in his chair, nearly knocking over the caffeinated ice coffee she'd bought him, and looked at her.

She was munching a piece of pizza at her desk, reviewing something on the screen in front of her, making notes on a handheld, probably because she didn't trust Flint with her confidential files as much as he didn't trust her.

"Where'd you get this?" he asked.

She looked up in surprise. He shook the piece of pizza at her.

"We have an Italian bakery in the building," she said. "It costs a fortune, but it makes the late nights worth it."

He was beginning to understand her tastes. Always the best in everything, which cost money. He wondered if lawyers made that kind of money, particularly lawyers who followed their principles.

He could pull her financials, he supposed, but he wouldn't do it here, in her office on her computer. He made himself focus on the work.

He'd gotten a lot done since he downloaded all of the files. He had hoped the important stuff was flagged somehow, but everything had been organized in a numbering system that he didn't entirely understand.

He looked first at the files outside that system. They were the ship's log and its manifold, and the information that had come with it when Paloma had bought it, long before he was born. He could have gotten lost in the ship itself—the logs were complete: the former owners' travels were also kept, as if that was important to the ship itself.

Maybe it was at the time; he didn't know shipping laws from nearly a century before. He had no idea if the Port of Armstrong required vehicles to hang onto the information about every place they'd been, every person they'd come into contact with.

He'd looked through the manifold enough to discover when Paloma had bought the ship, then downloaded the information of the ship's travels from that date on onto his own personal chip. He figured that was a good place to start.

The remaining files that weren't in the system were also ship related: cargo lists, instructions for each and every upgrade, and old computer records from systems that the ship no longer had.

Some of those systems didn't want to talk to the one in Van Alen's office. He downloaded those onto his personal chip as well, hoping that he'd be able to find a system—or enough privacy—to figure out what was on them.

Then he faced the daunting task of figuring out what those numbered files were.

First, he had Van Alen's system give him a count of the numbered files, and winced when he got the result. Well over a million. And if each file contained other files within it, he could be looking at tens of millions, certainly not something he could finish in a single night, like he had told Van Alen. Probably not something he could finish in a month.

"You look discouraged," she said.

He resisted the urge to cover the screen. He'd forgotten about his pizza. The piece had congealed on the plate beside his workstation.

"There's a lot here," he said.

"Too much? You want an assistant?"

"I can go through it," he said. *Just not in one night.*

"I have a good computer team," she said, and then bit her lower lip. "Although I'm sure you're better."

"Not better," he said. "But we don't know what's here. It's better to keep it confidential."

"My assistant's back with your clothes," Van Alen said. "You want him to bring them in?"

Flint shook his head. "I can get them on a break."

"They're going to think we're doing untoward things in here," she said.

"I thought you had confidential meetings all the time," he said.

"Not ones that took all night and required new clothes afterward," she said.

He smiled. He supposed it did look bad. But that didn't bother him. He would rather have this look like a tryst than a lawyer protecting her client from justice.

"You know," he said after a moment, "you were so hung up on that officer-of-the-court thing. If I get charged with this and the charge sticks, you'll be harboring a fugitive."

She smiled for the first time in the entire conversation. "My job then is to get you to turn yourself in. No one asks the attorney where the fugitive was, just if she knows how to contact him."

"Technically, you should turn me in now."

"Technically," she said, "I haven't been informed you're missing."

She'd already thought of that angle. He wasn't sure if he was relieved or not.

"I'm not sure what Paloma was hiding here," he said. "I thought it would be obvious. It's not."

"Maybe that's how the HazMat team downloaded it."

He shook his head. He'd already thought of that.

But he hadn't considered one thing: maybe the important files were the newest ones. He turned back to the screen.

"Did I give you an idea?" Van Alen asked.

"You did," he said, letting her think that her mention of the HazMat team was important. He separated the files by date, relieved to see that the HazMat team's download hadn't destroyed the origin dates of the files.

He wouldn't have wanted to go deep in those files, to find out what the dates were. That would have only added more time.

The dates worked. Most were more than forty years old. But about fifty had been accessed in the last five years. And only a few had been opened in the last few months.

"Bingo," he whispered, and hoped that Van Alen hadn't heard.

37

KI BOWLES COULD GET LOST IN INFORMATION. THAT WAS HER favorite part of reporting. Not the interviews, not finding the story before anyone else, not even the on-air part. What she loved the most was digging into minutiae and finding gold.

And, she realized, it had been a long time since she'd done anything quite this detailed.

She had missed it.

Since she cleaned up her office, she had made some tea and settled at her desk. She'd actually had to shoo off the remaining 'bot, which had sent her a message along her links, some prerecorded thing that let her know it was programmed to provide whatever beverage she wanted.

She wanted to make her own beverage, she told the damn thing. She was tired of being out of control of her life.

The shortness of her response had surprised her. But the work, as slight as it was—actually getting the mug, adding the preboiled water from the tap, and putting in a teabag (filled with real tea from India on Earth)—felt good.

It felt productive.

It felt right.

Just like sitting in her office did now, her feet up, the tea mug steaming beside her, as information scrolled across the screen in front of her. Behind her, some vids downloaded, previous reporters from different parts of the Moon covering similar stories.

All on the history of Retrieval Artists.

She'd even found stored lectures by business professors, criminologists, and corporate historians, all of which she planned to watch as she got this story underway.

But first, she went for the accepted knowledge. She went to the most popular encyclopedia site on Armstrong's net (not wanting to clutter up her mind with any differences throughout the Alliance, or even in other Moon-based cities), and scanned everything they had on Retrieval Artists, from vids to write-ups to reports for children.

She wanted to find how Retrieval Artists as a group got their start, and since they were considered to straddle a legal line, how they were able to stay in business and even flourish.

The encyclopedia wouldn't answer those questions, but it might give her a beginning.

She dug in even deeper, going through all the files, enjoying the very act of finding information, feeling her brain revive.

She hadn't realized how much she had come to hate her job.

Nor had she realized, until this very moment, how much she had identified with that job.

Which meant that she had come to hate herself.

38

FLINT WAS BEGINNING TO FIGURE OUT THE NUMBERING SYSTEM. The first seven digits were case numbers. The next four digits referred to the year. The last two digits referred to the head attorney, either the one who initiated the case or the one whose name went out on the bill.

He resisted the urge to glance at Van Alen, who had moved from pizza and iced coffee to a glass of wine and relaxation on her couch. She looked like a woman who had downloaded a drama of some kind and was watching it on her link instead of on a screen.

She seemed relaxed.

He went back to the files. The oldest ones were mostly Paloma's from her abandoned legal practice. They were filled with minutiae—official letters, billing statements, vids of confidential meetings and/or real-time transcripts of the same meetings. Each file had one hundred or more items in it, all of them tiny, all of them building toward something.

And if the case went to some kind of trial, then the file mushroomed into a well of files, some of them originating at WSX, and others originating elsewhere. Many of the files that originated elsewhere were police files and prosecution notes. Apparently, Paloma had spent most of her time as a criminal defense attorney.

As much as these files fascinated Flint, they seemed too old to mean anything. Although he knew he was prejudging. But he had so little time, maybe even less than the day he'd told Van Alen.

The old Paloma files did help him in one other way, though. They helped him realize the numbering system. He figured out the case numbers first. Then he stumbled on the last two-digit system by opening a file that didn't have Paloma's name on it at all.

Claudius Wagner had started the file, and it ran concurrent with the other old files Flint had found in the system.

This one was also a criminal defense case, and while it was interesting, Flint couldn't tell how it applied.

It took him another hour to realize that Paloma had taken *all* of the firm's files from the five years before she left. Before that, she only had her own. But for that last five year period, she took every single file WSX had generated.

Why? Blackmail?

He couldn't tell. Not from what he had in front of him. He wondered if it was in the ghost files he'd pulled out of his own computer system before rebuilding it. He'd found, about a year after Paloma had left, that she hadn't cleaned the system thoroughly. Most of her Retrieval Artist files were still in that computer, just hard to access.

In those days, he'd been more ethical. He'd set those files aside, then scrubbed the machine.

He hadn't looked at them at all.

He wanted to look at them now.

But he knew returning to the office was a form of suicide. He hadn't lied when he told Van Alen that he believed he'd be a suspect for some time.

The last thing he wanted was to be a suspect under arrest, which wouldn't allow him to figure anything out.

He sighed, and did do a quick search of the files, to see if any of them lacked the numerical system. They didn't.

All of these files were from WSX. All of them.

Had Paloma done her best to wipe these files out of WSX's systems? If so, had she done a better job than she had in the Retrieval Artist office?

Or had she left those ghosts in the machines she sold to Flint on purpose, so that he could find them?

If she had stolen everything from WSX and wiped their machines, how had they continued functioning?

He hadn't heard anything about a law firm losing its records, but that wouldn't be broadcast, not even within the police department. It would mire down dozens of current cases, and call hundreds of others into question.

It would also ruin WSX's reputation.

He leaned back in his chair and frowned at the screen. But, from what he could see (and granted, he wasn't seeing everything), none of the dates went past Paloma's tenure as a lawyer. She went back to WSX as a Tracker, if her words were to be believed, and then became a Retrieval Artist.

Had she brought copies of the files back with her? If so, then why was it so important that she keep these?

Or had she only brought back a few?

Or none at all?

Was this how she got work again with her old firm?

Flint stood, feeling overwhelmed. He wanted to send Paloma a message. It would be so much easier if he could just ask her what this was about.

But he couldn't.

Had she been disappointed that he hadn't asked her about the information he'd found on his own computers all that time ago? Or had all of this been some sort of happy accident? Was this even what she had in mind when she made that holographic recording?

He couldn't tell.

He felt the press of time, and he had no way to figure out what information was important and what information wasn't.

"Dammit," he whispered, then caught his breath. He hadn't expected to say that aloud.

But Van Alen still looked lost in her drama, her wine, and her relaxation. Except for her open and moving eyes, he would have thought her asleep.

He sat back down.

He'd have to approach this two ways: first, he'd look at the newest files; and second, he'd have this less sophisticated system scan all the files for deaths just like Paloma's, for bombs like the one that went off in the *Dove*.

He'd find something.

He had to.

Paloma had counted on him, and even now, he didn't want to let her down.

39

NYQUIST STOOD IN FLINT'S OFFICE, WONDERING HOW A MAN COULD let a place go to seed like this. The filters were off. Moon dust had seeped through every crevice. The air was full of it, making him cough, taking his already overtaxed lungs and turning them inside out.

If he had a choice, he would leave. But he didn't. He had to find Flint, and he had to do it soon.

It was obvious Flint wasn't here, although someone had been here in the last twenty-four hours. The systems were off. The computers were down.

That raised all kinds of suspicions, making him wonder if Flint had let this place go for reasons Nyquist hadn't figured out yet.

Had Flint known he would become a fugitive? If so, wouldn't he have planned better? Wouldn't he have gone to the *Emmeline* instead of the *Lost Seas*?

Had this Murray been right all along? Was Flint the wrong man, even though he had been the last one in the *Dove*?

But Flint had also been the last person Paloma contacted. His arrival at that crime scene might have been staged.

Nyquist stepped deeper into the office. The lights were on reserve, making everything seem blue and fuzzy around the edges. He would have to get techs here to download the computers if there was an arrest warrant on Flint.

Nyquist needed to check that first.

He sent some messages along his links. A few nonurgent ones had stacked up since he stepped inside here. One from the Brownie Bar, reporting that Flint hadn't been in all day. Another viewed all the security vids from the various university libraries and found no trace of Flint in the last twenty-four hours.

He hadn't logged on to any public links either, nor had he sent traceable messages along his own.

If he wasn't at his apartment—and Nyquist had sent a team there too—then he had somehow disappeared.

Nyquist shuddered. Flint wouldn't do that, would he? He wouldn't Disappear. He knew the consequences and the costs. He knew how difficult it was.

But it was a logical solution to someone who had just murdered a police-evidence technician. And it was something Flint might have been contemplating since he caused—or discovered—Paloma's death.

If it turned out that Flint wasn't at his office, Nyquist would contact the lawyer that had been with him and see what she knew. Some corporate lawyers, who weren't used to dealing with actual criminals, occasionally gave their clients up.

He could hope for that.

He could hope that this entire evening hadn't happened, although he wouldn't do him any good.

Nyquist slipped behind the desk and booted up the system. It creaked on, barely functioning, just like the environmental equipment.

He checked his links again. Still no warrant had been issued.

To hell with them. He had an investigation to run. Who would check the time logs between Flint's office and the warrant's issue? Who would care, if Nyquist caught a cop-killing criminal?

Or discovered something else, something that might help solve Paloma's murder.

40

FLINT WAS EATING COLD PIZZA AND DRINKING MORE ICED COFFEE. Apparently, Van Alen had ordered an entire battalion's worth of iced coffee and had it placed in a nearby refrigeration unit.

He was still trying to decipher the conundrum of the files. The most recently accessed ones had all been Claudius Wagner's cases— the Wagner that Paloma had been involved with; the one she had had children with.

The one she had left.

The files looked straightforward. But Flint had never gone over legal case files before. He had always started the file as a police officer— registering the complaint, delineating the evidence, making certain each bit of information was recorded in the proper place.

From there, the file went to the district attorney's office, and with luck, he never heard about it again.

Of course, he hadn't had much of that luck over the years. He'd had to testify, had to sit in on conferences where the DA threatened to have him testify, and sometimes he had to come down to the office to explain what he had actually done.

But none of that included expanding the file. The bills; the notations; the letters, written and vid. Some of these files had contracts in various drafts, and a few had wills. All of them seemed to cover more than one incident, and that alone confused Flint more than he wanted to admit.

"They finally did it."

Van Alen's voice came to him from far away. Flint blinked, then rubbed his eyes. He sighed and turned around.

She hadn't left her perch on the couch. Her wine glass was empty, and she looked sleepy.

"Did what?" he asked.

"Issued an official arrest warrant," she said. "Up until now, you were wanted as a material witness. Now they're accusing you of the crime."

"It's being broadcast?" he asked. If so, that was bad. Then people on the streets would be looking for him. Those with comparison software might even scan his face and compare it to whatever image the police department was broadcasting.

"No," Van Alen said. "We've got about an hour before that happens. I was notified. As a courtesy."

Flint grabbed that iced coffee. The cup was sweating. He looked at it. It was more like watered coffee now. He wondered how long it had been sitting beside him.

"You were notified." That took a moment to process. "You're not my attorney of record."

She smiled, then slipped her shoes back on. "You're not normally that slow, Miles. Of course I am. I got you into the *Lost Seas*. That puts me on record."

Of course it did. But for a civil action, not a criminal one. But he didn't have a criminal lawyer, so naturally, the system would contact the only lawyer of record.

"You're supposed to surrender me," Flint said.

"If I know where you are," she said.

"Do you?"

"You've seemed far away to me all evening," she said. "I think I'm going home and sleeping off this wine. Maybe in the morning, I'll be able to find you. I will, won't I?"

He wasn't sure. He'd have to look at that warrant himself. If things seemed too bad for him, he wouldn't turn himself in.

"You'll be able to find me," he said with certainty. Whether he let her find him was another matter.

"I'm bringing the change of clothing in here, along with some pastries and a few other snacks. There's no reason to leave the office," Van Alen said. "You have a shower, a comfortable couch, and a computer system. With that, the clothing and the food, you won't need anything else."

Except the freedom to go anywhere he wanted. He wouldn't have that, not until this warrant was resolved.

"You any closer to figuring this out?" Van Alen asked.

Flint shook his head. "I'm not sure why she saved these files. I hope it'll become obvious over time, but right now, I don't have that time."

"We could get you some help," Van Alen said.

He ignored that. "Can I ask you one question?"

"Sure," she said.

"Say I'm a lawyer in your firm. Do I have access to your files?"

"Everyone here is bound by the same confidentiality that I am," Van Alen said, a bit defensively.

"No," Flint said. "I'm not talking about here. I'm talking in general."

"In general," Van Alen said, "it's all privileged. A lawyer keeps her own records, but her secretary and her assistants are all part of that privilege. And so, by extension, is the rest of the firm and anyone we might hire from the outside for that particular case. Can I ask why?"

"If I were that lawyer in your firm," Flint said, deciding not to answer directly, "and I take all of the firm's records—"

"Is that what you have?" she sounded breathless. "All of the records of WSX?"

"—if I were to take all of the records," Flint said, a little louder. Her reaction had disconcerted him. "If I had done that, but hadn't released them to anyone, am I violating anything?"

"You mean if you copied them and took them out of the building?"

Flint nodded.

"It depends," she said. "If you took them without permission, you're probably violating something, but it would be an internal matter if you hadn't given them to anyone else. If you took them and gave them to someone outside the firm, then that's a violation of privilege. If you took all of this firm's records and gave them away, I'd prosecute you to the end of time. I'd find every charge I could make and I'd double it. I'd make sure you were ruined."

"But I could ruin you," Flint said.

"In that instance, you could," Van Alen said. "The law firm would be forever known as one that lost *all* of its records to a junior associate. There'd be no amount of talk or spin or even legal wrangling that would repair the damage."

Flint nodded.

"So, is that what you have? All of WSX's records?" That breathlessness again. She'd gone up against Justinian enough that she probably wanted to see what was here. Flint couldn't let her do that.

He stood, shoved his hands in his pockets, and paced. It felt good to move. "If I had the records, and I made sure you knew about it, but I assured you they were somewhere safe. If I did that, and then vowed I'd never use them unless you pissed me off or violated some agreement or something, we'd have a stalemate, wouldn't we?"

Van Alen crossed her arms. "You're not going to tell me what you have, are you?"

"It's need to know, remember?" he said. "I'm not sure what you need to know yet."

"Then why are you asking these questions?" she asked.

"I'm trying to figure things out."

"If you had the records and you threatened to release them, and if I couldn't find them but I knew you had them, yes, we'd probably have a stalemate. Although if you were a junior associate, I doubt you'd be smart enough to take me on like this. I'd outthink you."

"What if I'm your partner?" Flint asked.

"You mean like Lucianna Stuart and Claudius Wagner?" Van Alen asked.

Flint nodded.

"If I were Lucianna Stuart," Van Alen said, "I wouldn't threaten exposing the firm. It has my name, too."

"But she changed her name," Flint said.

Van Alen smiled. "Then I'd threaten one of two things. Either I'd threaten to steal all the important clients and build a firm of my own—"

"Which she clearly didn't do," Flint said.

"Or I'd leak information, bit by bit, stuff that no one wanted out."

"But you could get in trouble for that. All that confidentiality that we discussed," Flint said.

Van Alen's smile grew wider. "There are ways around that if you're smart enough. Subtle enough. Tough enough."

Flint felt a chill.

"WSX still stands," Van Alen said, obviously noting his changed expression.

"But they want something that was on that ship," Flint said.

"You think she had them in a tough position?"

"I think that's obvious," Flint said, "but I don't know why, and I don't know if this is even connected to her death."

"But you can find out, right?" Van Alen asked.

"Given time," Flint said.

"Well, then," she said, shrugging one shoulder in an almost careless gesture. "We'll have to get you the time."

She headed toward the door.

"One more thing, Maxine." It felt odd to use her first name, but she had used his. He wanted to keep them on equal footing.

"What?" she said.

"Are you helping me because I'm your client or because you hope I hold the key to destroying WSX?"

"I don't see those reasons as mutually exclusive," she said, and let herself out the door.

41

FLINT WAS GOOD. THERE WAS VERY LITTLE ON THE SYSTEMS IN HIS office, and what was there could be confirmed in the public record. There seemed to be some irregularities, but given the state of the equipment, Nyquist couldn't be sure.

He was halfway through that search when the arrest warrant finally got issued. At that moment, he felt good enough to bring in a tech team.

Before they arrived, he went over every centimeter of that messy office, making certain no bomb would surprise them, no booby trap would get anyone whom he'd called in to work on this case.

When the team finally got there, Nyquist was reasonably sure nothing would harm them.

He couldn't be positive, though, because he knew that Flint was better at computers than he was. The best Nyquist could do was warn the team, and remind them that this man had killed by remote control earlier that evening.

"There's no reason to doubt," Nyquist said, "that he won't try it again."

Then Nyquist left. He needed to go to his office, but he went to his apartment first because he couldn't go any longer without a shower.

His apartment looked neglected, probably because it was. It was three small rooms, barely enough for one person, and certainly not enough to show off to a certain female security chief, not without fumigating it and throwing away all the clutter that had accumulated in his few hours at home every night.

The shower felt like heaven. A shower with real water was one of the few luxuries he allowed himself. The hot water peeled off Moon dust from Flint's office. Nyquist watched the dust swirl in the water and realized that Flint's clothing had been covered in the stuff when he hurried to the scene of Paloma's murder.

Flint had been in his office when he got the news of the death—or the message from Paloma, as he had insisted. Or he had killed her, then changed his clothes, gone to his office, and walked around in the dust, knowing how trace evidence worked. He had hurried to Paloma's building, still covered in dust, and planned to use that as an alibi.

Except he had worn a tech suit when he had gone into Paloma's apartment, and he had taken that suit with him. If he had planned to use the dust as evidence, he would have left the suit, right?

Nyquist sighed. He had no idea. Flint had outthought him more than once, and Nyquist simply had to concede that Flint was smarter.

Once a cop started from that premise, he was often able to overcome the smarter opponent. He wouldn't try to outsmart the opponent; instead, he would use good old-fashioned police work to establish a solid case with a lot of evidence.

Nyquist shut off the shower, got out, and looked at the pile of clothes he had forgotten to put into the cleaning tube. They were covered with dust, and some of it had gotten onto the floor. The problem with that stuff was that it was impossible to remove once it had gotten on things.

If Flint had had the environmental problem in his office for more than a few days—and judging by the depth of that dust, he had—then he would have tracked dust everywhere he went. If he had murdered Paloma, he would have left moon dust inside her apartment.

Nyquist would simply need the techs to check for it—and then, of course, they'd have to match it to the samples removed from Flint's office.

He sent a message down his link asking the techs who'd worked Paloma's apartment to look for Moon dust. He also sent a message asking the team in Flint's office to take samples of Moon dust from various areas, and from various depths, just in case.

He got clothes out of his closet, then paused. Flint's reaction in Paloma's apartment had seemed real. No matter what Nyquist thought of Flint now, that much seemed true. And if he started from that premise, then he knew Flint wasn't a suspect.

Nyquist sighed. How many times had he told rookies that gut wasn't enough to go on? Gut could get confused—like his was right now. His gut hated Flint for setting that bomb, and yet knew that Flint hadn't faked his reaction in the apartment.

Nyquist decided not to focus on that. He would investigate as best he could. He got dressed, spending a little more time than usual with his hair and his clothing, just because DeRicci was on his mind (he smiled at himself for that). He put one pistol against his hip, like he always did, and another near his ankle. He checked his chips, making sure the warning chips were functioning and the recording chips didn't need downloading. Everything seemed fine, despite the explosion. Then he grabbed an apple—one of the expensive greenhouse-grown ones instead of the synthetic nutrient filled things (another of his luxuries)—and headed out the door.

As he hurried down the stairs, he checked his links one final time to make sure nothing serious had happened while he was cleaning the crawly stuff off himself. Nothing had. Just the techs, acknowledging his requests.

It was nice to know that other people worked through the night just like he was.

Sometimes he wondered how far he could stretch himself before he collapsed into a puddle of nerve endings.

He supposed he would eventually find out.

42

KI BOWLES HAD HAD THREE CUPS OF TEA AND SHE WAS WIRED. She couldn't sit still, so she read files on her left eye link as she walked around the room. The little 'bot followed her, so she finally shut the damn thing off, glad that she didn't have a cat.

The Retrieval Artist system all started because of a corporation named Environmental Systems Incorporated. Bowles recognized the name. What local wouldn't? ESI had been around forever. Before she had started her research, she would have said that ESI had been around since the beginning of time, but that wasn't accurate.

ESI had simply been around since the beginning of colonization.

Two Earth-based entrepreneurs founded ESI before anyone even thought of colonizing the Moon. In the beginning, ESI had created environmental systems for Earth's more dangerous landscapes—deserts, oceans—all those places humans wanted to dwell but couldn't without help.

Bowles skipped most of that. Corporate history, especially the kind written for encyclopedias and schoolrooms, was as dry as history got. But she started to pay attention when she got to the Moon.

ESI developed the first functioning dome, which was initially used by researchers and early entrepreneurs, the folks who had eventually deemed the Moon livable. The first dome was named Armstrong after the first person to walk on the Moon. The dome barely covered enough area to house Bowles' apartment building and the apartment building next door, and the dome's ceiling certainly wasn't high enough to accommodate either of them.

As Armstrong grew, that dome got incorporated into other domes, and so when local historians said the original dome remained in Old Armstrong, they were technically correct. Only the original dome was in pieces slabbed together with other pieces, instead of in its original formation.

Finally Bowles got tired of pacing. She went back to her desk and continued the research, learning that ESI expanded its services to other Moon domes, and then to Mars, and then to all of the colonized regions in the known universe. Wherever there were humans, there was ESI in one form or another.

ESI often brought the first team of humans to a hostile environment. The humans used ships or temporary domes and then examined the environment, figured out what they needed to do to sustain human life, and often did it.

Without contacting the indigenous population.

In fact, in this solar system, the indigenous population was often unrecognizable as life to the early colonizers. It wasn't until some scientist realized that the mold attacking a temporary dome was actually an army of tiny creatures trying to save its major city that anyone within Earth's government realized they were doing something wrong.

Over time, the politicians and diplomats got involved. Various Earth governments made different treaties with newly discovered alien governments (sometimes to great misunderstanding, since neither group could communicate well with each other) and corporations sometimes made agreements as well.

ESI had its own first-contact wing in the early days, and it made fewer missteps than the Earth governments did.

But it made missteps, some of which became major issues decades later.

Eventually, Earth formed a single government that actually governed the entire population of the planet (before, Earth had forms of a single government, none of which had any real regulatory function on a worldwide basis). Once that government formed, it began negotiating with other alien groups, like the Disty.

Human scholars worked with businesses and politicians so that trade could expand throughout the known universe, which was also growing. Trade expansion meant that rules and regulations had to have some kind of wide-ranging legal basis.

Finally, what the various governments agreed on was that each legal entity (sometimes a planet or a moon had more than one ruling government) continued to govern its own territory. Crimes committed in that territory by aliens would be prosecuted according to the territory's laws.

This reduced havoc and allowed trade, but it also caused all sorts of cultural repercussions, including the famous one that all Armstrong's schoolchildren learned. Early human colonists on one planet were put to death for stepping on a particularly rare flower.

That was the beginning of an internal revolt among humans themselves.

Bowles scanned much of this. It was familiar territory for her, even as an art history major.

Humans, so the internal mythology went, hated unjust laws. Even ancient religious texts like the Bible and the Koran dealt with humans who refused to follow laws that they did not believe in. Human philosophers from Henry David Thoreau to Alain Nygen argued throughout Earth's history that humans had a right to disobey any law they felt was unjust, so long as they paid the consequences.

Unfortunately, within the Earth Alliance, those consequences weren't just jail time or the loss of a hand, as they had been on Earth. They often meant the loss of a firstborn child or the hideous death of the so-called perpetrator, usually without any public hearing or trial.

Old ways of civil disobedience did not work any longer. Human companies had to choose between working with nonhuman members of the Earth Alliance or giving up on interstellar trade.

Environmental Systems Incorporated was at the edge of all the debate. ESI often went into the new cultures before anyone else, setting up systems, digging into whatever ground was there, looking for water supplies or minerals or ways of setting up septic systems. ESI employees were dying by the hundreds, many of them subject to laws that humans couldn't stomach, and ESI was facing an internal crisis.

So some smart CEO came up with the first Disappearance Service. It was a subcorporation of a subcorporation of ESI, something other cultures couldn't track without extensive knowledge of Earth-based business law, which those cultures did not have. The service helped the law-breakers' entire families start a new life, with new names and new skills and in a new place.

Other corporations started the same thing, and then independent Disappearance Services appeared. Such services were illegal, but their illegality couldn't be proven without actual proof that the service knew the person who disappeared was a wanted criminal. Record keeping became baroque, then byzantine, then nonexistent.

After a while, nonhuman governments within the Alliance refused to do business with humans, saying that humans reneged on the legal sides of the agreement. So human prosecutors' offices and police departments developed wings that tracked Disappeareds. Trackers found Disappeareds and brought them to justice. Eventually, some Trackers founded their own business and charged a premium for finding missing humans.

And some of those Trackers realized they could charge even more if they refused to bring the Disappeared to justice. They would find the Disappeared for the family—to let the person know that the charges had been dropped, or that they'd inherited a fortune, or that their uncle was wanted for murder and they were the only witness and could they come home? These Trackers were even shadier than the original group, and finally, in an effort to build up their image, they started calling themselves Retrieval Artists.

Early on, a lot of Retrieval Artists were prosecuted for harboring fugitives, but then the entire profession grew smart. And useful.

Once again, ESI was at the forefront. When it negotiated an agreement with a native government that then changed the legal ramifications of what ESI had done in its initial phase, ESI became the first corporation to have in-house Retrieval Artists whose job it was to bring back the highly trained, highly skilled person in hiding.

Bowles found the entire concept fascinating. There was more than one story here, maybe more than one series. She could look at Disappearance Services, at Trackers, and at various governments, as well as Retrieval Artists.

From what she could tell, with just an evening's cursory search, the early records had vid interviews with returned Disappeareds, the founder of ESI's first Disappearance Service, and even some early Retrieval Artists.

She had stumbled onto a gold mine, a gold mine of history and stories that had been there all along. If she hadn't known this stuff, none of her viewers would either.

The implications were far-reaching, going back to the early days of the Alliance and agreements people still argued about. The compromises every human put up with in order to live in a multiethnic, multicultural, multispecies universe were in stark relief here.

If she handled the information correctly, she could become not just an expert on Retrieval Artists, but on human cultural, business, and legal history and its daily ramifications for the Moon and the Earth Alliance.

It would take a long time to establish, but it would be worth her time.

She would become more than Ki Bowles, InterDome's most famous reporter. She would become Ki Bowles, the Moon's expert on all matters pertaining to the known universe.

She would be a source, not a grubby digger for information. She would be important. And, if she was honest with herself, that was all she ever really wanted.

43

WHEN NYQUIST REACHED THE FIFTH FLOOR OF THE FIRST DETECTIVE Division, he was surprised to realize he wasn't the only person from the morning shift still working a case. Three other detectives from morning were at their desks, researching or digging through files or completing a report.

Nyquist nodded at all of them, got words of concern from one who'd heard about the bombing at the port, and then he went into his closet-sized office.

He was too wired to sleep. He couldn't interview suspects at this late hour—not without cause—and he didn't need to be on the street looking for Flint. Patrol units were doing that. Flint's arrest warrant had been flagged as high priority.

Instead, Nyquist was going to review the evidence the techs had processed and he was going to go over backgrounds on everyone from Flint to the Wagners to see what he missed.

But first, he was going to moonlight on the case he'd been forbidden to investigate, the one he was involved in, the *Dove* bombing.

If anyone examined his records, he would simply say he was following the suspect in his own current case, the Paloma murder case, and he would leave it at that. Let some internal affairs officer figure out which case Nyquist was working on.

After all, the *Dove* belonged to Paloma. Flint, one of the primary suspects in her murder, was the last person to leave it before it blew. Nyquist had to retrace Flint's steps from the moment he entered the port until the moment he left it.

Nyquist knew no one had done more than a cursory search of the port's security videos. Everyone, from the techs to Space Traffic to the detectives, was focused on finding Flint, not on developing a case against him.

Nyquist would work on that case, because he learned about his suspects from their actions. Flint had a reason for being on the *Dove* after he learned that Paloma had been murdered. Whether it was to establish an alibi—after all, why would an ex-cop be that dumb?—or whether it was to set the bomb, Nyquist couldn't tell at the moment.

He wanted to be able to tell eventually.

So he fed an image of Flint into his creaky old computer system, had it match that image with the various security vids he'd gotten from the port, and then he watched a fairly continuous thread of images of Miles Flint.

Even alone, Flint had looked upset and distracted. Once or twice, the later vids caught the outline of a laser pistol under Flint's clothing, which didn't surprise Nyquist. Flint was an ex-cop, after all.

He had hurried like a man with somewhere important to go, but the images of his face that the vids had captured all showed a man who seemed lost, upset, and distraught.

Nyquist leaned on his forearms, careful not to touch the desktop screen. Flint went through the various sections of the port like a man on automatic pilot. When he finally reached Terminal 25, he paused, frowned, and seemed to come into himself.

Nyquist expected Flint to go straight to the *Dove*, but he didn't. Instead, he went to his own ship, the *Emmeline*. And there, Nyquist got a surprise.

The InterDome reporter, Ki Bowles, was waiting for him. She stood as if she had expected him. He seemed surprised to see her, but that could have been acting.

They exchanged words, and Flint started toward his ship. Then he stopped, and told her—quite visibly—to go. She did.

Nyquist turned up the audio, but all he got was ambient noise, clangs, and audio announcements. The port's security system wasn't designed for sophisticated audio pickup, particularly in the high-end areas like Terminal 25. Wealthy yacht owners expected their privacy, and they got it to the best of the port's ability, as long as the port could also provide them with the security that they so amply paid for.

When Nyquist couldn't get the audio from the interchange, he ran a program to read their lips. Only, he couldn't get much from that, either. Flint clearly told Bowles to leave, but whatever they had said before that was garbled or made no sense.

The program didn't get a good enough look at either of their mouths to do an accurate lip-read.

Nyquist sighed. That meant he had to interview Ki Bowles about her meeting with Flint. Had she known he was going to do something? Or was she there to ask him about Paloma's death?

He clicked his screen on InterDome and scanned for Ki Bowles latest report. What he got was weeks old.

He frowned. Was she on background? Had she filed something and he searched for it wrong? He couldn't' remember seeing her on the vidcasts recently, but that didn't mean much. He didn't watch the news unless he had to.

Maybe he had set up the parameters of the search wrong. He re-programmed his search through InterDome's latest downloads while he continued to watch the port's security vid.

Eventually he would figure out what Miles Flint was up to.

Eventually everything would make sense.

44

VAN ALEN'S OFFICE WAS FILLED WITH ODD, UNFAMILIAR NOISES. Bangs and creaks and groans. It took Flint awhile to realize these were normal building noises, things that happened every hour of every day, and regular employees of the place no longer even noticed.

Flint stood, moving away from the computer, trying to keep the blood flowing. He was getting tired, and he couldn't be.

He had a long, long way to go.

It did feel odd, though, being the only one in this opulent room, with its executive shower through the side door, and the complete kitchen just outside the main area. He wasn't used to working in places like this. It either showed that Van Alen trusted him or that she had her confidential information locked up where no one could find it.

He didn't bother to look. He had more than enough to do.

He raised his arms above his head, clasped his hands together, and stretched, listening to his back crack. Then he helped himself to more iced coffee, knowing that at some point the caffeine would simply make his heart race instead of keeping him awake.

Finally, he returned to the files.

The sheer volume of them overwhelmed him. He needed a plan of attack. But he wasn't even sure where to start. Some of the files he had examined were so mundane that he couldn't see how they were relevant.

So he rubbed his eyes and thought. Finding anything relevant would be luck at this point. Or he had to figure out where Paloma hid the relevant files, if there were any. For all he knew, she had simply stolen the files from her old firm as a form of leverage.

Then why go to such lengths to protect them?

Or was she protecting something else?

He took another sip of the iced coffee, feeling it shiver down his throat. Maybe he was overthinking this. Maybe he should simply take the old-fashioned approach, as if Paloma were any client, not his mentor.

What did he know?

He knew that she had left the firm and taken the files. He knew that she had fought to protect those files.

He knew that she lied routinely and easily, with no thought to the consequences.

He stopped, rubbed his eyes, and sighed. He was bitter, and he couldn't be. He had to let go of his emotions and think.

Paloma left the firm and changed her name. Yet she stayed connected as a Tracker and then as a Retrieval Artist. Those facts had to be important.

And the files he'd looked at, everything he'd scanned, showed that everything here came from her days as a lawyer.

So, logically, something toward the end of her tenure made her quit.

For the first time in an hour, his pulse quickened and he knew it wasn't because of the caffeine. He finally had a plan of attack. He finally knew how to approach this.

He went for the most recent file with the numbers indicating the case belonged to Lucianna Stuart, the lawyer who became Paloma.

He opened the first subfile and felt his stomach churn.

He was looking at a long-range photograph of a collapsed dome. Subsequent photographs showed the same dome in more detail, bodies twisted in the wreckage.

He wasn't sure he wanted to read this, but it was the first dramatic thing he'd found all night.

And somehow, he knew, it was important.

Maybe important enough to cost Paloma her life.

45

DeRicci could have gone home. One of the perks of this new job was that she didn't have to work long hours unless there was a Moon-wide crisis.

But there was no real reason to go home. Work, even when it was routine, was a lot more interesting than anything in her apartment.

She had let two of her assistants go, keeping only Popova here in case she needed to bounce something off of someone. Popova claimed to have no life as well. Sometimes DeRicci tested her, trying to see how much Popova would take before admitting she had a date or a boyfriend or a secret hidden life.

So far, Popova hadn't admitted anything, and DeRicci found that a bit disappointing.

She also found the files she was scanning disappointing. The list of quarantined ships was curious. The ships themselves seemed to have no pattern. Some had sat in their positions for decades. Some predated Terminal 81. Those made sense. They had gotten lost in the data systems, misfiled or overlooked once the terminal opened. No one thought to check on them, even though many of those ships hadn't been accessed in nearly a century.

She shuddered to think about the mess that would cause—the legal hassles in tracing long-term ownership, and the destructive capability of whatever it was that caused the ships to be quarantined in the first place.

The quarantines were generally nonspecific. Sometimes DeRicci couldn't even tell which organization had issued the quarantine, whether it had come from the port itself or from the ship's logs (some quarantines were mandatory if the ship traveled to a certain planet or among certain alien groups) and often the quarantine didn't seem to apply to the cargo and/or crew of the ship, most of whom had scattered long ago.

All of them would have to be tracked down. They'd have to go through decon and then they'd have to make a list of everyone they'd come into contact with, sometimes over the space of years.

DeRicci felt overwhelmed just thinking about that.

She got up and walked to the door, pulling it open and peering at Popova. Popova leaned over her desk screen, half asleep as she ran her finger along the touch screen.

"You hungry?" DeRicci asked.

Popova snapped into an upright position, her long black hair swaying around her like a robe. "Sorry?"

"You wanna get something for us to eat?" DeRicci asked.

"Sure," Popova said. "What do you want?"

"Whatever's open nearby and cheap," DeRicci said. "I'm buying."

Popova nodded as it became clear that she was the person in charge of ordering. She already knew DeRicci's food preferences, and the kinds of things that DeRicci believed could be eaten at a desk without permanently staining it.

DeRicci slipped back to her office and went back to the list of quarantined ships. She sorted the list, placing the ownership of the vessel at the very top. And let out a sigh of annoyance when she realized most vessels were owned by holding companies related to more holding companies related to subsidiaries related to corporations.

Only a few were independently owned.

And one name stopped her. A name she hadn't expected.

In the middle of the list, she found a space yacht quarantined ten years ago.

Its owner was someone she'd heard of but never met.

Claudius Wagner. Father of Justinian. And the lover—or maybe the husband—of a woman once known as Lucianna Stuart.

Paloma.

46

THE SUBFILES IN LUCIANNA STUART'S LAST CASE SEEMED TO GO
on forever. Flint finally looked at the system count for them, and discovered 450 subfiles. More files lurked in each subfile. This case alone
would take him weeks.

He waded through motions and court orders and legal documents
by the hundreds. He quickly learned how to scan them for the most
important information.

He also found vids, more still photos, and a pile of holographic
imagery, none of which he opened. The still photos were disturbing
enough.

From what he could glean on a cursory examination, Lucianna
Stuart had been the primary attorney for a large corporation named
Environmental Systems Inc. ESI had existed long before Lucianna was
born, and still continued. Flint recognized the company name from
hundreds of products he'd seen all over Armstrong, most of those
products having to do with heating ducts and sonic toilets and individual environmental systems.

ESI was an Earth corporation, but it had affiliates all over the
known universe. ESI had a branch in Armstrong, its second-largest
corporate headquarters after the one in Beijing on Earth. When Stuart
merged with Wagner and Xendor to form the biggest law firm on the
Moon, she brought ESI with her. Then she was a small attorney in a

phalanx of attorneys from firms all over the Earth Alliance. Most of the other attorneys handled the local cases, but the big cases—the ones that could bankrupt ESI—eventually came to WSX, mostly because of Lucianna Stuart's expertise.

Which was how she got the dome case.

Flint stopped drinking the iced coffee as he read these files, and moved to plain water. He needed something that wouldn't upset his stomach further.

These files were upsetting it enough.

From what he could gather with his cursory review, the dome case began simply enough. ESI won a bid to build a dome on the fifth moon of S'Dem. The fifth moon had no atmosphere, like this Moon, and the dome building seemed like an easy task for ESI, until Flint looked deeper in the documentation.

ESI wasn't building the dome for human habitation. It was building the dome for the Riayet, a race that survived in an atmosphere filled with a toxic mix of unbreathable chemicals, most of which Flint had never heard of. The Riayet swam through this thick atmosphere and incorporated it into their skin, making them almost inseparable from the environment itself.

Building a dome that would sustain them would be a difficult task. Spaceships that they built on their own often malfunctioned because of the heaviness of the atmosphere.

The Riayet had never colonized an area before because of their unusual environment. While they'd been able to make their off-world vessels work, at least most of time, they'd never been able to sustain off-world travels for more than a few Earth months.

ESI swore it could change that, and when the Riayet laid claim to the fifth moon of S'Dem, they hired ESI to build the dome.

The ESI engineers studied Riayet systems for nearly a decade, familiarizing themselves with the Riayet's most important needs. They ran simulations on Ria, the Riayet's home planet, managing to get the Riayet colonists to survive for more than a year in an artificial environment.

Using the lessons learned on Ria, the ESI engineers built a fully functional dome on the fifth moon. The dome seemed fine, although it had the usual problems—breakdowns, a few cracks—and one unexpected problem: the weight of the Riayet atmosphere caused half the moon's surface beneath the dome to slip. Apparently, the moon's crust wasn't as thick in some areas as it was in others, and couldn't handle the incredible mass of buildings, population, and heavy atmosphere.

The dome, now braced unevenly on broken ground, started to fail.

ESI corporate headquarters in Armstrong contacted Lucianna Stuart, letting her know that the ESI engineers believed they had miscalculated. They hadn't tested the entire surface of the planned settlement on the fifth moon. They had only tested a representative sample—and that sample was on the part of the colony that hadn't slipped.

ESI, used to doing calculations for human domes only, hadn't factored in the impact of the atmosphere, which was ten times heavier than air. It had assumptions, based on the faulty analysis of the fifth moon's surface, and those assumptions had proven to be false.

The dome couldn't be fixed. It would fail.

The Riayet government had sent ships to attempt an evacuation of the dome, but ESI's engineers also believed that a full-scale evacuation might make the dome even more unstable. Only a handful of dome exits could be used, and then only by a small group of Riayet.

The ESI representative who visited Lucianna Stuart told her that thousands of Riayet would die because of ESI's errors, and asked her how to contain ESI's liabilities. Primarily, ESI wanted to keep the incident quiet, so that it could continue its expansion into nonhuman domes.

After learning that, Flint got up and walked into the bathroom. It had hot and cold running water, a perk most apartments did not have. He splashed cold water on his face, mostly to clear his head. His hands were shaking. He didn't like any of this. He wanted to wake up, discover that he'd had a horrible nightmare in which he had learned that Paloma was someone else. Then he would lie in his bed, relieved, that everything had been a dream.

He dried off with a towel that was labeled real cotton. It felt soft against his skin. He didn't know what cotton was, but he did know he'd never felt anything like it before. The Moon-made materials he was used to felt scratchy by comparison.

He got himself another glass of water, and returned to the computer, knowing he had to learn more, even though he didn't want to.

Once it became clear to Lucianna Stuart that the ESI engineers were right—the dome would fail and thousands of Riayet would die—she came up with a plan to save the corporation, its reputation, and its future.

She sent in more engineers. Instead of evacuating as many Riayet as possible, Lucianna Stuart told ESI to send in a hundred of its best engineers, many of whom had worked on the Riayet dome in the first place. They were instructed to do whatever they could to shore up the dome, sustain the atmosphere, and begin repairs.

The corporation knew nothing would work. As Lucianna Stuart—a young, black-haired Paloma without the wrinkles—said in a vid conference, "The company line becomes, 'We would never send our own people in if we thought the dome was going to collapse.' "

She had said that with great calm, as if ordering a hundred needless human deaths on top of thousands of Riayet ones meant nothing to her.

Flint froze at the computer.

What right had she to talk with him about ethics? Why had she been so concerned with the rules and regulations of Retrieval Artists, with the smallest detail that could, as she had said when she trained him, save lives?

Was she atoning?

If so, she hadn't even come close to succeeding. On her plate were the hundred dead engineers and the Riayet who could have been saved.

All to keep alive a corporation that went on to build two other failed domes before getting out of the nonhuman dome business altogether.

Flint had no idea how many other bits of advice she had given over all of her years as an attorney, nor what else he would find in the files.

He wasn't sure he wanted to continue looking. He had no real death to avenge. Paloma's death was small justice for all the lives she had cost.

But he didn't know for certain if her death had come because of this or something else she had done. Maybe something horrible she had done as a Retrieval Artist, something someone might blame on him, since he had bought her business.

He leaned back in his chair, took a deep breath, and forced himself to continue.

Somewhere in these files was the answer he was looking for.

But now he wasn't sure he wanted to know what it was.

47

NYQUIST PRESSED HIS RIGHT INDEX FINGER AGAINST THE OUTER DOOR at Ki Bowles apartment building. The building, and the neighborhood it was in, were a surprise. Nyquist expected a rich and famous reporter to live in nicer surroundings.

Instead, her apartment building was as middle-class as his, with worse security. His finger carried his police identification, but as the door swung open, he reflected that a lot of other buildings required more than the single ID. It was too easy to replicate. Many middle-income apartment complexes had systems that included retinal scans, voice print ID, and confirmation from the local precinct.

This system required none of that.

Nyquist stepped in the building's foyer. An androgynous voice asked him what his business was. He said that he had to see Ki Bowles over a police matter.

The inner door opened, followed by the elevator doors. He stepped inside, and the elevator took him to Bowles' floor. He wondered if he should warn her about the poor state of security in this building. If he were a stalker who had fixated on Bowles because of her vid reports, he would have easy access to her.

Her apartment door was well lit. An exterior security system, one that she had purchased, winked around the door frame, obvious and much more effective than the building's security. He stood a foot away from the door, touched the light that extended outward from it, and heard a different androgynous voice ask him his business.

He repeated himself.

Then the system requested identification. He held up his finger, but the system insisted on a retinal scan. He had to wait another minute as the system confirmed everything.

While he waited, he realized he no longer needed to tell Bowles that her security was lax.

The door opened, and Ki Bowles stood behind it. In person, she was smaller than he expected, and younger. Deep shadows made her eyes seem sunken and the lack of makeup on her face gave her skin a sallow tinge. Apparently, she hadn't gone for the on-air enhancements—the kind that made vid people look normal on-screen and like mannequins offscreen.

She waited for him to speak—a nice tactic that he usually liked to use.

He introduced himself, and said he was investigating the death of Paloma. He did not apologize for arriving at her apartment so late in the evening.

Bowles' eyebrows went up. "What does this have to do with me?"

"I understand you spoke to Miles Flint earlier today."

"Briefly," she said.

"I'd like to discuss that conversation if we could." He glanced down the hall at the still-open elevator doors. "Somewhere private."

She sighed. The security lights went from bright to dim, but the system was still on. He would have to step through it and be analyzed by the system, something he normally didn't mind. But on this night, after all those decontamination exams, he really didn't want light to probe him again.

Still, he stepped through. Except for a momentary blip in his links, he felt nothing.

Bowles stepped away from the door. The main room had a lot of furniture that looked curiously unused. She pushed the door closed. A small 'bot scurried in as if it were going to get fired if it didn't perform its little duties.

"I saw Miles Flint," she said. "He told me to leave him alone. I did. I didn't know that Paloma had died when we spoke."

"Have you spoken to him since?" Nyquist asked.

"Is he a suspect?" Bowles asked.

"We're looking for him in connection with something else," Nyquist said.

"A different crime?" Bowles asked.

Nyquist nodded.

"Are you going to enlighten me?" She asked.

"No. It'll only clutter up the questions I have to ask you." Then Nyquist gave her a small smile. "Besides, you'll just look up the police database the moment I leave."

She grinned. "How do you know I'm not doing that already?"

He didn't know. He had no idea how extensive her links were. He hoped she'd pay attention to this conversation instead of the information she downloaded, but he'd have no real way of telling.

"Why were you waiting for Mr. Flint?" Nyquist asked.

To his surprise, Bowles turned away. She snapped her fingers, and the 'bot vanished for a moment, then reappeared, a steaming mug of tea on its saucer-shaped top.

"To be honest," Bowles said as she took the tea, "I wasn't there to see Flint."

"You were on the dock near his ship."

She nodded. She cradled the mug in her hands. The 'bot scuttled away without offering Nyquist anything. He felt awkward standing in front of the door. She made sure he knew what an unwelcome visitor he was.

"So you wanted to see him, right?" Nyquist asked.

"Actually..." Bowles sighed, then turned, still holding the tea. The mug had to be warm against her hands. "I just went there to think."

"Terminal 25? You're telling me you were at Flint's ship by coincidence."

Bowles' lips twisted. She might have been trying to smile, but Nyquist wasn't really sure. "You do know I was fired today, right, detective?"

"I wondered," he said. "There's no formal announcement, but you're no longer listed in any of InterDome's databases, except for old vid reports that hadn't been archived yet."

She walked into the seating area and perched on the edge of a chair. He followed, even though she hadn't indicated that he should.

"So you went to see Flint because you were fired?"

"Oh," she said, "I hadn't been fired yet. Supposedly, I got fired because I was in Terminal 25. Your links get shut down there. My boss tried to contact me to send me to the Paloma crime scene. When I didn't answer, he sent me a termination message. He was just waiting for an excuse, and I gave him one. They haven't liked me at InterDome since I took on Security Chief DeRicci."

And lost. Nyquist remembered that series of reports. He watched them later, after the crisis ended, and then saw the vindication of De-Ricci which had come from the governor-general. He hadn't thought of those reports at all when he came here. If he had, he might have approached this interview differently. Ki Bowles had a nasty side, one that didn't seem to mind destroying other lives.

Maybe it was a form of poetic justice that someone had just destroyed hers.

Nyquist didn't say anything about the DeRicci reports. He didn't even want to think about them—how angry they'd made him, how he'd wanted to jump to Noelle's defense, even though he had no more to say than any man would in the first stages of infatuation.

Instead, he focused on the case and made sure he thought of Ki Bowles as nothing more than a source, someone who had information that he didn't.

"I still don't understand," he said. "Why were you near Flint's ship?"

She sighed, then sipped from the mug of tea. "Because," she said, "I was thinking of my future."

He waited. He had a sense that if he pressed, she might stop, and she was just getting to the important part.

She swirled the mug, looking at the liquid as if it could tell her something. "You might think it odd, but I kinda admire Miles Flint."

Whatever Nyquist had expected her to say, it hadn't been that.

"Have you ever seen the footage of the day-care incident?" She raised her head and faced Nyquist.

"Day-care incident?" He remembered something about Flint's past and children, but the specifics never really registered.

"Flint's daughter was killed in a day-care by one of the workers. Turns out that worker killed other children—shaking them too hard—but it took a second visible death before anyone saw the pattern." Bowles continued to swirl the mug. The liquid would peek over the edge as if it were contemplating escape, and then disappear again. "That's what started Flint on his journey from computer tech to Retrieval Artist."

"Some journey," Nyquist said.

Apparently, Bowles didn't hear his sarcasm. "I think it has an ethical base. I think he tried to make things better as a police officer, then realized he couldn't enforce certain laws. So he became independent. I've talked to him. He's really firm about the way people should behave."

"Retrieval Artists break the law," Nyquist said.

"Some laws aren't just," Bowles said.

"Do you believe that?"

She shrugged. "I don't know enough about it."

"So how does this all connect to your visit to Flint's dock this morning?"

She glanced at him, the look almost coy. "I was thinking about changing my life. How I didn't like it. I've made some compromises that…"

Her voice trailed off, almost as if she realized who she was talking to.

"I almost went to Flint's office to talk to him. He's the only person I know who has changed his life so drastically, and for reasons that I'm not really clear about, but which seem noble to me."

"You think he's noble?"

Something in Nyquist's tone must have warned her away from the topic. Her expression changed. It became harsh, her eyes piercing.

He saw the fierce intelligence that had made her one of the Moon's most famous reporters.

"You think he killed his mentor, don't you?" she asked.

"Yes," he said.

"You want me to confirm that?" she asked. "Let you know that I saw him covered with blood or something?"

"I haven't asked that," Nyquist said. "I just want you to tell me what happened."

"Starting with why I was there."

He nodded.

"Which makes no sense to you." Her smile was almost wistful. "It barely makes sense to me. But I was using him as inspiration. Then he showed up. At first, I thought he was a figment of my imagination. But he was too upset. I'd never seen him like this."

"Like what?"

"As if he were coming apart from the inside out," she said. "He was barely holding himself together."

"Figuratively?" Nyquist said.

She nodded. "He was a mess, too. Usually, I never notice how he's dressed, but today his clothes were askew and covered with Moon dust. He looked like he'd been working doing hard labor or something. He was carrying a bag of something."

The tech suit. "Then what?"

"He was surprised to see me. He thought I was there to ambush him on a story. I had no idea about the story until later. He ordered me away, and I left."

"That's it?" Nyquist asked.

She swirled the mug again. "I was embarrassed. I felt like I'd been caught doing something wrong."

"Were you doing something wrong?" Nyquist asked.

She sipped, thought for a moment, then took another sip before setting the mug down. "I suppose I was. I should have been accessible. I should have been checking my links and going after stories. I should have been asking you questions this morning about what you found in Paloma's apartment."

"Do you regret that?"

She shook her head. "I don't. I liked Paloma. She was mysterious, in a good way. I always had it in the back of my mind to interview her, maybe get her take on the way the society worked. Maybe I was setting up a news story on the ways that laws could be unjust, I don't know."

He studied her for a moment. That was the second time she'd mentioned unjust laws. Was she sending him some kind of message? She didn't seem to have that kind of guile.

"What did Flint do after he told you to leave?"

"He started to go into his ship," she said, "then he realized I was still there. He told me to go again, and waited outside until I left. I don't know what he did after that."

"What did you do?"

"I went to a coffee shop, downloaded my messages, and realized I'd lost my job."

"Did you wait for Flint so that you could talk to him?"

Her smile was rueful. "He would never consider talking to me. I'd hurt a friend of his. He thinks I'm some kind of evil incarnate."

"Are you?" Nyquist asked, mostly because he couldn't help himself. He had that opinion of her as well, and her candor was surprising him.

"Evil?" She gave a small laugh. "Just careless, I think. And a little stupid. Maybe too arrogant, although that's taken a hit today."

Nyquist let that ride for a moment. When it became clear that Bowles wasn't going to say anything else, he asked, "Did you see Flint later?"

"I came home," she said. "They threw me out of InterDome. They sent my stuff here. I've been in this lovely apartment—"

And it was her turn to use sarcasm now.

"—since I left the port."

"Do you think Flint was capable of killing Paloma?" Nyquist asked, mostly because the question was routine. He'd ask any witness that of any suspect.

"No," Bowles said with incredible firmness. "He's got a moral streak that's deeper than any I've ever seen. I doubt he could kill anyone."

Nyquist frowned. He'd never had that sense of Flint. But then, he'd never realized that hard-bitten reporters could have crushes—and not see those crushes for what they were.

"You contact me if you think of anything else," he said.

She nodded, then let out one of those dry laughs again. "Normally, I'd bargain with you," she said. "I'd tell you to let me know if the story got more interesting. But I can't now."

"What're you going to do?" he asked, because he was curious.

"I'm not sure yet." She was clearly lying. She made direct eye contact when she lied, unlike most people, who looked away. She looked away when she revealed herself.

Why lie about her future?

"You know, if you're still a reporter or hoping to do the story of the century and you use anything from this interview—"

"I'm within my legal rights," she said. "I'm a participant. We haven't had any confidential discussions here."

But the statement seemed rote. Her heart wasn't in it, and neither was his. She didn't have more to tell him, and the security vids backed that up.

"Still," he said.

She laughed, and this time, the sound was sad.

"Don't worry, detective," she said. "No one wants to hear what I have to say anymore."

But the self-pity didn't seem like a natural fit for her. He reflected on that as he left the apartment. She was doing something, and it had something to do with Flint.

Nyquist just didn't know what.

48

Van Alen's office building had grown quiet. Apparently, the sources of some of the noises were other attorneys working late. Or maybe cleaning 'bots, making certain the office was tidy for the following day.

One cleaning 'bot—an upscale model with actual eyes—peeked into Van Alen's office, startling Flint. In a voice that sounded like grating Moon dust, the 'bot apologized, said it had no idea that Ms. Van Alen was holding a meeting, and quietly eased out.

Flint didn't even try to correct the little machine. Instead, he forced himself to continue reading the files on Paloma's last case as a lawyer. Buried beneath the images of the dead, beneath the legal arguments meant to hide Environmental Systems Incorporated's very real liability in all of this, was a single note: the families of the dead engineers had decided to sue ESI.

When that case got thrown out because "no sane management would send a hundred of its best people inside a dome that they knew would collapse," the families nearly gave up. Then someone inside ESI leaked a vid of the meeting with Lucianna Stuart, the one in which she established those very words as a defense.

The families tried for a new lawsuit, but the evidence got suppressed due to attorney-client privilege. The rumors started, but no one could track down the truth behind the statements that ESI had deliberately sent in its own people to die.

But the families, most of whom had seen the vid, made their own decision. If they were going to pay by losing a loved one, then the architect of that policy would pay too.

They went to one of the most efficient assassin's guilds in the known universe. The families put out a permanent death warrant on Lucianna Stuart. The assassins, part of the Bixian Government, issued a curse on everything she owned. The curse was a signal to everyone in the assassin's guild that Lucianna Stuart was a target. If any of them should find her, they should kill her and collect the very large fee.

Flint let out a small sigh. The curse that had been on the *Lost Seas*. It had come out as a quarantine in the registers, but now it finally made sense, since he could find no record of the *Lost Seas* ever going near Bixian territory.

Lucianna Stuart learned about the curse. For a reason that Flint couldn't figure out from the files, she didn't disappear. She stayed in plain sight, going so far as to legally change her name. The maneuver wasn't as silly as it sounded. Local laws weren't something that other races and other governments easily understood.

Something obvious like a legal name change kept Paloma in Armstrong's system—she still owned everything, including her part of the law firm—but she didn't collect on what she owned. She put the records in storage on the *Lost Seas* and vanished into her new identity as Paloma, independent Tracker, a woman who eventually became a Retrieval Artist.

The deception was enough to keep the Bixian assassins away from her, and to let her continue her life in Armstrong.

And to retain her ties to WSX.

Flint stood. He walked to the window and stared at the city. The windows had some kind of tint on them that made it impossible to see in. The tint also spoiled the view, although there were those in Armstrong who felt that the city had no views.

Paloma hadn't agreed with that. She had taken an apartment with a spectacular view, bought with Flint's money, because she hadn't had any money of her own.

But that had to be a lie, just like everything else had been. She had to have been accruing funds, any profits the firm had made.

He'd have to trace that money, as well. She probably had it paid to some escrow account somewhere, under the name Lucianna Stuart, and she probably hadn't touched the funds for fear of the very thing that had happened to her this morning.

He felt an odd mix of pity and revulsion. She had let so many people die, and she hadn't cared. All she had done was protect herself, ESI, and her law firm.

Nothing more.

And he had studied with her. Let her tell him things about ethics and the way that Retrieval Artists should behave.

Had she been laughing at him the entire time? Had she seen him as a dumb little puppet who hung onto her every word?

If that was the case, why had she trusted him with all of this?

He had no answers. So he went back to the files because he could do nothing else. And as he passed the section about the curse, he froze.

He hadn't heard of the Bixians before today. He had no idea how they killed. Some species used ritual killings so that the act could be traced back to them. The Disty had a distinctive, and messy, method of retribution called a Vengeance Killing.

Perhaps the Bixians had the same thing.

He tapped into the computer on the desk next to the one he was using. Van Alen hadn't given him permission to use any other system, but she wasn't here. He'd leave tracks, so that she would know he never touched confidential files.

Instead, he had the elaborate network system she paid extra for search for information on Bixian assassinations. He particularly had the system look for things the Bixian murders had in common.

He was sure he would find them. And he had a hunch he'd recognize them from the crime scene he'd been to that morning.

The scene of Paloma's death.

49

NYQUIST'S OFFICE LOOKED LESS WELCOMING THAN IT HAD AN HOUR ago. The light from the screen on his desk illuminated the darkness, glowing upward, making the entire place seem eerie. He had shut off the main lights when he left to interview Bowles, but he had kept the computer screen up because he knew he'd be back to further examine the security vid.

He wasn't sure it would tell him much.

The interior lights slowly rose as he stepped into the office. He shoved the door closed, not wanting any interruptions. He needed to do more research, and he needed to do some thinking.

He wasn't getting anywhere by this scattered approach.

He had just settled at his desk, reviewing the port's security vid from the moment Bowles left, when someone knocked on his door.

"What?" he said in a tone designed to discourage anyone from ever knocking again.

Noelle DeRicci peeked her head around the door. She grinned at him. "Thought you wouldn't see me again tonight, didn't you?"

He blinked, wondering if he was having a flashback. Their dinner had seemed like it had taken place days ago.

"Shouldn't you be at home, relaxing?" he asked, hoping that he didn't sound too harsh.

She slipped inside, apparently taking his words as an invitation to enter. She carried a bag that smelled faintly of bread. His stomach rumbled. To think he'd believed he'd never be able to eat again. He barely made it a few hours after the explosion before his traitorous stomach developed a mind of its own.

"You looked a bit frazzled earlier," she said. "I thought I'd bring a midnight snack."

"You're too kind," he said.

She pulled two cups from the bag. The rich aroma of expensive coffee filled the room, and he felt a shiver of pleasure go through him. How had she known that he needed real coffee right now?

"I'm not kind," she said. "I have some news for you that I thought I'd deliver in person before I go home and relax."

She said the words with enough bite that he knew she had heard his bitterness. Then she opened the bag and pulled out some croissants, and something that looked like real butter.

Late-night snack food, just like she had promised. Expensive late-night snack food. Just a little bit of heaven. Lord knew he could use it right now.

"I'm sorry if I was rude," he said. "It's been a very bad night. I should have gone home after dinner."

She smiled, setting the food on cloth napkins that also came out of the bag. She slipped two croissants toward him, then handed him a butter knife.

"You're on a case," she said. "It's a nasty one. And I'm about to give you a few answers, and create even more questions."

She was still standing, apparently waiting for an invitation to sit. He waved at her, indicating the only other chair in the room.

"What've you got?" he asked.

She told him about the Bixian Government, the assassinations, and the meaning of the curses. She explained everything the professor had told her, and when she finished, he sent a message to the techs who'd worked Paloma's apartment. He asked them to check the evidence for traces of a Bixian presence, either in the DNA, the goo that the system had initially thought was biochemical, or in the blood spatter. He also tapped his own system for information on Bixian assassinations, patterns, and methodology.

"There's more," DeRicci said. "Remember the other ships under quarantine? I found one that might interest you."

She sent an image to his link of a ship that looked like a midlevel space yacht, one built maybe three decades before. It had been top-of-the-line then, but was little more than a derelict now.

"Is this one of the quarantined ships?" he asked.

She nodded. "It's got a curse on it from the Bixian Government. The only other ship in Armstrong's port, at least that I could find, that has this curse."

He waited.

And she smiled. "It's owned by Claudius Wagner."

"What the hell did they do?" Nyquist asked. "How did they get assassins after them?"

"Good question," DeRicci said. "And I've got a better one."

"What?" he asked.

"Have you seen Claudius Wagner in the past few years?"

"I've never seen any Wagner before tonight," Nyquist said.

DeRicci shook her head. "On vids, in the news, making speeches. These lawyers aren't invisible. Justinian's all over the nets, pontificating about this or that, used as an expert here or a well-placed source there."

"But his brother isn't," Nyquist said. He knew that about Justinian.

"His brother isn't The Wagner of Wagner, Stuart, and Xendor," DeRicci said. "He's the lesser Wagner."

Nyquist blinked. "Are you saying Justinian should be a lesser Wagner?"

"Have you seen notification of Claudius's death? How come Justinian is running the firm? Did Daddy step down? And if he did, how come no one's ever reported it?"

"I suppose you've looked," Nyquist said.

"Curiosity." She picked up a croissant. "It's one of my biggest vices."

"Do you think he disappeared?" Nyquist asked.

DeRicci shrugged. "He's still getting paid. He has active accounts all over Armstrong. But curiously, no funds are ever withdrawn."

"So he's alive," Nyquist muttered. "Just missing."

"Or underground somewhere."

"Or hiding in plain sight," Nyquist said. "Like Paloma."

DeRicci raised her eyebrows. "There's no name change on file. Nothing from Claudius Wagner in years. I haven't had a chance to go back too far, but it looks like the man just stopped spending money, going to work, visiting his family, and pursuing his once-public career."

"I suppose this happened about the time the ship got cursed," Nyquist said.

DeRicci nodded.

He wanted to kiss her, but he didn't. Instead, he took one of the cups of coffee. "You don't know how much this means," he said.

She tapped the cup, apparently thinking he was referring to the food. "Believe me, I do."

But she didn't. He'd been feeling angry and alone ever since the blast. Now he felt like someone supported him. Someone was helping him, even though she didn't have to.

And it revived him, more than the information had. More than the croissant had.

"Still," he said, wishing the urge to kiss her would go so that he could think again. "Thanks."

She smiled. "You're welcome," she said. Then she leaned across the desk, kissed his cheek, waggled her fingers in a good-bye wave, and left, all before he could say anything else.

Not that he knew what to say.

He almost went after her, but he didn't.

He had a case to finish, a crime to solve, a murderer—probably her closest friend—to catch.

When it was over, she might not like Nyquist any more.

But he wouldn't worry about that now. He'd worry later, when he was done, and then, if she still liked him, if she still supported him (and she had, hadn't she, even knowing that Flint might be the culprit? She had come to Nyquist), then he would go to her office and kiss her.

Not on the cheek. But like he'd imagined—and would continue imagining all night long.

50

FLINT STUMBLED ON THE FILE NEARLY AN HOUR LATER. HE'D BEEN about to give up and take a nap on Van Alen's sofa. The sofa had been calling to him, looking more and more comfortable each time he glanced at it. He wondered if it had actually been programmed to look softer at night to encourage the late-night worker to take a much-needed rest.

He avoided the thing. He wouldn't let himself leave his desk, except to glance at the system on the desk next to him, to see what kind of information it had found. It was still trolling through files and notes and vids from all over the known universe. There had to be a lot of information on Bixian assassinations, since this machine was taking its own sweet time.

He wasn't taking any time at all. He was barely looking at the files he opened, just glancing enough to see how old they were. But he did look at subfiles.

And it was in his glance at the subfiles that he found what he'd been looking for.

An updated file, one that had last been accessed a week ago.

He opened that file only to discover that millions of subfiles existed within it. These files didn't use the WSX numbering system. Instead, they had a simpler system—a name and a date. Sometimes the name was the client's name; sometimes it was a case name. But the dates were always accurate.

Flint had the system sort the entire modern file by date, so that the most recent floated to the top. It contained dozens of Justinian Wagner's case files. They appeared to have been dumped into the file on the same date, and that file had a cryptic notation on its header—IG in place of the name.

As he scrolled through the information, Flint found the IG signature several times, but all of the cases within differed. Most of them had been handled by Justinian or a minor lawyer, and all of them involved different cases.

The files were grouped by month or year, however, and it became clear to Flint that this latter notation simply acknowledged when the files were dumped into the folders, not when they originated.

He looked at files not marked IG. They were older—five years or more—and they seemed familiar.

It took him a while to remember he'd seen ghosts of some of them in the system that he had bought from Paloma when he bought the office. At the time, he had thought Paloma had been careless when she cleaned out the office before she left.

Now he wasn't so certain.

Had she left them for him to find?

If so, why?

He frowned at the machine, then double-checked the *Lost Seas* logs. No one had accessed the ship since the curse had been placed on it, before Paloma's name change.

So she had sent files wirelessly into the vessel, hoping, apparently, that they'd go into storage and no one would find them.

She had used the *Lost Seas* as a kind of backup, and also as a secure storage site.

Flint glanced at the couch. It no longer beckoned. He wanted to see what these modern files had in common, why Paloma felt all of this was worth saving.

Justinian had acted like they were the only existing copies.

Which was plain odd. Data duplicated. Just taking it from one office to another made an extra copy. To have only a single copy of a piece of information was almost impossible.

Unless someone deliberately wiped it out.

Flint frowned at the file names scrolling in front of him.

"You could have left me a hint," he muttered.

But she hadn't. She had just left him the files.

As if that would be enough.

51

Nyquist ate the last of the croissant. His fingers were covered with buttery grease, and flakes of food had fallen down the front of his shirt, but he didn't care.

The treat had been wonderful, reviving, and the visit from DeRicci had buoyed his spirits.

He had gone back to the security vid with renewed confidence, feeling like he might have a shot at solving this thing.

He was going over the vid moment by moment, when he got a message from the techs. It was long and complicated, and as he opened it, he felt his breath catch.

The information he'd requested while DeRicci was here had come back. Mixed in the so-called biochemical goo, there was Bixian DNA. The assassins had killed Paloma, and, given the amount of Bixian biological material mixed in with her blood, she had probably managed to kill the Bixian, as well.

Which begged the question: where had the body gone?

Of course, he didn't know what a Bixian looked like, so maybe he had passed the thing and not even noticed. He used the police database to find an image of a Bixian, then had it projected across the room as a hologram.

Bixians were long and thin, like a rope or a snake, with grayish-green skin. There were no distinguishing characteristics that he could see, no fingers or eyes. He couldn't even see a mouth or any sexual organs.

He asked the system to show the mouth, and a suckerlike object protruded from the middle of the rope. Then he asked for sexual characteristics, and slices of silver appeared in a zigzag pattern along one side of the rope. The zigzags went in slightly different patterns for all five genders.

Nyquist had never understood cultures with more than three genders—if truth be told, he had trouble thinking of the nonreproductive third that so many species had as a gender at all.

He asked the system to show him other appendages—he knew better than to ask for arms or legs—and got a few mystery parts—things protruding from the center of the rope or the bottom of the rope or the top. One of those mystery parts had something labeled filaments, which apparently allowed Bixians to develop tools the way humans had when they started using their opposable thumbs.

But the system couldn't show him any eyes or any ears, even though the information on the Bixians said they had stupendous hearing and a multilevel sense of touch.

When he asked the system to show him how the assassins functioned, the holo became a blur of color. The rope-like Bixian whirled so fast that Nyquist couldn't see what it did.

Nyquist had to have the system slow down to one-one-hundredth time in order to see what had happened. Prey in the form of a human (which was as tall as the Bixian was long) stood beside the Bixian. The Bixian then started to spin. Its ropelike body, which had previously been smooth, became sharp, with scales—Nyquist didn't know what other term to use—sticking out like tiny knives. The Bixian whirled and, as it whirled, it also wrapped itself around the victim, crushing it and slicing it in the same movement.

Nyquist sped up the program, then asked for a view of the aftermath. The typical human victim of a Bixian assassination looked like Paloma—the entire body crushed as if each bone had been broken (often they were) and the skin flayed. Death happened so quickly that it looked like the victim's skin was intact because the heart had stopped. No blood flowed out of the wounds.

But Paloma had managed to kill one of the Bixians. How had she done that? These things moved too quickly for the human eye to see.

Had she had some kind of warning? He got no sense of it from the security vid, and there had been nothing on the body itself.

He kept the holo up in this office, the fake victim curled on the floor and the deadly Bixian still in attack posture with all scales extended outward. Then he went back to the report from the techs.

The techs said that Bixian assassinations were rare on the Moon and Bixians themselves almost never came here. Which was why their DNA hadn't been programmed into the security system at the apartment complex. They had been identified as biochemical goo because of the toxic makeup of their skin.

Any Bixian that traveled from one point to another should have left a slime trail, and there was none. The techs went through the interior and the exterior of the building and found nothing, leading them to believe that the Bixians had an accomplice—someone or something that had carried them into the building.

Nyquist felt his breath catch. Paloma had returned to the building with shopping bags, but those bags were never found. He peered at the holo, and asked the system to show him how small Bixians could get.

The Bixian image curled itself into a ball that looked solid. It was about the size of a human head.

Something that size could fit into one of the shopping bags.

A wounded Bixian? Who had carried it out? And why?

Nyquist leaned back. A wounded Bixian would have triggered the security alarms. When those went off and the building shut down, residents were ordered to evacuate. They had maybe three minutes to leave.

He returned to the security vid.

He'd been looking at Paloma's arrival, not at the evacuation. The vid seemed to have been tampered with for the arrival, but that might have just been some kind of blip that momentarily halted the system. If the Bixians had known that their own DNA would set off the biochemical triggers, then their slime trail would have done it. The moment they touched Paloma, their DNA would have been in the air. They knew they only had minutes to get out of the building.

They would have had a plan for this, just like they would have had a plan for a building with much less security.

He scanned the security vid, looking for the exits, looking at the evacuees.

He almost missed it. A man, at the edge of the crowd coming out of the stairwell, his body blocked by nearly a dozen panicked people. As he went through the front door, the security vids caught the edges of a bag in his right hand. Then he turned and headed across the lawn, the vid catching a full image of a bag in his left.

Nyquist backed the vid up and froze it on the partial image of the man's face.

"Gotcha," Nyquist whispered, then instructed the reconstruct program to build an image of the man's face.

52

FLINT HAD FINALLY GROWN TIRED OF COLD PIZZA. HIS STOMACH rebelled at the richness and he had to download an automatic calmer so that he wouldn't get ill. The problem was that he needed to nibble while he worked, just to stay awake. He found some real apples, clearly grown in the greenhouses outside the dome, and chewed on one while he continued searching the files.

He had no idea how late it was. He had no idea that offices could be so quiet. He figured in a law firm like this one, someone would arrive early. So far, no one had. The 'bots had cleaned the place, and now all the noises had ceased.

It was just him, the silence, and the files Paloma had left him.

He could make a few assumptions about the modern files. Many of them came from Paloma's days as a Tracker and Retrieval Artist for the firm. She copied her own files into this, with notes about things happening in the law firm.

Claudius Wagner's name was prominent in these files. She kept an eye on him and what he did. She also kept copious notes on Environmental Systems Incorporated, although she didn't have access to most of their files any longer.

Then, about four years before she retired as a Retrieval Artist, the subheadings for the files changed. That was when IG became one of the headings, and when Claudius's name stopped being so prominent.

At least, Flint assumed Claudius stopped being prominent. It was impossible to tell without going through all the files. But Justinian was the one who featured prominently in the later files, and from what Flint could tell, Justinian was as ruthless as his mother had been. Justinian often advised clients to do something which cost lives, giving the appearance of solving a problem when the problem was unsolvable.

Ironically, Claudius, whom Flint had always assumed was the megalomaniac, never quite gave advice that put humans in harm's way. He seemed to have no compunction about alien or native deaths, however, and often found ways to cover a company's complicity in native deaths on new worlds.

That was why ESI kept WSX after Lucianna Wagner became Paloma. Because Claudius saved them countless times. He was the one who advised them to expand their in-house Disappearance program, so that middle managers, opening new projects in poorly explored worlds, felt safe.

The other addition Claudius made to ESI's Disappearance Service was a lump-sum severance pay to the unfortunate employee. Unlike most Disappeareds, ESI's Disappeareds had money to go with their new identities.

Flint let out a small breath and kept searching. Finally, he gave up and looked at Bixian assassinations, just because he needed to get out of the files for a while.

What he found astonished him. Not the violence with which the Bixians killed, but the relentlessness with which they pursued their contracts.

Essentially, anyone targeted for Bixian assassination remained a target until the assassination was successful.

Nothing Paloma could have done would have ever taken the curse off her ship. She had to hide from the assassins all her life.

Flint leaned back in his chair and steepled his fingers. Why, then, had they caught up to her now? She'd been successful in avoiding them for decades. If anything, she was less visible than she had been.

And she'd had warning. The Bixians did not give warning. So someone had tipped her off. But who?

The same person who had given her the files after she quit being a Retrieval Artist?

IG. Of course. IG stood for her other son, Ignatius. The first Wagner of Wagner, Stuart, and Xendor whom Flint had met.

Flint hadn't been impressed. Ignatius, the one who'd tried to hire him a few years ago. When Flint had told Paloma, she hadn't mentioned that Ignatius was her son. Instead, she'd said, *He was never the brightest Wagner. But that should mean nothing. Most of the Wagners are geniuses, especially with multicultural law. Ignatius is merely brilliant.*

Back then, Flint remembered, there had been some kind of power struggle at WSX, and Ignatius hadn't been pleased with the way the firm was going.

The firm, under the leadership of his brother, Justinian.

Claudius no longer seemed to have a hand in anything.

Had he disappeared as well?

Flint found no evidence of that, but that didn't mean anything. There was so much evidence of other crimes, of horrible, nasty cover-ups, that he felt like he was drowning in information.

He needed a focus.

He needed to start with the very last file added to the cache in the *Lost Seas*. He would read that file all the way through and see if it held any clues.

Then he would watch Paloma's holo will again, and see if she made a reference to that old file, something he might understand now.

He wasn't sure what else to do.

53

IT DIDN'T TAKE NYQUIST LONG TO FIND OUT THE IDENTITY OF THE man who had carried the Bixian assassin out of Paloma's building. He was Ken McKinnon, a small-time criminal who had a long list of arrests and few convictions. Often he performed jobs like the one he had done for the assassins, carrying a bag, opening a door, driving an aircar.

He was usually so far removed from the crime that pinning anything on him was difficult. Even this one would be hard to prove. He could say that he found the bags in the elevator or near the stairs and decided to take them out of the building.

At worse, he'd be convicted of petty theft, and that was only if the owner of the bags had brought charges. She wouldn't, of course, since she was dead.

Nyquist got up, poured himself more coffee from the communal pot in the hallway—the good stuff that DeRicci had brought was long since gone—and returned to his office. The exhaustion he had felt earlier had vanished. He wasn't sure if he had gotten his second wind or if he had simply gone beyond exhaustion. All he knew was that he felt good for the first time in hours.

Maybe that was because the pieces were falling into place.

Not that he was happy with all the pieces. When he had discovered that McKinnon was his mystery man, Nyquist also learned that McKinnon's file had been accessed that afternoon.

Seemed that the street cops had been called to a loud and violent altercation near McKinnon's apartment. They arrived to find the walls spattered with blood, some biochemical goo on the ground, and McKinnon propped up against the wall, his bones shattered, two bags crumpled at his side.

The biochemical goo turned out to be some kind of trail, and it led out of the building. The techs had traced it to the street, but didn't know what it was.

Nyquist had the computer compare the information the McKinnon techs had picked up on the goo with the information his techs had brought back: the substance was the same.

The Bixian assassins had killed McKinnon, then slithered to the street where, presumably, they had some kind of vehicle waiting.

Nyquist would never know for sure, since McKinnon's building had no security systems. McKinnon's links had failed the moment the Bixians had touched him, and, from what little the techs had gathered, the Bixians had touched him through the bags. He had already deleted any reference in his own links as to what he had done that morning; apparently, the Bixians had waited until he completed that task before taking him out.

This had all happened twelve hours earlier. Nyquist sent street cops and Space Traffic after any Bixians in Armstrong (none were registered, which was not a surprise), but he had no hope they'd be found. They had probably caught the first shuttle off the Moon, or taken their own vehicle, whatever that was, out of the port. He would have Space Traffic trace this, but he doubted they'd find much.

The assassins were gone, and the man who had assisted them dead. Someone had to have hired them, though, and for a specific reason.

Nyquist started a search of alien legal databases to see if there was any precedent for getting the Bixian assassins' guild to admit who had paid them to put a curse on someone.

Paloma's curse had existed for a long time, but the Bixians had only caught up with her recently. Maybe if Nyquist figured out why, he would know who was behind the killings.

He reached for more coffee when a message pinged through his links. He got a recorded image of one of the techs, telling him that the bomb placed in the *Dove* had been set months ago by Paloma herself. The bomb had a fail-safe protecting two people from harm; one was Paloma and the other was Miles Flint. Anyone who entered the ship without Paloma or Flint beside them would die.

He shuddered, the explosion as real to him as if it had happened moments ago. He wiped at his face, surprised to find it smooth and not coated with blood.

He made himself take a deep breath. Obviously, Flint had nothing to do with the bombing. He probably hadn't even known the bomb existed.

Assassins killing Paloma, Paloma setting the bomb. Both things that Nyquist had suspected Flint of probably had nothing to do with him. Certainly the charges behind the warrant were no longer valid.

Nyquist probably should find Flint and talk with him, but finding him would prove difficult as long as there was a warrant. Nyquist sent an order through the regular links, revoking the warrant and clearing Flint of all charges. Nyquist also expunged the record, so that no one would consider Flint a criminal.

Nyquist felt a bit of relief, not just because of DeRicci and the potential conflict between him and her old partner, but also because he hadn't completely misjudged Flint. He'd trusted the man from the moment they'd met, then felt betrayed by him during the bombing.

Now maybe he could use Flint's first-rate mind and his knowledge of Paloma to help him figure out who killed her.

But first, he wanted to see the man who had first pointed the finger at Flint.

Nyquist wanted to talk to Justinian Wagner.

54

VAN ALEN HAD ARRIVED WITH BREAKFAST. SHE BROUGHT A VERITABLE feast—some kind of fake-egg dish, doctored to taste like the real thing, a cheese-and-rice dish, a fruit salad, and pastries of every type. She set the food on the conference table near the windows. She did not say hello.

Flint shut down the screen the moment she walked in, and encrypted it so that only he could open it. Then he apologized to her for the mess near the desk.

"I don't really care," she said. "I have celebration food."

"It looks like breakfast to me," Flint said.

"All right." She grinned. "It's a cross between breakfast and celebration food."

"You found out why I'm searching these files," he said.

"I found out that you are no longer under suspicion of anything. The warrant's not only been lifted, but it's been expunged. The police department sent me notification during my three-hours of shut-eye. I suspect the expunging is due to one of two things: one, the detective in charge knows he overreacted, or two, the entire department is afraid of me. I prefer to believe that it's two, but you can choose whichever option you like, so long as you don't contradict me."

Flint grinned. "I won't."

"See?" she said, sitting down. "Celebration news."

"And I've been up all night. Let me shower before I join you." Flint didn't go near the table, not yet anyway. "Trust me, you'll appreciate it."

"I trust you," she said, as Flint went into the bathroom.

He wasn't sure how he felt about the lifted warrant. It certainly made his life easier—he could work in his office now or in the *Emmeline*—but on the other hand, it might just be a ruse to get him back into the open.

On the third hand (the alien example, as DeRicci used to say), the expunging was a way to let him know that they wouldn't reissue the warrant, at least on the bombing. Maybe on Paloma's murder, but not on the bombing.

Van Alen's interruption was timely. He'd planned to shower before she arrived, but he'd gotten caught up in the work and had forgotten to look at the time. He'd read through the files, saw more work for ESI, including some kind of cryptic mention to a past lawsuit connected with the dome, and signs of confusion about this from Justinian. Flint had found no mention of Claudius at all.

The last file placed into the *Lost Seas* had contained all sorts of internal memos about keeping the ESI account.

Flint couldn't see why ESI was thinking of leaving.

He also watched the hologram again. Paloma had looked tired and, if it were possible, scared. Her apologies seemed real enough, but there was something in her gaze, something he had missed earlier—a calculation or maybe a determination, something that was directed at him, and yet beyond him, as if she expected him to do something she hadn't quite explained.

He wondered if he was too tired to know what that something was, or if he still didn't have enough information.

He also wondered if he had made up the entire look, if his interpretation was based on his new knowledge of Paloma, and not on anything that was actually there.

Flint dressed in the clothes that Van Alen had brought him the night before. The shower and the change of clothing had refreshed him. The fruit salad that Van Alen brought and those pastries—he couldn't face the egg or cheese thing—helped revive him as well.

He was just finishing the fruit when Van Alen's assistant poked her head in the door.

"May I speak to you alone?" she asked Van Alen.

Van Alen didn't even look up from her meal. She was wearing a sedate suit this morning, all black, with pants covering her long and spectacular legs. She looked even more professional than she had the day before.

"How about sending the information along a secure link?" she asked the assistant.

"I kinda wanted to see your reaction," the assistant said.

That got Van Alen's attention, and Flint's as well.

"To what?" Van Alen asked.

The assistant looked at Flint as if she wasn't sure she should speak in front of him. Apparently, she sent a message to Van Alen's link because Van Alen frowned and said, "Well, I don't know. I can't make up my mind without information. Is the person who wants to see me a client?"

"Not exactly," the assistant said.

"Does the visit concern a confidential case?"

The assistant shrugged.

"Then what is the problem?" Van Alen snapped.

"I can step out of the room," Flint said.

"And I can hold client meetings in the conference room. Prunella is being deliberately obtuse." Van Alen peered at her assistant. "Well?"

The poor woman with the unfortunate name gave Flint an apologetic glance. "It's just so odd."

"And getting odder," Van Alen snapped.

"Ignatius Wagner is here to see you."

Flint froze. Van Alen's frown deepened. "Ignatius?"

The assistant nodded. "He said this does not concern a case."

"Okay," Van Alen said.

"He also said he knows you represent Miles Flint and that's why he's here." She gave Flint a sideways glance, as if the unusual aspects of the last twenty-four hours were his fault, which, he supposed, they were.

"Well, then, I don't see what the problem is," Van Alen said.

"He said there might be a conflict of interest," the assistant said.

Van Alen rolled her eyes, then she sighed. "Give us a minute, would you?"

"You and Mr. Wagner?"

"Me and Mr. Flint," Van Alen said, waving a hand.

The assistant backed out of the room, closing the door quietly. Flint set aside the remains of his meal. He stood. "He knows I'm here."

"So?" Van Alen said. "You're not wanted by the police any longer."

"But the Wagners aren't real happy with me right now," Flint said, and he wasn't sure he wanted to deal with the younger son, not after all the files he'd looked at the night before. He wasn't sure how to handle a man who seemed to know what was going wrong with the family business and whose solution seemed to have something to do with stealing files for his mother.

"We're going to have to deal with them sometime," Van Alen said.

Flint frowned at her, then got up and went to the desks. He shut down their screens, made sure the handheld went into his pocket, and cleaned up all evidence of his late-night work session. Van Alen had the 'bots come in and take away the remaining food. She kept the coffee and the fresh-squeezed orange juice, something that had proven both too sweet and too acidic for Flint's tastes.

"All right," she said, wiping her hands on that black suit and leaving no crumbs. "You ready?"

"No," he said, even though he knew it wouldn't make any difference.

Van Alen gave him an indulgent grin, then had her assistant send in Paloma's youngest son.

Ignatius Wagner hadn't changed in the two years since Flint had last seen him. He still looked like a man who used slimness enhancers to control his weight, but overate to compensate. His fingers were manicured, like his brother's, but he didn't use enhancers that helped project his emotions, and for that Flint was relieved. If his emotions projected, the entire room would reek of sadness.

"A Wagner in my office," Van Alen said. "Such an honor."

Ignatius gave her half a smile. He didn't look like Paloma, except around the eyes. Flint had never noticed that before. Ignatius had the same birdlike look, an almost alien intensity that made him seem shrewder than he was.

"Don't play me, Maxine," he said. "May I sit?"

He didn't even look at Flint. Flint remained beside the desks, watching him, waiting to be noticed.

"Feel free," Van Alen said. "Mind if I lean?"

And without waiting for an answer, she leaned on the edge of her desk, like she had when she first talked to Flint. That, apparently, was the posture she took with potential clients who made her nervous.

"To what do we owe this visit?" she asked.

Now he glanced at Flint. "My brother has decided to hate you."

It was an interesting choice of words. Flint kicked out the chair that he'd been sitting in most of the night and eased himself onto it. "Your brother should know better than to let emotions cloud his judgment."

"You don't really know my brother, Mr. Flint," Ignatius said. "He frightens ruthless people."

The folks who frightened ruthless people were generally reckless people, but Flint didn't say that.

"Are you here for Mr. Flint or for me?" Van Alen asked.

"Both of you, if you'd believe it," Ignatius said.

Van Alen looked at Flint. "You know Mr. Flint isn't a lawyer."

Ignatius nodded. "And I also know that Mr. Flint's presence negates confidentiality. I'm hoping he'll see me as a potential client, like you will, and we won't have to deal with the legalities beyond that."

Ignatius was a lawyer, too, and a good one. Just not as good as his brother. But, Flint recalled, few people were.

"Will you be able to keep this conversation confidential, Miles?" Van Alen asked.

He wasn't sure. "You're not a client, and your brother has threatened to sue me. I'm not sure it's in my best interest to talk to you."

Ignatius gave him a small, almost rueful grin. "In the world my brother plays in, that's correct. It's not. But I'm not him. My mother trusted you. She believed you could do all the things she couldn't. I have a hunch she loved you more than she ever loved us."

"Mr. Wagner," Van Alen said, "let me remind you that so far this meeting isn't confidential."

"I know," he said again. "It's just that I need both of you."

Flint slouched even more in the chair, pretending a relaxation he didn't feel.

Ignatius looked at Flint. His round cheeks quivered as if he were holding back an emotion so great it threatened to consume him.

Van Alen sighed. "Why do you need us?"

Ignatius turned back toward her. "Because you're the only two people I know who can help me disappear."

55

THE LAW OFFICES OF WAGNER, STUART, AND XENDOR FILLED ONE OF
Armstrong's oldest buildings. But unlike most old buildings on Armstrong, this one had been kept up. It was in the center of the city—what
had once been the very edge of the dome—and it was the first building
made of Moon brick. The bricks themselves were more like blocks, huge
bits of manmade stone piled on top of each other, reinforcing the fact
that the building (and, by implication, its occupants) had great weight.

Nyquist had walked by the building hundreds of times, but he had
never gone inside. He'd actually first seen it as part of his history class
in high school. The teacher had taken everyone on a walking tour of
Armstrong to show the old landmarks.

He remembered this one, partly because the building's style mimicked
Old Earth fashion in a way that no one thought possible on the Moon, and
partly because the building had once been the City Center. Forty years
after it had been built by one of the Moon's first real estate developers to
prove that solid, permanent buildings could exist in this odd environment,
the city had taken over the building in lieu of tearing it down.

The building still had the pretension of a city office building. It occu-
pied its own block, and had matching (but smaller) buildings across the
street. The WSX building ruled the neighborhood—and it didn't look
like a benevolent despot, either. Buildings several blocks away mimicked
its Moon-brick style, though without the same kind of success.

The entire neighborhood here seemed large, pretentious, and stuffy. Nyquist couldn't imagine Flint anywhere near this place. Paloma the Retrieval Artist seemed out of place as well. But Justinian Wagner looked like a man who'd been born in this building. His façade wasn't as weighty as the building's, but it would be over time.

Nyquist splayed his fingers against the door's reader, letting it know who he was. The building attached to his links, and with a force that only government offices used, pulled his identification. He felt the pull because he was meant to. Apparently, Wagner, Stuart, and Xendor wanted its visitors to know what kind of clout it had.

The door swung open, and an android so lifelike that it looked more human than a number of the criminals Nyquist had arrested bowed to him. The android wore a black silk suit with a red ascot. Its face was modern Armstrong handsome—a solid chin, firm features, and high cheekbones.

The android's eyes, however, were off. They were a bluish-silver that seemed unnatural against the café au lait skin and black hair. The eyes had a moist look that was clearly fake—no android needed moist eyes—and a shine that didn't come from within.

"Detective," the android said in a surprisingly deep, masculine voice. The few androids Nyquist had seen—and that was very few, given how expensive and mostly useless the things were—had androgynous voices even if they had definite masculine or feminine features. "Your visit is unplanned."

The android made it sound as if Nyquist had arrived naked and unshowered. "Justinian Wagner."

The android swayed a moment. Nyquist looked past it into darkness. The front of the building had some kind of holo blocker, not allowing the entrant to see inside, even though he had gone through the main door.

The android's swaying stopped. Nyquist wondered if the swaying was some kind of design flaw or a way to let people know the android was accessing information, like a wait message on a particularly slow link.

"Mr. Wagner generally does not take visitors before 9 A.M. He also does not see anyone without an appointment. But considering the case you are working on, he will make an exception at this time."

The android's wet gaze moved toward Nyquist, as if seeing him for the first time. Those eyes had to be some kind of camera, to be used not just by the android's recording systems, but by whatever poor human slob had the job of monitoring the thing.

"Mr. Wagner's generosity knows no bounds," Nyquist said, deliberately heavy on the sarcasm.

The black wall opened very slowly, revealing little except bits of light and color.

"You have thirty minutes," the android said. "Then Mr. Wagner must insist that you leave."

"I'll take all the time that I want," Nyquist said, slipping through the open door.

"Wait!" The android followed him. "You didn't get the instructions to Mr. Wagner's office."

"Send them to my link," Nyquist said.

He really didn't want them. He wanted the chance to examine the offices. He wanted to see what the wealthiest law firm on the Moon looked like.

A map superimposed itself over his left eye, with specific instructions in a multitude of languages as well as little footprints along route, showing him where to go. Another image, larger than the map, appeared, demanding that he choose a language before he continued.

He tried to avoid doing anything, but the system wouldn't let him. He also couldn't walk more than a meter without an alarm going off in his head.

Normally, he would have ignored it all and simply blundered through it, but he'd had enough of invasive noises in the past twenty-four hours. Even though his own private systems had repaired the damage to his hearing, it was still on shaky grounds. Too much blaring sound would give him a headache he didn't need.

He picked English, just to be perverse, and all the other languages disappeared. The silly footprints did not.

At least he could see. The map was a sophisticated one that used the images he saw to help him find his way.

The main floor of the building looked like a lobby, but it wasn't one. Even though there were artfully arranged chairs around rounded wood tables set off from other groupings by what looked like real plants, no one sat in those chairs. A desk toward the back, which would have had a receptionist two decades before, stood empty except for another android, this one with female features and breasts larger than necessary.

Near some of the plants, humans in business suits sat at single-chair desk units, bent over screens or holding clear screens in their hands. The little feet on the map sent him around those desks—presumably, the average visitor didn't even see them—but Nyquist misstepped, ignoring the warning signs that flashed in front of his left eye, and nodded as he passed those desk-chair combos.

People cursed as he went by. A few of them clutched their clear screens to their chests, as if to hide what was on them, even though the clear screens had gone dark. A few others glared at him, and one woman shook her head, a half smile on her face. She understood what he was doing—disrupting the work, examining the office—and a part of her clearly approved.

When Nyquist reached the far end of the floor, however, he had no choice but to follow the map. None of the elevators led to Wagner's office. Only a special elevator, with a special passkey, would take him there.

He walked past a row of shabbily dressed men, all seated in wooden chairs, as if waiting for someone to notice them, and headed toward the elevator. One of the men reached for him, then grimaced, as something—probably internal—stopped him.

Nyquist peered at the man with his right eye, then compared the image he got to recent criminal database downloads. The man wasn't on any of them, but he did match the image of a Tracker who was in trouble with the police department in Glenn Station for asking for triple fee after a particularly tough recovery of a dangerous Disappeared.

Nyquist shook his head to show his disgust. The only Tracker who had enough funds to hire a place like WSX for his defense probably had overcharged all of his clients.

The elevator that took him to Wagner's office was more of a lift. When the gilded doors slid open, they revealed a mirrored platform. As he stepped on the mirror, his map vanished. He was no longer privy to the layout of the office.

The platform first took him sideways, down a corridor that he hadn't seen on the map before it vanished. Then he realized he was on a slight incline. By the time he reached the wide-open doorway that led him into Wagner's office, he had no idea how far up he had traveled, although he still had a sense of how far he had gone horizontally.

Unless he missed his guess, he was in the exact center of the block that the building stood on. And unless architects had changed over the centuries, he was probably on the middle floor, as well, in the exact center of the building itself.

The open doors led to a cone-shaped reception area that was filled with light from the dome. Nyquist glanced up, just like he was supposed to, and saw the dome glittering above him. In this part of the city, the dome had been rebuilt. The material above him was so see-through that the dome looked touchable.

He finally understood why Paloma had wanted an apartment attached to the dome, and he wondered if this office had initially been hers.

A distracted woman—he glanced at her eyes, and sure enough, she was as human as anyone working in this place could be—reached his side.

"Happy to see you, Detective," she said in a harried tone. "Mr. Wagner only has about thirty minutes—"

"So I heard."

"—so I'm afraid I'll have to hurry you through the preliminaries."

Preliminaries included a body scan, which revealed the two legal weapons he carried as a part of his police duties. No one removed the weapons, just recorded their make, model number, and the fact that the laser pistols were charged. The scan also shut off many of his internal links, but not the emergency links established by the city government. Nor did this scan seem to note the personal links that he didn't have running. He always received notification when those things went through a hard external shutdown.

Preliminaries also included the rules of the office—"Any word spoken in Mr. Wagner's office is by law confidential," the woman said as she imparted the misinformation with complete sincerity—and the best way to exit the building, which wasn't the way he came.

Once he'd gone through all that, he was allowed to step into Wagner's inner sanctum.

It was as impressive as Nyquist would have imagined, and he wondered how much of it was for show. He had no idea how someone could work in a place that seemed to be composed mostly of light. Light flowed from the modified skylight that opened to the dome, and fake sunlight flowed up from the floor. A mini filter, also composed of a light-like substance—something he could walk through but also see—made sure the light didn't glare.

The filter around Wagner's desk had some red tones, for warmth, and some blue tones, probably to impart a sense of intellectualism.

Wagner's enhancements, which had looked so fake in the detective headquarters, seemed natural here. They seemed to absorb the light and make it part of Wagner. He looked taller than he was, and the glow gave him an importance that he probably had nowhere else.

Nyquist would wager that Wagner insisted on having settlement conferences here, where the other attorneys were not just at a physical disadvantage because of the building's obvious impressiveness, but they were at an emotional one, too.

This place was Wagner's stage, and he used it to great advantage.

Wagner left his desk, which was made of some kind of blond substance that looked like wood (for all Nyquist knew, it was wood) that both took in and enhanced the light, and extended his manicured hand.

Nyquist suppressed the shudder that he felt coming on as he stared at that hand, remembering how moist and manipulative it had felt when he first touched it. He shook it and the sensation was just as uncomfortable as it had been before. He was proud of himself for not grimacing.

"To what do I owe this honor?" That was the second time someone had used the word *honor* to describe this visit, and instead of flattering Nyquist, it put him on edge.

"I need to talk with you about your family," Nyquist said.

"You have information on the will?" Wagner asked.

"I've got some," Nyquist lied. "But most of it is being looked at by our forensic information team."

Wagner winced. "From the *Dove*, I assume."

Nyquist nodded, lying again.

"You haven't gotten anything from the *Lost Seas*? Flint used some kind of legal trick to take all of my mother's information and—"

"That's between you and Flint," Nyquist said.

"Well." Wagner smiled. The look was still too oily for Nyquist's tastes. "At least we have the warrant now. Since he's a criminal, he won't have a lot of standing in court."

Nyquist didn't mention that the warrant had been canceled and that Flint was, for all intents and purposes, cleared. He wanted Wagner to cooperate. "I actually came to talk with you about your family."

Wagner pointedly looked at the door. "I told you all you need to know last night."

"You told me a lot," Nyquist said, doing his best to suck up. Sucking up wasn't his natural tendency. He was bad at it, and even worse when he tried hard. So he had to pretend that he liked this guy. Which he most decidedly did not. "But we've run across a few things in our investigation—"

"I'm sure my brother can deal with anything new that you might have," Wagner said. "I'll page Ignatius. He'd be able to give you the family history and how we believe Miles Flint insinuated himself into our mother's lives."

"You did a fine job of that last night," Nyquist said. "What I really need to know is how come your mother's ship the *Lost Seas* and your father's space yacht *Xendor's Folly* have both been cursed by the Bixian Government."

Wagner gave him such a look of surprise that Nyquist wished he had pressed the photochip on his hand. No one ever blindsided Wagner, apparently, and yet Nyquist had.

"Your mother legally changed her name shortly thereafter," Nyquist said. "It's a trick some people use instead of disappearing, particularly when they're dealing with aliens who don't understand our laws."

Wagner's face had frozen, almost as if he couldn't decide which emotion to assign it.

"As for your father, I can't find any record of him at all after the Bixian Government cursed *Xendor's Folly*. Who is Xendor, by the way?"

Wagner waved a hand in dismissal. "He was only part of the firm in the beginning. His heirs, who live off-Moon, get a small share of the profits."

Nyquist shivered at the word *profits*. He knew law offices made money; he even knew some of them got spectacularly rich, but he never really thought of them as profit-making machines, like most other businesses.

"*Xendor's Folly* is an interesting name for a ship," Nyquist said.

"My father is an interesting man," Wagner said, and Nyquist noted the present tense. Good. Old Man Wagner was still alive. Nyquist just had to find him.

"Did your father disappear?" Nyquist asked.

Wagner laughed. "Wagners can't disappear. We have too many enemies. Most of the Disappearance Services wouldn't work with us, and we couldn't trust those who did."

"Is that why your mother tried the low-rent version of disappearing?" Nyquist asked.

Wagner stiffened his shoulders, as if an insult to his mother was an insult to him. "My mother continued to work at the firm. If she really wanted to vanish, she wouldn't have done that."

"Unless she was being threatened by assassins who paid less attention to looks and legal dodges, and more attention to jobs, habits, and places of residence."

"Are you saying the Bixians do that?" Wagner asked.

"You know they do," Nyquist said. "Where's your father? He hasn't had a case in more than a decade. We have no record of him speaking to the press, going to fundraisers, or even golfing on that out-dome course he likes so much. His condo hasn't been used in a long, long time, yet he has an escrow account that all his… profits… from the firm go to. He's changed his name, just like Paloma did, hasn't he?"

Wagner finally decided on an emotion. It was disgust. He walked back to his desk. The lighting in the room seemed to have notched down a bit. Maybe the lights were set to respond to whatever fake emotion he generated.

"My parents had a case that I can't access," Wagner said. "It was before my time. The files are missing. I'm pretty sure your Mr. Flint has them. Which is illegal, by the way."

"How would he get them?" Nyquist asked.

"He took them last night from the *Lost Seas*. If you people had acted quicker on that warrant of yours, my firm's files would be back in my hands."

Interesting, Nyquist thought. But he didn't say anything. "This case got them in trouble?"

"It was my mother's. We were told that was why she had to stay away from us. Because someone wanted to kill her and would find her if she came near us."

Wagner spoke with such sarcasm that it almost sounded real. Maybe he *was* bitter about this.

"And your father?" Nyquist asked.

"Wasn't involved, so far as I can tell, since I haven't seen the files." Wagner splayed his hands across the surface of his desk. Nyquist wondered if that was a command to record or an instruction for someone else to listen in. It didn't seem like a smooth enough movement to be a habit.

"But he disappeared too."

"It's not disappearing." Wagner took his hands off the surface, then leaned back and folded those hands over his stomach. "He's still here. Just not visible."

Maybe the movement hadn't turned anything on. Maybe it had shut things off. Maybe the staff didn't know what happened to the senior Wagner.

"One day, he calls me into his office, which was a big deal. I wasn't even a junior partner then, just a flunky lawyer with the boss's last name and a lot of potential." Once again, Wagner used sarcasm. Nyquist had an even stronger sense that Wagner was being truthful.

But Nyquist was in Wagner's office. There could be mood elevators and sincerity-altering scents filtered through the place. They weren't exactly illegal, just ill-advised.

"My father told me that he had to step away from the firm, and he didn't trust the junior partners to take it over. He was going to give me his voting shares, make me an equal partner, and then he was going to behave like Mother did. I had to swear not to say anything to anyone, not even my brother. My father claimed he would tell my brother."

"Did he?" Nyquist asked.

Wagner shrugged. "I have no idea. I saw my father only twice after that, and both times he spent downloading information into my personal systems so that I would understand how the firm worked. Even then, I ended up being the dumb man in the partners' meetings for nearly a year."

It seems like he hated that. It probably humiliated him, the man who liked to be on top of everything.

"Do you know where your father is?" Nyquist asked.

Wagner studied him for a moment. "How important is this?"

"It may mean the difference between solving your mother's murder and not," Nyquist said.

Wagner tilted his head back as if he were considering it.

"Particularly given what you just told me," Nyquist said. "That Flint has those files and your father is the only other person who knows what's in them."

"I didn't say that last," Wagner said.

"But you implied it," Nyquist said.

Wagner nodded. "You'll find my father's apartment one floor up from my mother's. My mother chose to name herself after the dove, a bird most Terrans associate with peace. My father calls himself Hawke. I assume that's to spite her."

Such a lovely relationship those two had. Nyquist shook his head slightly. "Will he talk to me?"

Wagner shrugged. "I don't know and I don't care. I think you're better served finding Flint, and getting my inheritance back to me. I can tell you what's going on then."

"Knowing what Flint is searching for will help me just as much," Nyquist said.

Wagner nodded.

"You don't have any ideas, do you?" Nyquist asked.

"I'd check Flint's finances," Wagner said. "Flint's supposed to have money, but maybe he doesn't. I can't think of any other reason for the man to be so eager to get Mother's things."

"You think he'd blackmail you?"

"Mother always threatened to do that," Wagner said, "If the firm ever revealed who and where she was."

"So there's something important in those files," Nyquist said.

"Why else would she go to the trouble of hiding them?" Wagner asked.

To keep them away from you, Nyquist thought, but made sure those words never came out of his mouth. "Did she take those files after you became head of the firm?"

Wagner's lips thinned, then he shook his head. "Why?"

"It just seems odd to me," Nyquist said. "You claim your father knew what was in them. There's no real reason to hide the files, then, is there?"

"She needed leverage against the firm," Wagner said.

"Yet she continued to work here."

"My mother was a duplicitous, difficult woman who clearly did not care for niceties like loyalty and confidentiality. I'm sure she planned to divulge the contents of those files to outsiders if the firm betrayed her in any way," Wagner said.

"Outsiders," Nyquist said. "Like the press?"

Wagner shrugged, and this time it looked deliberate. "I have no idea. I rarely spoke to her, I never saw the files, and the genesis of all this happened when I was a child."

"And your father never told you."

"Why should he?" Wagner snapped.

"Because he gave you control over his firm," Nyquist said. "You say that Xendor's no longer involved. Neither was your mother. Your father was the only senior partner left, right?"

"So?" Wagner asked.

"If he wanted the firm to survive, wouldn't he have told you how to defend it?" Nyquist asked.

Wagner's eyes narrowed. They glinted with a malevolence that made Nyquist want to step backward, away from this man.

"Why don't you ask him?" Wagner said.

"Looks like I'll have to," Nyquist said. "I'm going to have to tell him how I found him."

Wagner's smile was cruel. "I think he'll figure that one out on his own."

56

"Disappear?" Van Alen said. "A thousand different Disappearance Services all over the known universe can help you disappear."

Ignatius Wagner crossed his arms. Van Alen hadn't moved from the front of her desk, but her body had tensed. Flint wondered if Ignatius had noted the change. The man didn't seem observant, but sometimes people who didn't seem to be watching saw the most.

Ignatius's entire body was shaking. Lightly, so that it was barely visible. His hands quivered and he kept them clasped together, finally pinning them between his knees so that they wouldn't inspire the rest of his body to shake.

"Obviously, I know about Disappearance Services," Ignatius said, "since my family's firm has tried to destroy a few of them."

"And succeeded, I might add," Van Alen said.

"All the while, protecting a few Disappeareds," Flint added, thinking of one in particular who had caused deaths all over the Moon the year he met Ignatius.

"We're not very consistent," Ignatius said. "Just ruthless."

Flint studied him. This kind of nervousness would be hard to fake.

"Well," Van Alen said, "if you're familiar with the services, why not use one?"

"You think one of them would help a Wagner?" Ignatius asked. "They'd probably think it was a setup."

"Isn't it?" Van Alen asked.

Ignatius didn't answer.

Flint leaned forward and draped his hands over the edges of his knees in a relaxed version of Ignatius's posture. The movement was deliberate, a subtle way to let Ignatius know that Flint had noted the shaking. "Why not get Environmental Systems Incorporated to let you use their Disappearance Service?"

Ignatius literally jumped. Flint had never seen anyone do that before. Ignatius turned toward Flint, almost as if he were going to caution him, then thought the better of it.

"ESI is my brother's account," Ignatius said.

Van Alen didn't understand what Flint was getting at, obviously, since she hadn't been privy to the files, but she was quick enough to realize something was going on.

"If we decide to help you," she said, "what would our role be?"

"It's not just me," Ignatius said. "It's my wife and my sons, too. We have to get out of here. I can't approach a service myself, not one that has any connection to the firm, and the others are just going to suspect me. I was hoping you could go to them in confidence, get all the legal documents, transfer the funds—all acting as my lawyer, and then help me get to wherever it is they take you when you do disappear."

Flint leaned even farther forward, as if by doing so he could see inside Ignatius's mind.

"I can do some of that," Van Alen said. "But they'd want to meet with you. That's how it's done."

"I know," Ignatius said. "Could we do it in your office? As a confidential thing?"

Van Alen looked at Flint. He shrugged. Ignatius seemed sincere, but there was no way to tell. Everything about this moment seemed off-kilter.

"Why do you need to disappear?" Flint asked.

"You asked about ESI," Ignatius said. "You've read the files."

"I know a few things," Flint said, "mostly about why your mother changed her name decades ago. I saw nothing pertaining to you."

That last was a lie. The recent files had all come from Ignatius, but Flint had yet to determine what they meant and why Ignatius had given them to her.

"Don't you see?" Ignatius said. "Mom's dead."

Flint nodded. "She was killed by Bixian assassins. I figured that much out."

Van Alen looked at him sharply.

"Someone had to hire them," Flint said. "I know who that was, too, not that it matters. All of this was decades ago."

"But they never found her. They didn't know how to go through the legal walls she set up. The assassins stake their targets, the buildings, the life patterns, but they're not detectives. They don't know how to go into a culture and figure it out the way Retrieval Artists and Trackers can."

Ignatius sounded almost desperate. He clasped his hands tighter, as if they held him together.

"I still am not sure what you're driving at," Flint said.

"Oh for God's sake," Ignatius said. "Someone had to tell those bastards where Mother was."

"I'm sure a lot of people knew," Flint said.

"But only a few knew about the Bixian assassins, the curse, and Mother," Ignatius said. "And only one had a reason to send them after her."

Van Alen was frowning. "I'm even more lost than Miles," she said. "Who had reason to kill your mother?"

Ignatius ran a hand over his mouth. He was shaking so badly that he looked like he would come apart.

"Justinian," he whispered. "Justinian told those bastards where Mom was. And I know it's only a matter of time before he comes after me."

57

PALOMA'S BUILDING LOOKED DIFFERENT THAN IT HAD THE DAY OF her murder. People were scattered all over the main lobby, talking or heading either to the elevators or out of the building. The black floor and the spectacular view didn't dominate quite as much when the building was full as they had when it was empty.

Nyquist did find himself looking for people trailing 'bots with shopping bags, like Paloma had done the day she died. Had she known those things could be used to secret her murderers away? Had the escape route—the bags—been one of opportunity, which prevented McKinnon from searching her apartment for something more suitable?

Nyquist would have to check. But not yet. First, he wanted to meet Claudius Wagner.

Nyquist didn't take the elevators. They still had an association with Paloma's murder. Instead, he took the stairs all the way to the ninth floor. He requested that the building not announce him or his purpose for coming here, and he made that request official, so building protocol couldn't override him.

As he left the stairwell, he was struck at how different this floor was from Paloma's. The black marble that seemed ubiquitous downstairs had been replaced here with Moon-made tile. The tile was set in a pattern he'd seen in adobe buildings in Tycho Crater, and never associated with Armstrong.

Maybe Paloma hadn't been the one who had placed the WSX building in the old City Center. Maybe it had been Claudius Wagner.

The only door besides the elevators and the stairwell had a carved moon pattern on its brown surface. Nyquist reached up to knock, and the door knocked for him—the little moon rose and made a clacking sound that simulated the sound of fists rapping on permaplastic.

"State your business." The voice was male, deep, and sounded annoyed.

"Detective Bartholomew Nyquist." Nyquist placed his hand up so that the door could read his standard identification from his palm chip. "I'm here about the murder of a woman downstairs. She died yesterday. Her name was Paloma."

"Proceed," the voice said.

"Regulations state that all official interviews must be conducted face-to-face."

"Why is this official?" the voice asked.

"Because I'm interviewing everyone in the building," Nyquist said.

"I hadn't heard that," the voice responded.

"We've just gotten to this phase," Nyquist said.

"And you're starting here?" the voice asked.

"There's evidence that the killer waited on an upper floor," Nyquist said. "It makes sense to start with the nearest floor above the murder site."

The door slid open, and the faint scent of incense wafted out. Nyquist stepped inside an apartment as dark as Paloma's had been light. The walls on either side contained more Moon tile, but the pattern was hard to see. Lights, recessed into the ceiling, probably brought the pattern to life, but no one had turned them on.

Nyquist rounded the corner and stepped into the living room. This apartment had no view of the dome and the Moon landscape beyond, at least from the main room. Maybe the bedrooms had it, or maybe this was one of the cheaper apartments, built to make the building "accessible" to all income levels.

A single chair dominated the main room, with screens, 'bots and high-end entertainment equipment all around that chair. Suddenly, the darkness made sense. Claudius Wagner spent most of his time in that chair, looking at imaginary landscapes, living an unreal life.

The man himself came out of the kitchen, wiping his hand on a towel. He was tall, with a mane of silver hair and a nose that suggested another explanation for the last name he'd adopted.

"Charles Hawke," he said, extending his hand.

Nyquist stared at it for a moment, then took it. "Bartholomew Nyquist."

"I was sorry to hear about the murder," Claudius said.

"Let's not play games, Mr. Wagner," Nyquist said. "Your son told me where you were."

Claudius let his hand drop. He studied Nyquist for a moment. Claudius's face had none of the enhanced emotionality of his son's. Instead, he seemed like an athletic man content to live alone, enjoying his entertainments and solitude.

He seemed to consider whether to continue lying about who he was. Then he shook his head slightly.

"Ignatius talked to you?" he said with a bit of disbelief.

"Justinian."

Claudius let out a small breath, then turned away. He walked back into the kitchen. Nyquist followed and was surprised to find an elaborate room filled with all the best cooking equipment and some old-fashioned features, like a presettlement camp stove mounted against the wall.

"What does he want?" Claudius asked, his back to Nyquist.

"Justinian? I'm not sure," Nyquist said. "*I* want to know why your ship *Xendor's Folly* was cursed by the Bixian Government, and why you've changed your name."

Claudius pressed a button on the far wall, and watched as an orange liquid mixed with ice filled a nearby glass. His hand shook as he brought the glass to his lips. "Someone told the Bixians where to find my wife."

The word choice interested Nyquist. "I never knew you and Paloma married."

Claudius's lips twisted, then he shrugged. "We had our own arrangement."

"But not a legal one," Nyquist said.

"She wouldn't," Claudius said. "She didn't want to tie her fortunes to mine."

"Even though you ran a business together."

Claudius turned, leaned against the counter, and tilted his head slightly. His expression had gone flat. Maybe he had been as good an attorney as his son, after all.

"You've done your homework, haven't you?" Claudius said.

Nyquist waited. He thought it interesting that Claudius stopped here. "I thought you and Paloma hated each other."

Claudius laughed. "You don't handle divorce cases, do you?"

"Only street cops do, and usually before anyone has spoken to a lawyer."

Claudius nodded. "Well, the passion that starts the relationship can sometimes turn dark. People are unwilling to let go of each other, so they hang on and use anger to substitute for all that raw sexuality."

Nyquist didn't move. Claudius was revealing a lot, and Nyquist had to think that was on purpose. This man didn't seem like someone who did anything by accident.

"So you two were angry at each other," Nyquist said.

"We had quite a feud." Claudius took that glass and had another sip, then poured the rest of the beverage into a recycler. "We would make up occasionally. The boys don't know that."

Nyquist would never think of Justinian as a boy. "You'd made up before she died."

Claudius nodded. "That's why she moved here after she got all that money. It was an easy way to see each other."

And it would be easy to confirm, with vid records from the building and eyewitness accounts from other neighbors. Claudius had to know that as well.

"Your sons didn't know that, either?"

"My sons thought my wife was moving here to keep an eye on me."

"Is that true as well?"

Claudius's smile was sad. He set the glass near the recycler, and then walked to the only visible chair.

"Lucianna didn't need to keep an eye on me," he said. "She knew what I was up to. She helped me years ago."

"When you did your modified disappearance."

Claudius nodded. He pushed a few mechanical items—games? Nyquist wasn't close enough to tell—aside and sat down heavily, like a man who knew extreme exhaustion.

That was the sense Nyquist was getting. This man had a bland expression that covered deep emotion. He wasn't more emotional than his son, nor was he any less tricky. But he was mourning Paloma's death.

"You still haven't answered my question," Nyquist said. "Why did you and your wife have to vanish?"

Claudius sighed. "I can't answer you, detective. I swore an oath."

"What kind?" Nyquist asked, not willing to make any assumptions.

"Client confidentiality. I will tell you that we had the same client—I took over the account when she had to leave—and believe me, I was surprised at what I found. Then a few things happened, some information leaked, old cases resurfaced, old angers did, as well, and suddenly I found myself subjected to the same treatment as Lucianna. We figured the name changes and the habit changes would be enough. And you know, they were, until yesterday."

"What do you think changed?" Nyquist asked.

"I think someone offered my son the same deal I got offered." Claudius spoke with great bitterness.

"What would that be?"

Claudius shook his head. "I can't go into detail."

"Be vague."

"This client is a long-term client, and this case is one of many. Lucianna kept most of her records and she didn't let me see the files, although she told me what was in them when I asked that year before I moved here."

Nyquist nodded. He hoped he'd be able to pull the details out later.

"The client took some of Lucianna's advice, but not all of it. The circumstances happened again, in a different environment, but with the same results, and the client acted in the same way. Only the new case brought the old one up again, and stirred up anger...." he paused. "This can't be making sense to you."

"I'll figure it out," Nyquist said.

"We managed to get some of it calmed, using extralegal means, very similar to what we had done before. And the result was the same as the ones before," Claudius said. "The hurt party hired the Bixians at the advice of the previous hurt party."

"And that's how you ended up here," Nyquist said.

Claudius nodded. "It's not so bad, really. I can see my children. I can live my life. I find I don't miss the firm at all."

But the implication hung between them. He would miss Paloma.

"You said you were offered a deal," Nyquist said.

"Yeah." Claudius pressed the armrest on the chair and it reclined. Even though the position was more relaxed, he seemed less so. His body was too taut to be look comfortable.

"What was it?"

"That I give up the client's files. Say that I advised them to take those extralegal measures. Admit my and the firm's culpability—not in public, mind you, just to the families—and pay a steep fine."

"Steep?"

"More money than you can earn in a lifetime, Detective. More money than everyone on your force can."

"So you disappeared rather than pay out money."

"First of all," Claudius said, putting his hands behind his head, "I haven't completely disappeared. Secondly, I was supposed to admit to both cases. I couldn't. I only knew the one, and what little I knew of the other came from a discussion with my wife. I'd have to allocute to the details of both cases, and I couldn't, not without the files—"

"Which your wife had," Nyquist said.

"Which she wouldn't relinquish," Claudius said. "She thought the allocution a very bad idea, even if it were supposedly confidential."

"She didn't think it would be?" Nyquist said.

"She said we had an obligation to our client," Claudius said. "She was right about that."

"But?"

Claudius closed his eyes. He looked even tenser than before.

"Mr. Wagner?"

He sighed, touched the armrest again, and let the chair come back to an upright position. Then he stood and walked to the kitchen again. He stopped for a moment, then came back into the main room. It was a slow-motion version of pacing, and Nyquist suspected Wagner had been doing it since he heard of Paloma's murder.

"We'd have to admit guilt," Claudius said. "*I* would have had to admit guilt. And culpability in a bunch of—"

He stopped just in time, which showed how upset he really was. Nyquist suspected that Claudius would never have made a slip like that if he had been thinking clearly.

"Culpability in a major crime," Claudius said. "A horrible crime, if the truth be told. And what's worse is that these bastards hadn't learned from it. They did it again. So my guilt is compounded by the fact that they should have known better."

He touched the chair, but didn't sit. Nyquist let him talk.

"Isn't it funny?" Claudius said, looking down at the chair. "I would rather have given up my life and risk a hideous death than admit that I had anything to do with those cases."

"You no longer feel that way?"

Claudius ran his hand over the top of the chair, almost as if he were caressing it. "I guess I never believed anyone would find us. I guess I never really believed we'd be called to account. And here we are."

"You said that your son received the same deal."

"Either they've done it again, which I doubt. I haven't heard news about it, and believe me, I watch. Or my son was told he could bring us in, pay the fine, and betray the client. Rumor has it that the client is looking for new attorneys. So my son had to be considering it."

"Your son was looking for a way out, one that didn't include vanishing." Nyquist guessed, hoping he was right.

Claudius nodded. "I think he was going for a half measure. I think he wanted the files. He'd hand them over, and maybe some money, and not admit anything. After all, he wasn't involved."

"But you and your wife were," Nyquist said.

"It can be argued by a good attorney that the real culprit here is my wife. There is no proof in my files that I suggested anything other than the client do exactly as my wife advised them years ago. And if I had no records of what she advised them, then all that the attorney would have to say is that I added the sentence 'Because it seemed to work the first time.' I had no liability. The firm had no liability. We'd gotten rid of the trouble-maker."

"Your wife," Nyquist said.

"By firing her, not killing her," Claudius said.

"But you didn't fire her," Nyquist said.

"It looked like we did."

"Only she'd contradict that," Nyquist said.

"She might have." His hand clenched into a fist. "My son is a good attorney."

"Meaning what?" Nyquist asked.

"Meaning," Claudius said, speaking very slowly, "it's better to have the files without the witness than the witness without the files."

"You think your son killed your wife," Nyquist said.

"I think my son covered his ass." Claudius pounded once on the seat back, then rested his fist again.

"But he didn't get the files," Nyquist said.

"He will." Claudius looked up, his gaze empty. "He's a good attorney. He'll get what he wants."

58

VAN ALEN LED FLINT OUT OF HER OFFICE. SHE SENT TWO ASSISTANTS inside to sit with Ignatius. Her excuse was that the assistants had to give him a new-client questionnaire, but that rationale fooled no one, least of all Ignatius. He knew, as well as everyone else, that Van Alen wanted to talk about him to Flint.

A few employees, scattered in the main area, seemed surprised to see Flint. Either they hadn't known he was there, or they had forgotten. The area was bathed in Dome Daylight, filtering through the windows on either side.

Van Alen pulled him into a small conference room. It had paneled walls and a small wood table in the center. Blinds covered the window here, making it seem like night again.

"Do you believe him?" she asked.

"Ignatius?" Flint sat in one of the chairs. The upholstery was thick but hard, a kind of leathery material built for looks and not comfort. "I don't know."

"We have to figure it out," she said. "Because if I help him and they use it against me somehow...."

Flint rubbed a hand over his face. He had trusted her, and so far she had come through. He thought of the files, and of Paloma's body, crumpled against the wall of her apartment. Then he thought of those experts, sent into a dome that no one could save, on Paloma's suggestion.

But Paloma had trusted him for reasons he hadn't yet understood, and he—not Justinian—was the one who had custody of all those files.

Which gave a lot of credence to Ignatius's story.

"I'd trust him," Flint said. "But only so far. I'd keep him in your office, where he can't link up to anyone, send for his family and have them come here, and then bring in whatever Disappearance Service you're going to use. I'd use the best one you know, but I'd bring in the leaders of three or four and pay all of them for their time. That way, if there's a leak from your office, no one will know which Disappearance Service helped Ignatius."

"And Justinian will have to go after all of them to get to his brother." Van Alen smiled. "I know three services that have never had a leak or a bad employee. I'll bring them all in."

"Bring five in, two that have leaks, and describe Ignatius's appearance to them. Have them prepare a false identity for him, and then have him back out. Do not include the family."

Van Alen smiled at him. "You're devious."

Flint shrugged.

"I can do you one better. I can send another client in his place. A double disappearance, if you will."

"No," Flint said. "If Ignatius is right and Justinian is willing to turn these assassins on his own family, he might send them after Ignatius's new identity. You've seen how poorly these assassins research. You could be dooming your own client."

Van Alen actually shuddered. "All right. It'll take me a while to set this up."

She got up, and waited for him to stand. Then she put her hand on the door, but didn't open it.

"Should I worry about planning someone's disappearance with a Retrieval Artist in the room?"

Flint smiled. "Some day, I'll tell you how I got all my money."

"Hmm?" She asked.

He patted her on the shoulder, surprised to find that the suit she wore was silk. "No," he said. "You have my word. I will never retrieve anyone from Ignatius's immediate family."

"I note that you didn't mention his whole family," Van Alen said.

"I reserve the right to hunt down Justinian if he decides to flee," Flint said.

"And Claudius," Van Alen said. "Don't forget him."

Flint started, surprised that he had forgotten Old Man Wagner. "And Claudius," he said, realizing what he had to do next.

59

THE SECURITY SYSTEM RANG. NYQUIST STARTED, AMAZED HE'D heard it too. Most of these systems were internally linked—only the owner of the apartment could hear the alarms.

Claudius looked surprised. He frowned at Nyquist as if the security alarm was Nyquist's fault. Claudius moved away from the chair, headed toward the door, and then stopped.

"What?" he said.

The system translated that rude question into the same who-are-you-and-what-do-you-want message that Nyquist heard.

"Building security, sir," a male voice said. "We understand you have an unexpected visitor."

Slowly, an image of the man outside the door appeared on the inside of the door. He was short and round, a bit greasy-looking to be security in such a high-end building, but Nyquist had seen worse. He had two packets of tools on either hip—a style Nyquist hadn't seen in decades. Usually, the maintenance team carried tools on their hips, and security simply had a visible weapon.

"I do have an unexpected visitor," Claudius said, giving Nyquist an odd look.

"Would you like us to remove him for you, sir?"

Nyquist shook his head. Claudius didn't seem to notice. He headed toward the door.

Nyquist grabbed his arm and made a motion to cut off all sound to the security system. Claudius pressed a chip on his forefinger, then stared at him.

"I'll leave if you have trouble with me," Nyquist said. "Just don't let someone else you don't know into your apartment."

Claudius's eyes went flat. "You think my son'll come after me?"

"I'm sorry," Nyquist said, "but you did just accuse him of killing your wife."

"She didn't raise him. I did. Justinian has a relationship with me."

That meant nothing, Nyquist knew. From the beginning of the profession, detectives looked to family members first if one of their own was murdered.

"Besides," Claudius said. "I'm no threat. I'm not a witness or a participant in any of the so-called crimes."

In theory, and only if you wanted to argue technicalities. But Nyquist didn't say that, either.

Instead, he said, "Bixian assassins killed your wife. Do you know what they look like?"

Claudius gave a quick nod.

"Then you know they could be in those pouches."

The security system rang again. "Sir?" the man outside said. "Are you all right?"

Claudius pressed his forefinger again. "Fine," he said.

"Do you need assistance, sir?"

"No," Claudius said. "Thank you."

"Our pleasure, sir."

The man moved away from the door. Nyquist and Claudius watched the displayed image until the man went into the elevator.

"See?" Claudius said. "Nothing to worry about."

"Check with the building control," Nyquist said. "See if they sent anyone."

"You're being paranoid."

"You're not being paranoid enough."

Claudius shook his head, but went to a wall panel, anyway. He moved so that Nyquist couldn't see what he was doing, but Nyquist heard the automated building response.

Then Claudius gasped. He backed away, shaking his right arm as if it were on fire.

It took Nyquist a moment to realize what was going on. Something had wrapped itself around the arm, something that had taken the color of the arm.

It was smaller than he expected, thinner, but he recognized the extended scales, like little knives slicing into Claudius's skin.

Nyquist cursed and grabbed his laser pistol. He wasn't sure what the best thing to do was. If he burned the thing on Claudius's arm, would it make the thing stronger? Weaker? Would he kill the thing?

Nyquist aimed laser pistol, remembering only at the last second that Bixian assassins worked in pairs.

60

Flint led the way back to Van Alen's office. He didn't tell her his plans. She might get angry with him, but he already knew her well enough to know that she would play along.

He opened the door. Ignatius was seated at the table where Flint and Van Alen had had their breakfast. The assistants were beside him, guarding him so that he couldn't see the confidential material, but also asking him questions that Flint, as another new client, had never been subjected to.

Ignatius stood as Flint and Van Alen entered. He gave Van Alen a watery smile. "That's quite an introductory procedure you have."

"I like to cover all bases," she said. She nodded to her assistants, who left as quickly as they had arrived.

As the door clicked shut behind them, Van Alen opened her mouth, but Flint spoke first.

"We'll help you," he said, "on one condition."

Ignatius's entire face shut down. He apparently hadn't expected any conditions—not real ones, anyway. He must have thought they were past that stage.

Van Alen, bless her, didn't even shoot Flint a glance. Instead, she waited beside him as if she had designated him to speak for her.

"Tell me where your father is."

Ignatius shook his head ever so slightly. "I don't know."

"You know," Flint said. "When I first met you, you told me that Paloma had told your father I was the most trustworthy person she had ever known."

Ignatius's mouth opened, then closed, in obvious surprise. "I told you that?"

Flint nodded. "I can even show you the record, since it was in my office, when you were trying to feed me information on the Tey case. Do you remember that?"

"I mentioned my father?" Ignatius sounded stunned.

"It must have been a slip," Flint said, "because at that point, your father hadn't been visible for years. Your mother shouldn't have had any contact with him. Yet you mentioned both of them, and they had talked about me, someone your mother theoretically should never have discussed with your father because they were estranged."

Ignatius swallowed hard. Van Alen watched with a slight smile on her face. Rather than being upset, apparently she seemed amused.

"So," Flint said, "your father is nearby and has had contact with your mother. I would guess that they aren't estranged at all, that that was just for show, just like her separation from the firm was for show."

Ignatius bit his lower lip. It was clear why he was the lesser Wagner. He had no ability hide his emotions at all.

"Tell us where your father is, and we'll help you disappear."

"Why?" Ignatius asked. "Why should I tell you?"

"You want help, don't you?" Van Alen asked.

Ignatius nodded. "But my father...I promised...why would you need to know."

"Because," Flint said harshly. "Your brother killed your mother. Does he know where your father is?"

"Oh." Ignatius put his head in his hands. "Oh, God."

Van Alen shot Flint a look of complete surprise and approval. Flint wondered what she expected out of this. The files? He would have to discuss that with her later.

Ignatius raised his head.

"All right," he said. "I'll tell you. Just get me and my wife and my kids out of here. Please."

"We will," Van Alen said in that crisply professional voice of hers. Flint had found it soothing the day before, and Ignatius seemed to find it soothing now. "Let me tell you our plan."

Flint held up a hand. "Claudius first."

"Upstairs," Ignatius said. "He lives upstairs from Mother. He calls himself Hawke. They loved each other, Mr. Flint. Whatever they did, remember that, okay?"

"You don't know what they did?" Van Alen asked.

Ignatius shook his head, that small, sad movement again. "I'm the lesser Wagner, remember, Ms. Van Alen? I really don't know much of anything."

"If that's true," Flint said, "then you're getting out just in time."

61

CLAUDIUS WASN'T SCREAMING; HE KEPT FLAILING HIS RIGHT ARM as if he could shake off the assassin. Nyquist wasn't even sure Claudius knew what he was doing—the man's face had gone gray and his eyes were glassy.

Nyquist fired the laser pistol. The shot grazed the assassin, and turned it a brilliant orange.

Now Claudius screamed. He dropped to his knees, and that was when Nyquist saw the second one, wrapped around Claudius's left foot. The things must have come in as he and Claudius dickered with the fake security man.

Nyquist shot again, and this time, the thing on Claudius's arm exploded.

Alarms went off all over the building—warning alarms, first about a shot being fired, and second announcing a biochemical contamination.

"The building will be evacuated," the androgynous voice said.

Nyquist grabbed his other laser pistol from his ankle holster and shot at the thing around Claudius's leg.

"You have five minutes to leave before all systems get shut down…."

Claudius stopped screaming. He reached for the thing on his leg, not noticing that his right hand was no longer there. He was spraying blood everywhere.

He would die in a matter of minutes if Nyquist didn't get that bleeding stopped.

"Anyone contaminated must remain inside...."

Nyquist shot a third time, but he couldn't seem to hit the damn thing. Or maybe it had some kind of shield.

Or maybe it could morph itself enough to protect against the weapon, once it knew what the weapon was.

"If your apartment does not let you out, then you have been contaminated...."

Claudius grabbed the thing with his left hand. It seemed to absorb his skin, but he looked determined, yanking and pulling and trying to force the thing off of him.

"Remain inside until HazMat teams arrive...."

Nyquist glanced into the kitchen. There had to be other weapons. This man couldn't live in supposed exile without weapons.

Could he?

"Do not worry...."

Claudius gurgled once, then fell forward. Nyquist stepped back. He was covered in blood.

"The situation is under control."

And he couldn't see the assassin. They were stuck in here together—and it wouldn't let him out alive.

62

FLINT FELT LIKE A FUGITIVE TRAVELING IN A BORROWED AIRCAR, headed toward Paloma's building. Van Alen had loaned him the car, since he wasn't sure if the warrant was off his. This car moved smoothly but wouldn't speed—damn lawyers, anyway—and he wanted to hurry.

He had to talk to Claudius about those files. Maybe the old man knew more than Ignatius had.

Flint also wanted to warn Claudius. If Ignatius felt threatened, then Claudius might be in trouble as well.

The buildings near Paloma's apartment loomed like growths coming out of the dome. This area of Armstrong felt sinister to him now.

And he knew that was because of Paloma's death.

It felt odd, heading to Paloma's apartment building, knowing she wasn't going to be there. He found it amazing that part of him knew she was dead, and another part refused to believe it. A third part was angry at her, and a fourth understood what she'd been doing.

Somewhere along the way, she'd regretted her actions. Whether it was because of the forced exile, or the lost parts of her life, or because she had some kind of ethical conversion, Flint would never know.

But she obviously learned how ruthless her son Justinian had become, and she knew he needed to be stopped. She tried to set up Flint as the person who would stop her son, but Flint never read the files she "accidentally" left in his business computer. He had too many ethics for that.

Then Flint took a long trip after his last case, and during that time, Paloma must have realized that her son had targeted her. She made the will, and she set up the bombs to protect it.

What she should have done was stop her son herself. But obviously, she hadn't had the strength to shut down her own firm. Her only other choice would have been to neutralize Justinian, and from everything Flint was beginning to understand, the only way to do that—besides destroying the firm—was to kill the man.

Paloma had done neither.

She wanted Flint to do it, and he had been gone.

He parked the aircar in the lot across the street, just as he had done the day before. Then he hurried into the elevator, and as he went down, he realized that people were streaming out of Paloma's building.

Again.

Another evacuation.

He was too late.

63

DeRicci had just finished talking to the mayor about the quarantined ships scattered throughout the port. The mayor understood the need for discretion in dealing with these ships, but he was worried; he thought there might be some kind of health hazard.

DeRicci didn't. She figured the bad stuff should have happened by now, and she told him that. He wanted some time to think—which meant he wanted to consult with someone smarter—and she let him.

That was when Popova pushed open her door.

"Paloma's building has just sent another biochemical contamination alarm," Popova said.

"Bixians?" DeRicci asked.

"I assume so, since the alarm is the same," Popova said.

"Send as many street cops as you can," DeRicci said. "Inform Armstrong's HazMat teams to get there, and have some techs go as well."

"Shouldn't we go through the mayor or the chief of police?" Popova said.

"And let those bastards get away again? Are you kidding?" DeRicci asked. "Never mind. I'll do it."

Then she sent half a dozen emergency messages through her links, giving orders.

Popova still stood by the door, watching, as if she had never seen anything like this before. Not that there was much to see. A woman using her links looked like a woman staring into space.

"What do you want?" DeRicci snapped when she was finished.

"I thought I should tell you the other thing in person," Popova said.

DeRicci waited.

"The information I have from building security is that the last person to enter the place was Detective Bartholomew Nyquist."

DeRicci's heart skittered. Damn that Popova. She was too observant. She saw how interested DeRicci was in Nyquist.

"You think he's tied to the Bixians?" DeRicci asked.

"No," Popova said. "But so far, it looks like he hasn't gotten out."

64

NYQUIST ORDERED HIS LINKS TO SHUT DOWN HIS PAIN RECEPTORS. Claudius lay across the floor, his hands gone, his eyes open. The blood pooled around him. Nyquist would've thought the man had drowned in it if he hadn't known better.

He couldn't see the second assassin. The first one was a blob of goo against the open panel, just like in Paloma's apartment.

But the second one...

It had detached itself from Claudius's leg, probably the moment he died, and had slithered somewhere. And that had happened when Nyquist was looking for another weapon.

Just a glance away, and he'd lost sight of the damn thing.

He couldn't send for help, either. His links had shut down.

He didn't know if the building had done that or the assassins.

He wouldn't be able to tell.

He circled, holding both pistols, looking at the floor, the ceiling, the walls. The assassin-thing had to be here somewhere.

It couldn't have slithered out, could it?

He circled and circled, waiting for the damn thing to attack.

65

They wouldn't let him in the building.

Flint stood outside, staring upward. No one had come out for ten minutes now, and no one was going inside, not until the HazMat teams cleared the place.

The building itself looked dark and unwelcoming. With everything shut down, it seemed uninhabited, a thing rather than a place.

He had a bad feeling about this, and he wasn't sure why.

The residents had crowded around him, some of them talking in low tones to the others, complaining about the dangers of the building, complaining that it wasn't what they had been promised.

He wanted to snap at them, to tell them that someone might be dying in there, but he didn't.

He stood and waited, and while he waited, he checked the faces around him against the last known image of Claudius Wagner.

So far, he hadn't found the man, but that meant nothing. Claudius might not have been in the building when the biohazard occurred.

He might not know anything was wrong.

But Flint doubted that, just like he doubted this second biohazard was a coincidence.

He sent a message to Van Alen through his links, warning her about the situation, and telling her to keep Ignatius away from the news. If the man tried to come here, he might die. It might all be a ruse to get Ignatius away from Van Alen's building.

Van Alen sent a message back instantly: the negotiations were proceeding with the various companies. Ignatius and his family were in an isolated part of the building, and she would make sure they heard nothing.

Flint thanked her and severed the link. He shifted from foot to foot. He thought of breaking in, but he knew the building's hazard systems were too tight for that. Some random protection system might even harm him, just because the building would see him as a threat.

So he had no choice.

He waited—and hoped this was all a false alarm.

66

DERICCI ARRIVED JUST AFTER THE LAW ENFORCEMENT TEAMS SHE'D sent for. Her aircar parked right next to a HazMat van.

She was breathing harshly, Popova's warnings still ringing in her ears. She wasn't being professional. She should let the Armstrong police handle this.

She was too involved.

Damn right she was.

Nyquist was in there. She'd seen what Bixian assassins could do, and she was trying not to think about it.

But she was failing.

She got out of the aircar and wasn't surprised to see Flint at the edge of the crowd, talking to one of the street police, gesturing toward the building.

She hurried toward them, caught something about a Wagner, and grabbed Flint's arm.

"Nyquist is in there," she said. "It's the same alarm that went off with the Bixians. We're going in."

Flint seemed to process that without a blink. "You stay."

"No," she said, and then she turned to the man Flint had been talking to. "You make sure that no one with these specs gets out of the building."

She linked to him quickly, sent him all the information about Bixian DNA.

"Make sure your teams search for that—bags, clothes, purses, anything that can carry something small and ropelike. Got it?"

"Yes, sir," the man said.

"And let us in."

"Sir, no civilians—"

"We're not civilians, dammit," she said, and shoved her way forward, still clinging to Flint's arm. He was hurrying with her. They got to the door, she held out her hand—her identification blaring—and they hurried inside. Someone handed them HazMat suits, and DeRicci flung them back.

"Noelle," Flint said. "We might need those."

"Do you know how those things kill?" she asked. She didn't wait for his answer. "There's a Wagner in here? Is that what Nyquist had come for?"

"The father. Ninth floor."

"Let's go." She hurried up the stairs, not seeing if he followed. She took them two at a time, and realized just how out of shape she was.

What would she do if she ran into one of those assassins? She had no idea. She didn't even have a weapon.

She wondered if Flint did.

The door to the ninth floor was open. The hallway was empty. She sprinted across it, breathing hard, and hammered on the only apartment door.

Flint stopped beside her and pushed her back. Then he did something—she couldn't see what—and the door opened.

The blood propelled her forward. A man was sprawled near the wall, his hands gone. She didn't recognize him.

She kept going, even though Flint was shouting at her. She didn't hear the words—she wouldn't listen to the words—and she ended up in what had been the kitchen.

Before someone shot it up.

Before Nyquist shot it up.

In a desperate attempt to survive.

67

"MILES!" DERICCI SCREAMED. "MILES, HELP ME. HE'S STILL BREATHING."

Flint had been searching the room with all his sensors on, making certain there were no Bixian assassins here. He figured one was a gooey mark on the wall, but he couldn't see the other.

"Miles!" DeRicci called. "*Now!*"

She was on her hands and knees beside Nyquist, clutching an area near his chest. He was bleeding too heavily for one person to stop it all.

Flint didn't go to her. Instead, he headed to the hallway and shouted for a medic. At the same time, he sent an emergency message down his links. He wasn't sure what would work in here and what wouldn't. He just knew he had to do both.

DeRicci was still yelling for him, and as he sprinted back in, he grabbed a soft coat from the closet. He was ripping it as he headed into the kitchen, hoping the second assassin was gone.

Then he no longer had to hope.

The dead assassin lay a few meters from Nyquist.

It looked like Nyquist had given it his all. He'd shot up the entire kitchen, but that had no effect. Then he'd found a good old-fashioned knife, and sliced as he was being sliced.

Somehow that had worked.

The assassin had survived long enough to slither away before it just flattened out.

Flint assumed the juices around it were some kind of life fluid. He'd leave that to the techs to figure out.

Since he and DeRicci hadn't been attacked, he also assumed there wasn't a third one.

He knelt beside DeRicci, who was putting pressure on a wound near Nyquist's heart, and tied off everything he could think to tie off. Nyquist's eyes were fluttering, but Flint wasn't sure he could see.

Then the medics burst in and shoved both Flint and DeRicci away. DeRicci wouldn't leave the area, even though she was covered in blood. Obviously, she and Nyquist had been friends, maybe more than friends, judging by the desperation in DeRicci's eyes, and she wasn't about to leave him.

Flint didn't want to either, but he knew he would just get in the way. It was amazing, the way Nyquist had managed to fight off those things. He wouldn't have survived if Flint and DeRicci hadn't gotten here so quickly.

That thought made him walk over to the other man. He had to be Claudius Wagner. Flint couldn't really get a sense of what the man had looked like, only that he had died a horrible death.

Like Paloma's.

Flint shuddered and realized it wasn't over yet.

Justinian had done this. He'd let the assassins know where both of his parents were.

He had killed by remote, just like his mother had, thinking his hands were clean because he hadn't done the actual murder. He hadn't even contracted for it. All he had done was impart a small piece of information, one the assassins had overlooked for decades.

Flint tasted bile against the back of his throat.

Ignatius was afraid of the man, his own brother, and why not? It would be impossible to prove that Justinian had sent the assassins after his parents.

Even if Flint tried, Justinian had all the resources of the Moon's largest and most influential law firm at his disposal.

If Flint went into that firm—or Justinian's home—and tried to take out the man, he'd still face those resources. Flint's own life would end if he ended Justinian's.

When DeRicci calmed, Flint would tell her what he suspected. But he also knew that she lacked the clout to take on WSX.

There was only one way to stop this man.

The way that he feared from the beginning.

And Flint would have to act fast.

68

Ki Bowles had never been summoned to a law office before. She spent the entire aircar trip to Van Alen and Associates worrying that this might have something to do with her firing. She had already warned her manager and her own attorney just in case.

So she was extremely surprised to be ushered into Maxine Van Alen's huge office, only to find Miles Flint sitting in a chair next to the desk. He looked a lot more relaxed than he had the day before, but something about him—the wariness in his gaze, the grief lines on his face—made him seem older than he ever had.

Van Alen stood beside him, looking imperial. She had always intimidated Bowles, who couldn't even ask for an interview with her, and now the feeling was worse.

"First," Van Alen said, "you need to sign a confidentiality agreement. Then we'll talk to you."

The agreement, sent across her links, seemed to go on forever. It was an actual document with vid text and links to explanations of legal terminology.

Flint fidgeted while Bowles examined it. He clearly wasn't as relaxed as he seemed.

When she finished signing it, Van Alen asked her if she was afraid of Wagner, Stuart, and Xendor.

Bowles almost said, "Hell, I'm afraid of *you*. Imagine how I feel about them." But she didn't.

Instead, she said flippantly, "Who isn't?"

"Well, if you can't stand up to them, we'll get someone else."

Bowles held out a hand. "I signed your damn agreement. At least tell me what you want before determining that I can't do it."

So Flint told her about Paloma being married to Old Man Wagner, and how they both died hideously, and that somewhere in the files of WSX was the reason for everything.

"You have exclusives for the rest of your life if you want them," he said.

"You realize I'm no longer with InterDome," she said.

"You wouldn't be getting this offer if you were," Van Alen said. "I'll be marketing everything for you. We probably won't go to Moon-based media, since WSX is tied to most of them. Are you interested? It's a long term project."

Interested? She felt like she had just come back to life. But she tried not to let her feelings show.

Instead, she turned to Flint. "Why me? You could have gone with a dozen people. You could have done it yourself. Why are you going with me?"

He studied her for a moment. Then he shrugged, almost as if to say, *You asked*.

"You're ruthless, Ki," he said.

She winced. Why did everyone say that about her?

He continued, "You want the story more than you want to protect people's lives and reputations. You have no real ethics. If you think you can bring someone down, you will, without regard to the effect on their lives."

She felt her cheeks warm. "If this is about Noelle DeRicci—"

"The governor-general stopped you from destroying her. I'll *help* you destroy Justinian Wagner. But you have to be as ruthless—more ruthless—than you were in going after Noelle. Will you do it?"

"And if the evidence doesn't warrant going after him?" Bowles asked, feeling insulted. "What then?"

Flint gave her a small smile. "It does. You put this stuff out, and it'll destroy WSX."

"How?" Bowles asked.

"We have their legal files," Van Alen said. "Decades of them. Files the firm has lost or misplaced. Files the firm won't give back to its own clients because it doesn't have them. That alone will bring down WSX. That kind of carelessness will make sure clients leave in droves."

"The rest will speak for itself," Flint said.

Bowles turned to Van Alen. "What about you? Isn't this unethical for you, too?"

Van Alen shrugged. "I'm not reading the files. I'm just representing Mr. Flint, who is the legal owner of those files. It's unethical if I read those files or use them in a case that I'm trying against WSX. Believe me, I was tempted. But this is a much better plan."

"Are you willing?" Flint asked.

Bowles straightened her back. She hated his characterization of her. But she had to admit, she was tempted. If this worked—and it would be a real gamble; it would be hard to take on the largest law firm on the Moon—then she had not just made her career, she'd found her own place in history.

"Hell, yeah," she said. "What do we do next?"

69

FLINT LET HIMSELF OUT OF THE OFFICE WHILE VAN ALEN EXPLAINED all the legal ramifications to Bowles. They'd have to keep her under control. They wouldn't let her break any news without backups and all their legal ammunition in place.

This would bring down Justinian Wagner, but it would happen slowly. And while it did, Flint had to pretend he didn't care. He had already decided to give Paloma's entire estate to Justinian. That way, Justinian had no reason to come after him. Flint would reload the information onto the *Lost Seas*, making sure it looked like the information had never been removed. Then he would give Justinian the official handheld with the material, and say that he hadn't made other copies.

It was a lie, of course, but a lie that Justinian might believe, given that Flint wasn't going to keep anything else from the estate for himself. Justinian would have trouble believing anyone would give back such wealth, even if he didn't need it.

Flint didn't need it and didn't want it. He was already doing what Paloma wanted. She wouldn't care if her estate went to her son while Flint, Van Alen, and Bowles used the time it bought them to bring Justinian down.

Van Alen had been worried that Justinian would send a Bixian assassin after Flint, but he reminded her that Justinian hadn't hired the assassins. He had just informed them where his parents were.

Justinian wouldn't hire any assassins himself—it was too hands-on. And he would have no reason to, once he had all of Paloma's files.

Besides, Wagner had no idea that Flint had damaging information against him that existed outside those files. For once, the size of the files worked in Flint's favor. He could say that in the few hours that he owned them, he had no time to look at them, particularly since he'd been a fugitive for much of that time.

Wagner would believe that as well. He might be worried that Flint had made copies, but since Flint was handing him both the original files (in the *Lost Seas*) and the handheld (which Flint cleaned up as much as he could so that there would be no record of the other backups), Wagner would probably think Flint hadn't had time to make copies.

Since it would take months for Flint to give Bowles the right information in the right order, Wagner would think Flint had nothing. Wagner would relax.

Flint would have to work hard. He was going to take his copies to the *Emmeline*, since his office still needed cleaning and probably some kind of debugging, given that the police had most likely searched it. He'd probably have to rent a place, either on Earth or Mars, to keep a secondary backup, somewhere far from Armstrong that Wagner wouldn't think of looking.

But that was minor.

When the first story, the one about the lost files, appeared, WSX was doomed.

It was only a matter of time.

Flint wished it could be faster. He wished he had been faster. Maybe he would have been able to help Nyquist.

It was clear that Nyquist would survive now. He'd have an awful recovery—maybe not even a full one—but he would make it.

Flint knew what that was like. He'd been crushed during a case, but not sliced, and the months of pain, the nanobots repairing things, the medical personnel poking this and that, wasn't anything he'd wish on someone he admired.

Hell, he'd barely wish it on someone he disliked.

DeRicci hadn't left Nyquist's side since the medics took him to Armstrong's best hospital. Flint stepped in to make sure that Nyquist got the best care—usually detectives couldn't afford the highest-level doctors—and then he let DeRicci take care of things. She found Nyquist's mother, and got the woman on a bullet train to Armstrong, but DeRicci had also made clear she—not his mother—would oversee his care.

Flint thought that was a hell of a commitment from someone who hadn't known him three months before.

But Flint was learning about commitments. Paloma would be alive if she hadn't had any personal relationships, just like she had recommended to him. Not only had she violated that, but she hadn't even tried to keep herself separate from her family.

Had she known how this would end up? Was this why she had advised him that way?

He shook his head.

He still hadn't processed everything he'd learned about Paloma. He figured it might take as long to understand how he felt about her as it took to destroy her law firm.

He sank into a chair in the hallway.

He really and truly was on his own now. And the only way to prevent being blindsided like this again was to make sure he stayed on his own.

Like Paloma had recommended.

All those years ago.

ABOUT THE AUTHOR

INTERNATIONAL BESTSELLING WRITER KRISTINE KATHRYN RUSCH has won or been nominated for every major award in the science fiction field. She has won Hugos for editing *The Magazine of Fantasy & Science Fiction* and for her short fiction. She has also won the *Asimov's Science Fiction Magazine* Readers Choice Award six times, as well as the Anlab Award from *Analog Magazine*, *Science Fiction Age* Readers Choice Award, the Locus Award, and the John W. Campbell Award. Her standalone sf novel, *Alien Influences*, was a finalist for the prestigious Arthur C. Clarke Award. *Io9* said her Retrieval Artist series featured one of the top ten science fiction detectives ever written. She writes a second sf series, the Diving Universe series, as well as a fantasy series called The Fey. She also writes mystery, romance and fantasy novels, occasionally using the pen names Kris DeLake, Kristine Grayson and Kris Nelscott.

The Retrieval Artist Series:

The Disappeared
Extremes
Consequences
Buried Deep
Paloma
Recovery Man
The Recovery Man's Bargain (A Short Novel)
Duplicate Effort
The Possession of Paavo Deshin (A Short Novel)
Anniversary Day
Blowback

The Retrieval Artist (A Short Novel)
The Impossibles (A Retrieval Artist Universe Short Story)

Made in the USA
San Bernardino, CA
22 December 2017